PRAISE FOR *The Line Between*

"Ever since *Last Unicorn,* one of the most beloved fantasies ever written, fantasy critics and readers have treasured [Beagle's] work, all the more so because he isn't prolific. For all their variety – 'Four Fables,' a children's story for all ages, a Sherlock Holmes pastiche, an old tar's tall tale, a sequel to one novel (*The Last Unicorn*) and a prequel to another (*The Innkeeper's Song,* 1993), and the germ of a prospective witch novel – all ten stories in this book are lucid and refreshing as spring water, full of amusement, humanity, and wisdom. Perhaps Beagle is incapable of genuinely dark fantasy, but his tall tale 'Salt Wine' touches the tonalities of R. L. Stevenson in 'The Bottle Imp' and W. W. Jacobs in 'The Monkey's Paw,' while on the other end of the spectrum, the *Last Unicorn* follow-up 'Two Hearts' is like Kenneth Grahame's 'Reluctant Dragon' with greater gravitas."
    Booklist, starred review

"Delicate shadings and subtle prose."
    Publishers Weekly

"Each one of the stories gathered here is aimed directly at the heart..."
    SF Site

"His third and best collection...a cornucopia of delights; mark this as a major contender for Collection of the Year."
    Locus

"At his best, Peter S. Beagle outshines the moon, the sun, the stars, the entire galaxy."
    Seattle Times

"Everything here is quite wonderful."
    Green Man Review

"A wonderful collection.... Each story is a gem.... Read it for any
reason you can find, but read it."
  SFRevu

"Everything Beagle writes is a pleasure to read."
  Denver Post

ABOUT PETER S. BEAGLE

"...One of my favorite writers."
  MADELEINE L'ENGLE, AUTHOR OF *A Wrinkle in Time* &
  A Swiftly Tilting Planet

"Peter S. Beagle illuminates with his own particular magic....
For years a loving readership has consulted him as an expert on
those hearts' reasons that reason does not know."
  URSULA K. LE GUIN, AUTHOR OF *A Wizard of Earthsea* &
  The Left Hand of Darkness

"...the only contemporary to remind one of Tolkien..."
  Booklist

"Peter S. Beagle is (in no particular order) a wonderful writer, a
fine human being, and a bandit prince out to steal readers' hearts."
  TAD WILLIAMS, AUTHOR OF *The Dragonbone Chair* &
  Tailchaser's Song

"It's a fully rounded region, this other world of Peter Beagle's
imagination...an originality...that is wholly his own."
  Kirkus

"[Beagle] has been compared, not unreasonably, with Lewis Carroll
and J.R.R. Tolkien, but he stands squarely...and triumphantly on
his own feet."
  Saturday Review

"Not only does Peter Beagle make his fantasy worlds come vividly, beautifully alive; he does it for the people who enter them."

POUL ANDERSON, AUTHOR OF *The High Crusade*

"Peter S. Beagle is the magician we all apprenticed ourselves to. Before all the endless series and shared-world novels, Beagle was there to show us the amazing possibilities waiting in the worlds of fantasy, and he is still one of the masters by which the rest of the field is measured."

LISA GOLDSTEIN, AUTHOR OF *The Red Magician*

"Peter S. Beagle would be one of the century's great writers in any arena he chose; we readers must feel blessed that Beagle picked fantasy as a homeland. Magic pumps like blood through the veins of his stories. Imparting passionately breathing, singing, laughing reality to the marvelous is his great gift to us all."

EDWARD BRYANT, AUTHOR OF *Cinnabar*

"Peter S. Beagle is our best modern fabulist in the tradition of Hawthorne and Twain."

JACK CADY, AUTHOR OF *The Night They Buried Road Dog*

WE NEVER TALK ABOUT MY BROTHER

We Never Talk About My Brother

Peter S. Beagle

TACHYON PUBLICATIONS | SAN FRANCISCO

Cover design and art by Ann Monn
Book design & composition by John D. Berry
The text typeface is FF Clifford

Tachyon Publications
1459 18th Street #139
San Francisco, CA 94107
(415) 285-5615
www.tachyonpublications.com

Edited by: Jacob Weisman

Trade paperback ISBN 10: 1-892391-83-X
Trade paperback ISBN 13: 978-1-892391-83-4

Printed in the United States of America by Worzalla

9 8 7 6 5 4 3 2 1

CONTENTS

TO JAKE AND PHIL,
AND GUNHILL ROAD

Introduction

BY CHARLES DE LINT

I THINK READING Peter Beagle was the first time I encountered an author who wrote fantasy novels set in this world we all live in. The only other one I can think of is James Branch Cabell, but he doesn't count because, while he was writing contemporary-to-him fantasy, the first part of the 20th century was still an "otherworld" so far as I was concerned. And while authors such as Robert Nathan were certainly writing their own contemporary fantasies before Peter, I came to their books only after having read any number of Peter's stories and novels.

As a reader, and later as a writer, I loved the immediacy of a contemporary setting, though like many writers in the 1970s, when I first tried my hand at fantasy I was as much locked into secondary worlds that pastiche Tolkien and Robert E. Howard as any of my peers. It took me a long time and more than a few books (many of which are still stuffed away in a box to never see the light of day) before I figured my way around it.

Peter doesn't seem to ever have had that problem. Like another one of my favourite authors, the underrated Parke Godwin, Peter appears to move effortlessly between settings and makes them his own. Contemporary. Historical. Secondary world. You'd never mistake a Beagle book as a clone of the work of some other writer.

That first book of his that I read was *A Fine and Private Place*, a novel I was recently delighted to discover holds up as well today as it did when I first encountered it. Better perhaps, since I'm older now myself and understand the motivations of some of the characters in ways I couldn't have when I first read it. That's another mark of a good writer: when their books still speak to you and can show you something new, no matter how many times you reread them.

What does all of this have to do with the stories in hand? Not much, or maybe everything.

The ability to bring any time and place alive – even if it has never existed – is only one small part of Peter's talent. More important, at least to this reader, is his ability to inhabit his characters.

Let me digress for a moment – I promise it will soon be relevant.

In music, singers touch us through their vocal skills, their tone (the quality of their voice), or their character – or more usually, some combination of the three. How we're touched is subjective, of course, and differs from listener to listener. But what's interesting is that a singer doesn't need to be adept at every part of the equation to be successful.

Take someone like Céline Dion. She's considered to be one of the world's best singers but I can't listen to her. She's all vocal gymnastics without character.

Now consider Tom Waits. His pitch is good, but you wouldn't consider him vocally skilled in a classical sense. The same goes for his tone, which can just as often resemble the growl of a misfiring engine or an animal's howl. But the character of his voice? Unparalleled. For those of us who love his music, that's what brings us back, time and again.

I don't care how technically proficient a singer is, or how gorgeous his or her tone. If a voice doesn't have character – if the singer doesn't inhabit the song and make me believe it – I'm not interested.

It's not quite the same in prose. Here the tone, which translates into the narrative voice of the character, is paramount. One writer's literary skills might be more rudimentary than another's (think, oh, Robert E. Howard as opposed to Michael Ondaatje), but if they can capture the right tone with their narration, then we'll believe in the character and want to follow the story wherever it might lead us. That's just the way it works. If we don't believe in the character, why bother reading?

Now, to stay with Howard for a moment, he's a good example of great tone, but like many writers, that tone doesn't vary much among his various stories because his characters are inevitably cut from a similar cloth. There are differences in detail, but we always know we're reading a Howard story.

That's because it's a lot more difficult to step into the skins of wildly-varying characters than someone who hasn't tried it might think. I read any number of writers who do one kind of character well, and I love them for it. But there are only a handful who can introduce us to any sort of a character, in any setting and time, and thoroughly inhabit that character's skin.

Peter's definitely one of those, and I offer the stories in this collection as indisputable evidence. His palette is rich with character colours and you'll never mistake one for another.

Listen to the narrative voice when you read "We Never Talk About My Brother" and compare its down-home, small-town, Middle American tone to the lyric high fantasy of *The Last Unicorn*. Or the middle-aged protagonist of *A Fine and Private Place* with the eleven-year-old narrating "Uncle Chaim and Aunt Rifke and the Angel." The distant voice telling us the story of "The Last and Only, or, Mr. Moscowitz Becomes French" bears not even a remote resemblance to the easy modernity of the characters in "Spook" trying to rid an apartment of an annoying ghost.

We care about these characters because we believe in them. We want foolish King Pelles to find redemption. We need to understand the strange, mystic chandail as much as the narrator Lalkhamsin-khamsolal does; if she hates these sea creatures so much, why does she go to such lengths to preserve the life of the one she finds helpless on the shore? In "The Tale of Junko and Sayuri," how far will Junko fall from his humanity using his wife's shapechanging abilities to further his ambition?

The last comment I want to make on these stories – and on Peter's writing in general – is that no matter whose story he chooses to tell, or where and when it's set, I doubt that his work will ever become uncomfortably dated. There's a timelessness to even his most contemporary stories that will not allow them to seem quaint fifty years from now. I know this because that first book of his I read still felt fresh when I reread it some forty-six years after its initial publication. I know this because everything I read by him taps into the deep well of True Story that never grows old.

But don't take my word for it. Read the stories that follow and see for yourself.

Charles de Lint
Ottawa, Summer 2008

WE NEVER TALK ABOUT MY BROTHER

Uncle Chaim and Aunt Rifke
and the Angel

This was the first story since my novel *A Fine And Private Place* that I drew specifically from my New York Jewish childhood. ("My Daughter's Name Is Sarah," based on a story from my mother's childhood, was published later than *A Fine and Private Place*, but written a few years earlier.) It is also powerfully influenced by three of my mother's four brothers, Raphael, Moses, and Isaac Soyer, who all became well-known painters in the New York realist style. As a child I spent a lot of time in my uncles' studios, whether visiting or actually posing for them, and Uncle Chaim's Greenwich Village *atelier* is based on my memory of Uncle Moses' workplace. Uncle Moses wasn't at all like my fictional Uncle Chaim in his speech and his mannerisms...but in terms of their attitudes toward their work, I do believe the real uncle and the imagined one would have understood each other.

MY UNCLE CHAIM, who was a painter, was working in his studio – as he did on every day except Shabbos – when the blue angel showed up. I was there.

I was usually there most afternoons, dropping in on my way home from Fiorello LaGuardia Elementary School. I was what they call a "latchkey kid," these days. My parents both worked and traveled full-time, and Uncle Chaim's studio had been my home base and my real playground since I was small. I was shy and uncomfortable with other children. Uncle Chaim didn't have any kids, and didn't know much about them, so he talked to me like an adult when he talked at all, which suited me perfectly. I looked through his paintings and drawings, tried some of my own, and ate Chinese food with him in silent companionship, when he remembered that we should probably eat. Sometimes I fell asleep on the cot. And when his friends – who were mostly painters like himself – dropped in to visit, I withdrew into my favorite corner and listened to their talk, and understood what I understood. Until the blue angel came.

It was very sudden: one moment I was looking through a couple of the comic books Uncle Chaim kept around for me, while he was trying to catch the highlight on the tendons under his model's chin, and the next moment there was this angel standing before him, actually *posing*, with her arms spread out and her great wings taking up almost half the studio. She was not blue herself – a light beige would be closer – but she wore a

3

blue robe that managed to look at once graceful and grand, with a white undergarment glimmering beneath. Her face, half-shadowed by a loose hood, looked disapproving.

I dropped the comic book and stared. No, I *gaped*, there's a difference. Uncle Chaim said to her, "I can't see my model. If you wouldn't mind moving just a bit?" He was grumpy when he was working, but never rude.

"*I* am your model," the angel said. "From this day forth, you will paint no one but me."

"I don't work on commission," Uncle Chaim answered. "I used to, but you have to put up with too many aggravating rich people. Now I just paint what I paint, take it to the gallery. Easier on my stomach, you know?"

His model, the wife of a fellow painter, said, "Chaim, who are you talking to?"

"Nobody, nobody, Ruthie. Just myself, same way your Jules does when he's working. Old guys get like that." To the angel, in a lower voice, he said, "Also, whatever you're doing to the light, could you not? I got some great shadows going right now." For a celestial brightness was swelling in the grubby little warehouse district studio, illuminating the warped floor boards, the wrinkled tubes of colors scattered everywhere, the canvases stacked and propped in the corners, along with several ancient rickety easels. It scared me, but not Uncle Chaim. He said. "So you're an angel, fine, that's terrific. Now give me back my shadows."

The room darkened obediently. "*Thank* you. Now about *moving...*" He made a brushing-away gesture with the hand holding the little glass of Scotch.

The model said, "Chaim, you're worrying me."

"What, I'm seventy-six years old, I'm not entitled to a hallucination now and then? I'm seeing an angel, you're not – this is no big deal. I just want it should move out of the way, let me work." The angel, in response, spread her wings even wider, and Uncle Chaim snapped, "Oh, for God's sake, shoo!"

"It is for God's sake that I am here," the angel announced majestically. "The Lord – Yahweh – I Am That I Am – has sent me down to be your muse." She inclined her head a trifle, by way of accepting the worship and wonder she expected.

From Uncle Chaim, she didn't get it, unless very nearly dropping his glass of Scotch counts as a compliment. "A muse?" he snorted. "I don't need a muse—I got models!"

"That's it," Ruthie said. "I'm calling Jules, I'll make him come over and sit with you." She put on her coat, picked up her purse, and headed for the door, saying over her shoulder, "Same time Thursday? If you're still here?"

"I got more models than I know what to do with," Uncle Chaim told the blue angel. "Men, women, old, young – even a cat, there's one lady always brings her cat, what am I going to do?" He heard the door slam, realized that Ruthie was gone, and sighed irritably, taking a larger swallow of whiskey than he usually allowed himself. "Now she's upset, she thinks she's my mother anyway, she'll send Jules with chicken soup and an enema." He narrowed his eyes at the angel. "And what's this, how I'm only going to be painting you from now on? Like Velazquez stuck painting royal Hapsburg imbeciles over and over? Some hope you've got! Listen, you go back and tell, "– he hesitated just a trifle – "tell whoever sent you that Chaim Malakoff is too old not to paint what he likes, when he likes, and for who he likes. You got all that? We're clear?"

It was surely no way to speak to an angel; but as Uncle Chaim used to warn me about everyone from neighborhood bullies to my fourth-grade teacher, who hit people, "You give the bastards an inch, they'll walk all over you. From me they get *bupkes, nichevo,* nothing. Not an inch." I got beaten up more than once in those days, saying that to the wrong people.

And the blue angel was definitely one of them. The entire room suddenly filled with her: with the wings spreading higher than the ceiling, wider than the walls, yet somehow not touching so much as a stick of charcoal; with the aroma almost too impossibly haunting to be borne; with the vast, unutterable beauty that a thousand medieval and Renaissance artists had somehow not gone mad (for the most part) trying to ambush on canvas or trap in stone. In that moment, Uncle Chaim confided later, he didn't know whether to pity or envy Muslims their ancient ban on depictions of the human body.

"I thought maybe I should kneel, what would it hurt? But then I thought, *what would it hurt?* It'd hurt my left knee, the one had the arthritis twenty years, that's what it would hurt." So he only shrugged a little and told her, "I could manage a sitting on Monday. Somebody can-celled, I got the whole morning free."

"Now," the angel said. Her air of distinct disapproval had become one of authority. The difference was slight but notable.

"Now," Uncle Chaim mimicked her. "All right, already – Ruthie left early, so why not?" He moved the unfinished portrait over to another easel, and carefully selected a blank canvas from several propped against a wall. "I got to clean off a couple of brushes here, we'll start. You want to take off that thing, whatever, on your head?" Even I knew perfectly well that it was a halo, but Uncle Chaim always told me that you had to start with people as you meant to go on.

"You will require a larger surface," the angel instructed him. "I am not to be represented in miniature."

Uncle Chaim raised one eyebrow (an ability I envied him to the point of practicing – futilely – in the bathroom mirror for hours, until my par-ents banged on the door, certain I was up to the worst kind of no good). "No, huh? Good enough for the Persians, good enough for Holbein and Hilliard and Sam Cooper, but not for you? So okay, so we'll try this one..." Rummaging in a corner, he fetched out his biggest canvas, dusted it off, eyed it critically – "Don't even remember what I'm doing with anything this size, must have been saving it for you" – and finally set it up on the empty easel, turning it away from the angel. "Okay, Malakoff's rules. Nobody – *nobody* – looks at my painting till I'm done. Not angels, not Adonai, not my nephew over there in the corner, that's David, Duvidl – not even my wife. Nobody. Understood?"

The angel nodded, almost imperceptibly. With surprising meekness, she asked, "Where shall I sit?"

"Not a lot of choices," Uncle Chaim grunted, lifting a brush from a jar of turpentine. "Over there's okay, where Ruthie was sitting – or maybe by the big window. The window would be good, we've lost the shadows already. Take the red chair, I'll fix the color later."

But sitting down is not a natural act for an angel: they stand or they fly; check any Renaissance painting. The great wings inevitably get crum-pled, the halo always winds up distinctly askew; and there is simply no way, even for Uncle Chaim, to ask an angel to cross her legs or to hook one over the arm of the chair. In the end they compromised, and the blue angel rose up to pose in the window, holding herself there effortlessly, with her wings not stirring at all. Uncle Chaim, settling in to work – brushes cleaned and Scotch replenished – could not refrain from remarking, "I always imagined you guys sort of hovered. Like hummingbirds."

"We fly only by the Will of God," the angel replied. "If Yahweh, praised be His name," – I could actually *hear* the capital letters – "withdrew that mighty Will from us, we would fall from the sky on the instant, every single one."

"Doesn't bear thinking about," Uncle Chaim muttered. "Raining angels all over everywhere – falling on people's heads, tying up traffic – "

The angel looked, first startled, and then notably shocked. "I was speaking of *our* sky," she explained haughtily, "the sky of Paradise, which compares to yours as gold to lead, tapestry to tissue, heavenly choirs to the bellowing of feeding hogs – "

"All *right* already, I get the picture." Uncle Chaim cocked an eye at her, poised up there in the window with no visible means of support, and then back at his canvas. "I was going to ask you about being an angel, what it's like, but if you're going to talk about us like that – badmouthing the *sky*, for God's sake, the whole *planet*."

The angel did not answer him immediately, and when she did, she appeared considerably abashed and spoke very quietly, almost like a scolded schoolgirl. "You are right. It is His sky, His world, and I shame my Lord, my fellows and my breeding by speaking slightingly of any part of it." In a lower voice, she added, as though speaking only to herself, "Perhaps that is why I am here."

Uncle Chaim was covering the canvas with a thin layer of very light blue, to give the painting an undertone. Without looking up, he said, "What, you got sent down here like a punishment? You talked back, you didn't take out the garbage? I could believe it. Your boy Yahweh, he always did have a short fuse."

"I was told only that I was to come to you and be your model and your muse," the angel answered. She pushed her hood back from her face, revealing hair that was not bright gold, as so often painted, but of a color resembling the night sky when it pales into dawn. "Angels do not ask questions."

"Mmm." Uncle Chaim sipped thoughtfully at his Scotch. "Well, one did, anyway, you believe the story."

The angel did not reply, but she looked at him as though he had uttered some unimaginable obscenity. Uncle Chaim shrugged and continued preparing the ground for the portrait. Neither one said anything for some time, and it was the angel who spoke first. She said, a trifle hesitantly, "I have never been a muse before."

"Never had one," Uncle Chaim replied sourly. "Did just fine."

"I do not know what the duties of a muse would be," the angel confessed. "You will need to advise me."

"What?" Uncle Chaim put down his brush. "Okay now, wait a minute. *I* got to tell you how to get into my hair, order me around, probably tell me how I'm not painting you right? Forget it, lady – you figure it out for yourself, I'm working here."

But the blue angel looked confused and unhappy, which is no more natural for an angel than sitting down. Uncle Chaim scratched his head and said, more gently, "What do I know? I guess you're supposed to stimulate my creativity, something like that. Give me ideas, visions, make me see things, think about things I've never thought about." After a pause, he added, "Frankly, Goya pretty much has that effect on me already. Goya and Matisse. So that's covered, the stimulation – maybe you could just tell them, *him*, about that..."

Seeing the expression on the angel's marble-smooth face, he let the sentence trail away. Rabbi Shulevitz, who cut his blond hair close and wore shorts when he watered his lawn, once told me that angels are supposed to express God's emotions and desires, without being troubled by any of their own. "Like a number of other heavenly dictates," he murmured when my mother was out of the room, "that one has never quite functioned as I'm sure it was intended."

They were still working in the studio when my mother called and ordered me home. The angel had required no rest or food at all, while Uncle Chaim had actually been drinking his Scotch instead of sipping it (I never once saw him drunk, but I'm not sure that I ever saw him entirely sober), and needed more bathroom breaks than usual. Daylight gone, and his precarious array of 60-watt bulbs proving increasingly unsatisfactory, he looked briefly at the portrait, covered it, and said to the angel, "Well, *that* stinks, but we'll do better tomorrow. What time you want to start?"

The angel floated down from the window to stand before him. Uncle Chaim was a small man, dark and balding, but he already knew that the angel altered her height when they faced each other, so as not to overwhelm him completely. She said, "I will be here when you are."

Uncle Chaim misunderstood. He assured her that if she had no other place to sleep but the studio, it wouldn't be the first time a model or a friend had spent the night on that trundle bed in the far corner. "Only no peeking at the picture, okay? On your honor as a muse."

The blue angel looked for a moment as though she were going to smile, but she didn't. "I will not sleep here, or anywhere on this earth," she said. "But you will find me waiting when you come."

"Oh," Uncle Chaim said. "Right. Of course. Fine. But don't change your clothes, okay? Absolutely no changing." The angel nodded.

When Uncle Chaim got home that night, my Aunt Rifke told my mother on the phone at some length, he was in a state that simply did not register on her long-practiced seismograph of her husband's moods. "He comes in, he's telling jokes, he eats up everything on the table, we snuggle up, watch a little TV, I can figure the work went well today. He doesn't talk, he's not hungry, he goes to bed early, tosses and tumbles around all night...okay, not so good. Thirty-seven years with a person, wait, you'll find out." Aunt Rifke had been Uncle Chaim's model until they married, and his agent, accountant and road manager ever since.

But the night he returned from beginning his portrait of the angel brought Aunt Rifke a husband she barely recognized. "Not up, not down, not happy, not *not* happy, just...*dazed,* I guess that's the best word. He'd start to eat something, then he'd forget about it, wander around the apartment – couldn't sit still, couldn't keep his mind on anything, had trouble even finishing a sentence. One sentence. I tell you, it scared me. I couldn't keep from wondering, *is this how it begins?* A man starts acting strange, one day to the next, you think about things like that, you know?" Talking about it, even long past the moment's terror, tears still started in her eyes.

Uncle Chaim did tell her that he had been visited by an angel who demanded that he paint her portrait. *That* Aunt Rifke had no trouble believing, thirty-seven years of marriage to an artist having inured her to certain revelations. Her main concern was how painting an angel might affect Uncle Chaim's working hours, and his daily conduct. "Like actors, you know, Duvidl? They *become* the people they're doing, I've seen it over and over." Also, blasphemous as it might sound, she wondered how much the angel would be paying, and in what currency. "And saying we'll get a big credit in the next world is not funny, Chaim. *Not* funny."

Uncle Chaim urged Rifke to come to the studio the very next day to meet his new model for herself. Strangely, that lady, whom I'd known all my life as a legendary repository of other people's lives, stories and secrets, flatly refused to take him up on the offer. "I got nothing to wear, not for meeting an angel in. Besides, what would we talk about? No, you just give her my best, I'll make some *rugelach*." And she never wavered from that position, except once.

The blue angel was indeed waiting when Uncle Chaim arrived in the studio early the next morning. She had even made coffee in his ancient glass percolator, and was offended when he informed her that it was as thin as rain and tasted like used dishwater. "Where I come from, no one ever *makes* coffee," she returned fire. "We command it."

"That's what's wrong with this crap," Uncle Chaim answered her. "Coffee's like art, you don't order coffee around." He waved the angel aside, and set about a second pot, which came out strong enough to widen the angel's eyes when she sipped it. Uncle Chaim teased her – "Don't get stuff like *that* in the Green Pastures, huh?" – and confided that he made much better coffee than Aunt Rifke. "Not her fault. Woman was raised on decaf, what can you expect? Cooks like an angel, though."

The angel either missed the joke or ignored it. She began to resume her pose in the window, but Uncle Chaim stopped her. "Later, later, the sun's not right. Just stand where you are, I want to do some work on the head." As I remember, he never used the personal possessive in referring to his models' bodies: it was invariably "turn the face a little," "relax the shoulder," "move the foot to the left." Amateurs often resented it; professionals tended to find it liberating. Uncle Chaim didn't much care either way.

For himself, he was grateful that the angel proved capable of holding a pose indefinitely, without complaining, asking for a break, or needing the toilet. What he found distracting was her steadily emerging interest in talking and asking questions. As requested, her expression never changed and her lips hardly moved; indeed, there were times when he would have sworn he was hearing her only in his mind. Enough of her queries had to do with his work, with how he did what he was doing, that he finally demanded point-blank, "All those angels, seraphs, cherubim, centuries of them – all those Virgins and Assumptions and whatnot – and you've never once been painted? Not one time?"

"I have never set foot on earth before," the angel confessed. "Not until I was sent to you."

"Sent to me. Directly. Special Delivery, Chaim Shlomovitch Malakoff – one angel, totally inexperienced at modeling. Or anything else, got anything to do with human life." The angel nodded, somewhat shyly. Uncle Chaim spoke only one word. *"Why?"*

"I am only eleven thousand, seven hundred and twenty-two years old," the angel said, with the a slight but distinct suggestion of resentment in her voice. "No one tells me a *thing.*"

Uncle Chaim was silent for some time, squinting at her face from different angles and distances, even closing one eye from time to time. Finally he grumbled, more than half to himself, "I got a very bad feeling that we're both supposed to learn something from this. Bad, bad feeling." He filled the little glass for the first time that day, and went back to work.

But if there was to be any learning involved in their near-daily meetings in the studio, it appeared to be entirely on her part. She was ravenously curious about human life on the blue-green ball of damp dirt that she had observed so distantly for so long, and her constant questioning reminded a weary Uncle Chaim – as he informed me more than once – of me at the age of four. Except that an angel cannot be bought off, even temporarily, with strawberry ice cream, or threatened with loss of a bedtime story if she can't learn to take "I don't *know!*" for an answer. At times he pretended not to hear her; on other occasions, he would make up some patently ridiculous explanation that a grandchild would have laughed to scorn, but that the angel took so seriously that he was guiltily certain he was bound to be struck by lightning. Only the lightning never came, and the tactic usually did buy him a few moments peace – until the next question.

Once he said to her, in some desperation, "You're an angel, you're supposed to know everything about human beings. Listen, I'll take you out to Bleecker, MacDougal, Washington Square, you can look at the books, magazines, TV, the classes, the beads and crystals...it's all about how to get in touch with angels. Real ones, real angels, never mind that stuff about the angel inside you. Everybody wants some of that angel wisdom, and they want it bad, and they want it right now. We'll take an afternoon off, I'll show you."

The blue angel said simply, "The streets and the shops have nothing to show me, nothing to teach. You do."

"No," Uncle Chaim said. "No, no, no, no *no*. I'm a painter – that's all, that's it, that's what I know. Painting. But you, you sit at the right hand of God – "

"He doesn't have hands," the angel interrupted. "And nobody exactly *sits* – "

"The point I'm making, you're the one who ought to be answering questions. About the universe, and about Darwin, and how everything really happened, and what is it with God and shellfish, and the whole business with the milk and the meat – *those* kinds of questions. I mean, I should be asking them, I know that, only I'm working right now."

It was almost impossible to judge the angel's emotions from the expressions of her chillingly beautiful porcelain face; but as far as Uncle Chaim could tell, she looked sad. She said, "I also am what I am. We angels – as you call us – we are messengers, minions, lackeys, knowing only what we are told, what we are ordered to do. A few of the Oldest, the ones who were there at the Beginning – Michael, Gabriel, Raphael – *they* have names, thoughts, histories, choices, powers. The rest of us, we tremble, we *hide* when we see them passing by. We think, *if those are angels, we must be something else altogether,* but we can never find a better word for ourselves."

She looked straight at Uncle Chaim – he noticed in some surprise that in a certain light her eyes were not nearly as blue as he had been painting them, but closer to a dark sea-green – and he looked away from an anguish that he had never seen before, and did not know how to paint. He said, "So okay, you're a low-class angel, a heavenly grunt, like they say now. So how come they picked you to be my muse? Got to mean *something*, no? Right?"

The angel did not answer his question, nor did she speak much for the rest of the day. Uncle Chaim posed her in several positions, but the unwonted sadness in her eyes depressed him past even Laphroaig's ability to ameliorate. He quit work early, allowing the angel – as he would never have permitted Aunt Rifke or me – to potter around the studio, putting it to rights according to her inexpert notions, organizing brushes, oils, watercolors, pastels and pencils, fixatives, rolls of canvas, bottles of tempera and turpentine, even dusty chunks of rabbit skin glue, according to size. As he told his friend Jules Sidelsky, meeting for their traditional weekly lunch at a Ukrainian restaurant on Second Avenue, where the two of them spoke only Russian, "maybe God could figure where things are anymore. Me, I just shut my eyes and pray."

Jules was large and fat, like Diego Rivera, and I thought of him as a sort of uncle too, because he and Ruthie always remembered my birthday, just like Uncle Chaim and Aunt Rifke. Jules did not believe in angels, but he knew that Uncle Chaim didn't necessarily believe in them either, just because he had one in his studio every day. He asked seriously, "That helps? The praying?" Uncle Chaim gave him a look, and Jules dropped the subject. "So what's she like? I mean, as a model? You like painting her?"

Uncle Chaim held his hand out, palm down, and wobbled it gently from side to side. "What's not to like? She'll hold any pose absolutely forever – you could leave her all night, morning I guarantee she wouldn't have moved a muscle. No whining, no bellyaching – listen, she'd make Cinderella look like the witch in that movie, the green one. In my life I never worked with anybody gave me less *tsuris*."

"So what's with – ?" and Jules mimicked his fluttering hand. "I'm waiting for the *but*, Chaim."

Uncle Chaim was still for a while, neither answering nor appearing to notice the steaming *varyniki* that the waitress had just set down before him. Finally he grumbled, "She's an angel, what can I tell you? Go reason with an angel." He found himself vaguely angry with Jules, for no reason that made any sense. He went on, "She's got it in her head she's supposed to be my muse. It's not the most comfortable thing sometimes, all right?"

Perhaps due to their shared childhood on Tenth Avenue, Jules did not laugh, but it was plainly a near thing. He said, mildly enough, "Matisse had muses. Rodin, up to here with muses. Picasso about had to give them serial numbers – I think he married them just to keep them straight in his head. You, me...I don't see it, Chaim. We're not muse types, you know? Never were, not in all our lives. Also, Rifke would kill you dead. Deader."

"What, I don't know that? Anyway, it's not what you're thinking." He grinned suddenly, in spite of himself. "She's not that kind of girl, you ought to be ashamed. It's just she wants to help, to inspire, that's what muses do. I don't mind her messing around with *my* mess in the studio – I mean, yeah, I mind it, but I can live with it. But the other day," – he paused briefly, taking a long breath – "the other day she wanted to give me a haircut. A haircut. It's all right, go ahead."

For Jules was definitely laughing this time, spluttering tea through his nose, so that he turned a bright cerise as other diners stared at them. "A haircut," he managed to get out, when he could speak at all clearly. "An angel gave you a haircut."

"No, she didn't *give* me a haircut," Uncle Chaim snapped back crossly. "She wanted to, she offered – and then, when I said *no, thanks,* after awhile she said she could play music for me while I worked. I usually have the news on, and she doesn't like it, I can tell. Well, it wouldn't make much sense to her, would it? Hardly does to me anymore."

"So she's going to be posing *and* playing music? What, on her harp? That's true, the harp business?"

"No, she just said she could command the music. The way they do with coffee." Jules stared at him. "Well, *I* don't know – I guess it's like some heavenly Muzak or something. Anyway, I told her no, and I'm sorry I told you anything. Eat, forget it, okay?"

But Jules was not to be put off so easily. He dug down into his *galushki poltavski* for a little time, and then looked up and said with his mouth full, "Tell me one thing, then I'll drop it. Would you say she was beautiful?"

"She's an angel," Uncle Chaim said.

"That's not what I asked. Angels are all supposed to be beautiful, right? Beyond words, beyond description, the works. So?" He smiled serenely at Uncle Chaim over his folded hands.

Uncle Chaim took so long to answer him that Jules actually waved a hand directly in front of his eyes. "Hello? Earth to Malakoff – this is your wakeup call. You in there, Chaim?"

"I'm there, I'm there, stop with the kid stuff." Uncle Chaim flicked his own fingers dismissively at his friend's hand. "Jules, all I can tell you, I never saw anyone looked like her before. Maybe that's beauty all by itself, maybe it's just novelty. Some days she looks eleven thousand years old, like she says – some days...some days she could be younger than Duvidl, she could be the first child in the world, first one ever." He shook his head helplessly. "I don't *know*, Jules. I wish I could ask Rembrandt or somebody. Vermeer. Vermeer would know."

Strangely, of the small corps of visitors to the studio – old painters like himself and Jules, gallery owners, art brokers, friends from the neighborhood – I seemed to be the only one who ever saw the blue angel as anything other than one of his unsought acolytes, perfectly happy to stretch canvases, make sandwiches and occasionally pose, all for the gift of a growled thanks and the privilege of covertly studying him at work. My memory is that I regarded her as a nice-looking older lady with wings, but not my type at all, I having just discovered Alice Faye. Lauren Bacall, Lizabeth Scott and Lena Horne came a bit later in my development.

I knew she was an angel. I also knew better than to tell any of my own friends about her: we were a cynical lot, who regularly got thrown out of movie theatres for cheering on the Wolfman and booing Shirley Temple and Bobby Breen. But I was shy with the angel, and – I guess – she with me, so I can't honestly say I remember much either in the way of conversation or revelation. Though I am still haunted by one particular moment when I asked her, straight out, "Up there, in heaven – do you ever see Jesus? Jesus Christ, I mean." We were hardly an observant family, any of us, but it still felt strange and a bit dangerous to say the name.

The blue angel turned from cleaning off a palette knife and looked directly at me, really for the first time since we had been introduced. I noticed that the color of her wings seemed to change from moment to moment, rippling constantly through a supple spectrum different from any I knew; and that I had no words either for her hair color, or for her smell. She said, "No, I have never seen him."

"Oh," I said, vaguely disappointed, Jewish or not. "Well – uh – what about his mother? The – the Virgin?" Funny, I remember that *that* seemed more daringly wicked than saying the other name out loud. I wonder why that should have been.

"No," the angel answered. "Nor," – heading me off – "have I ever seen God. You are closer to God now, as you stand there, than I have ever been."

"That doesn't make any sense," I said. She kept looking at me, but did not reply. I said, "I mean, you're an angel. Angels live with God, don't they?"

She shook her head. In that moment – and just for that moment – her richly empty face showed me a sadness that I don't think a human face could ever have contained. "Angels live alone. If we were with God, we would not be angels." She turned away, and I thought she had finished speaking. But then she looked back quite suddenly to say, in a voice that did not sound like her voice at all, being lower than the sound I knew, and almost masculine in texture, *"Dark and dark and dark...so empty...so dark..."*

It frightened me deeply, that one broken sentence, though I couldn't have said why: it was just so dislocating, so completely out of place – even the rhythm of those few words sounded more like the hesitant English of our old Latvian rabbi than that of Uncle Chaim's muse. He didn't hear it, and I didn't tell him about it, because I thought it must be me, that I was making it up, or I'd heard it wrong. I was accustomed to thinking like that when I was a boy.

"She's got like a dimmer switch," Uncle Chaim explained to Aunt Rifke; they were putting freshly washed sheets on the guest bed at the time, because I was staying the night to interview them for my Immigrant Experience class project. "Dial it one way, you wouldn't notice her if she were running naked down Madison Avenue at high noon, flapping her wings and waving a gun. Two guns. Turn that dial back the other way, all the way...well, thank God she wouldn't ever do that, because she'd likely set the studio on fire. You think I'm joking. I'm not joking."

"No, Chaim, I know you're not joking." Rifke silently undid and remade both of his attempts at hospital corners, as she always did. She said, "What I want to know is, just where's that dial set when you're painting her? And I'd think a bit about that answer, if I were you." Rifke's favorite cousin Harvey, a career social worker, had recently abandoned wife and children to run off with a beautiful young dope dealer, and Rifke was feeling more than slightly edgy.

Uncle Chaim did think about it, and replied, "About a third, I'd say. Maybe half, once or twice, no more. I remember, I had to ask her a couple times, turn it down, please – go work when somebody's *glowing* six feet away from you. I mean, the moon takes up a lot of space, a little studio like mine. Bad enough with the wings."

Rifke tucked in the last corner, smoothed the sheet tight, faced him across the bed and said, "You're never going to finish this one, are you?

Thirty-seven years, I know all the signs. You'll do it over and over, you'll frame it, you'll hang it, you'll say, *okay, that's it, I'm done* – but you won't be done, you'll just start the whole thing again, only maybe a different style, a brighter palette, a bigger canvas, a smaller canvas. But you'll never get it the way it's in your head, not for you." She smacked the pillows fluffy and tossed them back on the bed. "Don't even bother arguing with me, Malakoff. Not when I'm right."

"So am I arguing? Does it look like I'm arguing?" Uncle Chaim rarely drank at home, but on this occasion he walked into the kitchen, filled a glass from the dusty bottle of *grappa*, and turned back to his wife. He said very quietly, "Crazy to think I could get an angel right. Who could paint an angel?"

Aunt Rifke came to him then and put her hands on his shoulders. "My crazy old man, that's who," she answered him. "Nobody else. God would know."

And my Uncle Chaim blushed for the first time in many years. I didn't see this, but Aunt Rifke told me.

Of course, she was quite right about that painting, or any of the many, many others he made of the blue angel. He was never satisfied with any of them, not a one. There was always *something* wrong, something missing, something there but *not* there, glimpsed but gone. "Like that Chinese monkey trying to grab the moon in the water," Uncle Chaim said to me once. "That's me, a Chinese monkey."

Not that you could say he suffered financially from working with only one model, as the angel had commanded. The failed portraits that he lugged down to the gallery handling his paintings sold almost instantly to museums, private collectors and corporations decorating their lobbies and meeting rooms, under such generic titles as *Angel in the Window, Blue Wings, Angel with Wineglass,* and *Midnight Angel.* Aunt Rifke banked the money, and Uncle Chaim endured the unveilings and the receptions as best he could – without ever looking at the paintings themselves – and then shuffled back to his studio to start over. The angel was always waiting.

I was doing my homework in the studio when Jules Sidelsky visited at last, lured there by other reasons than art, beauty or deity. The blue angel hadn't given up the notion of acting as Uncle Chaim's muse, but never seemed able to take it much beyond making a tuna salad sandwich, or a pot of coffee (at which, to be fair, she had become quite skilled), summoning music, or reciting the lost works of legendary or forgotten poets while he worked. He tried to discourage this habit; but he did learn a number of Shakespeare's unpublished sonnets, and was able to write down for Jules three poems that drowned with Shelley off the Livorno coast. "Also, your boy Pushkin, his wife destroyed a mess of his stuff right after his death. My girl's got it all by heart, you believe that?"

Pushkin did it. If the great Russian had been declared a saint, Jules would have reported for instruction to the Patriarch of Moscow on the following day. As it was, he came down to Uncle Chaim's studio instead, and was at last introduced to the blue angel, who was as gracious as Jules did his bewildered best to be. She spent the afternoon declaiming Pushkin's vanished verse to him in the original, while hovering tirelessly upside down, just above the crossbar of a second easel. Uncle Chaim thought he might be entering a surrealist phase.

Leaving, Jules caught Uncle Chaim's arm and dragged him out his door into the hot, bustling Village streets, once his dearest subject before the coming of the blue angel. Uncle Chaim, knowing his purpose, said, "So now you see? Now you see?"

"I see." Jules's voice was dark and flat, and almost without expression. "I see you got an angel there, all right. No question in the world about that." The grip on Uncle Chaim's arm tightened. Jules said, "You have to get rid of her."

"*What*? What are you *talking* about? Just finally doing the most important work of my life, and you want me...?" Uncle Chaim's eyes narrowed, and he pulled forcefully away from his friend. "What is it with you and my models? You got like this once before, when I was painting that Puerto Rican guy, the teacher, with the big nose, and you just couldn't stand it, you remember? Said I'd stolen him, wouldn't speak to me for weeks, *weeks*, you remember?"

"Chaim, that's not true—"

"And so now I've got this angel, it's the same thing—worse, with the Pushkin and all—"

"Chaim, damn it, I wouldn't care if she were Pushkin's sister, they played Monopoly together—"

Uncle Chaim's voice abruptly grew calmer; the top of his head stopped sweating and lost its crimson tinge. "I'm sorry, I'm sorry, Jules. It's not I

don't understand, I've been the same way about other people's models."
He patted the other's shoulder awkwardly. "Look, I tell you what, anytime you want, you come on over, we'll work together. How about that?"

Poor Jules must have been completely staggered by all this. On the one
hand he knew – I mean, even *I* knew – that Uncle Chaim never invited
other artists to share space with him, let alone a model; on the other,
the sudden change can only have sharpened his anxiety about his old
friend's state of mind. He said, "Chaim, I'm just trying to tell you, whatever's going on, it isn't good for you. Not her fault, not your fault. People
and angels aren't supposed to hang out together – we aren't built for it,
and neither are they. She really needs to go back where she belongs."

"She can't. Absolutely not." Uncle Chaim was shaking his head, and
kept on shaking it. "She got *sent* here, Jules, she got sent to *me –* "

"By whom? You ever ask yourself that?" They stared at each other.
Jules said, very carefully, "No, not by the Devil. I don't believe in the Devil
any more than I believe in God, although he always gets the good lines.
But it's a free country, and I *can* believe in angels without swallowing all
the rest of it, if I want to." He paused, and took a gentler hold on Uncle
Chaim's arm. "And I can also imagine that angels might not be exactly
what we think they are. That an angel might lie, and still be an angel.
That an angel might be selfish – jealous, even. That an angel might just be
a little bit out of her head."

In a very pale and quiet voice, Uncle Chaim said, "You're talking about
a fallen angel, aren't you?"

"I don't know what I'm talking about," Jules answered. "That's the
God's truth." Both of them smiled wearily, but neither one laughed. Jules
said, "I'm dead serious, Chaim. For your sake, your sanity, she needs
to go."

"And for my sake, she can't." Uncle Chaim was plainly too exhausted
for either pretense or bluster, but there was no give in him. He said,
"*Landsmann,* it doesn't matter. You could be right, you could be wrong,
I'm telling you, it doesn't matter. There's no one else I want to paint anymore – there's no one else I *can* paint, Jules, that's just how it is. Go home
now." He refused to say another word.

In the months that followed, Uncle Chaim became steadily more silent,
more reclusive, more closed-off from everything that did not directly
involve the current portrait of the blue angel. By autumn, he was no lon-

ger meeting Jules for lunch at the Ukrainian restaurant; he could rarely be induced to appear at his own openings, or anyone else's; he frequently spent the night at his studio, sleeping briefly in his chair, when he slept at all. It had been understood between Uncle Chaim and me since I was three that I had the run of the place at any time; and while it was still true, I felt far less comfortable there than I was accustomed, and left it more and more to him and the strange lady with the wings.

When an exasperated – and increasingly frightened – Aunt Rifke would challenge him, "You've turned into Red Skelton, painting nothing but clowns on velvet – Margaret Keane, all those big-eyed war orphans," he only shrugged and replied, when he even bothered to respond, "You were the one who told me I could paint an angel. Change your mind?"

Whatever she truly thought, it was not in Aunt Rifke to say such a thing to him directly. Her only recourse was to mumble something like, "Even Leonardo gave up on drawing cats," or "You've done the best anybody could ever do – let it go now, let *her* go." Her own theory, differing somewhat from Jules's, was that it was as much Uncle Chaim's obsession as his model's possible madness that was holding the angel to earth. "Like Ella and Sam," she said to me, referring to the perpetually quarrelling parents of my favorite cousin Arthur. "Locked together, like some kind of punishment machine. Thirty years they hate each other, cats and dogs, but they're so scared of being alone, if one of them died," – she snapped her fingers – "the other one would be gone in a week. Like that. Okay, so not exactly like that, but like that." Aunt Rifke wasn't getting a lot of sleep either just then.

She confessed to me – it astonishes me to this day – that she prayed more than once herself, during the worst times. Even in my family, which still runs to atheists, agnostics and cranky anarchists, Aunt Rifke's unbelief was regarded as the standard by which all other blasphemy had to be judged, and set against which it invariably paled. The idea of a prayer from her lips was, on the one hand, fascinating – how would Aunt Rifke conceivably address a Supreme Being? – and more than a little alarming as well. Supplication was not in her vocabulary, let alone her repertoire. Command was.

I didn't ask her what she had prayed for. I did ask, trying to make her laugh, if she had commenced by saying, "To Whom it may concern..." She slapped my hand lightly. "Don't talk fresh, just because you're in fifth grade, sixth grade, whatever. Of course I didn't say that, an old Socialist Worker like me. I started off like you'd talk to some kid's mother on the phone, I said, 'It's time for your little girl to go home, we're going to be having dinner. You better call her in now, it's getting dark.' Like that, polite. But not fancy."

"And you got an answer?" Her face clouded, but she made no reply. "You didn't get an answer? Bad connection?" I honestly wasn't being fresh: this was my story too, somehow, all the way back, from the beginning, and I had to know where we were in it. "Come *on*, Aunt Rifke."

"I got an answer." The words came slowly, and cut off abruptly, though she seemed to want to say something more. Instead, she got up and went to the stove, all my aunts' traditional *querencia* in times of emotional stress. Without turning her head, she said in a curiously dull tone, "*You* go home now. Your mother'll yell at me."

My mother worried about my grades and my taste in friends, not about me; but I had never seen Aunt Rifke quite like this, and I knew better than to push her any further. So I went on home.

From that day, however, I made a new point of stopping by the studio literally every day – except Shabbos, naturally – even if only for a few minutes, just to let Uncle Chaim know that someone besides Aunt Rifke was concerned about him. Of course, obviously, a whole lot of other people would have been, from family to gallery owners to friends like Jules and Ruthie; but I was ten years old, and feeling like my uncle's only guardian, and a private detective to boot. A guardian against *what*? An angel? Detecting *what*? A portrait? I couldn't have said for a minute, but a ten-year-old boy with a sense of mission definitely qualifies as a dangerous flying object.

Uncle Chaim didn't talk to me anymore while he was working, and I really missed that. To this day, almost everything I know about painting – about *being* a painter, every day, all day – I learned from him, grumbled out of the side of his mouth as he sized a canvas, touched up a troublesome corner, or stood back, scratching his head, to reconsider a composition or a subject's expression, or simply to study the stoop of a shadow. Now he worked in bleak near-total silence; and since the blue angel never spoke unless addressed directly, the studio had become a far less inviting place than my three-year-old self had found it. Yet I felt that Uncle Chaim still liked having me there, even if he didn't say anything, so I kept going, but it was an effort some days, mission or no mission.

His only conversation was with the angel – Uncle Chaim always chatted with his models; paradoxically, he felt that it helped them to concentrate – and while I honestly wasn't trying to eavesdrop (except sometimes), I couldn't help overhearing their talk. Uncle Chaim would ask the angel to lift a wing slightly, or to alter her stance somewhat: as I've said, sitting remained uncomfortable and unnatural for her, but she had finally been able to manage a sort of semi-recumbent posture, which made her look curiously vulnerable, almost like a tired child after an adult party, playing at being her mother, with the grownups all asleep upstairs. I can close my eyes today and see her so.

One winter afternoon, having come tired, and stayed late, I was half-asleep on a padded rocker in a far corner when I heard Uncle Chaim saying, "You ever think that maybe we might both be dead, you and me?"

"We angels do not die," the blue angel responded. "It is not in us to die."

"I told you, lift your chin," Uncle Chaim grunted. "Well, it's built into *us*, believe me, it's mostly what we do from day one." He looked up at her from the easel. "But I'm trying to get you into a painting, and I'll never be able to do it, but it doesn't matter, got to keep trying. The head a *little* bit to the left – no, that's too much, I said a *little*." He put down his brush and walked over to the angel, taking her chin in his hand. He said, "And you... whatever you're after, you're not going to get that right, either, are you? So it's like we're stuck here together – and if we *were* dead, maybe this is hell. Would we know? You ever think about things like that?"

"No." The angel said nothing further for a long time, and I was dozing off again when I heard her speak. "You would not speak so lightly of hell if you had seen it. I have seen it. It is not what you think."

"*Nu?*" Uncle Chaim's voice could raise an eyebrow itself. "So what's it like?"

"*Cold*." The words were almost inaudible. "So cold...so lonely...so *empty*. God is not there...no one is there. No one, no one, no one...no one..."

It was that voice, that other voice that I had heard once before, and I have never again been as frightened as I was by the murmuring terror in her words. I actually grabbed my books and got up to leave, already framing some sort of gotta-go to Uncle Chaim, but just then Aunt Rifke walked into the studio for the first time, with Rabbi Shulevitz trailing behind her, so I stayed where I was. I don't know a thing about ten-year-olds today; but in those times one of the major functions of adults was to supply drama and mystery to our lives, and we took such things where we found them.

Rabbi Stuart Shulevitz was the nearest thing my family had to an actual regular rabbi. He was Reform, of course, which meant that he had no beard, played the guitar, performed Bat Mitzvahs and interfaith marriages, invited local priests and imams to lead the Passover ritual, and put up perpetually with all the jokes told, even by his own congregation, about young, beardless, terminally tolerant Reform rabbis. Uncle Chaim, who allowed Aunt Rifke to drag him to *shul* twice a year, on the High Holidays, regarded him as being somewhere between a mild head cold and mouse droppings in the pantry. But Aunt Rifke always defended Rabbi Shulevitz, saying, "He's smarter than he looks, and anyway he can't help being blond. Also, he smells good."

Uncle Chaim and I had to concede the point. Rabbi Shulevitz's immediate predecessor, a huge, hairy, bespectacled man from Riga, had smelled mainly of rancid hair oil and cheap peach *schnapps*. And he couldn't sing "Red River Valley," either.

Aunt Rifke was generally a placid-appearing, *hamishe* sort of woman, but now her plump face was set in lines that would have told even an angel that she meant business. The blue angel froze in position in a different way than she usually held still as required by the pose. Her strange eyes seemed almost to change their shape, widening in the center and somehow *lifting* at the corners, as though to echo her wings. She stood at near-attention, silently regarding Aunt Rifke and the rabbi.

Uncle Chaim never stopped painting. Over his shoulder he said, "Rifke, what do you want? I'll be home when I'm home."

"So who's rushing you?" Aunt Rifke snapped back. "We didn't come about you. We came the rabbi should take a look at your *model* here." The word burst from her mouth trailing blue smoke.

"What look? I'm working, I'm going to lose the light in ten, fifteen minutes. Sorry, Rabbi, I got no time. Come back next week, you could say a *barucha* for the whole studio. Goodbye, Rifke."

But my eyes were on the Rabbi, and on the angel, as he slowly approached her, paying no heed to the quarreling voices of Uncle Chaim and Aunt Rifke. Blond or not, "Red River Valley" or not, he was still magic in my sight, the official representative of a power as real as my disbelief. On the other hand, the angel could fly. The Chassidic wonder-*rebbes* of my parents' Eastern Europe could fly up to heaven and share the Shabbos meal with God, when they chose. Reform rabbis couldn't fly.

As Rabbi Shulevitz neared her, the blue angel became larger and more stately, and there was now a certain menacing aspect to her divine radiance, which set me shrinking into a corner, half-concealed by a dusty drape. But the rabbi came on.

"Come no closer," the angel warned him. Her voice sounded deeper, and slightly distorted, like a phonograph record when the Victrola hasn't been wound tight enough. "It is not for mortals to lay hands on the Lord's servant and messenger."

"I'm not touching you," Rabbi Shulevitz answered mildly. "I just want to look in your eyes. An angel can't object to that, surely."

"The full blaze of an angel's eyes would leave you ashes, impudent man." Even I could hear the undertone of anxiety in her voice.

"That is foolishness." The rabbi's tone continued gentle, almost playful. "My friend Chaim paints your eyes full of compassion, of sorrow for the world and all its creatures, every one. Only turn those eyes to me for a minute, for a very little minute, where's the harm?"

Obediently he stayed where he was, taking off his hat to reveal the black *yarmulke* underneath. Behind him, Aunt Rifke made as though to take Uncle Chaim's arm, but he shrugged her away, never taking his own eyes from Rabbi Shulevitz and the blue angel. His face was very pale. The glass of Scotch in his left hand, plainly as forgotten as the brush in his right, was beginning to slosh over the rim with his trembling, and I was distracted with fascination, waiting for him to drop it. So I wasn't quite present, you might say, when the rabbi's eyes looked into the eyes of the blue angel.

But I heard the rabbi gasp, and I saw him stagger backwards a couple of steps, with his arm up in front of his eyes. And I saw the angel turning away, instantly; the whole encounter can't have lasted more than five seconds, if that much. And if Rabbi Shulevitz looked stunned and frightened – which he did – there is no word that I know to describe the expression on the angel's face. No words.

Rabbi Shulevitz spoke to Aunt Rifke in Hebrew, which I didn't know, and she answered him in swift, fierce Yiddish, which I did, but only insofar as it pertained to things my parents felt were best kept hidden from me, such as money problems, family gossip and sex. So I missed most of her words, but I caught anyway three of them. One was *shofar*, which is the ram's horn blown at sundown on the High Holidays, and about which I already knew two good dirty jokes. The second was *minyan*, the number of adult Jews needed to form a prayer circle on special occasions. Reform *minyanim* include women, which Aunt Rifke always told me I'd come to appreciate in a couple of years. She was right.

The third word was *dybbuk*.

I knew the word, and I didn't know it. If you'd asked me its meaning, I would have answered that it meant some kind of bogey, like the Invisible Man, or just maybe the Mummy. But I learned the real meaning fast, because Rabbi Shulevitz had taken off his glasses and was wiping his forehead, and whispering, *"No. No. Ich vershtaye nicht..."*

Uncle Chaim was complaining, "What the hell *is* this? See now, we've lost the light already, I *told* you." No one – me included – was paying any attention.

Aunt Rifke – who was never entirely sure that Rabbi Shulevitz *really* understood Yiddish – burst into English. "It's a *dybbuk*, what's not to understand? There's a *dybbuk* in that woman, you've got to get rid of it! You get a *minyan* together, right now, you get rid of it! Exorcise!"

Why on earth did she want the rabbi to start doing pushups or jumping-jacks in this moment? I was still puzzling over that when he said, "That woman, as you call her, is an angel. You cannot...Rifke, you do not exorcise an angel." He was trembling – I could see that – but his voice was steady and firm.

"You do when it's possessed!" Aunt Rifke looked utterly exasperated with everybody. "I don't know how it could happen, but Chaim's angel's got a *dybbuk* in her –" she whirled on her husband – "which is why she makes you just keep painting her and painting her, day and night. You finish – really finish, it's done, over – she might have to go back out where it's not so nice for a *dybbuk*, you know about that? Look at her!" and she pointed an orange-nailed finger straight in the blue angel's face. *"She* hears me, *she* knows what I'm talking about. You know what I'm talking, don't you, Miss Angel? Or I should say, Mister *Dybbuk?* You tell me, okay?"

I had never seen Aunt Rifke like this; she might have been possessed herself. Rabbi Shulevitz was trying to calm her, while Uncle Chaim fumed at the intruders disturbing his model. To my eyes, the angel looked more than disturbed – she looked as terrified as a cat I'd seen backed against a railing by a couple of dogs, strays, with no one to call them away from tearing her to pieces. I was anxious for her, but much more so for my aunt and uncle, truly expecting them to be struck by lightning, or turned to salt, or something on that order. I was scared for the rabbi as well, but I figured he could take care of himself. Maybe even with Aunt Rifke.

"A *dybbuk* cannot possibly possess an angel," the rabbi was saying. "Believe me, I majored in Ashkenazic folklore – wrote my thesis on Lilith, as a matter of fact – and there are no accounts, no legends, not so much as a single *bubbemeise* of such a thing. *Dybbuks* are wandering spirits, some of them good, some malicious, but all houseless in the universe. They cannot enter heaven, and Gehenna won't have them, so they take refuge within the first human being they can reach, like any parasite. But an angel? Inconceivable, take my word. Inconceivable."

"In the mind of God," the blue angel said, "nothing is inconceivable."

Strangely, we hardly heard her; she had almost been forgotten in the dispute over her possession. But her voice was that other voice – I could see Uncle Chaim's eyes widen as he caught the difference. That voice said now, "She is right. I am a *dybbuk*."

In the sudden absolute silence, Aunt Rifke, serenely complacent, said, "Told you."

I heard myself say, "Is she bad? I thought she was an angel."

Uncle Chaim said impatiently, "What? She's a model."

Rabbi Shulevitz put his glasses back on, his eyes soft with pity behind the heavy lenses. I expected him to point at the angel, like Aunt Rifke, and thunder out stern and stately Hebrew maledictions, but he only said, "Poor thing, poor thing. Poor creature."

Through the angel's mouth, the *dybbuk* said, "Rabbi, go away. Let me alone, let me be. I am warning you."

I could not take my eyes off her. I don't know whether I was more fascinated by what she was saying, and the adults' having to deal with its mystery, or by the fact that all the time I had known her as Uncle Chaim's winged and haloed model, someone else was using her the way I played with my little puppet theatre at home – moving her, making up things for her to say, perhaps even putting her away at night when the studio was empty. Already it was as though I had never heard her strange, shy voice asking a child's endless questions about the world, but only this grownup voice, speaking to Rabbi Shulevitz Rabbi. "You cannot force me to leave her."

"I don't want to force you to do anything," the rabbi said gently. "I want to help you."

I wish I had never heard the laughter that answered him. I was too young to hear something like that, if anyone could ever be old enough. I cried out and doubled up around myself, hugging my stomach, although what I felt was worse than the worst bellyache I had ever wakened with in the night. Aunt Rifke came and put her arms around me, trying to soothe me, murmuring, half in English, half in Yiddish, "Shh, shh, it's all right, *der rebbe* will make it all right. He's helping the angel, he's getting rid of that thing inside her, like a doctor. Wait, wait, you'll see, it'll be all right." But I went on crying, because I had been visited by a monstrous grief not my own, and I was only ten.

The *dybbuk* said, "If you wish to help me, rabbi, leave me alone. I will not go into the dark again."

Rabbi Shulevitz wiped his forehead. He asked, his tone still gentle and wondering, "What did you do to become...what you are? Do you remember?"

The *dybbuk* did not answer him for a long time. Nobody spoke, except for Uncle Chaim muttering unhappily to himself, "Who needs this? Try to get your work done, it turns into a *ferkockte* party. Who needs it?" Aunt Rifke shushed him, but she reached for his arm, and this time he let her take it.

The rabbi said, "You are a Jew."

"I was. Now I am nothing."

"No, you are still a Jew. You must know that we do not practice exorcism, not as others do. We heal, we try to heal both the person possessed and the one possessing. But you must tell me what you have done. Why you cannot find peace."

The change in Rabbi Shulevitz astonished me as much as the difference between Uncle Chaim's blue angel and the spirit that inhabited her and spoke through her. He didn't even look like the crewcut, blue-eyed, guitar-playing, basketball-playing (well, he tried) college-student-dressing young man whose idea of a good time was getting people to sit in a circle and sing "So Long, It's Been Good to Know You" or "Dreidel, Dreidel, Dreidel" together. There was a power of his own inhabiting him, and clearly the *dybbuk* recognized it. It said slowly, "You cannot help me. You cannot heal."

"Well, we don't know that, do we?" Rabbi Shulevitz said brightly. "So, a bargain. You tell me what holds you here, and I will tell you, honestly, what I can do for you. *Honestly.*"

Again the *dybbuk* was slow to reply. Aunt Rifke said hotly, "What is this? What *help?* We're here to expel, to get rid of a demon that's taken over one of God's angels, if that's what she really is, and enchanted my husband so it's all he can paint, all he can think about painting. Who's talking about *helping* a demon?"

"The rabbi is," I said, and they all turned as though they'd forgotten I was there. I gulped and stumbled along, feeling like I might throw up. I said, "I don't think it's a demon, but even if it is, it's given Uncle Chaim a chance to paint a real angel, and everybody loves the paintings, and they buy them, which we wouldn't have had them to sell if the – the *thing* – hadn't made her stay in Uncle Chaim's studio." I ran out of breath, gas, and show-business ambitions all at pretty much the same time, and sat down, grateful that I had neither puked nor started to cry. I was still grandly capable of both back then.

Aunt Rifke looked at me in a way I didn't recall her ever doing before. She didn't say anything, but her arm tightened around me. Rabbi Shulevitz said quietly, "Thank you, David." He turned back to face the angel. In the same voice, he said, "Please. Tell me."

When the *dybbuk* spoke again, the words came one by one – two by two, at most. "A girl...There was a girl...a young woman..."

"*Ai*, how not?" Aunt Rifke's sigh was resigned, but not angry or mocking, just as Uncle Chaim's. "*Shah*, Rifkela" was a neither a dismissal nor an order. The rabbi, in turn, gestured them to silence.

"She wanted us to marry," the *dybbuk* said. "I did too. But there was time. There was a world...there was my work...there were things to see... to taste and smell and do and *be*...It could wait a little. She could wait..."

"Uh-huh. Of course. You could *die* waiting around for some damn man!"

"*Shah*, Rifkela!"

"But this one did not wait around," Rabbi Shulevitz said to the *dybbuk*.

"She did not wait for you, am I right?"

"She married another man," came the reply, and it seemed to my ten-year-old imagination that every tortured syllable came away tinged with blood. "They had been married for two years when he beat her to death."

It was my Uncle Chaim who gasped in shock. I don't think anyone else made a sound.

The *dybbuk* said, "She sent me a message. I came as fast as I could. I *did* come," though no one had challenged his statement. "But it was too late."

This time we were the ones who did not speak for a long time. Rabbi Shulevitz finally asked, "What did you do?"

"I looked for him. I meant to kill him, but he killed himself before I found him. So I was too late again."

"What happened then?" That was me, once more to my own surprise. "When you didn't get to kill him?"

"I lived. I wanted to die, but I lived."

From Aunt Rifke – how not? "You ever got married?"

"No. I lived alone, and I grew old and died. That is all."

"Excuse me, but that is *not* all." The rabbi's voice had suddenly, startlingly, turned probing, almost harsh. "That is only the beginning." Everyone looked at him. The rabbi said, "So, after you died, what did happen? Where did you go?"

There was no answer. Rabbi Shulevitz repeated the question. The *dybbuk* responded finally, "You have said it yourself. Houseless in the universe I am, and how should it be otherwise? The woman I loved died because I did not love her enough – what greater sin is there than that? Even her murderer had the courage to atone, but I dared not offer my own life in payment for hers. I chose to live, and living on has been my punishment, in death as well as in life. To wander back and forth in a cold you cannot know, shunned by heaven, scorned by purgatory...do you wonder that I sought shelter where I could, even in an angel? God himself would have to come and cast me out again, Rabbi – you never can."

I became aware that my aunt and uncle had drawn close around me, as though expecting something dangerous and possibly explosive to happen. Rabbi Shulevitz took off his glasses again, ran his hand through his crewcut, stared at the glasses as though he had never seen them before, and put them back on.

"You are right," he said to the *dybbuk*. "I'm a rabbi, not a *rebbe* – no Solomonic wisdom, no magical powers, just a degree from a second-class seminary in Metuchen, New Jersey. You wouldn't know it." He drew a deep breath and moved a few steps closer to the blue angel. He said, "But this *gornisht* rabbi knows anyway that you would never have been allowed this refuge if God had not taken pity on you. You must know this, surely?" The *dybbuk* did not answer. Rabbi Shulevitz said, "And if God pities you, might you not have a little pity on yourself? A little forgiveness?"

"Forgiveness..." Now it was the *dybbuk* who whispered. "Forgiveness may be God's business. It is not mine."

"Forgiveness is everyone's business. Even the dead. On this earth or under it, there is no peace without forgiveness." The rabbi reached out then, to touch the blue angel comfortingly. She did not react, but he winced and drew his hand back instantly, blowing hard on his fingers, hitting them against his leg. Even I could see that they had turned white with cold.

"You need not fear for her," the *dybbuk* said. "Angels feel neither cold nor heat. You have touched where I have been."

Rabbi Shulevitz shook his head. He said, "I touched you. I touched your shame and your grief – as raw today, I know, as on the day your love died. But the cold...the cold is yours. The loneliness, the endless guilt over what you should have done, the endless turning to and fro in empty darkness...none of that comes from God. You must believe me, my friend." He paused, still flexing his frozen fingers. "And you must come forth from God's angel now. For her sake and your own."

The *dybbuk* did not respond. Aunt Rifke said, far more sympathetically than she had before, "You need a *minyan*, I could make some calls. We'd be careful, we wouldn't hurt it."

Uncle Chaim looked from her to the rabbi, then back to the blue angel. He opened his mouth to say something, but didn't.

The rabbi said, "You have suffered enough at your own hands. It is time for you to surrender your pain." When there was still no reply, he asked, "Are you afraid to be without it? Is that your real fear?"

"It has been my only friend!" the *dybbuk* answered at last. "Even God cannot understand what I have done so well as my pain does. Without the pain, there is only me."

"There is heaven," Rabbi Shulevitz said. "Heaven is waiting for you. Heaven has been waiting a long, long time."

"*I am waiting for me!*" It burst out of the *dybbuk* in a long wail of purest terror, the kind you only hear from small children trapped in a nightmare. "You want me to abandon the one sanctuary I have ever found, where I can huddle warm in the consciousness of an angel and sometimes – for a little – even forget the thing I am. You want me to be naked to myself again, and I am telling you *no, not ever, not ever, not ever.* Do what you must, Rabbi, and I will do the only thing I can." It paused, and then added, somewhat stiffly, "Thank you for your efforts. You are a good man."

Rabbi Shulevitz looked genuinely embarrassed. He also looked weary, frustrated and older than he had been when he first recognized the possession of Uncle Chaim's angel. Looking vaguely around at us, he said, "I don't know – maybe it *will* take a *minyan*. I don't want to, but we can't just..." His voice trailed away sadly, too defeated even to finish the sentence.

Or maybe he didn't finish because that was when I stepped forward, pulling away from my aunt and uncle, and said, "He can come with me, if he wants. He can come and live in me. Like with the angel."

Uncle Chaim said, *"What?"* and Aunt Rifke said, *"No!"* and Rabbi Shulevitz said, *"David!"* He turned and grabbed me by the shoulders, and I could feel him wanting to shake me, but he didn't. He seemed to be having trouble breathing. He said, "David, you don't know what you're saying."

"Yes, I do," I said. "He's scared, he's so scared. I know about scared."

Aunt Rifke crouched down beside me, peering hard into my face. "David, you're ten years old, you're a little boy. This one, he could be a thousand years, he's been hiding from God in an angel's body. How could you know what he's feeling?"

I said, "Aunt Rifke, I go to school. I wake up every morning, and right away I think about the boys waiting to beat me up because I'm small, or because I'm Jewish, or because they just don't like my face, the way I look at them. Every day I want to stay home and read, and listen to the radio, and play my All-Star Baseball game, but I get dressed and I eat breakfast, and I walk to school. And every day I have to think how I'm going to get through recess, get through gym class, get home without running into Jay Taffer, George DiLucca. Billy Kronish. I know all about not wanting to go outside."

Nobody said anything. The rabbi tried several times, but it was Uncle Chaim who finally said loudly, "I got to teach you to box. A little Archie Moore, a little Willie Pep, we'll take care of those *mamzers*." He looked ready to give me my first lesson right there.

When the *dybbuk* spoke again, its voice was somehow different: quiet, slow, wondering. It said, "Boy, you would do that?" I didn't speak, but I nodded.

Aunt Rifke said, "Your mother would *kill* me! She's hated me since I married Chaim."

The *dybbuk* said, "Boy, if I come...outside, I cannot go back. Do you understand that?"

"Yes," I said. "I understand."

But I was shaking. I tried to imagine what it would be like to have someone living inside me, like a baby, or a tapeworm. I was fascinated by tapeworms that year. Only this would be a spirit, not an actual physical thing — that wouldn't be so bad, would it? It might even be company, in a way, almost like being a comic-book superhero and having a secret identity. I wondered whether the angel had even known the *dybbuk* was in her, as quiet as he had been until he spoke to Rabbi Shulevitz. Who, at the moment, was repeating over and over, "No, I can't permit this. This is *wrong*, this can't be allowed. No." He began to mutter prayers in Hebrew.

Aunt Rifke was saying, "I don't care, I'm calling some people from the *shul*, I'm getting some people down here right *away!*" Uncle Chaim was gripping my shoulder so hard it hurt, but he didn't say anything. But there was really no one in the room except the *dybbuk* and me. When I think about it, when I remember, that's all I see.

I remember being thirsty, terribly thirsty, because my throat and my mouth were so dry. I pulled away from Uncle Chaim and Aunt Rifke, and I moved past Rabbi Shulevitz, and I croaked out to the *dybbuk*, "Come on, then. You can come out of the angel, it's safe, it's okay." I remember thinking that it was like trying to talk a cat down out of a tree, and I almost giggled.

I never saw him actually leave the blue angel. I don't think anyone did. He was simply standing right in front of me, tall enough that I had to look up to meet his eyes. Maybe he wasn't a thousand years old, but Aunt Rifke hadn't missed by much. It wasn't his clothes that told me – he wore a white turban that looked almost square, a dark-red vest sort of thing and white trousers, under a gray robe that came all the way to the ground – it was the eyes. If blackness is the absence of light, then those were the blackest eyes I'll ever see, because there was no light in those eyes, and no smallest possibility of light ever. You couldn't call them sad: *sad* at least knows what *joy* is, and grieves at being exiled from joy. However old he really was, those eyes were a thousand years past sad.

"Sephardi," Rabbi Shulevitz murmured. "Of course he'd be Sephardi."

Aunt Rifke said, "You can see through him. Right through."

In fact he seemed to come and go: near-solid one moment, cobweb and smoke the next. His face was lean and dark, and must have been a proud face once. Now it was just weary, unspeakably weary – even a ten-year-old could see that. The lines down his cheeks and around the eyes and mouth made me think of desert pictures I'd seen, where the earth gets so dry that it pulls apart, cracks and pulls away from itself. He looked like that.

But he smiled at me. No, he smiled *into* me, and just as I've never seen eyes like his again, I've never seen a smile as beautiful. Maybe it couldn't reach his eyes, but it must have reached mine, because I can still see it. He said softly, "Thank you. You are a kind boy. I promise you, I will not take up much room."

I braced myself. The only invasive procedures I'd had any experience with then were my twice-monthly allergy shots and the time our doctor had to lance an infected finger that had swollen to twice its size. Would possession it be anything like that? Would it make a difference if you were sort of inviting the possession, not being ambushed and taken over, like in *Invasion of the Body Snatchers*? I didn't mean to close my eyes, but I did.

Then I heard the voice of the blue angel.

"There is no need." It sounded like the voice I knew, but the *breath* in it was different – I don't know how else to put it. I could say it sounded stronger, or clearer, or maybe more musical; but it was the breath, the free breath. Or maybe that isn't right either, I can't tell you – I'm not even certain whether angels breathe, and I knew an angel once. There it is.

"Manassa, there is no need," she said again. I turned to look at her then, when she called the *dybbuk* by his name, and she was smiling herself, for the first time. It wasn't like his; it was a faraway smile at something I couldn't see, but it was real, and I heard Uncle Chaim catch his breath. To no one in particular, he said, *"Now* she smiles. Never once, I could never once get her to smile."

"Listen," the blue angel said. I didn't hear anything but my uncle grumbling, and Rabbi Shulevitz's continued Hebrew prayers. But the *dybbuk* – Manassa – lifted his head, and the endlessly black eyes widened, just a little.

The angel said again, "Listen," and this time I did hear something, and so did everyone else. It was music, definitely music, but too faint with distance for me to make anything out of it. But Aunt Rifke, who loved more kinds of music than you'd think, put her hand to her mouth and whispered, *"Oh."*

"Manassa, listen," the angel said for the third time, and the two of them looked at each other as they music grew stronger and clearer. I can't describe it properly: it wasn't harps and psalteries – whatever a psaltery is, maybe you use it singing psalms – and it wasn't a choir of soaring heavenly voices, either. It was almost a little scary, the way you feel when you hear the wild geese passing over in the autumn night. It made me think of that poem of Tennyson's, with that line about *the horns of Elfland faintly blowing.* We'd been studying it in school.

"It is your welcome, Manassa," the blue angel said. "The gates are open for you. They were always open."

But the *dybbuk* backed away, suddenly whimpering. "I cannot! I am afraid! They will see!"

The angel took his hand. "They see now, as they saw you then. Come with me, I will take you there."

The *dybbuk* looked around, just this side of panicking. He even tugged a bit at the blue angel's hand, but she would not let him go. Finally he sighed very deeply – lord, you could feel the dust of the tombs in that sigh, and the wind between the stars – and nodded to her. He said, "I will go with you."

The blue angel turned to look at all of us, but mostly at Uncle Chaim.

She said to him, "You are a better painter than I was a muse. And you taught me a great deal about other things than painting. I will tell Rembrandt."

Aunt Rifke said, a little hesitantly, "I was maybe rude. I'm sorry." The angel smiled at her.

Rabbi Shulevitz said, "Only when I saw you did I realize that I had never believed in angels."

"Continue not to," the angel replied. "We rather prefer it, to tell you the truth. We work better that way."

Then she and the *dybbuk* both looked at me, and I didn't feel even ten years old; more like four or so. I threw my arms around Aunt Rifke and buried my face in her skirt. She patted my head – at least I guess it was her, I didn't actually see her. I heard the blue angel say in Yiddish, "*Sei gesund,* Chaim's Duvidl. You were always courteous to me. Be well."

I looked up in time to meet the old, old eyes of the *dybbuk*. He said, "In a thousand years, no one has ever offered me freely what you did." He said something else, too, but it wasn't in either Hebrew or Yiddish, and I didn't understand.

The blue angel spread her splendid, shimmering wings one last time, filling the studio – as, for a moment, the mean winter sky outside seemed to flare with a sunset hope that could not have been. Then she and Manassa, the *dybbuk*, were gone, vanished instantly, which makes me think that the wings aren't really for flying. I don't know what other purpose they could serve, except they did seem somehow to enfold us all and hold us close. But maybe they're just really decorative. I'll never know now.

Uncle Chaim blew out his breath in one long, exasperated sigh. He said to Aunt Rifke, "I never did get her right. You know that."

I was trying to hear the music, but Aunt Rifke was busy hugging me, and kissing me all over my face, and telling me not ever, *ever* to do such a thing again, what was I thinking? But she smiled up at Uncle Chaim and answered him, "Well, she got *you* right, that's what matters." Uncle Chaim blinked at her. Aunt Rifke said, "She's probably telling Rembrandt about you right now. Maybe Vermeer, too."

"You think so?" Uncle Chaim looked doubtful at first, but then he shrugged and began to smile himself. "Could be."

I asked Rabbi Shulevitz, "He said something to me, the *dybbuk,* just at the end. I didn't understand."

The rabbi put his arm around me. "He was speaking in old Ladino, the language of the Sephardim. He said, '*I will not forget you.*'" His smile was a little shaky, and I could feel him trembling himself, with everything over. "I think you have a friend in heaven, David. Extraordinary Duvidl."

The music was gone. We stood together in the studio, and although there were four of us, it felt as empty as the winter street beyond the window where the blue angel had posed so often. A taxi took the corner too fast, and almost hit a truck; a cloud bank was pearly with the moon's muffled light. A group of young women crossed the street, singing. I could feel everyone wanting to move away, but nobody did, and nobody spoke, until Uncle Chaim finally said, "Rabbi, you got time for a sitting tomorrow? Don't wear that suit."

We Never Talk About My Brother

The great songwriter Johnny Mercer insisted on sharing the royalties from "I Wanna Be Around to Pick Up the Pieces When Somebody Breaks Your Heart" with the Cincinnati department-store clerk who suggested the title to him, because he believed that the right title was at least half of a successful song.

Titles really are that valuable, and good ones rarely come to me at all, let alone easily: so I pay attention when they do. The title for this story popped into my head while I was headed out from a hotel room in Austin, Texas, so I mentioned it to the fellow driving me to the World Fantasy Convention that was my reason for being there. He asked me what it was about, and I said "I think it might be about a satyr."

Turns out I was wrong.

Therefore, since the world has still
Much good, but much less good than ill,
And while the sun and moon endure
Luck's a chance, but trouble's sure,
I'd face it as a wise man would,
And train for ill and not for good.

— A.E. Housman

NOBODY DOES ANYMORE, haven't for years – well, that's why you're here, ain't it, one of those "Where Are They Now" pieces of yours? – but it's funny, when you think about it. I mean, even after what happened, and all this time, you'd think Willa and I – Willa's my sister – you'd think we'd say at least Word One about him now and then. To each other, maybe not to anyone else. But we don't, not ever, even now. Hell, my wife won't talk about Esau, and she'd have more reason than most. Lucky you found me first – she'd have run you right on out of the house, and she could do it, too. Tell the truth, shame the devil, the only reason I'm sitting here talking to you at all is you having the mother wit to bring along that bottle of Blanton's Single Barrel. Lord, I swear I can*not* remember the last time I had any of that in the house.

Mind if you record me? No, no, you go ahead on, get your little tape thing going, okay by me. Doesn't make a bit of difference. You're like to think I'm pretty crazy before we're through, one way or another, but that don't make any difference either.

Well, okay then. Let's get started.

Last of the great TV anchormen, my brother, just as big as newsmen ever used to get. Not like today – too many of them in the game, too much competition, all sort of, I don't know, interchangeable. More and more folks getting the news on their computers, those little earphone gadgets, I don't know what-all. It's just different than it was. Way different. Confess I kind of like it.

But back then, back then, Esau was just a little way south of a movie star. Couldn't walk down the street, go out grocery shopping, he'd get jumped by a whole mob of his fans, his groupies. Couldn't turn on the TV and not see him on half a dozen channels, broadcasting, or being interviewed, or being a special guest on some show or other. I mean everything from big political stuff to cooking shows, for heaven's sake. My friend Buddy Andreason, we go fishing weekends, us and Kirby Rich, Buddy used to always tease me about it. Point to those little girls on the news, screaming and running after Esau for autographs, and he'd say, "Man, you could get yourself some of that so easy! Just tell them you're his brother, you'll introduce them – man, they'd be all over you! All *over* you!"

No, it's not a nickname, that was real. Esau Robbins. Right out of the Bible, the Old Testament, the guy who sold his birthright to his brother for a mess of pottage. Pottage is like soup or stew, something like that. Our Papa was a big Bible reader, and there was...I don't know, there was stuff that was funny to him that wasn't real funny to anyone else. Like naming me and Esau like he did.

A lot easier to live with Jacob than a funny name like Esau, I guess – you know, when you're a kid. But I wasn't all that crazy about my name either, tell you the truth, which is why I went with Jake first time anybody ever called me that in school, never looked back. I mean, you think about it now. The Bible Esau's the hunter, the fisherman, the outdoor guy – okay, maybe not the brightest fellow, not the most mannerly, maybe he cusses too much and spits his tobacco where he shouldn't, but still. And Jacob's the sneaky one, you know? Esau's come home beat and hungry and thirsty, and Jacob tricks him – face it, Jacob *tricks* him right out of his inheritance, his whole future, and their mama helps him do it, and God thinks that's righteous, a righteous act. Makes you wonder about some things, don't it?

Did he have a bad time of it growing up, account of his name? 'Bout like you'd expect. I had to fight his battles time to time, if some big fellow was bullyragging him, and my sister Willa did the same, because we were the older ones, and that's just what you do, right? But we didn't *see* him, you know what I mean? Didn't have any idea who he *was,* except a nuisance we had to take care of, watch after, keep out of traffic. He's seven years younger than Willa, five years younger than me. Doesn't sound like much now, but when you're a kid it's a lot. He might have been growing up in China, for all we knew about him.

I'm embarrassed to say it flat out, but there's not a lot I really recall about him as a kid, before the whole thing with Donnie Schmidt. I remember Esau loved tomatoes ripe off the vine – got into trouble every summer, stealing them out of the neighbors' yards – and he was scared of squirrels, can you believe that? Squirrels, for God's sake. Said they chased him. Oh, and he used to hurt himself a lot, jumping down from higher and higher places – ladders, trees, sheds and all such. Practicing landing, that was the idea. Practicing landing.

But I surely remember the first time I ever really looked at Esau and thought, wow, what's going on here? Not at school – in the old Pott Street playground, it was. Donnie Schmidt – mean kid with red hair and a squinty eye – Donnie had Esau down on his back, and was just beating him like a rug. Bloody nose, big purple shiner already coming up...I came running all the way across the playground, Willa too, and I got Donnie by the neck and hauled him right off my brother. Whopped him a couple of times too, I don't mind telling you. He was a nasty one, Donnie Schmidt.

Esau had quit fighting, but he didn't bounce up right away, and I wouldn't have neither, the whupping he'd taken. He was just staring at Donnie, and his eyes had gone really pale, both of them, and he pointed straight at Donnie – looked funny, I'm bound to say, with him still lying flat down in that red-clay mud – and he kind of whispered, "*You* got run over." Hadn't been as close as I was, I'd never have heard him.

"You got run over." Like that – like it had already happened, you see? Exactly – like he was reading the news. You got it.

Okay. Now. This is what's important. This is where you're going to start wondering whether you should have maybe sat just a little closer to the door. See, what happened to Donnie, didn't happen then – it had already happened a week before. Seriously. Donnie, he didn't disappear, blink out of sight, right when Esau said those words. He just shrugged and walked away, and Willa took Esau home to clean him up, and I got into a one-a-cat game – what you probably call "horse" or "catcher-flies-up" – with a couple of my pals until dinnertime. And Ma yelled some at Esau for getting into a fight, but nobody else thought anything more about it, then or ever. Nobody except me.

Because when I woke up next morning, everybody in town knew Donnie Schmidt had been dead for a week. Hell, we'd all been to the funeral.

I didn't see it happen, but Willa did – or that's what she thought, anyway. Donnie'd been walking to school, and old Mack Moffett's car went out of control somehow, crossed three lanes in two, three seconds, and pinned him against the wall of a house. Poor kid never knew what hit him, and neither did anyone who ever went over the car or gave poor Mack a sobriety test. The old man died a couple of months later, by the way. Call it shock, call it a broken heart, if you like – I don't know.

But the point is. The point is that Donnie Schmidt was alive as could be the day before, beating up on Esau on the playground. I remembered that. But I'd also swear on a stack of Bibles that he'd been killed in an accident the week before, and Willa would swear on the Day of Judgment that she was there. And we'd both pass any and every lie-detector test you want to put us through. Because we *know*, we know we're telling the truth, so it's not a lie. Right?

It's just not true.

Told you. Told you you'd be looking at me like that about now...no, don't say nothing, just *listen*, okay? There's more.

Now I got no idea if that was the first time he did it – made something happen by saying it already had. No idea. Like I said before, it was just the first time I ever really saw my brother.

Nor it didn't change a lot between us, him and Willa and me. Willa was all books and choir rehearsals, and I was all cars and trucks and hunting with my Uncle Rick, and Esau pretty much got along on his own, same as he'd always done. He was just Esau, bony as a clothes rack, all elbows and knees – Papa used to say that he was so thin you could shave with him – but if you looked closely, I guess you could have seen how he might yet turn out good-looking. Only we weren't looking closely, none of us were, not even me. Not even after Donnie. One of anything is still just one of anything, even if it's strange. You can put it out of your mind. So across the dinner table was about it for Willa and me. If we were home.

But while I wasn't really looking, I can't say I didn't pay a little more attention in the looking I did, if you know what I mean.

One time I do recall, when Esau was maybe twelve, maybe thirteen, in there somewhere. Must have been thirteen, because I was already out of high school and working five days a week to help with the rent. Anyway I'm up on the roof of the house on a Saturday, replacing a few shingles got blown off in the last windstorm. Hammering and humming, not thinking about much of anything, and suddenly I turn my head and there's Esau, a few feet away, squatting on his heels and watching me. Never heard him climbing up, no idea how long he's been there, but I know I don't like that look – sets me to thinking about the one he gave Donnie. What if he says to me, *"You* fell off the roof," and it turns out I'm dead, and been dead some while? So I say "Hey, you want to hand me those nails over there?" friendly and peaceable as you like. Probably the most I've said to him in a week, more.

So he hands me the nails, and I say thanks, and I go back to work, and Esau sits watching me a few minutes more, and then he asks, right out of nowhere, "Jake, you believe in God?"

Like that. I didn't even look up, just grunted, "Guess I do."

"You think God's nice?"

His voice was still breaking, I recall – went up and down like a seesaw, made me laugh. I said, "Minister says so."

He wouldn't quit on it, wouldn't let up. "But do *you* think God's nice?"

I dropped a couple of shingles, and made him go down and bring them back up to the roof for me. When he'd done that, I said, "You look around at this world, you think God's nice?"

He didn't answer for a while, just sat there watching me work. By and by he said, "If I was God, I'd be nice."

I set my eye on him then, and I don't know what made me do it, but I said, "You would, huh? Tell it to Donnie Schmidt."

I'd never said anything like that to him before. I'd never mentioned Donnie Schmidt since the funeral, because I knew in my mind – like Willa, like everyone else – that Donnie was dead and buried a week before him and Esau had that fight. Anyway, Esau's eyes filled up, which hardly ever happened, he wasn't ever a crier, and his face got all red, and he stood up, and for a minute I thought he actually was about to come at me. But he didn't – he just screamed, with that funny breaking voice, "I *would* be a nice God! I *would!*"

And he was off and gone, I guess down the ladder, though maybe he jumped, the way he was doing then, because he was limping a bit at dinnertime. Anyway, we never talked about God no more, nor about Donnie Schmidt neither, at least while Esau still lived here.

I never talked about any of this with Papa. He was pretty much taken up with his Bible and his notions and his work at the tannery, before he passed. But Ma saw more than she let on. One time...there was this one time she was still up when I come home from little Sadie Morrison's place, she as later married that Canuck fellow, Rene Arceneaux, and she said – that's Ma, not Sadie – she said to me, "Jacob, Esau's bad."

I said, "Ma, goodness' sake, don't say that. There's nothing wrong with the kid except he's kind of a pain in the ass. Otherwise I got no quarrel with him." Which was true enough then, and maybe still is, depending how you measure.

Ma shook her head. I remember, she was sitting right where you are, by the fireplace – this was their house, you know – just rocking and shelling peas – and she said, "Jacob, I ain't nearly as silly as everybody always thinks I am. I know when somebody's bad. Esau, he makes people into ghosts."

I looked at her. I said, "Ma. Ma, don't you never go round saying stuff like that, they'll put you away for sure. You're saying Esau kills people, and he never killed nobody!" And I believed it, you see, absolutely, even though I also knew better.

And Ma...Ma, whatever she knew, maybe she knew it because she was just as silly as folks thought she was. Hard to say about Ma. She said, "That girl last year, the one he was so gone on, who wanted to go off to New York to be an actress. You remember her?"

"Susie Harkin," I said. "Sure I remember. Plane crashed, killed everybody on board. It was real sad."

Ma didn't say nothing for a long time. Rocked and shelled, rocked and shelled. I stood and watched her, snatching myself a pea now and then, and thinking on how wearied she was getting to look. Then she said, almost mumbling-like, "I don't think so, Jacob. I'm *persuaded* she got killed in that crash, but I don't *think* so."

That's exactly how she put it – exactly. I didn't say anything myself, because what could I say – Ma, you're right, I remember it both ways too? I remember you telling me she gave him the mitten – that's the way Ma talks; she meant the girl broke up with him – and left, and I remember Susie doing just fine up there in the city, she even sent me a letter... but I also remember her and Esau talking about getting married someday, only then she stepped on that flight and never got to New York at all...I'm going to tell Ma that, and get her going, when the city health people already thought she ought to be off in some *facility* somewhere? Not hardly.

Things wandered along, way they do, just happening and not happening. Willa went all the way on to state college and become a teacher, and then she got married and moved all that way to Florida, Jacksonville Beach. Got two nice kids, my niece Carol-Ann and my nephew Ben. Ma finally did have to go away, and soon enough she passed too. Me, I kept on at the same hardware store where you found me, only after a while I came to own it – me and the bank. Married Middy Jo Staines, but she died. No children.

And Esau....well, he graduated the town high school like me and Willa – unless maybe we just think he did – and then the University of Colorado gave him a scholarship, unless they just think so, and he was gone out of here quicker than scat. Never really came home after that, except the once, which I'll get to in a bit. Got through college, got the job with that station in Baltimore, and the next time we saw him he was on the air, feeding stories to the network, the way they do – like, "And here's Esau Robbins, our Baltimore correspondent, to tell you more about today's tragic explosion," or whatever. And pretty soon it was D.C. and the national news, every night, and you look up and your baby brother's famous. Couldn't have been over thirty.

And looking good, too, no question about it. Grew up taller than me, taller than Papa, with Ma's dark hair and dark blue eyes, and that look – like he belonged right where he was, telling you things he knows that you don't, and telling them in that deep, warm, friendly voice he had. Lord, I don't know where he rented that voice – he sure didn't have it when he lived in this town. Voice like that, he could have been reciting Mother Goose or something, wouldn't have mattered. When you heard it you just wanted to listen.

I used to watch him on the TV, my brother Esau, telling us what's really doing in Afghanistan, in Somalia, in France, in D.C., and I'd look at his eyes, and I'd wonder if he ever even thought about poor nasty Donnie Schmidt. And I'd wonder how he found out he could do it, how'd he discover his talent, his knack, whatever you want to call it. I mean, how does a little boy, schoolyard-age boy – how does he deal with a thing like that? How does he even practice it, predicting something he wants to happen – and then, like that, it's true, and it's always been true, it's just a plain fact, like gravity or something, with nobody knowing any better for sure but me? Town like this, there's not a lot of people you can talk to about that kind of thing. Must of made him feel even more alone, you know?

The visit. Whoo. Yeah, well – all right. All right.

It wasn't hardly a real visit, first off. See, he'd already been the anchorman on that big news program for at least ten, twelve years when they got the notion to do a show on his return to the old home town. So they sent a whole crowd along with him – a camera crew, and a couple of producers, the way they do, and there was a writer, and some publicity people, and some other folks I can't recall. Anyway, I'll tell you, it was for sure the biggest thing to hit this place since Ruth and Gehrig barnstormed through here back in the Twenties. They were here a whole week, that gang, and they spent a lot of money, and made all the businesses happy. Can't beat that with a stick, can you?

And Esau walked through it all like a king – just like a king, no other word for it. They filmed him greeting old friends, talking with his old teachers, stopping in at all his old hangouts, even reading to kids at the library. Mind you, I don't remember him ever having any hangouts, and the teachers didn't seem to remember him much at all. As for the old friends...look, if Esau had any friends when we were all kids, I swear I don't recall them. I mean, there they were in this documentary thing, shaking his hand, slapping his back, having a beer with him in Henry's – been there fifty, sixty years, that place – but I'd never seen any of them with him as a kid, 'ceptin maybe a few of them were pounding on him, back before Donnie. Thing is, I don't imagine Esau was trying very hard to get the details right. Wouldn't have hardly thought we was worth the trouble. Willa thought she recognized one or two, and remembered this and that, but even she wasn't sure.

Oh, yeah, her and me, we were both in it. They paid for Willa to come from Florida – flew little Ben and Carol-Ann, too, but not her husband Jerry, cause they just wanted to show Esau being an uncle. They'd have put her and the kids up at the Laurel Inn with the crew, but she wanted to stay here at the old house, which was fine with me. Don't get to be around children much.

We didn't see much of Esau even after Willa got here, but a day or two before they wrapped up the film, he dropped over to the house for dinner, which meant that the whole crew dropped over too. We were the only ones eating, and it was the strangest meal I've ever had in my life, what with all those electricians setting up lights, and the sound people running cables every which way, and a director, for God's sake, a director telling us when to start eating – they sent out to Horshach's for prime rib – and where to look when the camera was on us, and what Willa should say to the kids when they asked for seconds. Carol-Ann got so nervous, she actually threw up her creamed corn. And Willa got so mad at the lighting guy, because Ben's got eye trouble, and the lights were so bright and hot... well, it was a real mess, that's all. Just a real mess.

But Esau, he just sat through it all like it was just another broadcast, which I guess to him it was. Never got upset about all the retakes – lord, that dinner must have taken three hours, one thing another – never looked sweaty or tired, always found something new and funny to say to the camera when it started rolling again. But that's who he was talking to, all through that show – not us, for sure. He never once looked straight at any of us, Willa or the kids or me, if the camera wasn't on him.

He was a stranger in this house, the house where we'd all grown up – more of a stranger than all those cameramen, those producers. He could just as well have been from another country, where everybody's great-looking, but they don't speak any language you ever heard of. With all the craziness and confusion, the lights and the reflectors, and the microphones swinging around on pole-things, I probably studied on my brother longer and harder than I'd ever done in my life before. There at that table, having that fake dinner, I studied on him, and I thought a few new things.

See, I couldn't believe it was just Esau. What I *could* believe is there's no such thing as history, not the way they teach it to you in school. Wars, revolutions, all those big inventions, all those big discoveries...if there's been a bunch of people like Esau right through time – or even a few, a handful – then the history books don't signify, you understand what I'm saying? Then it's all just been what any one of them wanted, decided on, right at this moment or that, and no great, you know, patterns to the way things happen. Just Esau, and whatever Others, and *you got run over*. Like that. That's what I came to think.

And I know I'm right. Because Susie Harkin was in that film.

Yeah, yeah, I know what I told you about the plane crash, the rest of it, I'm telling you this now. She walked in by herself, bright as you please, just before they finally got around to putting real food on the table, and sat right down across from Esau, between me and little Ben. The TV people looked at the director for orders, and I guess he figured she was family, no point fussing about it, and let her stay. He was too busy yelling at the crew about the lights, anyway.

Esau was good. I am here to tell you, Esau was *good*. There was just that one moment when he saw her...and even then, you might have had to be me or Willa, and watching close, before you noticed the twist of blank panic in his eyes. After that he never looked straight at her, and he sure never said her name, but you couldn't have told one thing from his expression. Susie didn't waste no time on him, neither; she was busy helping little Ben with his food, cutting his meat up small for him, and making faces to make him laugh. Ma had said "Esau makes people into ghosts," but I don't guess you'd find a ghost cutting up a boy's prime rib for him, do you? Not any kind of ghost I ever heard about.

When she'd finished helping Ben, she looked right up at me, and she winked.

As long as she'd been gone, Susie Harkin didn't look a day different. I don't suppose you'd ever have called her a beauty, best day she ever saw. Face too thin, forehead a shade low, nose maybe a bit beaky – but she had real nice brown eyes, and when she smiled you didn't see a thing but that smile. I'd liked her a good bit when she was going out with Esau, and I was real sorry when she died in that plane crash. So was Willa. And now here Susie was again, sitting at our old dinner table with all these people around, winking at me like the two of us had a secret together. And we did, because I knew she'd been dead, and now she wasn't, and *she* knew

I knew, and she knew *why* I knew besides. So, yeah, you could say we had our secret.

Esau didn't do much more looking at me during the dinner than he did at Susie, but that was the one time he did. I saw him when I turned to say something to Willa. It wasn't any special kind of a look he gave me, not in particular; it was maybe more like the first time I really looked at him, when he did what he did to Donnie Schmidt. As though he hadn't ever seen me either, until that glance, that wink, passed between Susie Harkin and me.

Anyway, by and by the little ones fell asleep, and Willa took them off to bed, and the crew packed up and went back to the Laurel Inn, and Susie right away vanished into the kitchen with all the dirty dishes – "No, I insist, you boys just stay and talk." You don't hear women say that much anymore.

So there we were, me and Esau, everything gotten quiet now – always more quiet after a lot of noise, you notice? – and him still not really looking at me, and me too tired and fussed and befuddled not to come straight at him. But the first thing I asked was about as dumb as it could be. "Squirrels still chasing you?"

Whatever he was or wasn't expecting from me, that sure as hell wasn't it. He practically laughed, or maybe it was more like he grunted in a laugh sort of way, and he said, "Not so much these days." Close to, he looked exactly like he looked on the TV – exactly, right down to the one curl off to the left on his forehead, and the inlaid belt buckle, and that steepling thing he did with his fingers. Really was like talking to the screen.

"Susie's looking fine, don't you think?" I asked him. "I mean, for having been dead and all."

Oh, that reached him. That got his attention. He looked at me then, all right, and he answered, real slow and cold and careful, "I don't know what you're talking about. What *are* you talking about?"

"Come on, Esau," I said. "Tomorrow I might wake up remembering mostly whatever you want me to remember, the way you do people, but right now, tonight, I'm afraid you're just going to have to sit here and talk to me –"

"Or *what?*" Those two words cracked out of him just like a whip does – there's the forward throw, almost gentle, like you're fly-fishing, and then the way you bring it back, that's what makes that sound. He didn't say anything more, but the color had drained right out of his eyes, same way it happened with Donnie Schmidt. Didn't look much like the TV now.

I asked him, "You planning to make me a ghost too? Kill me off in a plane crash a few weeks ago? I ought to tell you, I hate flying, and everybody knows it, so you might want to try something different. Me, I always wanted to get shot by a jealous husband at ninety-five or so, but it's your business, I wouldn't presume." I don't know, something just took me over and I didn't care what I said right then.

He didn't answer. We could hear Susie rattling things in the kitchen, and Willa singing softly to her kids upstairs. Got a pretty voice, Willa does. Wanted to do something with it, but what with school, and then there was Jerry, and then there was the trouble starting with Ma...well, nothing ever came of it somehow. But I could see Esau listening, and just for a minute or so he looked like somebody who really might have had a sister, and maybe a brother too, and was just visiting with them for the evening, like always. I took the moment to say, "Papa was funny, wasn't he, Esau? Getting us backwards like that, with the naming?"

He stared at me. I shrugged a little bit. I said, "Well, you think about it some. Here's Jacob, which I'm named for, cheating Esau out of his inheritance, tricks him into swapping everything due him for a mess of chicken soup or some such. But with us...with us, it kind of worked out t'other way round, wouldn't you say? I mean, when you think about it."

"I don't know what you're talking about." He said it in the TV voice, but his eyes still weren't his TV eyes, reassuring everyone that the world hadn't ended just yet. "Papa was as crazy as Ma, only different, and our names don't signify a thing except he was likely drunk at the time." He slammed his hand on the table, setting all the dishes Susie hadn't cleared off yet to rattling. Esau lowered his voice some. "I never stole *anything* from you, Jake Robbins. I wouldn't have lowered myself to it, any more than I'd have lowered myself to take along a lump of sand-covered cat-shit from this litterbox of a town, the day I finally got out of here. The one thing I ever took away was *me*, do you understand that, brother? Nothing more. Not one damn thing more."

His face was so cramped up with anger and plain contempt that I couldn't help putting a finger out toward him, like I was aiming to smooth away a bunch of rumples. "You want to watch out," I said. "Crack your makeup." Esau came to his feet then, and I really thought he was bound to clock me a good one. I said, "Sit down. There's ladies in the house."

He went on glaring in my face, but by and by he kind of stood down – didn't quite sit, you understand, but more leaned on the table, staring at me. He'd cracked his makeup, all right, and I don't mean the stuff they'd put on his skin for the filming. You wouldn't want that face telling you any kind of news right then.

"I bet Papa knew," I said. "Ma just had like a glimmer of the truth, but Papa...likely it's how come he drank so much, and read the Bible so crazy. It's his side of the family, after all."

Esau said it again. "I don't know what you're talking about," but there wasn't much what you might call conviction in the words. It's an odd thing, but he was always a real bad liar – embarrassing bad. I'd guess it's because he's never had to lie in his life: he could always make the lie be true, if he cared to. Handy.

I said, "I'm talking about genetics. Now there's a word I hadn't had much use for until recently – knew what it meant, more or less, and let it go at that. But there's a deal *to* genetics when you look close, you know?" No answer; nothing but that bad-guy stare, with something under it that maybe might be fear, and maybe not. I kept going. "Papa and his Bible. There's a lot in the Bible makes a lot more sense that way, genetics. What if...let's say all those miracles didn't have a thing to do with God, nor Moses, nor Jesus, nor Adam's left ball, whatever. What if it was all people like you? Two, three, four, five thousand years of people like you? The Bible zigs and zags and contradicts itself, tells the same story forty ways from Sunday, and don't connect up to nothing half the time, even to a preacher. But now you back off and suppose for one moment that the Bible's actually trying to record a world that keeps shifting this way and that, because people keep messing with it. What would you say about that, Esau?"

Nothing. Not a word, not a flicker of an eyelid, nothing for the longest time – and then, of all things, my brother began to smile. "Declare to goodness," he said, and it wasn't the smooth TV voice at all, but more like the way his mouth was born, as we say around here. "Even a blind hog finds an acorn once in a while. Continue, please. You have all my attention."

"No, I don't yet," I said back to him, "but I will. Because with genetics, it's a family thing. Somebody in a family has a gift, a talent, there's likely to be somebody else who has it too. Oh, maybe not the same size or shape of a gift, but close enough. Close enough."

I surely had his attention now, let me tell you. His hands were opening and closing like leaves starting to stir when a storm's coming. "Willa doesn't have that thing you have," I said, "none of it, not at all. She's the lucky one. But *I* do. Wouldn't have guessed it before, not even seeing what you'd done, but now I know better. That same power to mess with things, only I guess I never needed to. Not like you."

Esau started to say something, but then he didn't. I said, "I turned out pretty lucky myself. I had Middy Jo – for a while, anyway. I got a job suited me down to the ground. Didn't have nearly so many people to get even with as you had, and the ones I did I have I mostly forgot over time. I was always forgetful that way. Forget my head, it wasn't screwed on." Papa always used to say that about me, the same way he used to say Willa'd make some woman a great husband, because she could get the car started when he couldn't. Never yet heard old Jerry Flores complain.

"What you did to Donnie Schmidt," I said. "What you did to Susie. What I know you did to a few other folks, even though you made sure the rest of everybody didn't remember. It all scared me so bad, I would never gone anywhere *near* power like that, if I'd known I had it."

Esau's voice was sort of thickish now, like he was trying not to cry, which surely wasn't the case. He said, "You can't do what I do."

"You know better than that, Esau. Same way I know you've never bent reality towards even one good thing. I watch you on the TV, every night, just about, and everything you report on – it's death, it's all death, nothing but death, one way or another. A million baby girls left out on the street in China, a raft full of people capsizes off Haiti, some kid wipes out a whole schoolyard in Iowa, there's more people starving in Africa, getting massacred, there's suicide bombers and serial killers all over the place – it's you, it's your half of the genetics. It's what you are, Esau, and I'm sorry for you."

"Don't be." It was only a whisper, but it came at me like a little sideways swipe from one of those old-time straight razors, the kind Papa had. Esau said, "You're the good one." It wasn't a question. "Well, who'd have thought it? My loud-mouthed, clumsy, stupid big brother turns out to be the superhero in the closet, the champion with a secret identity.

Amazing. Just shows you something or other. Truly amazing."

"No," I said. "No, I don't care about that. I just wanted you to know I know. About the genetics and so forth." And then I said it – because he's right, I am stupid. I said, "You're trying to be the Angel of Death, Esau, and I'm just so sorry for you, that's all."

He'd been looking toward the kitchen, like he expected something – or maybe didn't expect it – but now he turned around on me, and I'm not ever about to forget what I saw then. It was like we were kids again, and he was screaming at me, "I *would* be a nice God! I *would!*" Except now the scream was all in his eyes: they were stretched wide as wide, like howling jaws, and the whites had gone too white, so they made the pupils look, not black, but a kind of musty, crumbly gray, like his eyes were rotting, nothing left in there but gray anger, gray pain, gray brick-lined schoolyards, where my brother Esau learned what he was. I'd been half-way joking when I'd said that about the Angel of Death. Not any more.

"Sorry for me, Jake?" It wasn't the razor-whisper, but it wasn't any voice you'd have recognized, either. Esau said, "*Sorry* for me? I'm on television, asshole. I'm a *star*. Have you the slightest notion of what that means? It means millions – *millions* – of people inviting me into their homes, listening to me, believing in me, *trusting* me. Hell, I'm a family member – a wise old uncle, a mysteriously well-traveled cousin, dropping by to tell them tales of the monsters and fools who run their lives, of the innocents who died horribly today, the people murdered to please somebody's god, the soldiers being sent to die in some place they never heard of, the catastrophes waiting to happen tomorrow, unless somebody does something right away. Which they won't, but that isn't *my* work. I can't claim credit there."

He smiled at me then, and it was a real smile, young and joyous as you like. He said, "Don't you understand? They *love* death, all those people, they love what I do – they *need* it, no matter how awful they say it is. It's built into the whole species, from the beginning, and you know it as well as I do. You may be the Good Angel, but I'm the one they hang out with in the kitchen and the living room, I'm the one they have their coffee with, or a beer, while I smile and lay on some more horror for them. Meaning no offense, but who wants what *you're* selling?"

"Those people who watch you don't know what they're buying," I said back. "Your stories aren't just stories, you aren't just reporting. You're making real things happen in the real world. I see you on the TV and I can feel all those things you talk about, and explain about, and tell folks to be afraid of, I can feel them coming true, every night. It's like Ma said, your stories kill people." He didn't turn a hair, or look away, and I didn't expect him to. I said, "And I keep wondering, how many like us might be doing the same right now, all over everywhere. Messing with people, messing with the world so nothing makes no sense, one day to the next, so most everybody gets run over in the end, like Donnie Schmidt. You suppose that's all we can do? That's all it's for, this gift we've got? This heritage?"

Esau shrugged. "No idea. It suits me." He gave me that smile again, made him look like a happier little kid than he ever was. "But why should it concern you, Jake? Are you planning to devote the rest of your life to writing letters to my sponsors, telling them I'm the source of all the pain and misery in the world? I'll be very interested in watching your efforts. Fascinated, you could say."

"No," I told him. "I've got a store to run, and I meet Earl Howser and Buddy Andreason for breakfast at Buttercup on Tuesdays, and it's not my place to chase around after you, fixing stuff. What I know's what I know, and it don't include putting the world back the way it ought to be. It's too late for that. Way too late for heroes, champions, miracles. Don't matter what our heritage was maybe meant for – your side got hold of it first, and you won long ago. No undoing that, Esau, I ain't fool enough to think otherwise. I'm still sorry for you, but I know your side's won, this side the grave."

He wasn't listening to me, not really. Just about all his attention was focusing on the kitchen right then, because Susie'd begun whistling while she was clattering pots in the sink. She could always whistle like a man, Susie could. Esau took a step toward the sound.

"I wouldn't," I advised him. "Best leave her be for a bit. What with one thing another, she's not real partial to you just now. You know how it is."

He stopped where he was, but he didn't answer. Halfway crouched, halfway plain puzzled – I've seen dogs look like that, when they couldn't figure what to do about that big new dog on the block. He said, real low, "I didn't bring her back."

"No," I said. "You couldn't have."

He didn't hear that right off; then he did, and he was just starting to turn when Susie came out of the kitchen, drying her hands on a dishtowel and asking, "Jake, would you like me to wash that old black roasting pan while I'm at it?" Then she saw Esau standing there, and she stood real still, and he did too. Lord, if I closed my eyes, I'd see them like that right now.

I stood up from the table, so that made three of us on our feet, saying nothing. Esau was breathing hard, and I couldn't hardly tell if Susie was breathing at all. That made me anxious – you know, considering – so I said, "Esau was just leaving. Wanted to say goodbye."

Neither of them paid the least bit of attention to me. Susie finally managed to say, "You're looking well, Esau. That's a really nice tie."

Esau's voice sounded like a cold wind in an empty place. He said, "You're rotting in the ground. You're bones."

"No." Susie's own voice was shaky, but stronger than his, some way. "No, Esau, I'm not. I refuse."

She sort of peeked past him at me as she said that, and Esau caught it. He turned.

"Susie stays," I said. I was madder than I ever remembered being, and I was wound up, ready to go at whoever, let's do it, just pick your weapons. And I was heavily spooked, too, because pretty much the only mixups I've been in my whole life, they were always about hauling some guy off my baby brother one more time. Heritage or not, I'm no fighter, never wanted to be one. It's just I always liked Susie.

As for the way Esau stared at me, it did clear up a few things, and that's about all I'm going to tell you. I looked back into those TV eyes, and I saw what lived in there, and I thought, well, anyway, I've still got a sister. If you can get through the rest of your life without ever having that feeling, I'd recommend it.

Esau said, "She goes back where she belongs. Now."

"She didn't belong there in the first place," I said to him. "Leave her be, Esau. She's got no business being dead."

"You don't know what you're doing," he said. His lips were twitching like they didn't belong to his face. "Stay out of it, Jake."

"Not a chance," I said. "I can't fix up all the things you do, what you've already done. Might be Superman, Spider-Man, Batman could, but it's not in me, I'm no hero. I'm just a stubborn man who runs a hardware store.

But I always liked Susie. Nice girl. Terrific whistler. Susie's not going back nowhere."

Even a little bit younger, I'm sure I'd have been showing off for her, backed away against the wall as she was, looking like a lady tied up for the dragon. But I wasn't showing off for anybody right then, being almost as scared as I was angry. Esau sighed – very dramatic, very heavy. He said, "I did warn you. Nobody can say I didn't warn you. You're my brother, after all."

I started to answer him, but I can't remember what I meant to say, because that was when Esau hit me. Not with his fists, but with such a blast of – I still don't know what to call it...hatred? Contempt? Plain meanness? – that it knocked me off my feet and right over my chair. For a moment I swear I thought I'd caught on fire. My head wouldn't work; *nothing* worked; it was like every single string in my body had been cut – I couldn't even flop around on the floor. I didn't know who I was. I didn't know *what* I was.

Susie screamed, and Esau hit me again. That time I did flop around, after I slid across the floor and fetched up against the wall. To this day I can't honestly explain how it felt – been trying to describe it to myself for years. Best I can do is that it wasn't like an electric shock, and it wasn't really like being burned, or beaten up either, although I was all over bruises next day. It was more...it was more like he was *unmaking* me, like he was starting to take me apart, atom by atom, molecule by molecule, so I wouldn't exist anymore – I wouldn't ever *have* existed, he'd never have *had* a brother. I could feel it happening, and I tell you, I'll never be scared of anything again.

But I didn't die. I mean, I didn't get *lost,* the way he wanted me to. Susie ran to me, but I managed to wave her off, because I didn't want her getting caught between us. Esau went on hammering me with whatever it was he had that let him smash planes out of the sky, trains off the tracks, set mudslides boiling down on little mud villages. But it wasn't hurting me any more, not like it had been. I was still me. He hadn't been able to make me not *be,* you understand?

I got my back against the wall and pushed myself up till I was on my feet. Took more time than you might think – I work, I don't work *out* – and anyway Esau just kept at me, like point-blank, coming close up to me now and knocking me this way and that, one belt of crazy rage after another. I couldn't do much about it yet, but he couldn't quite put me down again, either.

I did tell him to stop it. Same way he warned me, I told him to stop. But he wouldn't.

So I stopped him. Or the thing stopped him, the thing that had been rousing up in me all this time, while he was whupping the daylights out of me. It burst out of me like from a flamethrower, searing me – mouth, throat, chest, guts – way worse than anything Esau'd done to me, and slamming me back against the wall harder than he had. I couldn't see, and I couldn't hear a thing, and right that moment, that's when I did think I was going to die. Looked forward to it, too, just then.

When my eyes cleared some – ears took a lot longer – I saw Esau lying on the floor. He wasn't moving.

If it was just me, the way I was feeling, I'd likely have left him lying there till the neighbors started complaining. But...see, I already told you how Willa and me, we were always supposed to watch over our baby brother – protect him in those schoolyard fights, make sure he did his homework, all that – and I guess old habits die hard. I said, "Esau? Esau?" and when he didn't answer, I tried to get to him, but he seemed an awful long way off. Susie helped me. She'd been crying, but she stopped, and she got me to Esau.

He was trying to sit up by the time we reached him, and we helped him onto his feet in a while. He looked like pounded shit, excuse my French, what with his nice shirt in rags, and that tie Susie liked gone, and an arm of his suit jacket dangling by a few threads. I'd seen him wear that same jacket on the TV, I don't know how many times. His face was gray. I don't mean pale, or white – it was gray like old cement, old grout, and it was like the gray went all the way through. Susie and me, we might be the only people in the world ever saw him like that.

He actually tried to smile. He said, "I should have made you check your guns at the door. Where on earth did you pick up *that* trick?"

"Just got pissed off," I said. "And I'll do worse if you're not out of here in two minutes by Papa's watch. Susie stays."

Esau shrugged, or he tried to. "Got to catch a plane tomorrow, anyway. Back to the old grindstone." He looked at Susie. She kind of edged behind my shoulder some, and Esau's smile widened. He said, "Don't worry, my dear. You really should have stayed dead, you know, but it's not your fault." He turned back toward me. "Your doing, of course."

"Watching those folks pile in," I told him. My head was still ringing. "That whole crew, all those people come to paint up your homecoming for the world to see. Couldn't help thinking there ought to be someone like Susie there too. Like Donnie Schmidt. I swear, I was just thinking on it."

"Glad it wasn't Donnie who showed up," Esau murmured. He tugged on the loose arm of his ruined jacket; it came free, and he dropped it on the floor. "Sneaky old Brother Jake," he said. "You've likely got more of the family inheritance than I do. Just like in Papa's Bible, after all."

I was still feeling hollowed-out, burned-out, not by anything he'd done, but by whatever it was I'd had to do. I said, "I can't let you go on, Esau."

He smiled. "You can't kill me, Jake. We both know you better than that."

"You might not know me well enough," I said. "Gone as long as you've been. There's worse things than killing you. Maybe way worse."

And he saw. He looked into my eyes, for a change, and he saw what I had it in mind to do. "You wouldn't dare," he said in a whisper. "You wouldn't dare."

"I wouldn't dare *not* do it," I answered him straight. "You're a time bomb, Esau, you're a loaded gun. Didn't matter before, when I could pretend I didn't really know – but now, if I don't take the bullets out of you, I'm as bad you are. Can't see that I've got a choice."

He's Esau. He didn't beg, and he didn't bother with threatening. All he said was, "It won't be easy for you. It's my life you're talking about. I'll fight you for it."

"I know you will," I said. "And you'll have a better chance than Donnie Schmidt."

"Or me," Susie said, standing right next to me. "Goodbye, Esau."

He gave her a different kind of smile than he'd given me – practically kind, practically real. It looked nice on him. He said, "Goodbye, Susie. See you on the six o'clock." And he was away, that fast, vanished into the dark. I looked after him for some while, then said what I had to say, and closed the door.

Susie had heard me, of course. "He always meant to be a good God," I told her. "A good God, a good angel, whatever. Don't know how he got to be...what he was."

Susie picked up Esau's torn-off sleeve and turned it around and around in her hands, not looking at it, not looking at anything much. She said finally, "I read once, in India they've got gods that are also demons. Depends on their mood, I guess, or the time of year. Or maybe just their lunch."

"Well, I wasn't planning to go into the god business myself," I told her. "Really wasn't looking to set up in competition with any Angel of Death. Piss-poor job, you ask me. No benefits, no paid vacations. And damn sure no union."

Susie shook her head and laughed a little bit, but after that she got quiet again, and sort of broody. By and by, she said, "There's a union. There's always been others like you, Jake. The ones who mend the world."

"The world's no torn shirt," I said. My insides felt like they'd been scooped out, dragged over gravel and put back. "I got a store to run." Susie looked at me, didn't say anything. I said, "There's others like him out there, I don't know how many. Can't stop them all." I put my hand on Susie's shoulder to steady myself.

Willa came in behind us in her bathrobe, looked around at the dining room, and demanded, "What was all that tarryhooting around in here after we went to bed? Did you and Esau get to wrestling or something?"

"Kind of," I mumbled. "Boys with beers. I'll clean up, I promise."

Willa shrugged. "Your house. I was just afraid you'd wake up the kids. Esau already gone?" I nodded, and she peered at me in that older-sister way of hers. "You sure nothing happened between you two?" She wasn't expecting an answer, so I didn't have to fix one up. She studied Susie a lot more closely and carefully than she'd done during dinner, and there wasn't any question what she was thinking. But what Willa thinks and what Willa says never did spend a lot of time together. This time she just said, "Good of you to take the time with Ben, Susie. I was just frazzled out, dealing with those crazy TV people and Carol-Ann."

"It's been some time since I've been around children," Susie said. "I like yours."

Willa said, "Stay the night, why don't you? It's late, and there's a spare bedroom downstairs." As she left, she said over her shoulder, "And I make great Mexican eggs. My husband loves them, and *he's* Mexican."

Susie looked at me. I said, "If you aren't worried about compromising your reputation, that is, staying over in the house of a widower man.

There's still folks in this town would raise their eyebrows."

Susie laughed full-out then, for the first time. That was nice. She said, "I'm older than I look."

Well.

What else? The network never ran that show, of course, what with one thing another. Didn't get the chance. Seems like it all started turning bad for Esau, just about then, slow but steady. That stock-option business. Those people who sued the whole network about his fouled-up dirty-bomb story. The sexual harassment charges. *Those* got settled out of court, like a bunch of other stuff, but there was a mountain landing on his head and he couldn't duck it all. Still, he hung on like a bullrider. He's almost as stubborn as I am. Almost.

Tell the truth, he might have ridden that bull all the way home, if he'd still been selling the same kind of stories. But the things that had made him who he was, the big disasters and the common-man nightmares, somehow there just weren't as many of them as there had been. The news got smaller, and so did he.

Did I feel bad? Interesting, you asking me that. Yeah, I did feel bad for him, I couldn't help it. I still wonder how he felt when he woke up – the morning *after* the night he told the country all about those Kansas cult-murders, with the ritual mutilating and all – only it turned out they hadn't ever happened, even though he'd made them up just as pretty and scary as all the other lies he'd always made real. How's the Angel of Death supposed to do his job with clipped wings?

I got a call in the store that day. Picked up on the second ring, but when I said hello there wasn't anybody on the line.

The guns were the last straw. The automatics and the Uzis and what-ever in his office, in the dressing-room, those were bad enough, the tab-loids had a field day with those. But trying to go through Los Angeles air-port security with a pistol butt just sticking out of his coat pocket...lord, that did him in. Network hustled him out of there so fast, his desk was smoking behind him. That wasn't me, by the way, all those guns. That was just the state he was in by then. Poor Esau. All those years jumping off things, he still never did learn how to land.

Or maybe I should have chosen my words better as he walked away that night. Probably would have, if I'd had more time. All I knew then was I had to speak up before he did. Jam my foot in the door.

"My brother thinks he's an angel," I'd said. "He thinks he can change anything in the world just by saying so. But that's crazy. *He can't do that.*"

Didn't know what else to say. Might have had a little too much what we used to call *English* on it, but I done what I could.

Lord, don't I wish I had a movie of you for the last half-hour or so, the way you've been looking at me. You'd get to keep *that,* anyway, even though there won't be nothing on your tape tomorrow, nor nothing in your memory. Couple of hours, you couldn't even find this house again, same as your editor won't ever remember giving out this assignment. Because nobody talks about my brother anymore. Nobody's talked about him in years. And it's a sad thing, some ways, because being Esau Robbins every night, everywhere, six o'clock...that *mattered* to him. Being the Angel of Death, that *mattered* to him. They were the only things that ever filled him, you understand me? That's all he ever could do in his life, my poor damn brother – get even with us, with people, for being alive. And I took all that away. Stole his birthright and shut down the life he built with it. That don't balance the scales, nor make up for all he did, but it's going to have to do.

Esau Robbins no longer exists. He's not dead. He's just...gone. Maybe someday I'll go and look for him, like an older brother should, but right now gone is how it stays. Price of the pottage.

Thanks for the Blanton's, young man. Puts a smile on my face, and even though it isn't her drink Susie will certainly applaud your thoughtfulness.

You'll likely be finding a bonus in your next paycheck. Nobody in accounting will be able to explain why – and you sure as hell won't, either – but just you roll with it.

The Tale of Junko and Sayuri

I can't claim to know Japan. I don't speak the language, I have only a smattering of the
history, literature, and mythology, and I've only been there once, in the mid-1980s. But
during that visit I met an old man in a small town: a celebrated woodcarver officially
designated as a National Treasure, who spoke no English and loved jazz (we jammed
a little together, him on saxophone and me on guitar). He sold me a carving that I still
have, and which partly inspired this story of shapeshifting and true natures.

IN JAPAN, very, very, long ago, when almost anybody you met on the road
might turn out to be a god or a demon, there was a young man named
Junko. That name can mean "genuine" in Japanese, or "pure," or "obedi-
ent," and he was all of those things then. He served the great *daimyo* Lord
Kuroda, lord of much of southern Honshu, as Chief Huntsman, and was
privileged to live in the lord's castle itself, rather than in any of the outer
structures, the *yagura*. In addition, he was handsome and amiable, and all
the ladies of the court were aware of him. But he had no notion of this,
which only added to his charm. He was a very serious young man.

He was also a commoner, born of the poorest folk in a poor village,
which meant that he had not the right even to a family name, nor even
to be called Junko-*san* as a mark of respect. In most courts of that time,
he would never have been permitted to look straight into the eyes of a
samurai, let alone to live so intimately among them. But the Lord Kuroda
was an unusual man, with his own sense of humor, his own ideas of what
constituted a samurai, and with a doubtless lamentable tendency to treat
everyone equally. This was generally blamed on his peculiar horoscope.

Now at this time, it often seemed as though half of Japan were forever at war with the other half. The mighty private armies of the *daimyos*
marched and galloped up and down the land, leaving peasant villages
and great fortresses alike smoldering behind them as they pleased. The
shogun at Kyoto might well issue his edicts from time to time, but the sho-
gunate had not then the power that it was to seize much later; so for the
most part his threats went unheeded, and no peace treaty endured for
long. The Lord Kuroda held himself and his own people aside from war
as much as he could, believing it tedious, pointless and utterly impractical, but even he found it wise to keep an army of retainers. And the poor
in other less fortunate prefectures replanted and built their houses again,

and said among themselves that Buddha and the *kami* – the many gods of Shinto – alike slept.

One cold winter, when game was particularly scarce, Junko went out hunting for his master. Friends would gladly have come with him, but everyone knew that Junko preferred to hunt alone. He was polite about it, as always, but he felt that the other courtiers made too much noise and frightened away the winter-white deer and rabbits and wild pigs that he was stalking. He himself moved as quietly – even pulling a sledge behind him – as any fish in a stream, or any bird in the air, and he never came home empty-handed.

On this day, as Amaterasu, the sun, was drowsing down the western sky, Junko also was starting back to the Lord Kuroda's castle. His sledge was laden with a fat stag, and a pig as well, and Junko knew that another kill would load the sledge too heavily for his strength. All the same, he could not resist loosing one last arrow at a second wild pig that had broken the ice on a frozen stream, and was greedily drinking there, ignoring everything but the water. It was too good a chance to pass up, and Junko stood very still, took a deep breath – then let it out, just a little bit, as archers will do – and let his arrow fly.

It may have been that his hands were cold, or that the pig moved slightly at the last moment, or even that the growing twilight deceived Junko's eye, though that seems unlikely. At all events, he missed his mark – the arrow hissed past the pig's left ear, sending the animal off in a panicky scramble through the brush, out of sight and range in an instant – but he hit *something.* Something at the very edge of the water gave a small, sad cry, thrashed violently in the weeds there for a moment, and then fell silent and still.

Junko frowned, annoyed with himself; he had been especially proud of the fact that he never needed more than one arrow to bring down his prey. Well, whatever little creature he had accidentally wounded, it was his duty to put it quickly out of its pain, since an honorable man should never inflict unnecessary suffering. He went forward carefully, his boots sinking into the wet earth.

He found it lying half-in, half-out of the stream: an otter, with his arrow still in his flank. It was conscious, but not trying to drag itself away – it only looked at him out of dazed dark eyes and made no sound, not even when he knelt beside it and drew his knife to cut its throat.

It looked at him – nothing more.

"It would be such a pity to ruin such fur with blood," he thought. "Perhaps I could make a tippet out of it for my master's wife." He put the knife away slowly and lifted the otter in his arms, preparing to break its neck with one swift twist. The otter's sharp teeth could surely have taken off a finger through the heavy mittens, but it struggled not at all, though Junko could feel the captive heart beating wildly against him. When he closed his free hand on the creature's neck, the panting breath, so softly desperate, made his wrist tingle strangely.

"So beautiful," he said aloud in the darkening air. He had never had any special feeling about animals: they were good to eat or they weren't good to eat, though he did rather admire the shimmering grace of fish and the cool stare of a fox. But the otter, hurt and helpless between his hands, made him feel as though he were the one wounded, somehow. "Beautiful," he whispered again, and very carefully and slowly he began to withdraw the arrow.

When Junko arrived back at his lord's castle, it was full dark and the otter lay under his shirt, warm against his belly. He delivered his kill, to be taken off to the great kitchens, gravely accepted the thanks due him, and hurried away to the meager quarters granted him at the castle as soon as it was correct to do so. There he laid the otter on a ragged old cloak that his sister had given him when he was a boy, and knelt beside the creature to study it in lamplight. The wound was no worse than it had been, and no better, though the blood had stopped flowing. He gave the otter water in a little clay dish, but it sniffed feebly at it without drinking; when he put his hand gently on the arrow wound, he could feel the fever already building.

"Well," he said to the otter, "all I know to do is to treat you as I did my little brother, the time he fell on the ploughshare. No biting, now." With his dagger, he trimmed the oily brown fur around the injury; with a rag dipped in hot *nihonshu*, which others call *sake*, he cleaned the area over and over; and with herbal infusions whose use he had learned from his mother's mother, he did his best to draw the infection. Through it all the otter never stirred or protested, but watched him steadily as he labored to undo the damage he had caused. He sang softly now and then, old nonsensical children's songs, hardly knowing he was doing it, and now and then the otter cocked an ear, seeming to listen.

When he was done he offered the water again, and this time the otter drank from the dish, cautiously, never taking its eyes from him, but deeply even so. Junko then lifted it in the old cloak and set all upon his own *tatami* mat, saying, "I cannot bind your wound properly, but healing in open air is best, anyway. And now you should sleep." He covered the otter with his coat, then lay down near it on the *tatami* and quickly fell asleep himself. The otter was awake longer than he, its wide eyes darker than the darkness.

In the morning the gash in the otter's flank smelled far less of fever, and the little animal was clearly hungry. Knowing that otters eat mainly fish, along with such things as frogs and turtles, Junko dressed hurriedly and went to a river that was near the castle (the better for the *daimyo* to keep an eye on the boats that went up and down between the distant cities), and there he caught and cleaned several small fish and brought them back to his quarters. The otter devoured them all, groomed its fur with great care – spending half an hour on its exposed wound alone – and then fell back to sleep for the rest of the day, much of which Junko spent studying it, sitting crosslegged beside his *tatami*. He was completely captivated to learn that the otter snored – very daintily and delicately, through its diamond-shaped nose – and that it smelled only slightly of fish, even after its meal, and much more of spring-warmed earth, as deep in winter as they were. He touched its front claws and realized that they were almost as hard as armor.

When a highly placed serving woman suggested through another servant that she might possibly enjoy his company for tea, Junko made the most courteous apology he could, and went on staring at the otter on his sleeping mat. Towards evening the little creature woke up and lay considering him in its turn, out of eyes much brighter and clearer than they had been. He spoke to it then, saying, "I am very sorry that I hurt you. I hope you are better today." The otter licked its whiskers without taking its eyes from his.

During the days that passed, Junko told no one about the otter: neither the Lord Kuroda nor his wife, the Lady Hara, nor even his closest friend, the horsemaster Akira Yamagata, who might have been expected to understand his fascination. He fed and cared for the otter every day, cleaned and aired out his quarters himself, and saw the arrow wound closing steadily from the inside, as every soldier knows is the proper way of healing. And the otter lay patiently under his hands as he tended it, and shared his *tatami* at night; and if it did not purr, or arch itself back against his hands, as a cat will, when he stroked its beautiful, rich fur, nevertheless it never drew away from the contact, but looked constantly into his eyes, as though it would have spoken to him if it could. He fell into the habit of talking to it himself, more and more, and he named it Sayuri, because men have to name things, and Sayuri was his sister's name.

One morning he told the otter, "My lord will have me guide a hunt meeting with the Lord Sugihara, down on holiday from Osaka. I am not looking forward to it, because neither trusts the other for an instant, and it could all become very wearying, though certainly educational. But when I return, however late it may be, I will take you back to your stream and release you there. You are fully recovered now, and a castle is no place for a wild creature like yourself. Stay well and warm until I come back."

The meeting between the two lords was indeed tiresome, and the hunt itself extremely unsatisfactory; but it had at least the virtue of taking less time than he would have expected, so the sun was still in the sky when Junko climbed the stair to his quarters. He went slowly, remembering his promise to the otter, and finding himself curiously reluctant to keep it. "It will be lonely," he thought. "I will miss...what is it that I will miss?" He could not say, but he knew that it was a real thing. So he sighed and went on to his quarters and opened the door.

The otter was gone.

In its place there stood, waiting for him, the most beautiful young woman he had ever seen. She stood barely higher than his heart, wearing a blue and white kimono, and her face was the dawn shade of a tea-rose, and as perfectly boned and structured as the kites that children were competing with every spring even then. Junko stood gaping at her, not even trying to speak.

"Yes," she said quietly, smiling with small white teeth at his bewilderment. "I am indeed that otter you shot, and then nursed back to health so tenderly. I am quite well now, as you see."

"But," said Junko. "But."

The young woman smiled more warmly as he stumbled among words, finding only that one. "This is my true form, but I take other shapes from time to time, as I choose. And it is so pleasant to be an otter – even as they hunt and mate, and raise their children, and struggle to survive, they seem to be having such a joyful time of it. Don't you think so, my lord?"

Junko said "But" again, that being the only word he was quite master of. The woman came toward him, her long, graceful fingers toying with the knot of the *obi* at her waist.

"I could not return to my own form until today," she explained to him, "because I was wounded, which always keeps me from changing. I might very well have died an otter, but for your devoted care. It is only proper that I make you some little recompense, surely?"

She seemed so hesitant herself that the last words came out a shy question. But the *obi* had already fallen to the floor.

Later, in the night, propped on her elbow and looking at him with eyes even darker than the otter's eyes, she said, "You have never lain so with a woman, have you?"

Junko blushed in the darkness. "Not exactly. I mean, of course there were...No."

The young woman was silent for a time. Then she said, "Well, I will tell you something, since you have been so honest with me. Nor will I lie to you – I have mated, made love, yes, but never in this form. Only as a deer, or a wildcat, or even as a snow monkey, in the northern mountains. Never as a human being, until now."

"And you *are* human?" Junko asked her. "Forgive me, but are you sure you are not an animal who can change into a woman?" For there are all sorts of legends in Japan about such creatures. Especially foxes.

She chuckled against his shoulder. "I am altogether human, I promise you." After a moment, she added, "You named me Sayuri. I like that name. I will keep it."

"But you must have a name of your own, surely? Everyone has a name."

"Not I, never." She put a finger on his lips to forestall further questioning. "Sayuri will suit me very well."

And the beautiful young woman who had been an otter suited Junko very well herself. He presented her formally as his fiancée to the Lord Kuroda the next day, and then to the full court. He was awkward at it, certainly, never having been schooled in such regions of etiquette; but all were charmed by the young woman's grace and modesty, even so, despite the fact that she could offer nothing in the way of family history or noble lineage. Indeed, Lord Kuroda's wife, the Lady Hara, immediately requested her as one of her ladies-in-waiting. So all went well there, and Junko – still as dazed by his sudden fortune as the otter had been by his arrow – was proud and happy in a way that he had never known to be happy in all his life.

He and Sayuri were married in short order by the Shinto priest Yukiyasa, the same who had married Lord Kuroda to Lady Hara, which everyone agreed was good luck, and were given new quarters in the castle – modest still, but more fitting for so singular a couple. More, his master, as a wedding gift, saw to it that Junko was given proper hunting equipment to replace the battered bow and homemade arrows with which he had first arrived at court. There were those present at the ceremony who bit their lips in envy of such favor to a commoner; but Junko, in his desire that everyone share in his joy, noticed none of this. The Lord Kuroda did.

Early on the morning after their wedding, when few were yet awake, Junko and his bride walked in the castle garden, in the northeast corner, where the stream entered, and which was known as the Realm of the Blue Dragon. The days were cold still, but they walked close together and were content, saying very little. But the stream made Junko think of the strange and nearly fatal way in which he had met his Sayuri, and he asked her then, "Beloved, do you think you would ever be likely to change into an otter again? For I hurt you by mischance, but there are many people who trap otters for their fur, and I would be afraid for you."

Sayuri's laughter was like the sound of the water flowing beside them, as she answered him. "I think not, my lord. There are more risks involved with that form – including marriage – than I had bargained for." Then she turned a serious face to her new husband, holding his arm tightly. "But I would grieve were I forbidden to change shape ever again. It is a part of whatever I am, you must know that."

"'Whatever I am,'" Junko repeated slowly, and for a moment it seemed as though the back of his neck was colder than it should be, even on a winter morning. "But you assured me that you were altogether human. Those were your words."

"And I am, I am certain I am!" Sayuri stopped walking and turned him to face her. "But what else am I? No name but the one you gave me... no childhood that I can recall, except in flashes, like lightning, here and gone...no father or mother to present me at my own wedding...far more memories of the many animals I have been than of the woman I know I am. There *must* be more to me than I can see in your eyes, or in the jeweled hand mirror that was the Lady Hara's gift. Do you understand, husband?"

There were tears on her long black eyelashes, and though they did not fall, they reassured Junko in a curious way, since animals cannot weep. He put his arms around her to comfort her, saying, "Do as you will, as you need to do, my wife. I ask only that you protect yourself from all injury, since you cannot regain your human form then, and anything could happen to you. Will you promise me that?"

Then Sayuri laughed, and shook her head so that the teardrops flew, and she said, "I swear that and more. You will never again share your sleeping mat with anything furred, or with any more than two legs." And Junko joined in her laughter, and they went on with their walk, all the way across the garden to the southwest corner, which is still called the Realm of the White Tiger.

So they lived quite happily together for some years at the court of the *daimyo* Lord Kuroda. Junko served his master with the same perfect loyalty as ever, and went on providing more game than any other huntsman for the castle kitchens; while Sayuri continued to be much favored by the Lady Hara, joining her in her favorite arts of music, brush-painting, and especially *ikebana*, the spreading new discipline of flower arrangement. So skilled was she at this latter, in fact, that Lady Hara often sought her assistance in planning the decorations for a poetry recital in her own quarters, or even for a feast on the green summer island in the stream. Watching the two of them pacing slowly by the water together, the fringes of the great lady's parasol touching his otter-wife's thick and fragrant hair, Junko was so proud that it pained him, and made it hard to breathe.

And if, now and then, he awoke in the night to find the space beside him still warm but empty, or heard a rustle in the trees outside, or a sigh of the grass, that he was huntsman enough to know was no bird, no doe teaching her fawn to strip bark from Lord Kuroda's plum trees, he learned to turn over and go back to sleep, and ask no questions in the morning. For Sayuri was most often back by dawn, or very soon thereafter – always in human shape, as she had promised him – usually chilled beyond the bone and needing to be warmed. And Junko would warm her and never ask her to say where – and what – she had been.

She did not always leave the castle: mouse and bat were among her favorite forms, and between those two she knew everything that was taking place within its walls. More than once she shocked Junko by informing him that this or that high-ranking retainer was slipping into dusty alcoves with this or that servant girl; he learned before Lord Kuroda that the Lady Hara was again with child, but that it would be best the *daimyo* not know, since this one too would not live to be born. Animals know these things. As an owl, she might glide silently over the forest at night, and tell him if the deer had shifted their grazing grounds, as they did from time to time, or were lying up in a new place. In fox-shape, she warned of an approaching forest fire without ever seeing a flame; Junko roused the castle and gained great praise and credit thereby. He wanted earnestly to explain that all honor was due to his wife Sayuri, but this was impossible, and she seemed more than content with his gratitude and their somewhat unlikely happiness. So they lived, and the time passed.

One night it happened that she returned to their bed shivering, not with cold, nor with fear – there were several cats in the castle – but, as he slowly realized, with anger, which was not something he was used to from Sayuri. She might be by turns as calm and thoughtful as a fox, as playful as an otter, as gentle as a deer, fiercely passionate as any mink or marten, or as curious and mischievous as a red-faced snow monkey. All these moods and humors he had come in time to understand – but anger was a new thing entirely. He held her, and asked simply, "What is it, my love?"

At first she would not speak, or could not; but by and by, when the trembling passed a little, she whispered, "I was in the kitchen," – by this Junko knew that she had been in mouse-shape – "and the cooks were talking late over their own meal. And one said it was a shame that you had been passed over for the lord's private guard in favor of Yasunari Saito, since you had surely earned promotion a dozen times over. But another cook said," – the words were choking her again – "that it made no difference, because you were a commoner with no surname, and that it was miraculous that you were even in Lord Kuroda's home, let alone his retinue. *Miraculous* – after all you have done for them!" The tears of rage came then.

"Well, well," Junko said, stroking her hair, "that must have been Aoki. He has never liked me, that one, and it wouldn't matter to him if I had a dozen surnames. For the rest of it, things are the way they are, and that is...well, the way it is. Don't cry, please, Sayuri. I am grateful for what I have, and most grateful for you. Don't cry."

But later, when she had at last fallen asleep on his chest, he could not help brooding – only a little – about the unfairness of Saito's promotion. *Unfair* was not a word Junko had allowed himself even to think since he was quite small, and still learning the way things were, but it seemed to slither in his mind, and he could not get to grips with it, or make it go away. It was long before he slept again.

As has been said, the Lord Kuroda was a wise man, though not at all handsome, who saw more at a single dinner than many were likely to see in a week or a month. Riding out hunting one day, with Junko at his elbow, and they two having drawn a little apart from their companions, he said to him briefly and directly, "Saito is a fool, but his advancement was necessary, since I may well need his father's two hundred and fifty samurai one day." Junko bowed his head without answering. Lord Kuroda continued, "But it means nothing to me that you bring no warriors with you – nothing but your strength and your faithfulness. The next opening in my guard you shall fill."

With that he spurred ahead, doubtless to avoid Junko's stammering thanks. Junko was too overcome to be much of a hand at the hunt that afternoon; but while the others teased and derided him for this, Lord Kuroda only winked gravely.

Of course Sayuri was overjoyed at the news of the lord's promise, and she and Junko celebrated it with *nihonshu* and love, and then *shochu*, which is brewed from rice and sweet potatoes and a few other things. And afterward it was her turn to lie awake in the night, with her husband in her arms, and her mind perhaps full of small-animal thoughts. And perhaps not; who knows? It was all so long ago.

But it was at most a month before the horse of the samurai Daisuke Ikeda shied at a rabbit underfoot, reared, fell backwards and crushed his rider. There was much sorrow at court, for Ikeda was the oldest of the *daimyo*'s guard, and a well-liked man, but there was also a space in the guard to fill, and Lord Kuroda was as good as his word. Within days, Junko was wearing his master's livery, for all the world as though he were as good as Ikeda, or anyone else, and riding at his side on a fine, proud young stallion. And however many at court may have thought this highly unsuitable, no one said a word about it.

Junko also grieved for Ikeda, who had been kind to him. But his delight in his new position was muted, more than he would have expected, by his odd disquiet concerning that rabbit. Riding in the rear, as befit a commoner (it had been a formal procession, meant to impress a neighboring lord), he had seen the animal shoot from its hole, seemingly as blindly as though red-eyed Death were on its heels; and he had never known Ikeda's wise old horse to panic at an ambush, much less a rabbit. One worrisome thought led to another, and that to a third, until finally he brought them all to his wife. He had grown much in the habit of doing this.

Sayuri sat crosslegged on the proper new bed that the Lord Kuroda had given them to replace their worn *tatami,* and she listened attentively to Junko's fears, saying nothing until he was finished. Then she replied simply, "Husband, I was not the rabbit – I was the weasel just behind it, chasing it out of its burrow into the horse's path. Can you look at your own new horse – at your beautiful new livery – at this bed of ours – and say I have done wrong?"

"But Ikeda is dead!" Junko cried in horror. "Ask rather how I can look at his widow, at his children, at my master – at myself in the mirror now! Oh, I wish you had never told me this, Sayuri!"

"Then you should not have asked me," she answered him. "The weasel never meant for the good Ikeda to be killed – though he was old and should have retired from the guard long ago. The weasel only wanted the rabbit." She beckoned Junko to sit beside her, saying, "But is a wife not supposed to concern herself with the advancement of her husband's fortunes? I was told otherwise by the priest who married us." She put her arms around Junko. "Come, my love, take the good luck with the regrettable, and say as many prayers for Ikeda's repose as will comfort you." She laughed then: the joyous childlike giggle that never failed to melt even the sternest heart. "Although I think that *I* am more skilled at that than any prayer."

But Junko paced the castle all night, and wandered the grounds like a spirit; it was dawn before he could at last reassure himself that what she had told him was both sound and sensible. Ikeda's death had clearly been an accident, after all, and there was nothing in the least shameful in making the best of even such a tragedy. Sayuri's shapeshifting had brought about great good for him, however unintentional; let him give thanks for such a wife and, as he rode proudly beside the Lord Kuroda, bless the wandering arrow that had found an otter instead of a wild pig. "She is my luck," he thought often. "I should have given her that name, *luck,* instead of *little lily.*"

But he did, indeed, pray often at the family shrine erected for Daisuke Ikeda.

Now in time Junko came to realize that, while he had certainly been honored far beyond his origins in becoming part of Lord Kuroda's private guard, he had also attained a kind of limit beyond which he had no chance of rising. Above the guard stood his master's counselors and ministers: some of them higher in rank than others, some higher in a more subtle manner, unspoken and unwritten. In any case, their world was far out of reach for a nameless commoner, no matter how graciously favored by his lord. He would always be exactly what he was – unlike Sayuri, who could at least become different animals in her search for her true nature. And, understanding this, for the first time in his life Junko began to admit aloud that the world was unjust.

"Look at Nakamura," he would say resentfully to his wife over the teacups. "Not only does he review the guard when Lord Kuroda is away or indisposed – Nakamura, who barely knows a lance from a chopstick – he advises my master on diplomacy, when he has never been north of the Inland Sea in his life. And Hashimoto – Finance Minister Hashimoto, if you please – Hashimoto holds the position for no other reason than that he is Lady Hara's second cousin on her father's side. It is not correct, Sayuri. It is not *right.*"

Sayuri smiled and nodded, and made tea. She had become celebrated among the ladies-in-waiting for the excellence and delicacy of her *gyukuro* green tea.

And a few weeks later, Minister Shiro Nakamura, who loved to stroll alone in the castle gardens before dawn, to catch the first scent of the awakening flowers, was found torn in pieces by what could only have been a wolf. There were never many wolves in Japan, even then, but there was no question of the killer in this case: the great paw prints in the soft earth were so large that Junko suggested that the animal might well have come from Hokkaido, where the wolves were notably larger. "But how could a wolf ever find its way from Hokkaido Island so far south to Honshu?" he asked himself in the night. "And why should it do so?" He was very much afraid that he knew the answer.

The hunt that was immediately organized after the discovery of Minister Nakamura's still-warm body found no wolf of any species, but it did find blood in one of the paw prints, and on the blade of the antique dagger that Nakamura always carried. Sayuri was not at home when Junko returned; nor did she appear for several days, and even then she looked pale and faint, and spoke little. Junko made the excuse of illness to the Lady Hara, who sent medicines and dainties, plainly hoping that Sayuri's reported condition might betoken a new godchild. For his part, he asked no questions of his wife, knowing that she would tell him the truth. She always did.

It took more time, and a great deal of courteously muffled scandal and outrage at court before Junko ascended into the ranks of Lord Kuroda's advisors. He did not replace Minister Nakamura, but a station was created for him: that of Minister to the Lower Orders. When Junko's first speechless gratitude began to be replaced by stumbling bewilderment, Lord Kuroda explained to him, thus: "By now, my friend, you should know that I am not one of those nobles who believe that the commoners have no reason to exist, except that we give them the privilege of serving us. Quite a few, in fact," – and here he named a good eight or ten of the castle servants, ending with Junko himself – "show evidence of excellent sense, excellent judgment." He paused, looking straight into Junko's eyes. "And where there is judgment, there will be opinions."

By this Junko understood that he had been chosen to be a liaison – what some might call a spy – between the *daimyo* and all those who were not nobles, priests or samurai. The notion offended him deeply, but he had not attained his unusually favored position by showing offense. He merely bowed deeply to the Lord Kuroda, and replied that he would do his best to give satisfaction. The Lord Kuroda looked long into his eyes without responding.

So Junko, surname or no, became the first commoner ever accepted into a world his class had long been forbidden even to dream of entering. His and Sayuri's quarters were changed once again for rooms that seemed to him larger than his entire native village; they were assigned a servant of their own, and a new bed that, as Sayuri giggled, was "like a great snowdrift. I am certain we will yet find a bear sleeping out the winter with us." The haughtiness of Lord Kuroda's other counselors, and the sense that their servant despised them, seemed a small price to pay at the time.

Out of respect and gratitude to his master, Junko served him well as Minister to the Lower Orders. He provoked no disloyal or rebellious conversations, but only listened quietly to the talk of the stables, the kitchens, the deep storerooms and the barracks. What he thought Lord Kuroda should know, he reported faithfully; what seemed to him to be no one's business but the speakers' remained where he heard it. And Lord Kuroda appreciated his discreet ability to tell the difference, and told him so, even calling him Junko-*san* in private. And once – not very long before at all – that would have been more than enough.

But again he had collided with an invisible barrier. Precisely because the post had been invented especially for him, there was no precedent for promotion, nor any obvious position for him to step into whenever it should become vacant. Those who had always been kindly and amiable to Junko the castle's chief huntsman, now looked with visible contempt on Junko the Minister, Junko the jumped-up pet of the Lord Kuroda. Those below him took great pleasure in observing his frustration and discomfort; when they dared, they murmured as they passed him, "Did you think you were better than we are? Did you really believe they would let you become one of *them?* Then you were a fool – and now you are no one. No one."

Junko never spoke of his unhappiness to Lord Kuroda, but he expressed it once to his friend Akira Yamagata. The horsemaster, being a silent man, much more at ease with beasts than people, replied shortly, "Let demons fly away with them all. You cannot win with such folk; you cannot ever be even with them in their minds. Serve your master, and you cannot go wrong. Any horse will tell you that."

As for Sayuri, she simply listened, and arranged fresh flowers everywhere in their quarters, and made green *gyokuro* tea. When she walked with Junko in the castle gardens, and he asked her whether she felt herself any nearer to perceiving her true nature, she most often replied, "My husband, I know more and more what I am *not* – but as to what I *am...*" and her voice would trail away, leaving the thought unfinished.

Then she would add, quickly and softly, "But human – that, yes. I know I am human."

Now the most clever and ambitious of the Lord Kuroda's counselors, recently become Minister of Waterways and Fisheries, was a man named Mitsuo Kondo. Perhaps because he was little older than Junko, only now approaching his middle years, he went well out of his way to show his scorn for a commoner, though never in the presence of the *daimyo*. In the same way, Junko responded humbly to Kondo's poorly-veiled insults; while at home he confided to his wife that he often dreamed of wringing the man's thin neck, as he had so often done with chickens in his childhood. "Being of low birth, I am naturally acquainted with barnyards," he remarked bitterly to Sayuri.

It happened that on a warm night of early summer, Junko woke thirsty to an empty bed – he was quite used to this by now – and was still thirsty when he had drunk the last remaining green tea. Setting off to find water, barefooted and still drowsy, he had just turned into a corridor that led to the kitchens, when he heard the scraping of giant claws on a weathered *sugi*-wood floor, and flattened himself against the wall so hard that the imprint of the molding remained on his skin for hours afterward.

A huge black bear was lumbering down a passageway just ahead. It must surely have smelled his terror – or, as he imagined, heard the frantic beating of his heart – for it hesitated, then rose on its hind legs, turning toward him to sniff the air, growling softly. He saw the deep yellow-white chevron on the creature's breast, as well as the bright blood on its horrific fangs and claws, and he smelled both the blood and the raw, wild, strangely sweet odor of the beast itself. Even armed he might not be the creature's match; weaponless, he knew this was the moment of his death. But then the bear's great bulk dropped to the floor again, turning away, and his forgotten breath hissed between his teeth as the animal moved slowly on out of his sight, still growling to itself.

Junko did not go back to his quarters that night, but sat shivering where he was until dawn, tracing a trail of dead moss between two floorboards over and over with his forefinger. Then at last he slipped warily back into the new bed where Sayuri had laughingly imagined a bear keeping them company. She was sound asleep, not even stirring at his return. Junko lay still himself, studying her hands: one partly under her head, one stretched out on the pillow. There was no blood on any of the long fingers he loved to watch moving among her flowers. This was not as reassuring to him as it might once have been.

The hunt for Minister Kondo went on for days. The blood trail was washed away by a sudden summer rain, except for the track leading from his private offices, and there were other indications that he had been carried off by some great animal, or something even worse. For all his dislike of Kondo, Junko took a leading part in the hunt – as did Lord Kuroda himself – from its earliest moments to the very last, when it was silently agreed that the Minister's body would never be found. Lord Kuroda commanded ten days of mourning, and had a shrine created in Minister Kondo's memory on his own summer island. It is still there, though no one today knows whom it was meant to honor.

Even after the proper period of remembrance had passed, the empty place among the *daimyo*'s counselors remained unfilled for some considerable while. Few had liked Kondo any more than Junko did; all had feared his ambition, his gifts, and his evil tongue, and many were happy that he was gone, however horrified they may have been at the manner of his departure. But Lord Kuroda was clearly grieved – and, more than that, suspicious, though of what even he could not precisely say. Wolves and bears were common enough in Honshu in those days, but not in Honshu gardens and palaces; nor was the loss of three important members of his court, each under such curious circumstances, something even a mighty *daimyo* could easily let pass. The tale had already spread through the entire province, from bands of half-naked beggars huddled muttering under bridges to courts as great as his own. There was even a delicate message from the Shogun in Kyoto. Lord Kuroda brooded long over the proper response.

Junko came to feel his master's contemplative eyes on him even when he was not in Lord Kuroda's presence. At length, to ease his mind, he went directly to the *daimyo* and asked him, "Lord, have I done wrong? I pray you tell me if this is so." For he knew his own silent part in the three deaths, and he was afraid for his wife Sayuri.

But Lord Kuroda answered him gently, "Your pardon, loyal Junko, if I have caused you to be more troubled than we all are, day on day. I think you know that I have often considered your country astuteness to be of more plain practical aid to me than the costly education of many a noble.

Now I wonder whether you might have any least counsel to offer me regarding the terrible days through which we are passing." He permitted himself a very small, sad chuckle. "Because, just as everyone in my realm knows his station, my own task is to provide each of them with wisdom, assurance and security. And I have none to offer them, no more than they. Do you understand me, Junko?"

Then Junko was torn in his heart, for he had never lost his fondness for the Lord Kuroda, and it touched him deeply to see the *daimyo* so distressed. But he shook his head and murmured only, "These are indeed dark times, my lord, and there is nothing that would honor my unworthy self more than to offer you any candle to light your way. But in all truth, I have no guidance for you, except to offer sacrifice and pay the priests well. Who but they can read the intentions of the *kami?*"

"Apparently the gods' intentions were for my priests to leave me," the Lord Kuroda replied. "Half of them ran off when Minister Nakamura's body was discovered, and you yourself have seen the rest vanishing day by day since Kondo's has *not* been discovered. In a little the only priest left to me will be my old Yukiyasa." He sighed deeply, and turned from Junko, saying, "No matter, my friend. I had no business to place my own yoke upon your shoulders. Go to your bed and your life, and think no more of this. But know that I am grateful...grateful." And as he shuffled away, disappearing from sight among his bodyservants, it seemed to Junko for the first time that his master was an old man.

He repeated the conversation to Sayuri, generally satisfied with the way he had responded to the *daimyo*'s queries, but adding in some annoyance, "I expected him to offer me Kondo's position, but he never mentioned it. It will surely come, I am certain."

Sayuri had grown increasingly silent since the night of the black bear, more and more keeping to their quarters, avoiding her many friends and interests, shirking her duty to the Lady Hara when she dared; most often taking refuge in sleep, where she twitched and whimpered as Junko had never known her to do. Now, without looking at him, she said, "Yes. It will come."

And so it did, in good time, and with little competition, whether direct or stealthy, for rising to high rank at the court of Lord Kuroda more and more clearly involved risking a terrible end. There was no one who openly connected the deaths with the steady advancement of the peasant Junko – Junko-*san* now, to all, by special order – nor, certainly, with his charming and modest wife – but there were some who pondered, and one in particular who pondered deeply. This was Yukiyasa.

Yukiyasa was the Shinto priest who had married Sayuri to Junko. As the Lord Kuroda had predicted, he was the only priest who had not fled the court, and the only person who seemed able to rouse Sayuri from her melancholic torpor. Out of his hearing, he was called the Turtle, partly due to his endlessly wrinkled face and neck, but also because of his bright black eyes that still missed nothing – not the smallest change in the flowing of the sea or the angle of the wind, not the slightest trembling of the eyelashes of a woman fearing to show fear for her husband far away in battle. If age had slowed his step, it seemed to have quickened his perceptions: he could smell rain two days off, identify a Mongolian plover before others could be sure it was even a bird, and hear a leaf's fall or a fieldmouse's squeak through the castle walls. But he did look more and more like a turtle every season.

Junko instinctively avoided the old priest as much as he could, keeping clear of the *inari* shrine he maintained, except for the *Shogatsu Matsuri*, the New Year's festival. But Yukiyasi visited with Sayuri almost daily – in her quarters, if she did not come to the shrine – reading to her from the *Kojiki* and the *Nihon shoki*, teasing and provoking her until she had no choice but to smile, often remarking that she should one day consider becoming a Shinto priest herself. She always changed the subject, but the notion made her thoughtful, all the same.

"Today he said that I understood the way of the gods," she reported to Junko one spring evening. "What do you suppose he meant by that?"

They were walking together in the Realm of the Blue Dragon, still their favorite part of the castle gardens, and Junko's attention was elsewhere at the moment, contemplating the best use of the numerous waterways and fisheries that ran through the Lord Kuroda's vast domain. Now, his notice returning to his wife, he said, "The *kami* have always been shapeshifters; look at the foxes your friend's shrine celebrates. Perhaps he senses..." He did not finish the sentence.

Sayuri's grip on his arm tightened enough to hurt him. "No," she said in a small voice. "No, that cannot be, cannot. I change no longer. Never again." Her face had gone paler than the moon.

"The bear?" He had never meant to ask her, and immediately wished he could take back the question. But she answered him straightforwardly, almost in a rush, as the melting snows had quickened the measure even of Lord Kuroda's gentle stream.

"I was so frightened to be the bear. I didn't like it at all. It was a terrible thing."

"A terrible thing that you were – or a terrible thing you did?" He could not keep his own words from tumbling out.

"Both," she whispered, "*both*." She was crying now, but she resisted strongly when Junko tried to hold her. "No, no, you mustn't, it is too dangerous. I am sorry, so sorry, I so wish your arrow had killed me. Then Ikeda would be alive, and Nakamura, and Kondo –"

"And I would still be what I was born," Junko interrupted her. "Junko the hunter, lower than any cook – because a cook is at least an artist, while a huntsman is a butcher – Junko, with his peasant ways and peasant accent, barely tolerable just as long as he keeps to his place. If it were not for you, my otter, my wolf –"

"*No!*" She twisted away from him, and actually ran a few paces off before she turned to stare at him in real horror. It was long before she spoke again, and then she said quietly, "We have quite traded places, have we not, my husband? You were the one who grieved for the poor victims of my shape-changing, and it was I who laughed at your foolish concern and prided myself upon the improvements I brought to your fortunes, as a good wife should do. And now..." She faltered for a little, still looking at him as though *he* were the strange animal she had never seen before. "Now you turn out to be the shapeshifter, after all, and I the soft fool who'll have none of it, no more. Not even for love of you – and I loved you when I was an otter – not even for the sake of at last learning my own being, my own soul. That can go undiscovered forever, and welcome, and I will remain Sayuri, your wife, no more and no less. And I will tend three graves, and pray at the shrine, and live as I can with what I have done. That is how it will be."

"'That is how it will be,'" Junko mimicked her. "And I? I am to rise no higher at this court, where the old men despise me and the young ones plot against me – all because you have suddenly turned nun?" He moved toward her, his eyes narrowing. "Yukiyasa," he said slowly. "It's the Turtle, isn't it? That horrible antique, with his foul-smelling robes and his way of shooting his head out and blinking at people. It's Yukiyasa who has put all this into your head, I know it. I swear, if I really *could* change my shape—"

But Sayuri covered his mouth with her hand, crying, "Don't! Don't ever say that, I beg you! You have no idea what that is like, what that *is*, or you would never say such a thing." In that moment, the look in her beautiful dark eyes made Junko think of the black bear rising on its hind legs and turning to sniff the air for him, and he was afraid of her. He did not move, nor did he try to speak, until she took her hand away.

Then he said, not mockingly this time, but as soothingly as he knew how, "Well, we have come a very long way together—too long a way for us to turn on each other now. I ask pardon for my thoughtlessness and my stupidity, and I promise never to speak of...what we will not speak of, ever again. Such advancement as I can win on my own, that will I do, and be well satisfied with my own nature, and my own fate. Will that content you, my wife?"

"That will content me, husband," she whispered after a little. She did not resist when Junko put his arms around her, but he could feel the fear in her body, and so he added lightly, "And I promise also never to say another word concerning your Turtle, for I know how much his wisdom and kindness mean to you. Not a word—not even if you were indeed to become a priest, as he wishes you to do. So." He stroked her hair, as she had always liked him to do. "Shall we go on with our walk?"

And Sayuri laughed for the first time in a long while, and she nodded and put her arm through his, and they walked on together.

But it was not true, though, to do him justice, Junko tried earnestly, for a while, to believe it so. Even while taking his new post as Minister of Waterways and Fisheries with all seriousness—descended as he was from river people who had manned weirs, dams and sluices throughout Honshu and Shikoku for generations—he could not help coveting another position: that of Masanori Morioka, Chief Minister for Dealing with Barbarians. This ranked just under the Lord Kuroda himself—in another country, Morioka would have been called Prime Minister—and where the *daimyo* was aging visibly, Morioka was only a year or two older than Junko himself. Far more important, he came of high samurai family, and, since Lord Kuroda and the Lady Hara had no children, he might already have been chosen to succeed his lord when the time came. Junko was increasingly certain of this: the Lord Kuroda was no one to leave his lands in chaos while his relatives went to war over so rich a prize. It must be Murioka; there could be no doubt of it.

In the past, this would have mattered little to the Junko whose only concern was whether the rains had brought enough new grass for the deer, and if the snow monkeys' unusually thick coats might foretell an evil winter. But it mattered now to this Junko, and – again to be fair – he did his best to conceal his jealousy from his wife. In this he failed, because he talked in his sleep almost every night, and Sayuri's heart shivered to decipher his mumblings and his whispered rants. She would lie as close to him as she could then, hoping somehow to absorb his aching resentment into her own body, and wishing once again, deeply and dearly, that she had died an otter.

As the Lord Kuroda grew more frail, and Morioka steadily assumed a greater share of the *daimyo*'s responsibilities, Junko's anger and envy became more and more plain to see, and not only by his wife. Lady Hara spoke of it with some disquiet to Sayuri; and Akira, the taciturn horsemaster, told Junko that he needed to ride out more, and to spend more time in the company of horses than of courtiers, and less time fretting over childish matters that he could not control in any case. And it was Lord Kuroda himself, having summoned Junko to him in private, who was the one to ask, "Have I done wrong, then? What troubles you, Junko-san?" For he always showed a tenderness toward Junko that made certain spiteful folk grumble that the *daimyo* had fathered him in secret on a peasant woman.

Then Junko, for a moment, was ashamed of his bitterness, and he knelt before Lord Kuroda and put his hands between the hard old hands that trembled only a little, even now, and he whispered, "Never have I had anything from you but goodness beyond my worth. But would that I enjoyed the opportunity to serve you that others have earned – perhaps through ability, perhaps...not."

By this Lord Kuroda knew that he was speaking of Masanori Morioka. He responded with unaccustomed sternness, "Minister of Waterways and Fisheries you are, and I would never permit even Morioka to trespass on a single one of the duties and privileges that your honorable service has won for you. But we must always remember that all barbarians believe themselves to be civilized, and dealing with such people while keeping the dangerous truth from them requires a subtlety that few possess. You are not one of them, Junko-*san*."

He smiled at Junko then, leaning stiffly forward to raise him to his feet. "Nor am I, not really. It is a matter of training from one's childhood, my friend – learning to sense and walk, even in the dark, the elusive balance between humility and servility, candor and courtesy, power and the appearance of power. Masanori Morioka is far better at this game than I ever was, even when I was young. Let the worst come, I will have no fears for my realm in his hands."

With those words, the worst had indeed come to Junko; with those words Morioka was doomed. Yet he managed to keep his answer calm and slow, saying merely, "In his hands? Is it so decided, lord?"

"It is so decided," his master replied.

Junko drew himself to his full height and bowed deeply, holding his arms rigid at his sides. "Then I also must retire from the court, since Minister Morioka and I dislike each other too greatly to work together after you are gone. While you remain, so will I."

But the Lord Kuroda smiled then: not widely, which was not his way, but with a certain sad warmth that was new to his kind, ugly face. He responded only, "In that case I will stay alive just as long as it befits me to do so," and with a small flick of his fingers gave Junko leave to withdraw.

On the way to his quarters, he briefly encountered Morioka, who bowed mockingly to him, saying nothing until Junko had returned the bow and passed on. Then he called after him, "And how go the mighty consultations with our *daimyo*?" for he knew where Junko had been, and he had his own envy of the Lord Kuroda's feeling for Junko.

"As well as your great battles," Junko answered him, and Morioka scowled like a demon-mask, since he had never borne arms for Lord Kuroda or any other, and everyone at court knew *that*. So they went on to their separate destinations; and Junko, reaching home, flung himself down on the bed and wept with a terrifying ferocity. Nor could he stop: it was as though the tears of rage that had been building and swelling within him since his stoic childhood had finally surged out of his control, and were very likely to flood him as the cyclones still did every year to his family's sliver of farmland. He was all water, and all bitterness, and nothing beyond, ever.

He continued biting the bedclothes to muffle his weeping, but Sayuri heard him just the same, and came to him. At first she drew back in something close to fear of such violent anguish; but in a little she sat on the edge of the bed and put her hand timidly on his shoulder, saying, "Husband, I cannot bear to see you so. What in this world can possibly be such an immeasurable grief to you? Speak to me, and if I cannot help you, I will at least share your sorrow. Share it with me now, I beg you."

And she said all else that good wives – and good husbands, as well – say at such moments; and after a long while Junko lifted his head to face her. His eyes and nose and mouth were all clotted with tears, and he looked as children look who have been punished for no reason they can understand. But behind the tears Sayuri saw a hot and howling anger that would have turned him to a beast then and there, if it could have done. In a thick, shaking voice he told her what the Lord Kuroda had told him, ending by saying, more quietly now, "You see, it was all for nothing, after all. All of it, for nothing."

Sayuri thought at first that he was speaking of his long, difficult climb up from his poor peasant birth to the castle luxury where they sat together on a bed whose sheets were of Chinese silk. But Junko, his voice gone wearily flat and almost toneless, went on, "Everything you did for me, for us – Ikeda, Nakamura, Kondo – it was all wasted, they might just as well have been spared. Yes – they might as well have remained alive."

"Yes," Sayuri repeated dazedly. "They might have remained alive." But then she shook off the confused stupor that his words had brought about, and she gripped his wrists, saying, "But Junko-*san,* no, I never killed for your sake. I was a bear, a wolf, a weasel after a rabbit – I was hungry, not human. In those beast forms I did not even know who those men were!"

"Did you not?" the fierce question came back at her. "Be honest with yourself, my wife. Did the wolf never know for a moment that tearing out the throat of Isamu Nakamura would benefit a certain peasant who dreamed of becoming a counselor to a *daimyo?* What of the bear – surely the bear must have known that carrying off the previous Minister of Waterways and Fisheries would open the way –"

"*No!* No, it is not true!" Still holding his wrists tightly, she shook him violently. "The animals were innocent – *I* was innocent! It was coincidence, nothing more –"

"Was it?" They stared at each other for a moment longer, before Sayuri released Junko's wrists and he turned away, shaking his head. "It doesn't matter, it is of no importance. Whatever was true then, you will take no more shapes, and *I*...I will stay not one day after Lord Kuroda is gone. We will retire to my home village, and I will be a big man there, and you the most beautiful and accomplished woman. And why not? – we deserve it. And they will give us the very grandest house they possess, in my honor, and it will be smaller than this one room, and smell of old men. And why not? We have served the great *daimyo* faithfully and well, and we deserve it all."

And saying this, he walked away, leaving Sayuri alone to bite her knuckles and make small sounds without tears.

The old priest Yukiyasa found her so when he came to read to her, since she had not appeared at the shrine. Having performed her wedding, he regarded her therefore as his daughter and his responsibility, and he lifted her face and looked long at her, asking no questions. Not did she speak, but placed one hand over his dry, withered hand and they stood in silence, until her mind was a little eased. Then she said, in a voice that sounded as ancient as his, "I have done evil, and may do so again. Can you help me, Turtle?" For he knew perfectly well what he was called, but she was the only one permitted to address him by that name.

Yukiyasa said, "Often and often does evil result where nothing but good was meant. I am sure this is true in your case."

But Sayuri answered, "What I intended – even if it was not quite I who intended it – is of no importance. What I did is what matters."

The priest peered at her, puzzled as he had not been in a very long time, and yet with a curious sense that he might do best to remain so. He continued, "I have many times thought that in this world far more harm is wrought by foolish men than by wicked ones. Perhaps you were foolish, my daughter. Are you also vain enough to imagine yourself the only one?"

That won him a fragment of a smile, coming and going so swiftly that it might have been an illusion, and perhaps was. But Yukiyasa was encouraged, and he said further, "You *were* foolish, then," not making a question of it. "Well, so. I myself have done such things as I would never confess to you – not because they were evil, but because they were so *stupid* –"

Sayuri said, "I change into animals. People have died."

Yukiyasa did not speak for a long time, but he never took his eyes from Sayuri's eyes. Finally he said quietly, "Yes, I see them," and he did not say whether he meant wolves or bears, or Daisuke Ikeda, Minister Shiro Nakamura or Minister Mitsuo Kondo. He said, "The *kami* did this to you before you were born. It is your fate, but it is not your fault."

"But what *I* did is my fault!" she cried. "Death is death, killing is killing!" She paused to catch her breath and compose herself, and then went on in a lower tone. "My husband thinks that I killed those men to remove them from his path to power in the court. I say *no, no, it was the animals, not me* – but what if it is true? What if that is exactly what happened? What should I do then, Turtle, please tell me? Turtle, please!"

The old man took her hands between his own. "Even if every word is true, you are still blameless. Listen to me now. I have studied the way of the *kami* all my life, and I am no longer sure that there is even such a thing as blame, such a thing as sin. You did what you did, and you are being punished for it now, as we two stand here. The *kami* are never punished. This is the one thing I know, daughter, with all my years and all my learning. The *kami* are never punished, and we always are."

Then he kissed Sayuri on the forehead, and made her lie down, and recited to her from the *Kojiki* until she fell asleep, and he went away.

Passing the courtyard where the *daimyo*'s soldiers trained, he noticed Junko watching an exercise, but plainly not seeing it. The old priest paused beside him for a time, observing Junko's silent discomfort in his presence without enjoying it. When Junko finally bowed and started away – still without speaking, discourteous as that was – Yukiyasa addressed him, saying, "I will give you my advice, though you do not want it. Whether for a good reason or a bad one, it would be a terrible mistake for you ever again to order your wife, in words or in your thoughts, to become so much as a squirrel or a sparrow. A good reason or a bad one. Do you understand me?"

Then Junko turned and strode back to him, his face white, but his eyes wide with anger, and his voice a low hiss. "I do *not* understand you. I do not know what you are talking about. My wife is no shapeshifter, but if she were, I would never make such a request of her. Never, I have *sworn* to her that I would never – "

He halted, realizing what he had said. Yukiyasa looked at him for a long moment before he repeated, "In words or in thoughts," and walked slowly on to the shrine where he lived. Junko stared after him, but did not follow.

But by this time he was too far lost in envy of Masanori Morioka to give more than the briefest consideration to the Shinto priest's warning. True to his promise to her, he held himself back from urging Sayuri to remember, in so many words, that there was no future for them in a court commanded by Morioka. Even so, he found one way or another to put it into her mind every day; and every night he awoke well before dawn, hoping to find her gone, as had happened so many times in their life together. But she continued to slumber the night through, though often enough she wakened him with her twitching and moaning, which once would have moved him instantly to soothe and comfort her. Now he only turned over with a disappointed grunt and drowsed off again. He had always had the gift of sleep.

Finally, on a night of early autumn, his desire was granted. The moon was high and small, leaves were stirring softly in a warm breeze, and the space beside him was empty. Junko smiled in the darkness and rose quickly to follow. Then he hesitated, partly from fear of just what he might overtake; partly because it would clearly be better to be aroused by running feet in the corridors and the dreadful news about Minister Morioka. But it was impossible for even him to close his eyes now, so he donned a kimono and paced their quarters from one end to the other, impatiently pushing fragile screens aside, cursing when he tripped over pairs of Sayuri's *geta*, and listening for screams.

But there was no sound beyond the soft creaking of the night, and finally the silence became more than he could endure. Telling himself that Sayuri, in whatever form, would surely know him, he drew a long breath and stepped out into the corridor.

Standing motionless as his eyes grew accustomed to the darkness, he saw and heard nothing, but he smelled...or almost smelled...no, he had no words for what he smelled. The wild odor of the bloody-mouthed black bear was lodged in his throat yet, as was the scent of the wolf fur clutched in the dead fingers of Minister Nakamura. But this was a cold smell, like that of a great serpent, and there was another underneath, even colder – *burned bone*, Junko thought, though that made no sense at all; and then, even more absurdly, *bone flames*. He turned to look back at the entrance to his quarters, but it seemed already far away, receding as he watched, like a sail on the sea.

There was no choice but to go on. He wished that he had brought a sword or a *tanto* dagger, but only samurai were permitted to carry such weapons; and for all his kindly respect and affection, the Lord Kuroda had never made any exception for Junko. When he was in Morioka's place, he would change *that*. He moved ahead, step by step, cautiously feeling his way between splashes of moonlight.

Masanori Morioka's quarters were located a floor above his own – closer to the *daimyo*'s, which was something else to brood about, and tend to later. He started up the stair, anxious neither to alert nor alarm anyone, and beginning to wonder – all was still *so* quiet – whether he had misread Sayuri's absence. What if she had merely gone scurrying in mouse-shape, as she had once been fond of doing, skittering in the castle rafters as a bat, or even roving outside as any sort of small night thing? How would it look if he were surprised wandering himself where he had no reason to be at such an hour? He paused, very nearly of a mind to turn back... and yet the serpent-smell had grown stronger with each step, and so near now that he felt as though he were the creature exuding it: as though the coldly burning bones were, in some way, his own.

Another step, and another after, moving sideways now without realizing that he was doing so, the serpent-smell pressing on him like a smothering blanket, making his breath come shorter and shallower. Once he lurched to one knee, twice into the wall, unsure now of whether he was stumbling upstairs or down...then he did hear the scream.

It was a woman's scream, not a man's. And it came, not from Minister Morioka's quarters, but from those of the Lord Kuroda and the Lady Hara.

For an instant, Junko was too stupefied to be afraid; it was as though the strings of his mind had been cut, as well as those of his petrified body. Then he uttered a wordless cry that he himself never heard, and sprang toward the *daimyo*'s rooms, kicking off his slippers when they skidded on the polished floors.

Lady Hara screamed again, as Junko burst through the rice-paper door, stumbling over the wreckage of shattered *tansu* chests and *shoji* screens. He could not see her or Lord Kuroda at first: the vast figure in his path seemed to draw all light and shape and color into itself, so that nothing was real except the towering horns, the cloven hooves, the sullen gleam of the reptilian scales from the waist down, the unbearable stench of simmering bone...

"*Ushi-oni!*" He heard it in his mind as an insect whisper. Lord Kuroda was standing between his wife and the demon, legs braced in a fighting stance, *wakizashi* sword trembling in his old hand. The *ushi-oni* roared like a landslide and knocked the sword across the room. Lord Kuroda drew his one remaining weapon, the *tanto* he carried always in his belt. The *ushi-oni* made a different sound that might have been laughter. The dagger fell to the floor.

Junko said, "Sayuri."

The great thing turned at his voice, as the black bear had done, and he saw the nightmare cow-face, and the rows of filthy fangs crowding the slack, drooling lips. And – as he had seen it in the red eyes of the bear – the unmistakable recognition.

"My wife," Junko said. "Come away."

The *ushi-oni* roared again, but did not move, neither toward him, nor toward Lord Kuroda and Lady Hara. Junko said, "Come. I never meant this. I never meant this."

Out of the corner of his eye, Junko saw the *daimyo* moving to recover his fallen dagger. But the *ushi-oni*'s attention was all on Junko, the mad yellow-white eyes had darkened to a dirty amber, and the claws on its many-fingered hands had all withdrawn slightly. Junko faced it boldly, all unarmed as he was, saying again, "Come away, Sayuri. We do not belong here, you and I."

He knew that if he turned his head he would see a blinking, quaking Minister Morioka behind him in the ruined doorway, but for that he cared nothing now. He took a few steps toward the *ushi-oni*, halting when it growled stinking fire and backed away. Junko did not speak further, but only reached out with his eyes. *We know each other.*

He was never to learn whether the monster that had been – that *was* – his wife would have come to him, nor what would have been the result if it had. Lady Hara, suddenly reaching the limit of her body's courage, uttered a tiny sigh, like a child falling asleep, and collapsed to the floor. The *ushi-oni* began to turn toward her, and at that moment the Lord Kuroda lunged forward and struck with all the strength in his old arm.

The *tanto* buried itself to the coral-ornamented hilt in the right side of the demon.

The *ushi-oni*'s howl shook the room and seemed to split Junko's head, bringing blood even from his eyes, as well as from his ears and nose. A great scaled paw smashed him down as the creature roared and reeled in its death agony, trampling everything it had not already smashed to splinters, dragging ancient scrolls and brush paintings down from the walls, crushing the Lord Kuroda family shrine underfoot. The *ushi-oni* bellowed unceasingly, the sound slamming from wall back to broken wall, and everyone hearing it bellowed with the same pain, bleeding like Junko and like him holding, not their heads and faces, but their hearts. When the demon fell, and was silent, the sound continued on forever.

But even forever ends, and there came a time when Junko pulled himself to his feet. He found himself face to face with Minister Morioka, pale as a grubworm, gabbling like an infant, walking as though he had just learned how. Others were in the room now, all shouting, all brandishing weapons, all keeping their distance from the great, still thing on the floor. He saw the Lord Kuroda, far away across the ruins, bending over Lady Hara, carefully and tenderly lifting her to her feet while staring strangely at Junko. Whatever his face, as bloody as Junko's own, revealed, it was neither anger nor outrage, but Junko looked away anyway.

The *ushi-oni* had not moved since its fall, but its eyes were open, unblinking, darkening. Junko knelt beside it without speaking. The fanged cow-lips twitched slightly, and a stone whisper reached his ear and no other, shaping two words. *"My nature..."* There were no more words, and no sound in the room.

Junko said, "She was my wife."

No one answered him, not until the Lord Kuroda said, "No." Junko realized then that the expression in his master's eyes was one of deepest pity. Lord Kuroda said, "It is not possible. An *ushi-oni* may take on another shape if it wishes, being a demon, but in death it returns to its true being, always. You see that this has not occurred here."

"No," Junko answered him, "because this *was* Sayuri's natural form. This is what she was, but she did not know it, no more than I. I swear that she did not know." He rose, biting his lower lip hard enough to bring more blood to his mouth, and faced the *daimyo* directly. He said, "This was my doing. All of it. The weasel, the wolf, the bear – she meant only to help me, and I...I did not want to know." He looked around at the shattered room filled with solemn people in nightrobes and armor. "Do you understand? Any of you?"

The Lord Kuroda's compassionate manner had taken on a shade of puzzlement; but the Lady Hara was nodding her elegant old head. Behind Junko, Minister Morioka had at last found language, though his stammering voice retained none of its normal arrogance. He asked timidly, "How could an *ushi-oni* not know what it was? How could such a monster ever marry a human being?"

"Perhaps because she fell in love," the Lady Hara said quietly. "Love makes one forget many things."

"I cannot speak for my wife," Junko replied. "For myself, there are certain things I will remember while I live, which I beg will not be long." He turned his eyes to Minister Morioka. "I wanted her to kill you. I never said it in those words – *never* – but I made very sure she knew that I wanted you out of my way, as she had removed three others. I ask your pardon, and offer my head. There can be no other atonement."

Then the Minister shrank back without replying, for while he had no objection to the death penalty, he greatly preferred to see it administered by someone else. But the Lord Kuroda asked in wonder, "Yet the *ushi-oni* came here, to these rooms, not to Minister Morioka's quarters. Why should she – *it* – have done so?"

Junko shook his head. "That I cannot say. I know only that I am done with everything." He walked slowly to retrieve the *daimyo*'s sword, brought it to him, and knelt again, baring his neck without another word.

Lord Kuroda did not move or speak for a long time. The Lady Hara put her hand on his arm, but he did not look at her. At last he set the *wakizashi* back in its lacquered sheath, the soft click the only sound in the ravaged room, which seemed to have turned very cold since the fall of the *ushi-oni*. He touched Junko's shoulder, beckoning him to rise.

"Go in peace," he said without expression, "if there is any for you. No harm will come to you, since it will be known that you are still under the protection of the Lord Kuroda. Farewell...Junko-*san*."

A moment longer they stared into one another's eyes; then Junko bowed to his master and his master's lady, turned like a soldier, and walked away, past smashed and shivered *tengu* furniture, past Minister Morioka – who would not look at him – through the crowd of gaping, muttering retainers, and so out of the Lord Kuroda's castle. He did not return to his quarters for any belongings, but went away barefoot, clad only in his kimono, and he looked back only once, when he smelled the smoke and knew that the servants were already burning the body of the *ushi-oni* that was also his wife Sayuri. Then he went on.

And no one ever would have known what became of him, if the old priest Yukiyasa had not been the patient, inquisitive man that he was. Some years after the disappearance of Minister Junko, the commoner who had ridden at the right hand of a *daimyo* for a little while, Yukiyasa left his Shinto shrine in the care of a disciple, picked up his staff and his begging bowl, and set off on a trail long since grown cold. But it was not the first such trail that he had followed in his life, and he possessed the curious patience of the very old that is perhaps the closest mortal approach to immortality. The journey was a trying one, but many peasant families were happy to please the gods by offering him lodging, and peasants have long memories. It took the priest less time than one might have expected to track Junko to a village that barely merited the title, on a brook that was called a river by the people living there. For that matter, Junko himself was not known in the village by his rightful name, but as Toru, which is *wayfarer*. Yukiyasa found him at the brook in the late afternoon, lying flat on his belly, fishing for salmon by the oldest method there is, which is tickling them slowly and gently, until they fall asleep, and then scooping them into a net. There were already six fish on the grass beside him.

Junko was coaxing a seventh salmon to the bank, and did not look up or speak when the old priest's shadow fell over him. Not until he had landed the last fish did he say, "I knew it was you, Turtle. I could always smell you as far as the summer island."

Yukiyasa took no offense at this, but only chuckled as he sat down. "The incense does cling. Others have mentioned it."

Neither spoke for some time, but each sat considering the other. To the priest's eye, Junko looked brown and healthy enough, but notably older than he should have. His face was thinner, his hair had turned completely white, and there was an air about him, not so much of loneliness as of solitude, as though what lived inside him had left no room for another living being, or even a living thought. *He chose a good name,* Yukiyasa thought. "You do well here, my son?"

"As well as I may." Junko shrugged. "I hunt and fish for the folk here, and mend their poor flimsy dams and weirs, as I was raised to do. And they in turn shelter me, and call me *Wayfarer*, and ask no questions. I am where I belong."

To this Yukiyasa knew not what to say, and they two were silent again, until Junko asked finally, "Akira Yamagata, the horsemaster – he is well?"

"Gone these two years and more," the priest replied gently, for he knew of the friendship. Junko inquired after a few other members of Lord Kuroda's household, but not once about the *daimyo* himself, or about Lady Hara. Wondering on this, and thinking to provoke Junko beyond prudence, Yukiyasa began to speak of the successes of Masanori Morioka. "Since you...since you left, the ascent in his fortunes has been astonishing. He is very nearly a Council of Ministers in himself now – and the lord being old, and without children..." He shrugged, leaving the sentence deliberately unfinished.

"Well, well," Junko said mildly, almost to himself. "Well, well." He smiled then, for the first time at the puzzled priest, and it was a smile of such piercing amusement as even Yukiyasa had never seen in all his long life. "I am pleased for him, and wish him all success. Let him know of it."

"This after you sent an *ushi-oni* to destroy him?" It was not Yukiyasa's custom ever to raise his voice, but perplexity was bringing him close to it. "You said yourself that you wished Minister Morioka dead and out of your way. Sayuri died of that envy." Startled and frightened by the anger in his words, he repeated them nevertheless, realizing that he had loved the woman who was no woman. "She died because you were insanely, cruelly jealous of that man you praise now."

Junko's smile vanished, replaced, not by anger of his own, but by the same weary knowledge that had aged his face. "Not so, though I wish it were. You have no idea how I wish that were true." He was silent for a time, looking away as he began to gather the seven salmon into a rush-lined basket. Then he said, still not meeting the priest's eyes, "No. My wife died because she understood me."

"What nonsense is this?" Yukiyasa cried out. He was deeply ashamed of his loss of control, yet for once refused to restrain himself. "I warned you, I *warned* you, in so many words, never again to coax her to change

form – never to let her do it, for your sake and her own – and see what
came of your disregard! She yielded once more to your desire, set forth to
murder Minister Morioka, as she had slain others, and thereby rediscov-
ered the terrible truth she had forgotten for love of you. For love of you!"
The old priest was on his feet now, trembling and sweating, jabbing his
finger at Junko's expressionless face. "Understand you? How could she
understand such a man? She only loved, and she died of it, and it need
not have happened so. It need not have happened!"

The sky was going around in great, slow circles, and Yukiyasa thought
that it would be sensible to sit down, but he could not find his feet.
Someone was saying somewhere, a long way off, "She loved me when
she was an otter." Then Junko had him by the shoulders, and was guiding
him carefully through the long journey back to the grass and the ground.
In time the sky stopped spinning, and Yukiyasa drank cold brook water
from Junko's cupped hands and said, "Thank you. I am sorry."

"No need," Junko replied. "You have the right of it as much as anyone
ever will. But Sayuri knew something that no one else knew, not even I
myself." He paused, waiting until the priest's color had returned and his
heartbeat had ceased to shake his body so violently. Then he said, "Sayuri
knew that in my soul, in the darkest corner of my soul, I wished her to
go exactly where she did go. And it was not to Minister Morioka's quarters."

It took the priest Yuriyasa no time at all, dazed as he still was, to comprehend what he had been told, but a very long while indeed to find a
response. At last he said, almost whispering, "The Lord Kuroda loved
you. Like a son."

Junko nodded without answering. Yukiyasa asked him hesitantly,
"Did you imagine that if Sayuri...if Lord Kuroda were gone, you might
somehow become *daimyo* yourself?"

"'Like a son' is not like being a son," Junko replied. "No, I had no such
expectations. My master, in his generosity, had raised me higher than I
could possibly have conceived or deserved, being who I am – *what* I am.
In a hundred lifetimes, how should I ever hold any grievance against the
Lord Kuroda?"

Twilight had arrived as they spoke together, and fires were being
lighted in the nearest huts. Junko stood up, slinging the fish basket over
his shoulder. Looking down at Yukiyasa, his face appearing younger with

the eyes in shadow, he said, "But Sayuri knew the *ushi-oni* in me, the thing that hated having been shown all that I could not have or be, and that wished, in the midst of luxury, to have been left where I belonged – in a place just like this one, where not one person knows how to write the words *daimyo* or *shogun*, and *samurai* is a word that comes raiding and killing, trampling our crops, burning our homes. Do you hear what I am telling you, priest of the *kami*? Do you hear?"

He pulled Yukiyasa to his feet, briefly holding the old man close as a lover, though he did not seem to notice it. He said, very quietly, "I loved Lord Kuroda for the man he was. But from the day I entered his castle – a ragged, ignorant boy from a ragged village of which *he* was ignorant – I hated him for *what* he was. I spent days and years forgetting that I hated him and all his kind, every moment denying it in my heart, in my mind, in my bones." For a moment he put his hand hard over his mouth, as though to stop the words from coming out, but they came anyway. "Sayuri...Sayuri knew my soul."

A child's voice called from the village, the sound sweetly shrill on the evening air. Junko smiled. "I promised her family fish tonight. We must go."

He took Yukiyasa's elbow respectfully, and they walked slowly away from the river in the fading light. Junko asked, "You will rest here for a few days? It is a long road home. I know."

The priest nodded agreement. "You will not return with me." It was not a question, but he added, "Lord Kuroda has not long, and he has missed you."

"And I him. Tell him I will forget my own name before I forget his kindness." A sudden whisper of a laugh. "Though I am Toru now, and no one will ever call me Junko again, I think."

"Junko-*san*," Yukiyasa corrected him. "Even now, he always asks after Junko-*san*."

Neither spoke again until they had entered the village, and muddy children were clinging to Junko's legs, dragging him toward a hut further on. Then the priest said quietly, "She really believed she was human. She might never have known." Junko bowed his head. "Did you believe it yourself, truly? I have wondered."

The answer was almost drowned out by the children's yelps of happiness and hunger. "As much as I ever believed I was Junko-*san*."

King Pelles the Sure

My old friend, the novelist Darryl Brock, has described this as the best anti-war story he has ever read. My vote would probably go to William March's *Company K*, which I read at seventeen and have never since gotten out of my head, though I wish I could. Whatever the comparative ranking, I'm proud of this one.

ONCE THERE WAS A KING who dreamed of war. His name was Pelles.

He was a gentle and kindly monarch, who ruled over a small but wealthy and completely tranquil kingdom, beloved alike by noble and peasant, despite the fact that he had no queen, and so no heir except a brother to ensure an orderly succession. Even so, he was the envy of mightier kings, whose days were so full of putting down uprisings, fighting off one another's invasions, and wiping out rebellious villages that they never knew a single moment of comfort or security. King Pelles – and his people, and his land – knew nothing else.

But the king dreamed of war.

"Nobody is ever remembered for living out a dull, placid, uneventful life," he would say to his Grand Vizier, whom he daily compelled to play at toy soldiers with him on the parlor floor. "Peace is all very well – a fine thing, certainly – but do you ever hear ballads about King Herman the Peaceful? Do you ever listen to bards chanting the deeds of King Leslie the Calm, or read great national epics about King James the Docile, King William the Diplomatic? You do not!"

"There was Ethelred the Unready," suggested the Grand Vizier, whose back hurt from crouching over the carpet battlefield every afternoon. "Meaning unready for conflict or crusade, unwilling to slaughter needlessly. And King Charles the Good – "

"But it is Charles the Hammer who lives in legend," King Pelles retorted. "William the Conqueror – Erik Bloodaxe – Alfonso the Avenger – Selim the Valiant – Ivan the Terrible. Our own schoolchildren know *those* names...and why not," he added bitterly, "since we don't have any heroes of our own. How can we, when nobody ever even raids us, or bothers to challenge us over land or resources, or attempts to annex us, to swallow our little realm whole, as has happened to so many such lands in our time? Sometimes I feel as though I should send out a dozen heralds to proclaim our need of an enemy. I *do*, Vizier."

"No, sire," said the Grand Vizier earnestly. "No, truly, you don't want to do anything like that. I promise you, you don't." He straightened up, rubbing his back and smoothing out his robe of office. He said, "Sire, Majesty, if I may humbly suggest it, you would do well – as would every soul dwelling on this soil that we call home – to appreciate what you see as our insignificance. There is an old saying that there is no country as unhappy as one that needs heroes. Trust me when I say in my turn that our land's happiness is your greatest victory in this life, and that you will never know another to equal it. Nor should you try, for that would show you both greedy and ungrateful, and offend the gods. I urge you to leave well enough alone."

Having spoken so, the Grand Vizier braced himself for an angry response, or at least a petulant one, being a man in late middle age who had served other kings. He was both astonished and alarmed to realize that King Pelles had hardly heard him, so caught up was he in romantic visions of battle. "It would have to be in self-defense, of course," the king was saying dreamily. "We have no interest in others' treasure or territory – we're not that sort of nation. If someone would only try to invade us by crafty wiles, such as filling a wooden horse with armed soldiers and leaving it invitingly outside the gates of our capital city. Then we could set it afire and roast them all – "

He caught sight of the horrified expression on the Grand Vizier's face, and added hurriedly, "Not that we ever *would*, of course, certainly not, I was just speculating."

"Of course, sire," murmured the Grand Vizier. But his breath was turning increasingly short and painful as King Pelles went on.

"Or if they should come by sea, slipping into our port on a foggy night, we would be ready with a corps of young men trained to swim out with braces and augurs and sink their ships. And if they struck by air, perhaps dropping silently from the sky in dark balloons, our archers could shoot all them down with fire-arrows. Or if we could induce them to tunnel under the castle walls – oh, *that* would be good, if they tunneled – then we could..."

The Grand Vizier coughed, as delicately as he could manage it, given the panicky constriction of his throat. He said, "Your Highness, meaning absolutely no disrespect, you have never seen war – "

"Exactly, exactly!" King Pelles broke in. "How can one know the true meaning of peace, who has no experience of its undoubtedly horrid counterpart? Can you answer me that, Vizier?"

"Majesty, I have known that experience," the Grand Vizier replied quietly. "It was far from here, in a land I traveled to as a boy. I shared it with many brave and dear and young friends, who are all dead now – as I should have been, but for the courtesy of the gods, and the enemy's poor aim. You have missed nothing, my lord."

He seemed to have grown older as he spoke, and the king – who may have been foolish, but who was not a fool – saw, and answered him equally gently. "I understand what you are telling me, good Vizier. But this would be only a little war, truly – no more enduring or consuming than one of our delightful carpet clashes. A *manageable* war – a demonstration, one might say, just to let our rivals see that our people are not to be trifled with. In case they were thinking about trifling. Do you see the difference, Vizier? Between this war and yours?"

With another king, the Grand Vizier would have considered long and carefully before risking the truth. With King Pelles, he had no such fears, but he also knew his man well enough to recognize when hearing the truth would make no smallest difference to what the king decided to do. So he said only, "Well, well, be sure to employ great precision in choosing your foe – "

"*Our* foe," King Pelles corrected him. "Our *nation's* foe."

"*Our* foe," the Grand Vizier agreed. "We must, whatever else we do, select the weakest enemy available – "

"But that would be dishonorable!" the king protested. "Ignoble! Unsporting!" He was decidedly upset.

The Grand Vizier was firm in this. "We are hardly a nation at all; we are more like a shire or a county with an army. A distinctly small army. A more powerful adversary would destroy us – that is simply a fact, my king. You cannot *manage* a war without attention to facts."

He was hoping that his sardonic emphasis on the notion of managing such a capricious thing as war might deter King Pelles from the whole fancy, but it did not. After a silence, the king finally sighed and said, "Well. If that is what a war is, so be it. Consider our choices, Vizier, and make your recommendation." He added then, rather quickly, "But do arrange for a *gracious* war, if you possibly can. Something... something a little *tidy*. With songs in it, you know."

The Grand Vizier said, "I will do what I can."

As it turned out, he did tragically better than he meant. Perhaps because King Pelles had never wanted to know it, he truly had no notion of how deeply his land was hated for its prosperity on the one hand and coveted on the other. The Grand Vizier had hoped to engineer a very brief war for the king, quickly over, with minimum damage, disruption or inconvenience to everyone involved, and easily succeeded in tempting their little country's nearest neighbor to invade (in the traditional style, as it happens, by marching across borders). But his plan went completely out of control in a matter of hours. Wise enough to lure a weaker country into a foolish attack, he was as innocent, in his own way, as his king, never having considered that other lands might be utterly delighted to join with the lone aggressor he had bargained for. An alliance of territories which normally despised each other formed swiftly, and King Pelles's land came under siege from all sides.

Actually, it was no war at all, but a massacre, a butchery. There was a good deal of death, which was something else the king had never seen. He was still shaking and crying from the horror of it, and the pity, and his terrible shame, when the Grand Vizier disguised them both as peasant women and set them scurrying out the back way as the flaming castle came down, seeming to melt and dissolve like so much pink candy floss. King Pelles looked back and wept anew for his home, and for his country; and the Grand Vizier remembered the words of Boabdil's mother when the Moorish king looked back in tears from the mountain pass at lost Spain behind him. *"Weep not like a woman for the kingdom you could not defend like a man."* But then he thought that defending things like men was what had gotten them into this catastrophe in the first place, and decided to say nothing.

The king and his Grand Vizier scrambled day on wretched day across the trampled, smoking land, handicapped somewhat by their long skirts and heavy muddy boots, but running like a pair of aging thieves all the same. No one stopped them, or even looked at them closely, although there were mighty rewards posted everywhere for their heads, and they really looked very little like peasant women, even on their best days. But the country was in such havoc, with so many others – displaced, homeless, penniless, mad with terror and loss – fleeing in every direction, that no one had the time or the inclination to concern themselves with the identities of their poor companions on the road. The soldiers of the alliance were too busy looting and burning, and those whose homes were being looted and burned were too busy not being in them. King Pelles and the Grand Vizier were never once recognized.

One evening, dazed as a child abruptly awakened from a happy dream, the king finally asked where they were bound.

"I have relatives in the south country beyond those hills you see," the Grand Vizier told him. "A cousin and her husband – they have a farm. It has been a long time since I last saw them, and I cannot entirely remember where they live. But they will take us in, I am sure of it."

King Pelles sighed like the great Moor. "Better your family than mine. *My* cousins – my own brother – would demand a bribe, and then turn us over to the conquerors anyway. They are bad people, the lot of them." He huddled deeper into his ragged blanket, shrugging himself closer to their tiny fire. "But I am the worst by far," he added, "the worst, there is no comparison. I deserve whatever becomes of me."

"You did not know, sire," the Grand Vizier offered in attempted solace. "That is the worst that can be said of you, that you did not know."

"But you did, you *did,* and you tried to warn me, and I refused to listen to you. And you obeyed my orders, and now you share my fate, and my people's innocent lives lie in ruins, and it is my doing, and there is no atoning for it." The king rocked back and forth, then stretched on the ground in his blanket, as though he were trying to bury himself where he lay, whimpering again and again, "No atoning, no atoning." He hurt himself doing this, for the ground was shingly and rock-strewn. The Grand Vizier knew he would see the bruises in the morning.

"You were a good king," the Vizier said. "You meant well."

"*No!*" The word came out as a scream of agony. "I *never* meant well! I meant glory for myself – nothing less or more than that. And I knew it, I *knew* it, I knew it at the time, and still I had to go ahead, had to play out my toy battle with soft, breakable human bodies, breakable human souls. *No atoning...*"

There was nothing for the Grand Vizier then, but to say, as to a child, "Go to sleep, Your Majesty. What's done is done, and one of us is as guilty as the other. And even so, we must sleep."

But he himself slept poorly – perhaps even worse than King Pelles – in the barns and the empty cattle byres and the caves; and the king's piteous murmurings as he dreamed were hardly of any help. There was always the smell of smoke, from one direction or another; at times there would come noises in the night, which might as easily have been restless cows as pursuing spies or soldiers, but there was never any way for the Vizier to make certain of either. All he allowed himself to think about was the need to guide the king safely to shelter from one night to the next – further than that, his imagining dared not go, if he meant to sleep at all. *And even if we find my cousin – what was her husband's name again? – even if we do find their farm, what then?*

By great good fortune, they did find the Grand Vizier's cousin, whose name was Nerissa – her husband's name was Antonio – and were welcomed as though they had last visited only days ago, or a week at most. The little farm was a crowded place, since Nerissa and Antonio, with no children of their own, had gladly taken in their widowed friend Clara and her four, who ranged in age from six to seventeen years. Nevertheless, they received King Pelles and the Grand Vizier unhesitatingly: as Antonio said, "No farm was ever the worse for more hands in the fields, nor more faces around the dinner table. And whoever noticed the smudged and sunburned face of a farmworker who wasn't one himself? Have no fear – you are safe with us. In these times, there is no safety but family."

So it was that he who had been the king of all the land and he who had been its most powerful dignitary became nothing more than hands in the fields, and were grateful. Neither was young, but they worked hard and long all the same, and proudly kept even with Antonio and the others when it came time to bring the harvest home. And every evening, King Pelles told stories about wise animals and clever magicians to Clara's children, and later the Grand Vizier conducted an informal history lesson for the older ones, in which their mother often joined. Still an attractive woman, she had clear brown skin and dark, amused eyes which were increasingly attentive, as time passed, to whatever the Vizier said or did. Antonio and Nerissa saw this, and were glad of it, as was the king. "Your cousin has wasted his life on my foolishness," he said to Nerissa. "I am so happy that she will give it back to him."

When the Grand Vizier could do it without feeling intrusive, he listened – with the back of his head, perhaps, or the back of his mind – to the king's fairytales. They were not like any he had ever heard, and they fascinated and alarmed him at the same time. Few had what he would have considered happy endings, especially as a child – the gallant prince frequently failed to arrive in time to rescue the princess from the dragon, more often than not the poison was not counteracted, the talking cat could not always preserve his master from his own stupidity. Endings changed, as well, with each telling, and characters wandered from one story into a different one, often changing their natures as they did so. On occasion grief flowed into overwhelming joy, though that outcome was never something you might want to bet on. The Grand Vizier constantly expected the children to become frightened or upset, but they listened in obvious absorption, the younger ones crowding each other on the king's lap, and all four nodding silently from time to time, as children do to express trust in the tale.

Maybe it is the way he tells them, the Grand Vizier thought more than once, for King Pelles always had a special voice at those times, different than the way he spoke in the fields or at evening table. It was a low voice, with a calmness in it that – as the Vizier knew – had grown directly from suffering and remorse, and seemed to draw the children's confidence whether or not the words were understood.

Yet content as King Pelles was in his new life, fond of Clara's children as he was, warmed far deeper than his bones by being a true part of a family for the first time...even so, he still wept in his sleep, whispering brokenly, *"No atoning..."* The Grand Vizier heard him every night.

Winter was always hard in that kingdom, even in the south country, but the Grand Vizier was profoundly glad of it. The snow and mud closed the roads, for one thing: there would be no further pursuit of the king for a time, and who knew what might happen, or have happened, by spring? What news reached the farm suggested that a group of the king's former advisors had banded together to install a ruler of their choosing, and thus restore at least their notion of order to the kingdom, but the Vizier could not discover his name, nor learn any further details of the story. But he allowed himself to be somewhat hopeful, to imagine that perhaps – just *perhaps* – the hunt might have dwindled away, and that the king's existence might have become completely unimportant to the new regime. For the first time in his long career of service, the Grand Vizier dreamed a small dream for himself.

But with the thawing of the roads, with the tinkling dissolution of the icicles that had fringed the farmhouse's gables for many months, with the first tentative sounds of the frogs who had slept in the deep beds of the frozen streams all winter...the soldiers came marching. With the first storks, they came.

Martine, Clara's younger daughter, was playing by the awakening pond one afternoon, and heard their boots and the rattle of their mail before they had rounded the bend in the road. She, like all the others, had been told over and over that if she ever saw even one soldier she must run straight to the house and warn her mother's special friend, and the other one as well, the storyteller. She never waited to see these, but was up and away at the first sound, and through the front door in a muddy flash, crying, "They're here! They're here!"

Antonio had long since prepared a hiding place for King Pelles and the Grand Vizier in case of just such an emergency. It lay under the floor of his own bedroom, so cunningly made and so close-fit that it was impossible to tell which boards might turn on hinges, or how to make them open, even if you knew. The two men were down there, motionless in the dark, well before the soldiers had reached the farmhouse; until the first fist hammered on the front door, the only sound they heard was the beating of each other's hearts.

The soldiers were polite, as soldiers go. They trampled no chickens, broke nothing in the house, and kept their hands off Antonio's fresh stock of winter ale, last of the season. Filling the kitchen with their size and the noise of their bodies, they treated Nerissa and Clara with truly remarkable courtesy; and their captain offered boiled sweets to the children clustered behind them, even responding with a good-humored chuckle when little Martine kicked his shin. Nor did they ask a single question concerning guests, or visitors, or new-hired laborers. Indeed, they were so amiable and considerate, by contrast with what the family had expected, that it took Nerissa a moment longer than it should have to realize that they had not been sent for the king and the Grand Vizier at all.

They had come for her husband.

"You see, ma'am," the Captain explained, as three of his men laid hold of Antonio, who had bolted too late for the back door, "the war just keeps going *on*. Wars, I mean. It's chaos, madness, really it is, ever since that idiot Pelles started the whole thing. Everyone turning against everyone else – whole regiments changing sides, generals selling out their own troops – mutiny over *there*, rebellion *here*, betrayal *that* way, corruption *this* way...and what's a poor soldier to do but follow his orders, no matter who's giving them today? And my orders all winter have been to round up every single warm body, which means every able, breathing male with both legs under him, and ship them straightaway to the front. And so that's what I do."

"The front," Nerissa said numbly. "Which front? Where is the battle?"

The Captain spread his arms in dramatic frustration. "Well, I don't know *which* front, do I? As many of them as there are these days? Somebody else tells me that when we get there. Very sorry to be snatching away your breadwinner, ma'am – 'pon my soul, I am – but there it is, you see, and I put it to you, what's a poor soldier to do?" He turned irritably toward the soldiers struggling with Antonio. *"Hold* him, blast you! What's the bloody matter with you?"

In the moment that his gaze was not on her, Nerissa reached for her favorite butchering knife. Behind her, Clara's hand closed silently on a cleaver. Only Martine saw, and drew breath to scream more loudly than she ever had in her short life. But the Captain was never to know how close he was to death in that moment, because just then King Pelles walked alone into the kitchen.

He wore his royal robes, and his crown as well, which the children had never seen in all the time he had lived with them. Nodding pleasantly at the soldiers, he said to the Captain, "Let the man go. You will have a much richer prize to show your general than some poor farmer."

The Captain was dumb with amazement, turning all sorts of colors as he gaped at the king. His men, thoroughly astounded themselves, eased their grip on Antonio, who promptly burst free and headed for the door a second time. Some would have given chase, but King Pelles snapped out again, "Let him go!" and it was a king's order, prisoner or no. The men fell back.

"We weren't looking for you, sir," the Captain said, almost meekly. "We thought you were dead."

"Well, how much better for you that I'm not," the king replied briskly. "There will be a bonus involved, surely, and you certainly should be able to trade me to one side or another – possibly all of them, if you manage it right. I know all about managing," he added, in a somewhat different voice.

A young officer just behind the captain demanded, "Where is the Grand Vizier? He was seen with you on the road."

King Pelles shrugged lightly and sighed. "And that was where he died, on the way here, poor chap. I buried him myself." He turned back to the Captain. "Where are you supposed to take me, if I may ask?"

"To the new king," the Captain muttered in answer. "To King Phoebus."

"To my brother?" It was the king's turn to be astonished. "My brother is king now?"

"As of three days ago, anyway. When I left headquarters, he was." The Captain spread his arms wide again. "What do *I* know, these days?"

Even in his happiest moments on Nerissa and Antonio's farm, the king had never laughed as he laughed now, with a kind of delight no less rich for being ironic. "Well," he said finally. "Well, by all means, let us go to my brother. Let us go to King Phoebus, then – and on the way, perhaps we might talk about managing." He removed his crown, smiling as he handed it to the Captain. "There you are. Can't be king if you don't have a crown, you know."

Nerissa and Clara stood equally as stunned as the men who cautiously laid hands on the unresisting King Pelles; but the two youngest children set up a wail of angry protest when they began leading him away. They clung to his legs and wept, and neither the Captain nor their mother could part them from him. That took the king himself, who finally turned to put his arms around them, calling each by name, and saying, "Remember the stories. My stories will always be with you." He embraced the two women, saying to Clara in a low voice, "Take care of him, as he took care of me." Then he went away with the soldiers, eyes clear and a smile on his face.

If the Captain had looked back, he might well have seen the Grand Vizier, who came wandering into the kitchen a moment later, nursing a large bruise on his cheekbone, and another already forming on his jaw. Clara flew to him, as he said dazedly, "He hit me. I wouldn't let him surrender himself alone, so then he.... Call them back – I'm his Vizier, he can't go without me. Call them back."

"Hush," Clara said, holding him. "Hush."

In time the long night of wars, rebellions, and retaliations of every sort slowly gave way at least to truces born of simple exhaustion, and reliable news became easier to come by, even for wary hillfolk like themselves. Thus the Grand Vizier was able to discover that the king's brother Phoebus had quite quickly been overthrown, very likely while the soldiers were still on the road with their captive. But further he could not go. He never found out what had become of King Pelles, and after some time he came to realize that he did not really want to.

"As long as we don't know anything certainly," he said to his family, "it is always possible that he might still be alive. Somewhere. I cannot speak for anyone else, but that is the only way I can live with his sacrifice."

"Perhaps sacrifice was the only way he could live," suggested his wife. The Grand Vizier turned to her in some surprise, and Clara smiled at him. "I heard him in the night too," she said.

"*I* hear his stories," young Martine said importantly. "I close my eyes when I get into bed, and he tells me a story."

"Yes," said the Grand Vizier softly. "Yes, he tells me stories too."

The Last and Only,
or,
Mr. Moscowitz Becomes French

In one way this is the oldest story in the book; and in another, one of the newest. My memory is that I started it in the late 1960s, when my family and I had settled into our first house with real central heating, which was located in farming country just outside Watsonville, California. I sent an early version off to my agent, Elizabeth Otis, in New York, and in so doing initiated a sputtering cycle of rewrites and rejections that went on quietly in the background for a couple of years. By that time I'd stumbled into screen-writing, and for the next decade I largely abandoned prose fiction while in hot pur-suit of the first serious money I'd ever seen. "The Last and Only" languished in my bat-tered, dangerous filing cabinet until well past the turn of the new century, when Connor Cochran – once more exploring the dark continent of that cabinet with gun and cam-era – came across it and asked me to try again from a slightly different angle. What hap-pened next was the oddest collaboration I've ever experienced, in which one of the two writers at the table was a younger, hairier me whom I didn't always recognize and only barely remembered.

It often happens that stories have to wait a very long time for the author to catch up with what they already know. But usually not this long.

ONCE UPON A TIME, there lived in California a Frenchman named George Moscowitz. His name is of no importance – there are old families in France named Wilson and Holmes, and the first president of the Third Republic was named MacMahon – but what was interesting about Mr. Moscowitz was that he had not always been French. Nor was he entirely French at the time we meet him, but he was becoming perceptibly more so every day. His wife, whose name was Miriam, drew his silhouette on a child's blackboard and filled him in from the feet up with tricolor chalk, adding a little more color daily. She was at mid-thigh when we begin our story.

Most of the doctors who examined Mr. Moscowitz agreed that his affliction was due to some sort of bug that he must have picked up in France when he and Mrs. Moscowitz were honeymooning there, fif-teen years before. In its dormant stage, the bug had manifested itself only as a kind of pleasant Francophilia: on their return from France Mr. Moscowitz had begun to buy Linguaphone CDs, and to get up at six in the morning to watch a cable television show on beginner's French. He took to collecting French books and magazines, French music and painting and sculpture, French recipes, French folklore, French attitudes, and, inevitably, French people. As a librarian in a large university, he came in contact with a good many French exchange students and visiting professors, and he went far out of his way to make friends with them – Mr. Moscowitz, shy as a badger. The students had a saying among themselves that if you wanted to be French in that town, you had to clear it with Monsieur Moscowitz, who issued licenses and *cartes de séjour*. The joke was not especially unkind, because Mr. Moscowitz often had them to dinner at his home, and in his quiet delight in the very sound of their voices they found themselves curiously less bored with themselves, and with one another. Their companions at dinner were quite likely to be the ignorant Marseillais tailor who got all of Mr. Moscowitz's custom, or the Canuck coach of the soccer team, but there was something so touching in Mr. Moscowitz's assumption that all French-speaking people must be naturally at home together that professors and proletariat generally managed to find each other charming and valuable. And Mr. Moscowitz himself, speaking rarely, but sometimes smiling uncontrollably, like an exhalation of joy – he was a snob in that he preferred the culture and manners of another country to his own, and certainly a fool in that he could find wisdom in every foolishness uttered in French – he was marvelously happy then, and it was impossible for those around him to escape his happiness. Now and then he would address a compliment or a witticism to his wife, who would smile and answer softly, *"Merci,"* or *"La-la,"* for she knew that at such moments he believed without thinking about it that she too spoke French.

Mrs. Moscowitz herself was, as must be obvious, a patient woman of a tolerant humor, who greatly enjoyed her husband's enjoyment of all things French, and who believed, firmly and serenely, that this curious obsession would fade with time, to be replaced by bridge or chess, or – though she prayed not – golf. "At least he's dressing much better these days," she told her sister Dina, who lived in Scottsdale, Arizona. "Thank God you don't have to wear plaid pants to be French."

Then, after fifteen years, whatever it was that he had contracted in France, if that was what he had done, came fully out of hiding; and here stood Mr. Moscowitz in one doctor's office after another, French from his soles to his ankles, to his shins, to his knees, and still heading north for a second spring. (Mrs. Moscowitz's little drawing is, of course, only a convenient metaphor – if anything her husband was becoming French from his bones out.) He was treated with drugs as common as candy and as rare as turtle tears by doctors ranging from Johns Hopkins specialists to a New Guinea shaman; he was examined by herbalists and honey-doctors, and by committees of medical men so reputable as to make illness in their presence seem almost criminal; and he was dragged to a crossroads one howling midnight to meet with a half-naked, foamy-chinned old man who claimed to be the son of Merlin's affair with Nimue, and a colonel in the Marine Reserves besides. This fellow's diagnosis was supernatural possession; his prescribed remedy would cost Mr. Moscowitz a black pig (and the pig its liver), and was impractical, but the idea left Mr. Moscowitz thoughtful for a long time.

In bed that night, he said to his wife, "Perhaps it is possession. It's frightening, yes, but it's exciting too, if you want the truth. I feel something growing inside me, taking shape as it crowds me out, and the closer I get to disappearing, the clearer it becomes. And yet, it is me too, if you understand – I wish I could explain to you how it feels – it is like, 'ow you say..."

"Don't say that," Mrs. Moscowitz interrupted with tears in her voice. She had begun to whimper quietly when he spoke of disappearing. "Only TV Frenchmen talk like that."

"*Excuse-moi, ma vieille.* The more it crowds me, the more it makes me feel like *me*. I feel a whole country growing inside me, thousands of years, millions of people, stupid, crazy, shrewd people, and all of them me. I never felt like that before, I never felt that there was anything inside me, even myself. Now I'm pregnant with a whole country, and I'm growing fat with it, and one day – " He began to cry himself then, and the two of them huddled small in their bed, holding hands all night long. He dreamed in French that night, as he had been doing for weeks, but he woke up still speaking it, and he did not regain his English until he had had his first cup of coffee. It took him longer each morning thereafter.

A psychiatrist whom they visited when Mr. Moscowitz's silhouette was French to the waist commented that his theory of possession by himself was a way of sidling up to the truth that Mr. Moscowitz was actually willing his transformation. "The unconscious is ingenious at devising methods of withdrawal," he explained, pulling at his fingertips as though milking a cow, "and national character is certainly no barrier to a mind so determined to get out from under the weight of being an American. It's not as uncommon as you might think, these days."

"*Qu'est-ce qu'il dit?*" whispered Mr. Moscowitz to his wife.

"I have a patient," mused the psychiatrist, "who believes that he is gradually being metamorphosed into a roc, such a giant bird as carried off Sindbad the Sailor to lands unimaginable and riches beyond comprehension. He has asked me to come with him to the very same lands when his change is complete."

"*Qu'est-ce qu'il dit? Qu'est-ce que c'est, roc?*" Mrs. Moscowitz shushed her husband nervously and said, "Yes, yes, but what about George? Do you think you can cure him?"

"I won't be around," said the psychiatrist. There came a stoop of great wings outside the window, and the Moscowitzes fled.

"Well, there it is," Mrs. Moscowitz said when they were home, "and I must confess I thought as much. You could stop this stupid change yourself if you really wanted to, but you don't want to stop it. You're withdrawing, just the way he said, you're escaping from the responsibility of being plain old George Moscowitz in the plain old United States. You're quitting, and I'm ashamed of you – you're copping out." She hadn't used the phrase since her own college days, at Vassar, and it made her feel old and even less in control of this disturbing situation.

"Cop-out, cop-out," said Mr. Moscowitz thoughtfully. "What charm! I love it very much, the American slang. Cop-out, copping out. I cop out, *tu* cop out, they all cop out..."

Then Mrs. Moscowitz burst into tears, and picking up her colored chalks, she scribbled up and down and across the neat silhouette of her husband until the chalk screamed and broke, and the whole blackboard was plastered red, white, and blue; and as she did this, she cried "I don't care, I don't care if you're escaping or not, or what you change into. I wouldn't care if you turned into a cockroach, if I could be a cockroach too." Her eyes were so blurred with tears that Mr. Moscowitz seemed to be sliding away from her like a cloud. He took her in his arms then, but all the comfort he offered her was in French, and she cried even harder.

It was the only time she ever allowed herself to break down. The next day she set about learning French. It was difficult for her, for she had no natural ear for language, but she enrolled in three schools at once – one for group study, one for private lessons, and the other online – and she worked very hard. She even dug out her husband's abandoned language CDs and listened to them constantly. And during her days and evenings, if she found herself near a mirror, she would peer at the plump, tired face she saw there and say carefully to it, *"Je suis la professeur. Vous êtes l'étudiante. Je suis française. Vous n'êtes pas française."* These were the first four sentences that the recordings spoke to her every day. It had occurred to her – though she never voiced the idea – that she might be able to will the same change that had befallen her husband on herself. She told herself often, especially after triumphing over her reflection, that she felt more French daily; and when she finally gave up the pretense of being transformed, she said to herself, "It's my fault. I want to change for him, not for myself. It's not enough." She kept up with her French lessons, all the same.

Mr. Moscowitz, on his part, was finding it necessary to take English lessons. His work in the library was growing more harassing every day: he could no longer read the requests filed by the students – let alone the forms and instructions on his own computer screen – and he had to resort to desperate guessing games and mnemonic systems to find anything in the stacks or on the shelves. His condition was obvious to his friends on the library staff, and they covered up for him as best they could, doing most of his work while a graduate student from the French department sat with him in a carrel, teaching him English as elementary as though he had never spoken it. But he did not learn it quickly, and he never learned it well, and his friends could not keep him hidden all the time. Inevitably, the Chancellor of the university interested himself in the matter, and after a series of interviews with Mr. Moscowitz – conducted in French, for the Chancellor was a traveled man who had studied at the Sorbonne – announced regretfully that he saw no way but to let Mr. Moscowitz go. "You understand my position, Georges, my old one," he said, shrugging slightly and twitching his mouth. "It is a damage, of course, well understood, but there will be much severance pay and a pension of the fullest." The presence of a Frenchman always made the Chancellor a little giddy.

"You speak French like a Spanish cow," observed Mr. Moscowitz, who had been expecting this decision and was quite calm. He then pointed out to the Chancellor that he had standing and to spare, and that he was not about to be gotten rid of so easily. Even in this imbecile country, an employee had his rights, and it was on the Chancellor's shoulders to find a reason for discharging him. He requested the Chancellor to show him a single university code, past or present, that listed change of nationality as sufficient grounds for terminating a contract; and he added that he was older than the Chancellor and had given him no encouragement to call him *tu*.

"But you're not the same man we hired!" cried the Chancellor in English.

"No?" asked Mr. Moscowitz when the remark had been explained to him. "Then who am I, please?"

The university would have been glad to settle the case out of court, and Mrs. Moscowitz pleaded with her husband to accept their offered terms, which were liberal enough; but he refused, for no reason that she could see but delight at the confusion and embarrassment he was about to cause, and a positive hunger for the tumult of a court battle. The man she had married, she remembered, had always found it hard to show anger even to his worst enemy, for fear of hurting his feelings; but she stopped thinking about it at that point, not wanting to make the Chancellor's case for him. "You are quite right, George," she told him, and then, carefully, *"Tu as raison, mon chou."* He told her – as nearly as she could understand – that if she ever learned to speak French properly she would sound like a Basque, so she might as well not try. He was very rude to the Marseillais tailor these days.

The ACLU appointed a lawyer for Mr. Moscowitz, and, for all purposes but the practical, he won his case as decisively as Darrow defending Darwin. The lawyer laid great and tearful stress on the calamity (hisses from the gallery, where a sizeable French contingent grew larger every day) that had befallen a simple, ordinary man, leaving him dumb and defenseless in the midst of academic piranhas who would strip him of position, reputation, even statehood, in one pitiless bite. (This last was in reference to a foolish statement by the university counsel that Mr. Moscowitz would have some difficulty passing a citizenship test now, let alone a librarian's examination.) But his main defense was the same as Mr. Moscowitz's before the Chancellor: there was no precedent for such a situation as his client's, nor was this case likely to set one. If the universities wanted to write it into their common code that any man proved to be changing his nationality should summarily be discharged, then the universities could do that, and very silly they would look, too. ("What would constitute proof?" he wondered aloud, and what degree of change would it be necessary to prove? "Fifty percent? Thirty-three and one-third? Or just, as the French say, a *soupçon?*") But as matters stood, the university had no more right to fire Mr. Moscowitz for becoming a Frenchman than they would have if he became fat, or gray-haired, or two inches taller. The lawyer ended his plea by bowing deeply to his client and crying *"Vive* Moscowitz!" And the whole courthouse rang and thundered then as Americans and French, judge and jury, counsels and bailiffs and the whole audience rose and roared, *"Vive* Moscowitz! *Vive* Moscowitz!" The Chancellor thought of the Sorbonne, and wept.

There were newspapermen in the courtroom, and by that last day there were television cameras. Mr. Moscowitz sat at home that night and leaned forward to stare at his face whenever it came on the screen. His wife, thinking he was criticizing his appearance, remarked, "You look nice. A little like Jean Gabin." Mr. Moscowitz grunted. *"Le camera t'aime,"* she said carefully. She answered the phone when it rang, which was often. Many of the callers had television shows of their own. The others wanted Mr. Moscowitz to write books.

Within a week of the trial, Mr. Moscowitz was a national celebrity, which meant that as many people knew his name as knew the name of the actor who played the dashing Gilles de Rais in a new television serial, and not quite as many as recognized the eleven-year-old Racine girl with a forty-inch bust, who sang Christian techno-rap. Mrs. Moscowitz saw him more often on television than she did at home – at seven on a Sunday morning he was invited to discuss post-existential film or France's relations with her former African colonies; at two o'clock he might be awarding a ticket to Paris to the winner of the daily *My Ex Will Hate This* contest; and at eleven p.m., on one of the late-night shows, she could watch him speaking the lyrics to the internationally popular French song, *"Je M'en Fous De Tout Ça,"* while a covey of teenage dancers yipped and jiggled around him. Mrs. Moscowitz would sigh, switch off the set, and sit down at the computer to study her assigned installment of the adventures of the family Vincent, who spoke basic French to one another and were always having breakfast, visiting aunts, or making lists. "Regard Helene," said Mrs. Moscowitz bitterly. "She is in train of falling into the quicksand again. Yes, she falls. Naughty, naughty Helene. She talks too much."

There was a good deal of scientific and political interest taken in Mr. Moscowitz as well. He spent several weekends in Washington, being examined and interviewed, and he met the President, briefly. The President shook his hand, and gave him a souvenir fountain pen and a flag lapel, and said that he regarded Mr. Moscowitz's transformation as the ultimate expression of the American dream, for it surely proved to the world that any American could become whatever he wanted enough to be, even if what he wanted to be was a snail-eating French wimp.

The scientists, whose lingering fear had been that the metamorphosis of Mr. Moscowitz had been somehow accomplished by the Russians or the Iranians, as a practice run before they turned everybody into Russians or Iranians, found nothing in Mr. Moscowitz either to enlighten or alert them. He was a small, suspicious man who spoke often of his rights, and might, as far as they could tell, have been born French. They sent him home at last, to his business manager, to his television commitments, to his endorsements, to his ghostwritten autobiography, and to his wife; and they told the President, "Go figure. Maybe this is the way the world ends, we wouldn't know. And it might not hurt to avoid crêpes for a while."

Mr. Moscowitz's celebrity lasted for almost two months – quite a long time, considering that it was autumn and there were a lot of other public novas flaring and dying on prime time. His high-water mark was certainly reached on the weekend that the officials of at least one cable network were watching one another's eyes to see how they might react to the idea of a George Moscowitz Show. His fortunes began to ebb on Monday morning – public interest is a matter of momentum, and there just wasn't anything Mr. Moscowitz could do for an encore.

"If he were only a *nice* Frenchman, or a *sexy* Frenchman!" the producers and the publishers and the ghostwriters and the A&R executives and the sponsors sighed separately and in conference. "Someone like Jean Reno or Charles Boyer, or Chevalier, or Jacques Pépin, or even Louis Jourdan – somebody charming, somebody with style, with manners, with maybe a little ho-*ho*, Mimi, you good-for-nothing little Mimi..." But what they had, as far as they could see, was one of those surly frogs in a cloth cap who rioted in front of the American Embassy and trashed the Paris McDonald's. Once, on a talk show, he said, taking great care with his English grammar, "The United States is like a very large dog which has not been – *qu'est-ce que c'est le mot?* – housebro*k*en. It is well enough in its place, but its place is not on the couch. Or in the Mideast, or in Africa, or in a restaurant kitchen." The television station began to get letters. They suggested that Mr. Moscowitz go back where he came from.

So Mr. Moscowitz was whisked out of the public consciousness as deftly as an unpleasant report on what else gives mice cancer or makes eating fish as hazardous as bullfighting. His television bookings were cancelled; he was replaced by reruns, motivational speakers, old John Payne musicals, or one of the less distressing rappers. The contracts for his books and columns and articles remained unsigned, or turned out to conceal escape clauses, elusive and elliptical, but enforceable. Within a week of his last public utterance – "American women smell bad, they smell of fear and vomit and *l'ennui*" – George Moscowitz was no longer a celebrity. He wasn't even a Special Guest.

Nor was he a librarian anymore, in spite of the court's decision. He could not be discharged, but he certainly couldn't be kept on in the library. The obvious solution would have been to find him a position in the French department, but he was no teacher, no translator, no scholar; he was unqualified to teach the language in a junior high school. The Chancellor graciously offered him a departmental scholarship to get a degree in French, but he turned it down as an insult. "At least, a couple of education courses – " said the Chancellor. "Take them yourself," said Mr. Moscowitz, and he resigned.

"What will we do now, George?" asked his wife. "*Que ferons-nous?*" She was glad to have her husband back from the land of magic, even though he was as much a stranger to her now as he sometimes seemed to be to himself. ("What does a butterfly think of its chrysalis?" she wondered modestly, "Or of milkweed?") His fall from grace seemed to have made him kind again. They spent their days together now, walking, or reading Chateaubriand aloud; often silent, for it was hard for Mrs. Moscowitz to speak truly in French, and her husband could not mutter along in English for long without becoming angry. "Will we go to France?" she asked, knowing his answer.

"Yes," Mr. Moscowitz said. He showed her a letter. "The French government will pay our passage. We are going home." He said it many times, now with joy, now with a certain desperation. "We are going home."

The French of course insisted on making the news of Mr. Moscowitz's departure public in America, and the general American attitude was a curious mix of relief and chagrin. They were glad to have Mr. Moscowitz safely out of the way, but it was "doubtless unpleasant," as a French newspaper suggested, "to see a recognizable human shape insist on emerging from the great melting pot, instead of eagerly dissolving away." Various influences in the United States warned that Mr. Moscowitz was obviously a spy for some international conspiracy, but the President, who had vaguely liked him, said, "Well, good for him, great. Enjoy, baby." The government made up a special loose-leaf passport for Mr. Moscowitz, with room for other changes of nationality, just in case.

Mrs. Moscowitz, who made few demands on her husband, or anyone else, insisted on going to visit her sister Dina in Scottsdale before the move to France. She spent several days being taught to play video games by her nephew and enjoying countless tea parties with her two nieces, and sitting up late with Dina and her sympathetic husband, talking over all the ramifications of her coming exile. "Because that's the way I know I see it," she said, "in my heart. I try to feel excited – I really do try, for George's sake – but inside, inside..." She never wept or broke down at such points, but would pause for a few moments, while her sister fussed with the coffee cups and her brother-in-law looked away. "It's not that I'll miss that many people," she would go on, "or our life – well, George's life – around the university. Or the apartment, or all the things we can't take with us – that doesn't really matter, all that. Maybe if we had children, like you..." and she would fall silent again, but not for long, before she burst out, "But *me*, I'll miss *me!* I don't know who I'll be, living in France, but it'll be someone else, it won't ever be *me* again. And I did...I *did* like me the way I was, and so did George, no matter what he says now." But in time, as they knew she would, she would recover her familiar reliable calmness and decide, "Oh, it will be all right, I'm sure. I'm just being an old stick-in-the-mud. It *will* be an adventure, after all."

The French government sent a specially-chartered jet to summon the Moscowitzes; it was very grand treatment, Mrs. Moscowitz thought, but she had hoped they would sail. "On a boat, we would be nowhere for a few days," she said to herself, "and I do need to be nowhere first, just a little while." She took her books and CDs about the Vincent family along with her, and she drew a long breath and held onto Mr. Moscowitz's sleeve when the plane doors opened onto the black and glowing airfield, and they were invited to step down among the roaring people who had been waiting for two days to welcome them. "Here we go," she said softly. *"Allons-y.* We are home."

France greeted them with great pride and great delight, in which there was mixed not the smallest drop of humor. To the overwhelming majority of the French press, to the poets and politicians, and certainly to the mass of the people – who read the papers and the poems, and waited at the airport – it seemed both utterly logical and magnificently just that a man's soul should discover itself to be French. Was it not possible that all the souls in the world might be French, born in exile but beginning to find their way home from the cold countries, one by one? Think of all the tourists, the wonderful middle-aged tourists – where will we put them all? Anywhere, anywhere, it won't matter, for all the world will be France, as it should have been long ago, when our souls began to speak different languages. *Vive* Moscowitz then, *vive* Moscowitz! And see if you can get him to do a spread in *Paris-Match,* or on your television program, or book him for a few weeks at the Olympia. Got to make your money before Judgment Day.

But the government had not invited Mr. Moscowitz to France to abandon him to free enterprise – he was much too important for that. His television appearances were made on government time; his public speeches were staged and sponsored by the government; and he would never have been allowed, even had he wished, to endorse a soft drink that claimed that it made the imbiber twenty-two percent more French. He was not for rent. He traveled – or, rather, he was traveled – through the country, from Provence to Brittany, gently guarded, fenced round in a civilized manner; and throngs of people came out to see him. Then he was returned to Paris.

The government officials in charge of Mr. Moscowitz found a beautiful apartment in safe, quiet Passy for him and his wife, and let them understand that the rent would be paid for the rest of their lives. There was a maid and a cook, both paid for, and there was a garden that seemed as big as the Bois de Boulogne to the Moscowitzes, and there was a government chauffeur to take them wherever they wanted to go, whenever. And finally – for the government understood that many men will die without work – there was a job ready for Mr. Moscowitz when he chose to take it up, as the librarian of the Benjamin Franklin library, behind the Odeon.

He had hoped for the Bibliothèque nationale, but he was satisfied with the lesser post. "We are home," he said to his wife. "Having one job or another – one thing or another – only makes a difference to those who are not truly at home. *Tu m'comprends?*"

"*Oui,*" said Mrs. Moscowitz. They were forever asking each other that, *Do you understand me?* and they both always said *yes.* He spoke often of home and of belonging, she noticed; perhaps he meant to reassure her. For herself, she had come to realize that all the lists and journeys of the family Vincent would never make her a moment more French than she was, which was not at all, regardless. Indeed, the more she studied the language – the government had provided a series of tutors for her – the less she seemed to understand it, and she lived in anxiety that she and Mr. Moscowitz would lose this hold of one another, like children separated in a parade. Yet she was not as unhappy as she had feared, for her old capacity for making the best of things surfaced once again, and actually did make her new life as kind and rewarding as it could possibly have been, not only for her, but for those with whom she came in any sort of contact. She would have been very surprised to learn this last.

But Mr. Moscowitz himself was not happy for long in France. It was certainly no one's fault but his own. The government took the wisest care of him it knew – though it exhibited him, still it always remembered that he was a human being, which is hard for a government – and the people of France sent him silly, lovely gifts and letters of welcome from all across the country. In their neighborhood, the Moscowitzes were the reigning couple without really knowing it. Students gathered under their windows on the spring nights to sing to them, and the students' fathers, the butchers and grocers and druggists and booksellers of Passy, would never let Mrs. Moscowitz pay for anything when she went shopping. They made friends, good, intelligent, government-approved friends – and yet Mr. Moscowitz brooded more and more visibly, until his wife finally asked him, "What is it, George? What's the matter?"

"They are not French," he said. "All these people. They don't know what it *is* to be French."

"Because they live like Americans?" she asked gently. "George," – she had learned to pronounce it *Jhorj,* in the soft French manner – "everyone does that, or everyone will. To be anything but American is very hard these days. I think they do very well."

"They are not French," Mr. Moscowitz repeated. "I am French, but they are not French. I wonder if they ever were." She looked at him in some alarm. It was her first intimation that the process was not complete.

His dissatisfaction with the people who thought they were French grew more apparent every day. Friends, neighbors, fellow employees, and a wide spectrum of official persons passed in turn before his eyes; and he studied each one and plainly discarded them. Once he had been the kind of man who said nothing, rather than lie; but now he said everything he thought, which is not necessarily more honest. He stalked through the streets of Paris, muttering, "You are not French, none of you are – you are imposters! What have you done with my own people, where have they gone?" It was impossible for such a search to go unnoticed for long. Children as well as grown men began to run up to him on the street, begging, *"Monsieur Moscowitz, regardez-moi, je suis vraiment français!"* He would look at them once, speak or say nothing, and stride on. The rejected quite often wept as they looked after him.

There were some Frenchmen, of both high and low estate, who became furious with Mr. Moscowitz – who was *he*, a first-generation American, French only by extremely dubious mutation, to claim that they, whose ancestors had either laid the foundations of European culture, or died, ignorant, in its defense, were not French? But in the main, a deep sadness shadowed the country. An inquisitor had come among them, an apostle, and they had been found wanting. France mourned herself, and began wondering if she had ever existed at all; for Mr. Moscowitz hunted hungrily through all recorded French history, searching for his lost kindred, and cried at last that from the days of the first paintings in the Dordogne caves, there was no evidence that a single true Frenchman had ever fought a battle, or written a poem, or built a city, or comprehended a law of the universe. "Dear France," he said with a kind of cold sorrow, "for all the Frenchmen who have ever turned your soil, you might have remained virgin and empty all these centuries. As far back in time as I can see, there has never been one, until now."

The President of France, a great man, his own monument in his own time, a man who had never wavered in the certainty that he himself was France, wrote Mr. Moscowitz a letter in which he stated: "We have always been French. We have been Gauls and Goths, Celts and Franks, but we have always been French. We, and no one else, have made France live. What else should we be but French?"

Mr. Moscowitz wrote him a letter in answer, saying, "You have inhabited France, you have occupied it, you have held it in trust if you like, and you have served it varyingly well – but that has not made you French, nor will it, any more than generations of monkeys breeding in a lion's empty cage will become lions. As for what else you may truly be, that you will have to find out for yourselves, as I had to find out."

The President, who was a religious man, thought of Belshazzar's Feast. He called on Mr. Moscowitz at his home in Passy, to the awe of Mrs. Moscowitz, who knew that ambassadors had lived out their terms in Paris without ever meeting the President face-to-face. The President said, "M. Moscowitz, you are denying us the right to believe in ourselves as a continuity, as part of the process of history. No nation can exist without that belief."

"*Monsieur le Président, je suis désolé,*" answered Mr. Moscowitz. He had grown blue-gray and thin, bones hinting more and more under the once-genial flesh.

"We have done you honor," mused the President, "though I admit before you say it that we believed we were honoring ourselves. But you turn us into ghosts, *Monsieur* Moscowitz, homeless figments, and our grip on the earth is too precarious at the best of times for me to allow you to do this. You must be silent, or I will make you so. I do not want to, but I will."

Mr. Moscowitz smiled, almost wistfully, and the President grew afraid. He had a sudden vision of Mr. Moscowitz banishing him and every other soul in France with a single word, a single gesture; and in that moment's vision it seemed to him that they all went away like clouds, leaving Mr. Moscowitz to dance by himself in cobwebbed Paris on Bastille Day. The President shivered and cried out, "What is it that you want of us? What should we be? What is it, to be French, what does the stupid word mean?"

Mr. Moscowitz answered him. "I do not know, any more than you do. But I do not need to ask." His eyes were full of tears and his nose was running. "The French are inside me," he said, "singing and stamping to be let out, all of them, the wonderful children that I will never see. I am like Moses, who led his people to the Promised Land, but never set his own foot down there. All fathers are a little like Moses."

The next day, Mr. Moscowitz put on his good clothes and asked his wife to pack him a lunch. "With an apple, please," he said, "and the good Camembert, and a whole onion. Two apples." His new hat, cocked at a youthful angle, scraped coldly beside her eye when he kissed her. She did not hold him a moment longer than she ever had when he kissed her goodbye. Then Mr. Moscowitz walked away from her, and into legend.

No one ever saw him again. There were stories about him, as there still are; rumors out of Concarneau, and Sète, and Lille, from misty cities and yellow villages. Most of the tales concerned strange, magic infants, as marvelous in the families that bore them as merchildren in herring nets. The President sent out his messengers, but quite often there were no such children at all, and when there were they were the usual cases of cross-eyes and extra fingers, webbed feet and cauls. The President was relieved, and said so frankly to Mrs. Moscowitz. "With all respectful sympathy, Madame," he told her, "the happiest place for your husband now is a fairy story. It is warm inside a myth, and safe, quite safe, and the company is of the best. I envy him, for I will never know such companions. I will get politicians and generals."

"And I will get his pension and his belongings," Mrs. Moscowitz said to herself. "And I will know solitude."

The President went on, "He was mad, of course, your husband, but what a mission he set himself! It was worthy of one of Charlemagne's paladins, or of your – " he fumbled through his limited stock of nonpartisan American heroes – "your Johnny Appleseed. Yes."

The President died in the country, an old man, and Mrs. Moscowitz in time died alone in Passy. She never returned to America, even to visit, partly out of loyalty to Mr. Moscowitz's dream, and partly because if there is one thing besides cheese that the French do better than any other people, it is the careful and assiduous tending of a great man's widow. She wanted for nothing to the end of her days, except her husband – and, in a very real sense, France was all she had left of him.

That was a long time ago, but the legends go on quietly, not only of the seafoam children who will create France, but of Mr. Moscowitz as well. In Paris and the provinces, anyone who listens long enough can hear stories of the American who became French. He wanders through the warm nights and the cold, under stars and streetlamps, walking with the bright purpose of a child who has slipped out of his parents' sight and is now free to do as he pleases. In the country, they say that he is on his way to see how his children are growing up, and perhaps there are mothers who lull their own children with that story, or warn them with it when they behave badly. But Parisians like to dress things up, and as they tell it, Mr. Moscowitz is never alone. Cyrano is with him, and St. Joan, Roland, D'Artagnan, and Villon – and there are others. The light of them brightens the road for Mr. Moscowitz to see his way.

But even in Paris there are people, especially women, who say that Mr. Moscowitz's only companion on his journey is Mrs. Moscowitz herself, holding his arm or running to catch up. And she deserves to be there, they will tell you, for she would have been glad of any child at all; and if he was the one who dreamed and loved France so much, still and all, she suffered.

Spook

To describe this story in any detail would, I think, spoil the fun. I'll just say that it's one of my Joe Farrell adventures (Julie Tanikawa definitely figures in it, if only in absentia), that it takes place in Avicenna, the shadow-Berkeley that lives in the California of my imagination, and that it was inspired – as were both "King Pelles the Sure" and "Uncle Chaim and Aunt Rifke and the Angel" – by a long spell of staring at the paintings and sculptures of the splendid artist Lisa Snellings-Clark. I had a very nice time writing it, and can't wait to record the audiobook version. I think you'll be able to tell that.

WHEN THEY CAME OUT of the consultation with the *santero*, Farrell said, "Seventy-five bucks. For seventy-five bucks I can get an Eskimo and make my own ice." It was his favorite Marx Brothers line, employed often.

Ben said, "Come on, we learned *something*. At least we know it's bound to the house, can't even go round the block. You and Julie can find another place easy, it's a buyers' market right now. I'm sure you could get the deposit back."

"Julie loves that dump," Farrell said sourly. "Says she's finally got the north light exactly the way she wants it, and she'll never move again, ever. And she means it, I know her." He kicked a bottle into the gutter, and then felt guilty and went back and picked it up. "Buddies, lovers, partners – whatever the hell it is we are after twenty-five years – listen, if the Spook isn't gone when she gets back, I'll be sleeping at the restaurant with my clothes in a plastic bag. Live with an artist, you take your chances."

Ben grunted, not seeing much difference between the huge old loft and any of the studios Julie had always chosen since she settled for good in Avicenna. Cashing in a handful of sick-leave days from his job in Los Angeles, he had come up to help the two of them move in, finishing only a week before. There had been odd small occurrences from the first day – flickers of almost-movement in the rafters, and noises that were finally pronounced to be squirrel fights on the roof and in the vines outside the windows – but the thing he and Farrell were calling the Spook hadn't fully presented itself until the evening after Julie left to visit relatives in Seattle.

Farrell said, "Julie's grandmother. Grandma would know how to handle this."

"Her grandmother's dead," Ben said. After a moment he added, "Isn't she?" because one never quite knew with the Tanikawa family.

"Oh, yeah, long gone. But that doesn't mean a whole lot to those two." Farrell sighed. "No help for it. Not a thing to do but look up Andy Mac."

"Andy Mac." Ben stopped walking. Farrell turned, and they stood on the sidewalk, looking at each other. Ben said, "Couldn't we just have our tonsils out or something? Or go in for prostate surgery? I'll bet there's a two-for-one sale at Sisters of Mercy."

"Come on, it won't be *that* bad. Okay, Andy Mac's incredibly aggravating, and he smells sort of—"

"Dead."

"Dead, yes, granted. But he's the only man for the job, and we both know it. And one thing about him—he keeps his word."

"This is true. Which reminds me that he hates your guts. He despises me, but it's not nearly the same thing. Why on earth would he even consider helping you?"

"On the chance of getting even. Andy Mac likes getting even."

"Even for *what*? Now would be a really fine time to tell me."

"Long story. Long and unbelievably unedifying."

Ben said, "Then you find him. I don't care if you're being haunted by Hannibal Lecter, Truman Capote and the Bride of Frankenstein. You want him, you go find him."

So Farrell tracked down Andy Mac by himself, eventually finding him in a dubious Herrera Street bathhouse, and got him to agree to come over that evening. Andy Mac, as always, flatly refused any suggestion of payment for his services; but it was just as flatly understood – again, as always – that there would be much care and feeding involved, so as to avoid any mysterious power outage in the spirit world. Farrell had worked with Andy Mac before.

"You just have to know how to handle him. It's not an art—it's more like reading the simple instructions that came with the package. *Insert Tab A into Slot B...fold flap over...insert two C batteries, this way up...*Amazing how many people never read the instructions."

"The print's too small. And Andy Mac doesn't come from Office Depot. You're worrying me, Farrell. Again."

The new loft was in North Avicenna, right across from a community theatre given to staging poetry slams on Fridays. The location could hardly have been improved upon: apart from Julie's perfect north light, it lay within walking distance of the area hospital and her job as a part-time medical illustrator, and a short bicycle ride to the Gourmet Ghetto restaurant where Farrell worked as a *sous*-chef. Ben stayed with them whenever he came to town, in spite of the inevitable long flights of stairs – two, this time – and things occasionally falling down or off the walls. Like most houses in that part of Avicenna, it was very old. Farrell simply picked the things up, fixed them, and Krazy Glued them more or less back where they belonged.

"No way Andy Mac makes it up those stairs," Ben said with absolute certainty. "Twelve to seven against."

"I laid in a ton of smoked salmon. You know he'll trample babies and puppies for smoked salmon."

"Even so. Five to two."

Andy Mac made it, though he could be heard wheezing for a good five minutes before he knocked on the door. Farrell met him with a glass and a plate, and he grabbed both and sank into Julie's favorite overstuffed chair with a sound like a whalespout. For the next five minutes all he could say was "Jesus, Farrell...*Jesus*..."

Andy Mac was fifty-something: the size and general texture of the chair, only damper and stickier. His orange-freckled face always looked to Ben like a huge prizewinning Half-Moon Bay pumpkin just beginning to collapse of its own weight. His arms were disproportionally short, he sweated a good deal, and he had breath like a Chicago stockyard and little, flicky eyes the color of baby shit. He made his official living as a translator from the Finno-Ugric languages – there are more Hungarians and Estonians in Avicenna than one might think – and rumor credited him with a small sideline in blackmail, smuggling, and gentlemanly extortion. But he was also as learned a man as Farrell had ever known, who had more than once called him "the only medium worth a damn in the entire Bay Area – the only one who can really deliver, every time, on contact with that Other Place, whatever it actually is. In a pinch, that's worth a lot of lox and armpits."

"Sorry, Andy," Farrell said meekly. "I'm getting a little old for those stairs myself."

"Always been a liar," Andy Mac mumbled through a whiskey-soaked mouthful of salmon. "You *said* there'd be teacakes."

Farrell said, "Teacakes, bloody *hell*," and looked at Ben with what could only have been described as mute appeal. Ben said, "Olga's might still be open. I'll go see."

By the time he got back with the pastries (the local Russian bakery, two blocks away, really was called Olga From The Volga), Ben could hear the Spook through the door. It was zooming around the apartment like a mad parakeet, dive-bombing Farrell and howling in that thin, tinny voice, which was scarier for being so distant. The Spook looked like a cross between an airport windsock and a very weary broom. It was scarlet, and it had floppy, empty scarlet sleeves, and no face. Ben it only strafed now and then; Andy Mac it left strictly alone. But it went viciously, purposefully after Farrell, not simply swooping and stooping at him, but chittering wildly – and it was *words*, not just noise, Ben could tell that much. The thing was *after* Farrell, no question about it.

Farrell himself was in the closet, literally, scrunched back among the winter coats, yelling to Andy Mac, "What *is* it? What the hell *is* it?" From time to time he cautiously opened the closet door to peer out, and the Spook would immediately go for him like a cat after a chipmunk. Ben fully expected it either to slam into the door and knock itself out, or to pass right through it, but it merely veered away and waited around for another shot at Farrell. Andy Mac sat where he was, looking as bored as though he were watching TV or a kids' Thanksgiving Day pageant, even yawning once or twice. But his small eyes were stretched wider than Ben had ever seen them, and even his orange freckles looked pale.

"Well," he finally said. "There's a new one on me."

Ben asked, "Is it a ghost?" Andy Mac nodded slightly, and Farrell stuck his head out of the coat closet and said, "A ghost of *what*? A lampshade?"

"A man," Andy Mac said. "Ghosts don't always come back looking the way they did in life. Sometimes they just don't remember, they'll grab onto any shape that looks halfway familiar." On Andy Mac quiet and serious looked deeply impressive, in a sinister way. He said, "This one doesn't remember his own name, never mind what he looked like. But he knows how he died."

Dramatic pause. Andy Mac's voice dropped an octave. "He was murdered. Ambushed and strangled in his own house, in his own room. This room."

The Spook was obviously listening, bobbing up and down near the ceiling like a child's birthday balloon. Andy Mac went on, "A hundred and seventy years ago. Give or take."

Farrell called from the coat closet, "Not possible. This dump isn't *that* old – it just feels like it."

"Go argue with a ghost," Andy Mac said. "There was *some* house on this spot a hundred and seventy years ago, and he definitely died here, or he wouldn't be hanging around. Ghosts don't freelance."

"He's never bothered Julie." Farrell was edging halfway out of the closet for a second time. "Never showed up until she'd left for Seattle."

"Yes," Andy Mac purred. "That's because he doesn't think she murdered him."

The total silence that followed after Farrell's *"What?"* was broken at last by the Spook's yowl of vindication. Farrell yowled right back to match it. "For Christ's sake, I wasn't *born* a hundred-seventy years ago! Whoever murdered the thing – the guy, okay – it wasn't me. Tell it – *him* – tell him it wasn't me!"

Andy Mac took a huge bite of smoked salmon and washed it down with a slug of Johnnie Walker Black. "Go argue with a ghost," I said. "All they've got – all they *are* – are their memories, and they get them screwed up all the time. But once they lock into a thing the way they want to remember it –" he shrugged immensely – "that's it, game over. Not a lot to do about it."

"Nothing to do about it?" Spook or no Spook, Farrell was all the way out of the closet by then, practically shouting in Andy Mac's big face. "What are you talking about? There's got to be something we can do!"

Another vast, sweaty shrug, another mouthful of lox. "I don't do exorcisms. They're messy, and they only work on demons, anyway. This one's just an aggrieved householder with an obsession. Misguided, but one could sympathize. And after all, he can't really *hurt* you. In any significant way."

Farrell growled at him. Andy Mac considered, pulling at his lower lip, which made Ben feel slightly seasick. "Well, there's *one* thing..." Another dramatic pause, lasting so long that Ben put his hand on Farrell's shoulder, in case of accidents. He was confident that Farrell hadn't murdered the Spook, but he wasn't a bit sure about his intentions toward Andy Mac. But Farrell only said two words, both of them through his teeth. "What? Talk."

"What happened to those teacakes?" The phone rang as Ben was bringing them over, but no one even looked toward it. Andy Mac grabbed a fistful of the cookies and said, "Let's see what he wants. He knows he can't have the revenge he craves, but I'll bet he's got something in mind. Ghosts have agendas, like everybody else, and agendas go last."

The Spook dived at Farrell again, who shot back into the closet with a wail of despair, "Damn it, this shit has got to *stop!*" The ghost swerved away from the door once again and hung in the air, chittering like a pissed-off squirrel. Andy Mac heaved himself up and out of the armchair, cocking his head sideways, listening as intently as though the Spook were reciting Tonight's Seafood Specials. Then he started to laugh.

Andy Mac's laugh was rare, but legendary among his acquaintances. Julie had once compared it to a volcanic mud slide she had seen in the Philippines. He shook, and he coughed, and he rumbled and gurgled, and he twitched all over, and the corners of his mouth got wet. Even the Spook stopped carrying on to stare at him – eyeless and faceless as it was – and Andy Mac just kept laughing.

When he did stop, on an inhale that sounded like a moose pulling its feet out of a swamp, he yelled, "Farrell! Get out here!"

From the closet, Farrell answered, "Not a chance. I'm running cable in here and sending out for Chinese."

"Get out here," Andy Mac repeated. "Walter won't attack you." To the Spook, he added, "You don't mind me calling you Walter?"

The answer appeared to be in the affirmative. Farrell returned, slowly and cautiously, making sure to keep an escape route clear. The Spook's shrill snarl rose higher, but it stayed where it was. Andy Mac said, "Farrell, this is the late Walter Smith – at least, he *thinks* that might have been his name. Walter, meet Joe Farrell." He might have been introducing them at a faculty cocktail party.

"Tell him I didn't kill him," Farrell demanded. "I mean, I wouldn't mind killing him *now*, but I didn't do it *then*. Tell him!"

"Won't do any good. Doesn't even register." Andy Mac crunched down the last of the Russian teacakes and wiped his sugary hands on his pants. "Anyway. Walter is challenging you to a duel."

It was as though Farrell had been expecting something like this: Ben's memory afterward was that he himself was the one who protested "This is *crazy!*" while Farrell mostly looked back and forth between Andy Mac and Walter the Spook, while the phone rang unanswered again, and Ben went on making loud noises. Finally he said the obvious. "But what's the point of it? Even if he could hold a weapon, he can't hurt me – so what's in it for him? What kind of a revenge is that?"

"There are other weapons than swords and pistols," Andy Mac replied, "and other stakes than life and death. You can't hurt him either, obviously, and you get to choose the armaments, because you're the challenged party. But *he* gets to set the terms." He smiled like an oil spill. "If you win, Walter will never bother you again. Period. No strings, no small print. He'll be here, because he lives here, but you'll never see him. Fair enough?"

Farrell nodded. "And if he wins?"

"Ah," Andy Mac said. "Well. It appears that our Walter has conceived something of a *tendresse* for the absent Ms. Tanikawa. He gets a bit incoherent here, but he certainly thinks that she's much too good for the man who murdered him."

"Damn it, I *didn't* – " Farrell began, but then he stopped himself and said only, "Julie's not part of the deal. That is not negotiable."

Andy Mac shrugged. "If you lose, you leave. Nothing to do with your lady. You make what excuse you like – you even tell her the truth, if that's your idea of a good time – and you're permanently off the premises by dinnertime tomorrow, before Ms. Tanikawa returns on the following day. That simple."

"Not really," Farrell said. "If I tell Julie why I'm having to move – and yes, I will – she'll walk right out with me, like a shot, I promise you. Julie rather hates being manipulated." He grinned tauntingly up at the Spook fluttering overhead. "Where's your *tendresse* then, Walter, old buddy?"

The oil spill smile spread, and Andy Mac answered him. "Walter has listened often to Ms. Tanikawa expressing her own *tendresse* for this loft. He's willing to chance it."

Ben glanced anxiously at Farrell, remembering their morning's conversation. Julie wouldn't ever leave this loft, not even for Farrell, nor would he have expected her to. He'd been bluffing, and it hadn't worked. But Ben saw him recouping, gathering his psychic feet under him, bracing himself for whatever came next. He took a long, slow breath.

"All right," Farrell said. "All right, then. The duel will take place pre-cisely at dawn tomorrow. I'll choose the weapons then. Right now, it's late, and I'll require a peaceful night and morning to make my decision. I trust that won't be a problem?"

"No problem at all," Andy Mac answered for the Spook. "Just so the combat doesn't turn on manual dexterity."

"Me? Hardly." Farrell turned to Ben. "You'll be my second?"

"Like I've got a choice. What's a second expected to do?"

Farrell was brisk. "Oh, you check out the weapons, and you carry my body home if I lose, and you tell Julie I died bravely. The usual. You've seen the movie."

Andy Mac said that he'd second the Spook, out of fairness and necessity. "Like a public defender, backbone of our system." The phone rang once more, and this time Farrell picked it up. It was Julie, as the other two calls had been, letting Farrell know the time and number of her flight from Seattle. Andy Mac left, and Ben went to haul out the air mattress and sleeping bag he always used staying over with Farrell and Julie. When he came back, the phone call was finished, and Farrell was lying on his bed with his hands behind his head, staring at the ceiling. And where Walter the Spook spent the night, neither of them had the least idea.

Farrell didn't move or speak while Ben undressed and crawled into the sleeping bag; but then he murmured thoughtfully, more to himself, "I wonder who *did* kill old Walter Smith, all that time ago. Aggravating, never to know."

"Well, if he was anything like the way he is now, they could have sold tickets. Held a raffle." Farrell chuckled softly. Ben said, "About why Andy Mac hates you."

"I told you...long story."

"You also told me he went for the gig on the chance of getting even. What did you do to him, for God's sake?" Farrell did not answer. Ben said, "I really hate to call in old markers, but you remember that paper on *Moby-Dick*? You remember your grade? I do."

"You're a very hard man," Farrell said after a further silence. "You were a very hard five-year-old." He sighed. "It's not as long a story as all that, I just don't come out of it looking very good. Andy Mac's a snob and a showoff, but he's not a monster, not even a bad guy, really. He's got a whole lot to show off, lord knows, but it's not enough, it's never enough. And he has to be right, *has* to – it's that important to him. Anyway, some time back, years, there was this party, and he was working on impressing Julie – "

"Julie? I never thought Andy Mac liked girls that way."

"I don't think he really likes anybody that way. But he dearly likes making an impression, subject doesn't matter. So he was lecturing her about James Joyce and *Finnegans Wake* – and maybe I got jealous, maybe the devil made me do it, but I butted in and started talking about this Romanian linguistics professor, whom I made up on the spot, and how he had this big theory that Joyce was actually...what did I say, a Mason? No, I said the Romanian guy proved beyond doubt that Joyce was a Rosicrucian, and I quoted whole passages from his well-known book on Joyce – "

"Which, of course, Andy Mac knew by heart. Oh, lord, I see where this is going – "

"Right, he was great, really. Improvised better than I did – explained to Julie how *Finnegans Wake* was absolutely transparent, once you understood the code. And she looked at him, and then she looked at me, and people were listening...and I sort of wandered off – "

"And by and by, the word got back to him.... Oh, you're bad, Farrell. That was a terrible thing to do. I'm ashamed of you."

"What can I tell you? I was younger then."

"And you think he's still carrying a grudge about that?"

"I know he is."

Ben slept fitfully, and Farrell not at all, so both were up well before dawn. The Spook was still invisible, and Andy Mac wasn't due till showtime, so Ben made Eggs Benjamin, as requested – notorious on two continents or not – plus a pot of equally notorious coffee, and went for a walk in the still-misty streets to keep himself from staring and pacing and offering helpful suggestions. They had seen each other through other dawns, and other duels.

He had left his cell phone on, which was a good thing, because Farrell called halfway through his fourth time around the block. "Come on back – I need you to look up some stuff for me! *Hurry!*"

Ben ran up the two flights, sounding exactly like Andy Mac when he lurched through the door, and sat down at Julie's computer to look up stuff. He printed it out as he came across it, and Farrell sat there read-ing and reading; and for a few hours it was like the old times of studying together, trying to write dates and formulas all over shirt cuffs, and even fingernails. Farrell had always had the better memory, and if Ben had envied it then, he was glad of it now. They spoke very little.

They stayed at it until they heard Andy Mac at the door, which Ben opened before he could knock. It seemed to annoy him. He was dressed for opening night at the opera: evening clothes, white tie, gorgeous red-and-gold cravat, lacking only the silk hat. He looked surprised to see Ben in everyday street clothes, and more than a bit contemptuous as well. He said, "I understood that proper seconds wore proper clothing to a duel of honor."

"Well, I'm an *im*proper second."

Farrell looked up for a moment and waved languidly before he went back to reading. Ben said, "Hey, this isn't the Bois de Boulogne. We'll be ready come sunrise."

Andy Mac had to leave it at that, and leave it with no snacks this time, no Johnnie Walker Black to occupy him until the hour of the duel. Ben could watch him getting more and more annoyed, and couldn't help sym-pathizing: here he'd gotten totally, uncharacteristically, involved in an affair that not only wouldn't feed him, but was most likely going to turn out too weird even to dine out on. He said finally, "You know, it wouldn't hurt you to see the man's point of view."

Farrell didn't bother to look up this time. "He has no point of view. What he has is a thing about my girlfriend, and he'll make our lives hell if I don't get out and give her up. I'm sorry, but that's not a point of view. That's a hissy fit."

"But he was murdered!" Andy Mac bellowed.

Farrell shrugged, long and slow, and very deliberate. "That's not a point of view either. I didn't do it, and I'm tired of him saying I did. In this century, in this country, that's considered slander. I may very well sue."

"After all, you've only got *his* word for it," Ben added. "And we already know about *him*." To his own surprise, he was actually starting to enjoy this—especially watching the dampness spreading under Andy Mac's tux-edoed armpits. "Old Walter might be amusing himself, attacking Farrell and spinning all this shit out for you, just because he's bored out of his mind. It's not exactly much of a life he's got, is it?"

He swept his arm up toward the ceiling in a dramatic gesture, and that was when he saw Walter the Spook perched up in the rafters. To be accurate, not having anything to perch *with*, he was hovering, as hummingbirds do, and definitely vibrating like a hummingbird, ready for the duel, ready for his close-up. *Probably the most exciting thing that's happened to him in the last hundred years.* Ben couldn't help wondering what weapon he might have chosen if Farrell had been the challenger. Maybe he did have hands – though there had been no sign of any – maybe he could be hiding a couple of Derringers up in those empty, floppy scarlet sleeves. *Is a ghost simply what you always were, inside? What does it tell us that he's this?*

Andy Mac looked at his watch and said, "Sunrise in five minutes. I think we might get started."

"Dawn," Farrell said firmly. So they waited out the last five minutes, with Walter the Spook plainly struggling with a profound and passionate need to start diving at Farrell again, and Farrell peacefully ignoring everybody, looking through papers and making a few notes, as though he were prepping for a final. Ben stood by, waiting for instructions, as previously agreed. Farrell unplugged the phone.

"Okay," he said. "Now."

He said nothing more, but only sat there, smiling a little bit at nothing in particular. What seemed like another five minutes went by before Andy Mac finally said, "Now *what?*"

"Now I name the weapons," Farrell said. "And the terms." The smile broadened, but this time it was aimed directly at the Spook above their heads. Farrell said, "Bad poetry at twenty paces. To the death."

In the silence that followed, he added, *"Really* bad poetry," just before Andy Mac went up in smoke.

"What the *hell* are you talking about? You can't fight a duel with poetry!"

"You can with these," Farrell replied happily. "Trust me, it'll be like dueling with cobras, crocodiles." He was as purry and sleepy-eyed as a kitten serenely attached to a nipple. "Wait till you hear a couple of sparkling stanzas from Julia A. Moore...Margaret Cavendish, the Duchess of Newcastle...J. B. Smiley. Oh, your boy is toast already, Andy, burned toast. Honestly, I'd tell him to hang it up now, in the first round."

Whether or not Walter the Spook was capable, at this point in his career, of fully comprehending human speech, Ben had no idea, but he never doubted that the ghost got the gist. He was squalling like a buggered banshee before Farrell was half through; but instead of going for him, he flew down straight to Andy Mac, looking a bit like an old-fashioned ear trumpet as he yammered to him. Andy Mac was all attention, listening so intently that the listening was *visible:* Ben felt he could actually see the translation going on in his head, the frontal lobes and cerebellum wringing meaning out of angry gibberish. He couldn't help wondering whether Walter the Spook had originally spoken Estonian.

"Well," Andy Mac finally announced. "Speaking as Mr. Smith's second, I must immediately register a formal protest. It's shameful and immoral to force a person to fight with a weapon with which he is completely unacquainted, and with which you – I'm quite certain – are an expert." Farrell inclined his head modestly. "And for my own curiosity, how can such a duel possibly be considered a combat to the death? It may be absurd, and even humiliating, but there's nothing lethal about even the worst poetry."

Farrell didn't answer immediately. When he did, his voice was quiet and reflective, and not at all mocking. He said, "You know, Andy, in a way I owe your little red buddy something very important. Something I might never have realized without his intervention. Tell him I'm really grateful."

Andy Mac very clearly did not want to ask the question, but there was just as clearly no way not to. "Grateful for what?"

"For teaching me that I want to stay where I am," Farrell said. "It never used to matter to me. One place, one job, one pleasant, convenient other... it's always been like any other place, any other person, you know? But not now, some way. Not now." He stood up, again addressing himself to Walter the Spook. "Even if I moved out tomorrow, you still wouldn't have a chance with Julie. I'd find a place of my own – there's a neat little two-bedroom right by the restaurant – and she'd likely be over there when she wasn't working here. That's the way we've always lived, all these years – except sometimes *over there* was in another time zone, or another country. Or maybe *here* was, depending. A lot of years like that."

Andy Mac started to say something, but Farrell cut him off. "But not now. It's a funny thing," – he hesitated for a long moment – "but now I think that leaving this particular dump actually would mean some kind of death for me. So there's a certain lethal incentive, you could say, right?"

The Spook chattered furiously, but Andy Mac paid no heed. Farrell continued, "And as for what's at risk for the good Walter...well, I'm not just talking about sentimental Hallmark cards. I'm talking poetry so bad that a wise man would listen to it through smoked glass. Poetry that sets the blood cringing backwards in your veins – poetry from which one's very kidneys shrink, poetry that curdles the lymph glands and makes the teeth whine like dogs." His voice had acquired the half-taunting urgency of a carnival pitchman. "Poetry so horrid, the brain will simply refuse to recognize it as English, let alone verse. Be warned – oh, be warned – it's deadly stuff, toxic as the East River." He smacked his hands together, grinning a werewolf grin. "Let's *go!*"

He began stepping off twenty paces, while Walter the Spook dithered shrilly, and Andy Mac said, "You know I'm going to have to speak for him, translate for him. That's only fair."

"You're his second," Farrell said calmly, still counting, with his back to the others. "I want him to have every proper advantage." He turned at the far wall, where Julie habitually hung paintings and drawings she had doubts about and wanted to live with for awhile – she called it the "Parole Wall" – and said, "I'll even give him the first shot. Fair?"

"And the referee?" Andy Mac demanded. He glanced at Ben even more scornfully than usual. "Tonto here, your faithful, hairy sidekick? I don't think so."

"And risk your vengeance?" Ben answered. "You'd come to my house in the dead of night and steal my newspaper." Andy Mac didn't bother to respond. He was muttering to Walter the Spook, who was hovering at such an angle that – just for a moment – Ben thought he glimpsed a pair of tiny eyes as sharp as frost glittering further back than they should have been under the Little Red Riding Hood hood. But then they were gone, and Ben never caught sight of them again.

Farrell said, "A referee won't be necessary. Trust me, we'll know." He smiled cheerfully at Walter the Spook. "Go ahead, then. Hit me with the horror."

And to Ben's amazement, Walter reared back and did exactly that. The first volley caught both him and Farrell shockingly off guard, as Andy Mac listened carefully and then recited:

> *"Beautiful Railway Bridge of the Silv'ry Tay!*
> *Alas! I am very sorry to say*
> *That ninety lives have been taken away*
> *On the last Sabbath day of 1879,*
> *Which will be remember'd for a very long time."*

"McGonagall the Magnificent," Farrell said softly. "Wow. Tell Walter I'm very impressed. I'd have led off with Dr. Fuller, or someone like that."

Walter went straight through the poem, with Andy Mac's aid: all the way through the storm, the bridge's collapse and the ensuing train wreck, and onward to the inescapable moral.

> *"Oh! Ill-fated Bridge of the Silv'ry Tay,*
> *I must now conclude my lay*
> *By telling the world fearlessly without least dismay,*
> *That your central girders would not have given way,*
> *At least many sensible men do say,*
> *Had they been supported on each side with buttresses,*
> *At least many sensible men confesses,*
> *For the stronger we our houses do build,*
> *The less chance we have of being killed."*

Ben could feel the blood leaving his face, and Farrell himself looked, as he said, definitely impressed, and maybe a bit more. He said slowly, "McGonagall, is it? O-*kay*, McGonagall right back at'cha."

> *"Beautiful city of Glasgow, with your streets so neat and clean,*
> *Your stately mansions, and beautiful Green!*
> *Likewise your beautiful bridges across the river Clyde,*
> *And on your bonnie banks I would like to reside..."*

Neither Walter the Spook nor Andy Mac seemed much affected by this serve; nor, in all honesty, was Ben himself. It was bad, true, but not bad enough – it didn't belong in the same league with the first poem, and Farrell plainly knew it. He said, with some defiance, "It gets better," and continued:

> *"'Tis beautiful to see ships passing to and fro,*
> *Laden with goods for the high and the low,*
> *So let the beautiful city of Glasgow flourish,*
> *And may the inhabitants always find food their bodies to*
> *nourish..."*

But "The Tay Bridge Disaster" had plainly left Walter ahead on points, no question about it, and the Spook was strutting and squawking in the air like Tinker Bell on speed. Andy Mac was smiling all over his pumpkin face, as though he had just put through a successful 800 call to the spirit world. He listened attentively to the swaggering chatter, and announced "Nature's Cook."

"Cavendish," Farrell muttered. "Damn, *I* was going to come back with that one." He was actually looking somewhat alarmed. Walter recited:

> *"Death is the cook of Nature, and we find*
> *Meat dressed several ways to please her mind.*
> *Some meats she roasts with fevers, burning hot,*
> *And some she boils with dropsies in a pot.*
> *Some for jelly consuming by degrees,*
> *And some with ulcers, gravy out to squeeze..."*

Ben became aware of a sudden, desperate need to pee. He faced it for the cowardly reaction it was, whispered, "Right back" to Farrell and headed for the toilet while Walter went charging on through the Cavendish recipe book.

> *"In sweat sometimes she stews with savory smell*
> *A hodge-podge of diseases tasteth well.*
> *Brains dressed with apoplexy to Nature's wish,*
> *Or swims with sauce of megrims in a dish.*
> *And tongues she dries with smoke from stomachs ill..."*

Given a choice, Ben would gladly have stayed in the john long enough to get his mail there, but friendship comes with obligations, even for cowards. He got back in time for the Duchess's grand finale.

> *"Then Death cuts throats, for blood puddings to make,*
> *And puts them in the guts, which colics rack.*
> *Some hunted are by Death, for deer that's red,*
> *Or stall-fed oxen, knocked on the head.*
> *Some for bacon by Death are singed, or scalt,*
> *Then powdered up with phlegm, and rheum that's salt."*

There fell a deadly silence in the room when the last horrendous syllable had thudded to the floor. Farrell had clearly not bargained for this: they had both underestimated Walter the Spook, and for all their preparations Ben was beginning to think that they might just be outgunned. He whispered, "Moore. No more fooling around – *Moore.*"

Farrell nodded grimly. "All right," he said. "All right. Because there is a season for casual mercy – there is a season for fooling around – and then there is a time for Julia A. Moore. The Bible tells us so." Raising his voice, he announced, "Lament on the Death of Willie."

Andy Mac looked like the manager of a team facing the Yankees who had just been told that Mariano Rivera was coming in to pitch. Farrell shook himself once, like a wet dog, and went to work.

> *"Willie had a purple monkey climbing on a yellow stick,*
> *And when he sucked the paint all off it made him deathly sick;*
> *And in his latest hours he clasped that monkey in his hand,*
> *And bid goodbye to earth and went into a better land.*
> *Oh! no more he'll shoot his sister with his little wooden gun*
> *And no more he'll twist the pussy's tail and make her yowl, for*
> *fun.*
> *The pussy's tail now stands out straight; the gun is laid aside*
> *The monkey doesn't jump around since little Willie died."*

Silence followed this one too; but it was more like a sort of holy hush, even from Walter the Spook. The presence of simple greatness has that effect. Ben heard Andy Mac mumble, more to himself, "A hit, a very palpable hit," and agreed silently that sometimes only Shakespeare will do when you're talking about Julia A. Moore.

Andy Mac cleared his throat. "You must be in trouble, calling on the Goddess so early in the game. You do know that Emmeline Grangerford's poetry is Twain's parody of Moore?"

Farrell grinned at him. "You're stalling. The Sweet Singer of Michigan is beyond parody, beyond imitation – beyond category, as Duke Ellington used to say. Come on, hotshot – I'm waiting."

But Farrell's playing the Moore option had thrown the Spook off balance in his turn. He fumbled through a couple of minor responses – another McGonagall, and a couple by Dr. William Fuller – which Farrell brushed aside with J. B. Smiley's perfectly charming poem about the Kalamazoo insane asylum (*"The folks are not all of them crazy / Who hail from Kalamazoo"*) and Moore's poem about the death of Lord Byron, which ends with the magnificent and legendary rhyme:

> *"Lord Byron's age was 36 years,*
> *Then closed the sad career,*
> *Of the most celebrated 'Englishman'*
> *Of the nineteenth century."*

Farrell sighed as contentedly as though he had just finished making love. "Call me an elitist, but it doesn't *get* any better than that, I'm sorry."

Andy Mac faced the attack impassively; one would have had to know him and be looking for it to see Farrell's merciless grapeshot reaching him at all. But Walter the Spook was visibly wilting and paling under the bombardment, as escaped toy balloons always do, sooner or later. In a strange way, he did look like a fatally wounded duelist, stumbling in the air, lurching inevitably down toward stillness. It was over, obviously, and Ben – now that they could afford it – felt honestly sorry for him.

It was over...and then Walter the Spook played his ace.

Or maybe it was Andy Mac himself, getting even at last for an old humiliation. Whichever it was, Farrell and Ben were abruptly sandbagged, sideswiped by a great poet – no Sweet Singer of Michigan here, but Samuel Taylor Coleridge himself, celebrated author of *The Rime of the Ancient Mariner* and *Xanadu* – not to mention "To a Young Ass (Its Mother Being Tethered Near It)."

> *"Poor little foal of an oppressed race!*
> *I love the languid patience of thy face:*

And oft with gentle hand I give thee bread,
And clap thy ragged coat, and pat thy head..."

Ben had never read or heard the poem, but one look at his friend's stricken face told him that Farrell had.

"Or is thy sad heart filled with filial pain
To see thy wretched mother's shortened chain?
And truly, very piteous is her lot –
Chained to a log within a narrow spot,
Where the close-eaten grass is scarcely seen,
While sweet around her waves the tempting green!"

They looked at each other helplessly. Ben whispered, "Coleridge was a doper, wasn't he? Opium, hash, like that?" Farrell didn't answer.

Thoroughly revived, Walter the Spook rolled on, zooming above Andy Mac's head as the man recited, like a matador taking a victory lap. Farrell grunted slightly with each line, and seemed to roll with them, as though each were a blow slamming into him.

"Innocent foal! thou poor despised forlorn
I hail thee Brother – spite of the fool's scorn!
And fain would take thee with me, in the Dell
Of Peace and mild Equality to dwell,
Where Toil shall call the charmer Health his bride,
And Laughter tickle Plenty's ribless side!
How thou would toss thy heels in gamesome play,
And frisk about, as lamb or kitten gay!
Yea! and more musically sweet to me
Thy dissonant harsh bray of joy would be,
Than warbled melodies that soothe to rest
The aching of pale Fashion's vacant breast!"

Nobody said a word for a long while after he finished – nobody except Walter the Spook, who couldn't stop chattering in triumph, as though he were singing some kind of tribal conquest song over Farrell's body. Farrell neither moved nor spoke, unresponsive to anything or anyone.

Ben could not read his eyes, as he usually could, out of the long old friendship. *Nothing now. No one there.*

Andy Mac said, "Well." Farrell didn't answer. Andy Mac said, "I think we can consider this duel dueled, don't you? Throw in the towel, call it a TKO?"

"Coleridge," Farrell said wearily. "I wrote a thing about Coleridge in college, I just never thought..." His voice trailed off tonelessly.

"Well, it's as *I've* always said." If the self-satisfaction in Andy Mac's voice could have been tapped, it would have powered a fair-sized suburb. "In the end, it's always a matter of who's got the best lawyer. *Everything* comes down to the best lawyer."

Ben took a couple of steps toward him, without realizing that he had done so. Later, he had no memory of what he'd had in mind, except that the defeat on Farrell's face, combined with that triumphant purr, was more than he could bear. Farrell said, "I'll start packing. It never takes me long."

"Oh, take your time, by all means," Andy Mac said grandly. The Spook was chittering in his ear, and he was nodding steadily. "Walter is quite content to have received justice, at long last. He doesn't wish any further inconvenience to anyone, even his murderer." The oil spill smile took a victory lap itself. "No, of course not—*I* know you didn't do it, and *you* and Tonto here know it, so what does it matter what *he* thinks? He's just a little red flying whiskbroom, after all."

Farrell was already trudging toward the bedroom. Ben turned away, unable to watch him. He said to Andy Mac, "I don't know who killed him, a hundred-and-whatever years ago, but if I ever get my hands on him anytime—"

"Oh, please," Andy Mac said. "It's life, Tonto. Stop making such a bloody tragedy of it—it's just life. Your leader knows that, don't you, Farrell?"

Ben's father, a would-be song-and-dance man born out of his time, had raised him on a good many old vaudeville songs and comedy sketches, including a classic routine built around the recurring line, *"Slowly I turned..."* Ben had never fully understood what was supposed to be funny about the sketch, but he used the line occasionally, without comprehension, as his father most likely had. He thought of it then, absurdly, because on the word *tragedy* Farrell turned back—very, very slowly—to face Andy Mac and Walter the Spook. At the expression on his face the Spook stopped yodeling and went for the rafters, zipping straight up, like a helicopter, and Andy Mac said "What?" Farrell didn't speak. Andy Mac said "*What?*" again.

"Theophilus Marzials," Farrell said. Ben wasn't entirely sure whether it was a name or a curse, an incantation of some kind. But Andy Mac knew. He opened his mouth, but nothing came out. Farrell said, "A Tragedy."

"You can't do that," Andy Mac whispered. "That's like...you can't *use* Marzials. That's...that's not *fair*."

"Ah, it's just life, Andy," Farrell said. "And desperate times require desperate measures." He winked at Ben and announced again, "A Tragedy. By Theophilus Julius Henry Marzials, lesser Pre-Raphaelite poet, born in England of Belgian and English parents. Second son, and youngest of five children. Remind me to tell you how I learned it—there was a Kiowa Indian involved." Andy Mac closed his eyes as Farrell began.

> "*Death!*
> *Plop.*
> *The barges down in the river flop.*
> *Flop, plop.*
> *Above, beneath.*
> *From the slimy branches the grey drips drop,*
> *As they scraggle black on the thin grey sky,*
> *Where the black cloud rack-hackles drizzle and fly*
> *To the oozy waters, that lounge and flop*
> *On the black scrag piles, where the loose cords plop,*
> *As the raw wind whines in the thin tree-top.*
> *Plop, plop.*
> *And scudding by*
> *The boatmen call out hoy! and hey!*
> *All is running water and sky,*
> *And my head shrieks — 'Stop,' And my heart shrieks — 'Die...'*"

"The worst poem ever written in English," Andy Mac moaned softly. He had not opened his eyes. "Like bringing a nuclear weapon into a beach volleyball game."

Andy Mac played volleyball? On the beach? Ben decided not to think about that more than he absolutely had to. Farrell was giving the poem the serious works now, nodding with the rhythm, altering his tone to suit the line. Ben caught a glimpse of Walter the Spook, huddled in the shadows atop a huge old hutch that somehow managed to follow Julie everywhere she lived, despite Farrell's undying enmity. Even at that distance, with not a lot to go on, he looked sick and increasingly drained as Marzials rolled remorselessly on.

> *"And the shrill wind whines in the thin tree-top*
> *Flop, plop.*
> *A curse on him.*
> *Ugh! yet I knew – I knew –*
> *If a woman is false can a friend be true?*
> *It was only a lie from beginning to end –*
> *My Devil – My 'Friend'*
> *I had trusted the whole of my living to!*
> *Ugh; and I knew!"*

"No more!" Andy Mac's eyes were open, and his hands were out in piteous supplication. "It's done, you win, we give – please, no more!"

"Shh, shh," Farrell soothed him. "There's only a little more." He might have been a nurse or a torturer in that moment. Ben expected to see the poor Spook go *flop, plop* then himself, but he managed to shuffle out of sight along a curtain rod as Farrell was building to a rolling climax.

> *"Ugh!*
> *So what do I care,*
> *And my head is as empty as air –*
> *I can do,*
> *I can dare,*
> *(Plop, plop*
> *The barges flop*
> *Drip, drop.)*
> *I can dare! I can dare!*
> *And let myself all run away with my head*
> *And stop.*
> *Drop.*

Dead.
Plop, flop.
Plop."

There wasn't a great deal for anyone to say after that last *plop*, and nobody tried. Farrell managed to dig up at least some leftovers for Andy Mac, out of compassion for that sweat-soaked tuxedo, which would surely never be the same, and then Ben drove him back to the Herrera Street bathhouse. He was silent on the way, but just before getting out of the car he said, "He'll keep his word. They won't see him again."

"But they'll know he's there," Ben said. "I'd have trouble with that, a ghost watching everything."

Andy Mac chuckled, so softly that it was almost a whisper. "Ghosts watch everything we do, everywhere, all the time. Get used to it, side-kick."

He walked away slowly, shaking his head, and Ben drove back to the loft and settled down to serious coffee drinking. Placid by nature, he only got the shakes *after* a crisis, not *during*, and coffee always calmed him. Farrell was asleep, snoring as peacefully as though he hadn't spent the morning involved in a genuine duel to the death. Ben saw no sign of Walter the Spook. He drank coffee, made more, read the newspaper, and tried to get all the lines of "A Tragedy" out of his head. He never quite did, not all of them, but came in time to regard them as honorable wounds, sustained in a noble cause.

When Farrell woke up ravenous they scrambled everything in the pantry, and celebrated the victory with Farrell's prized stash of Aventinus beer; but they also did their best to talk about ordinary matters, with reasonable success. Ben did finally ask, "You planning to tell Julie about the Gunfight at the Booga-Booga Corral when she gets home?"

Farrell nodded. "Right away. She always finds stuff like this out, anyway—I might as well get points for candor. I think she might even be flattered, a bit. Not *too* flattered, but still. And she'll feel sorry for him, sure as hell, I know the woman." He sighed. "It's as I said, Ben—the poor guy really did teach me something I didn't want to know, and I do owe him, some way. Believe me, I've gotten used to way weirder stuff in my time, and so has Julie. Just so he's *quiet*. Quiet, I can live with. *And* invisible. We'll deal."

Ben said, "I stay with you guys, I always hate to go home."

"Oh, you're much better off in Los Angeles. There've been times when it was all I could do not to go home with you. Julie too, probably. Things just keep *happening* here." Another sigh; and then that bent, warped, crookedy smile that he had in the first grade. "Besides, you must never forget the immortal words of our Julia – the Goddess herself."

"Which are?"

"*'Literary is a work very difficult to do.'*"

"Amen and amen," Ben said. He reached for the last bottle of Aventinus, but Farrell slapped his hand.

The Stickball Witch

Everything in this story is as real and true of my 1940s/1950s Bronx childhood as I can remember it. One of my two closest childhood friends has already assured his grown kids that it happened exactly as recounted; and the other one would cheerfully swear the same, if properly remunerated.

This was written to be read aloud as the first of four season-themed podcasts for a delightful online magazine called *The Green Man Review*. It was my nod to Spring, and appears here in print for the first time.

I WAS A BOY, and it was spring in the Bronx. School would be out in less than two months. My friend Phil's folks had just gotten a television set, and he and I could watch Ralph Bellamy in *Man Against Crime* on Friday nights. There was a new war on in Korea, and red-haired Sandy Greenbaum was being even more insufferable than usual because her big brother Sam was some kind of aide to General Mark Clark, whose name she always pronounced in full, like an incantation. Or perhaps a prayer, I wonder now: who knows how frightened for Sam her family actually was? Maybe saying the general's whole name was a way of not stepping on a crack, not breaking the charm that would bring her brother home whole himself? What did I know? I was eleven years old, and she was obnoxious and had freckles.

I was eleven, and it was spring. The dogwood was blossoming in the cemetery down the block; the park two blocks away in the other direction was bright with budding goldenrod, and would be brilliant with forsythia and ragweed in another week or so. My allergy shots had already begun; but so, one after another, also like wildflowers in their season, had rollerskates and bicycles, jacks and Double Dutch and hopscotch (which we called "potsy") for the girls, catch and one-o'cat and schoolyard fights for the pure hell of fighting for the boys. And stickball. Between one day and the next, stickball again.

Stickball is – *was,* I guess; who plays it now? – street baseball, played with broomsticks and a specific kind of ball. It was manufactured by the Spalding Company – though I never heard it called anything but a *Spaldeen* – and was made of a particular kind of pink rubber, which emitted a flaky whitish powder when fresh, and smelled indescribably of...of spring, finally, and of laundry drying on apartment-building roofs and on lines strung between apartment windows, and sunlight lasting a little longer every day. In the Bronx in 1950, spring smelled like Spaldeens.

There were never enough players to make up two full teams; it was quite common for boys to play for both sides, as necessary. (Although choosing up sides, arguing over the fairness of which team got stuck with which fat or slow or stone-fingered kid, could easily take longer than the game itself.) As for the playing field, the ground rules literally varied with the parking along Tryon Avenue that afternoon. First and third bases were almost always cars, though we made do with bicycles or wagons when we had to; second and home were usually one manhole cover apart, though this might be affected by the spatial relationship of first and third. Since we were always short on fielders (if anyone actually had a glove, it usually wound up being a base), a hit that traveled as far as two manhole covers' distance was an automatic double; so, also, was a ball hit into traffic, wedged under a car or carried away forever by Richie Williams' damn dog. A three-manhole shot was a triple. Home runs... well, fat Stewie Hauser hit one once, far down the block toward the cemetery, and mean Joey Gonsalves hit one that he *said* was a homer, go argue with Joey Gonsalves. He had brothers.

Of course, we could have walked two blocks to the park and played on a real baseball diamond, but that was just the point of stickball. It had to be played with *sticks*, not real bats, balls and gloves; it *had* to be improvised, from equipment to the contours of the baselines, to the constantly evolving rules, which were quite likely to be significantly different over on Decatur Avenue, or DeKalb. You played baseball or softball in the park – stickball was for the street, only and always. Not all of life was that simple, even in 1950, even at the age of eleven, but stickball...oh, stickball, yes.

I wasn't good at stickball; let's have *that* clear. I wasn't one of those chosen last, or forced on one team or the other like a handicap, but I was a lot closer to that social class than to the stars like Stewie Hauser, Miltie Mellinger or J. T. Jones. The only athletic gift I had was that I could run, which wasn't much use in our game, since we didn't have stolen bases, the way they played down on Rochambeau Avenue. If I actually connected, I'd make it home well before anybody ran the ball down, but it didn't happen often. To this day, I remember every time that it did.

Today Tryon's lined with condos on both sides, but back then there were still a lot of trees, and a lot of one-family houses: thirty, forty years old, older, most still occupied by the original owners, who had built and settled in when the Bronx was still largely farming country, and my mother would often meet a cow or a goat on her way to school. Fragments of those farms survived in my own school years: they were usually inhabited by half-mad hermits who threw stones at kids trying to cut through their overgrown fields and blighted orchards. All gone now, of course, all leveled and paved over by the end of that decade. I'm not nostalgic. I just remember.

Tryon Avenue had a witch. Many streets did; it was almost a necessity to local tradition, back when a single block, a single apartment building, was an entire country for a child, complete with history, royalty, a peasant class, endless threats from outsiders, and a rich and varied folklore. The designated witch was always some old lady living alone, quite often foreign-born and oddly dressed (by our highly Puritanical standards for adults); and known to us, beyond any reasonable doubt, as implacably menacing, whether or not she'd done anything at all to merit the verdict. Whatever else they had in common, the universal factor – going all the way back to the Brothers Grimm, and surely beyond – was that any ball hit into their front yards, or their ragged little gardens, stayed there forever. We were often surprisingly daring – foolhardy, even, looking back – but we weren't crazy.

Mrs. Poliakov was *our* witch. She lived about halfway down the block, in a small gray house, which I keep seeing as stone, though I'm sure it wasn't, no more than it could have been gingerbread. Mrs. Poliakov almost never left the gray house; such deliveries as she needed came to her, as was more common in those days. Since we hardly kept exact track of just who went into the house and who came out, we were happy to spread – and, by and by, absolutely believe – a rumor that Mrs. Poliakov sometimes ate deliverymen, or turned them into...things. Which would certainly account for the absence of a Mr. Poliakov, after all. We thought hard about stuff like that. We had discussions. We *ruminated*.

She was a tiny woman, really, gray and nondescript as her house, but we equipped her with fangs (if you looked closely, which nobody was about to do), and with what the Italian kids called the *mal'occhio*, and the Puerto Ricans the *mal ojo* – the evil eye. My memory has her backing carefully down her front steps when she did come out, usually wrapped in an old tweed overcoat, no matter the weather. She always wore a man's battered felt hat, and she limped a bit on her right leg.

Spaldeens hit into Mrs. Poliakov's yard, as I've said, were lost balls, even though we could usually see them where they lay against her fence, often actually within reach through the wobbly, peeling slats. She never threw them back, of course, but she never got rid of them either, so there they lay like spoils of some mysterious war nobody but the participants remembered. We visualized her gloating over them, using them to cast spells, as we knew beyond question she did. For spite we threw other things into her yard at night – rotting garbage, dead animals, paper bags filled with patiently-collected dog and cat shit – and then ran like hell. I felt bad sometimes, thinking about it...but that'd teach *her* to be sitting up midnights, casting spells.

What changed everything – especially for me – was the day Chuck Golden dared me to go get the ball that I'd just fouled off into Mrs. Poliakov's front yard. (Anything in the street, including parked cars and Schwartz's fruit truck, was fair territory; the curbs were our foul lines.) Chuck Golden was a sawed-off loudmouth, but that Spaldeen happened to be our last one, and it was just wrong to quit playing on a Saturday, with the sun still high. Junius Dinkins, who usually had more sense, said, "You hit it, you oughta get it," and Stewie Hauser – always the second guy to do or say anything, said he double-dared me. So there it was. You couldn't walk away from a double-dare, even from a dumbshit like Stewie. I mean, you *could,* but the rest of your life wouldn't ever be worth living after that. I knew that then. Not believed. Knew.

But I also knew absolutely that if I entered that yard, I'd never come back. Not as myself, anyway – maybe as some kind of monster, which was almost tempting when I thought of Joey Gonsalves and all his brothers. What if Mrs. Poliakov grabbed me in her claws and dragged me into her house – that house we'd spent hours peopling with every horror we'd ever seen in a movie or a comic book? Oh, sure, my mom and dad would call the cops. But what good would the police be if I'd already been eaten, or fed into a meat grinder, or turned into furniture? I wasn't aware of it until later, but it was in that moment that I woke up to the realization that you couldn't depend on your parents in a *real* crisis, any more than you could on the police. I never managed to unlearn that discovery, though I did try.

But when you're eleven years old, there's no such thing as a choice between being a witch's afternoon snack or being a fink and a chickenshit. I made the best scene I could (having already seen *A Tale of Two Cities*) out of accepting my doom; and, rot them, the team played right back to me. They didn't exactly ask for any last messages to my nearest and dearest, but J. T. Jones shook my hand hard, and Miltie gave me back the immie he'd won off me two weeks before. And I handed my broomstick to Richie Williams – as formally as if it were a sword or a custom-made pool cue – and I made my legs walk me straight across the street and into Mrs. Poliakov's front yard.

I picked up the ball I'd hit, suddenly entertaining a mad notion of scooping up as many others as I could carry and racing back in triumph from behind enemy lines with an armload of trophies to flaunt, both at Chuck Golden and at Mrs. Poliakov. That vision lasted until I heard her voice, deep and rough as a man's. "Boy! You!"

She was standing on her top step, beckoning to me with an appropriately clawlike forefinger. For once she wasn't wearing that weird tweed topcoat, but a long dark wool skirt and blouse that made her look like our idea of a gypsy. The old fedora covered her scanty white hair, giving substance to our belief that she wore it even in bed. She said it a second time. "You!"

I'd never heard her voice before. None of us had, as far as I ever knew. As long as she'd lived in that gray house, she must have yelled at two or three generations of children to stay out of her yard. By the time we came along, it wasn't necessary anymore: the fear had been passed down to us with the legend, and however much we might mock her in private, she didn't have to say a word to scatter us when she wanted to. Our parents, when they noticed, teased us for scaredy-cats, but we knew what we knew.

Now I walked slowly toward her, feeling my friends' terror behind me, but unable to turn my head. I stopped at the bottom of Mrs. Poliakov's front steps. She looked at me out of eyes so gray they were almost black, eyes younger than the drooping, wrinkled lids under which they studied me. The grating, heavily-accented voice – Russian, I think now, but maybe Polish – said, "You ball, boy?"

"Uh," I said. "Uh, yes. My ball. Our ball."

"That game," Mrs. Poliakov said. "What game? *Lapta?*"

Oddly enough, I knew about *lapta*, because my mother was born in the Ukraine. *Lapta* involves a bat and ball, and a lot of running back and forth, but it's more like cricket than baseball. I said, "No, no *lapta*. Stickball. *Steeck-boll.*"

Mrs. Poliakov said, *"Steeck..."* and then "Sticks...ball," and about got it right. I nodded eagerly, "Stickball, that's it, we play it all the time. We don't mean to hit the balls into your yard, we're really sorry..." My own voice gradually dried up as I stared into those old, gray, relentlessly clear eyes. "Can we...could we have our ball back now? *Ball,* okay?" and I held the rescued Spaldeen up, so she'd understand what I was talking about. "Ball?"

Quicker than I can say this, she snatched that ball back from me, holding it over her head as though she expected me to jump for it. "No, *nyet,* no ball," and she pointed toward the street with her free hand. I thought she was telling me to get the hell out of her yard, but that wasn't it either, nor was she throwing me out when she grabbed my arm and started walking with me, saying, "Game, *hanh?* Show – show me *sticks*ball. You show."

And here we came, the two of us, marching as to war, back into the street where my friends were standing gaping at us, some of them backing away from a scary old neighborhood witch, none of them with a word to say. *She* was enjoying herself – you could actually see it in the glint of her eyes, and in the way she limped over to J. T. Jones and slapped the Spaldeen into his hand. "Sticksball, okay, *hanh?* Show."

I wonder less about how she guessed that J. T. was our pitcher than how she knew that we used a pitcher at all. Most teams didn't: no matter how much the rules vary, block to block, in the majority of stickball games the batter just tosses the ball up himself and times his swing to its descent. But we always had a real pitcher, even though that meant our taking turns at catcher; even if he had to pitch for both sides, as he mostly did. And J. T. was *good,* even throwing underhand, and he was honest as well; never took anything off his pitches when we were at bat, which pissed some guys off, but most of us were proud of him. He was a legend, at least in the North Bronx. At least on Tryon Avenue, and all the way to Jerome on one side, and down to Webster the other way. Down to White Plains Road, really.

We chose up sides again and started a new game; but who could keep his mind on playing, with that woman who'd terrified us all our lives standing there watching, her hands behind her back and a very slight smile on her whiskery old lips? J. T.'s hands were so sweaty the ball kept getting away from him, and Miltie Mellinger kept losing the broomstick when he swung, for the same reason – almost nailed me one time, the stick flew straight at my head. We hit, all right, so much that keeping score quickly became pointless. J. T. wasn't up to anything but just laying it in there, and even the weakest hitters like Howie Stern and Marv Cooper were slamming it over the parked cars and the green trees for the rest of us to run down. Not me, though: I struck out three or four times and slunk off to lean against Howie's father's Packard, which was our dugout. For all the scoring, nobody talked or cheered much, I remember that.

Mrs. Poliakov said *"Hanh,"* again, loudly, like a whale coming up to blow. She said, "Sticksball. Give me. Give." She held out her hand.

J. T. looked around at everyone before he put the Spaldeen into her hand. Stewie Hauser said, "Okay, relief pitcher coming in, pop that glove, *bubbe,"* and crouched down to catch. *Bubbe* is grandma, but nobody laughed. Mrs. Poliakov adjusted her fedora and turned the rubber ball slowly between the swollen-knuckled fingers of both hands, studying the Spalding logo intently for minutes before she looked up and repeated, "Okay." She gestured to Marv to stand in, even though he wasn't due up yet. He didn't argue. Mrs. Poliakov gave an arthritic little hop, clumsily imitating J. T.'s motion, and she pitched.

Marv never saw it. I'm not sure Stewie did, either, until he was yelling "Jesus *Christ,* sonofa*bitch!"* and sucking his fingers as the ball bounced away from him toward the sidewalk. J. T.'s mouth was open, and Richie Williams was actually crossing himself. Junius Dinkins was just saying softly, *"Naww,* man," over and over. And Mrs. Poliakov beckoned, as she had beckoned to me in her front yard, and the Spaldeen came back to her.

It rolled meekly then; later on, it came bouncing jauntily as though it knew the way better. Mrs. Poliakov was an awkward fielder; anyone who even made contact would easily have been on base by the time she picked the ball up. But none of us ever did – J. T. managed a couple of trickling fouls, but that was it. The Spaldeen either came in so impossibly fast and hard that after a little we were bailing out before she released it; or else the thing simply zigzagged, dodged our bats, curved around us, dropped literally out of sight, or changed its pink-rubber mind and backed up in mid-flight. Satchel Paige messed with batters' heads by warning and half-convincing them that he could make a baseball do all those things. Mrs. Poliakov was *doing* it, and doing it with a toy you could get at Lapin's corner store for forty-nine cents, with tax; cheaper, you buy a dozen. I will always believe – and so, I promise you, will anyone else who was there – that she could have done exactly the same thing with a pair of rolled-up gym socks.

Stewie Hauser hadn't stopped saying "Jesus *Christ!*" from that first pitch, and Miltie Mellinger kept mumbling, "It's a trick, she *does* something to the ball, a *spin.*" Chuck Golden, who always had to know more than you did, was explaining learnedly, "She's throwing a spitball, that's illegal. My dad told me about spitballs." Some of the girls jumping rope and pushing doll-carriages had stopped playing, and were staring from the sidewalk; there were even one or two adult onlookers, who could tell that *something* was going on. We ourselves would have quit, if we could, but Mrs. Poliakov wouldn't let us, not until she was good and ready. We'd have to keep dragging our broomsticks up there all night, if she wanted; through all eternity, if she chose. That we knew without a word.

All the same, she gave me my one great moment in sports, there in the cobblestone street, at five o'clock on a spring afternoon, with mothers already starting to call from windows about dinner and homework. When I stepped in for one last hopeless at-bat against her, she gave me a gray, snaggly grin – the only real smile anyone ever had from her – and she called in to me, "For you, boy. For brave!"

And she grooved one. It floated in chest-high, not veering, not dropping or hopping, just minding its own business, timing itself to my swing rather than the other way around. Shirley Temple couldn't have missed it. Miss Eschenberg, who taught fourth grade, couldn't have missed it. My seven-year-old brother couldn't have missed it.

And for once *I* didn't miss it. It vanished down the block, tearing through leaves, knocking down twigs, soaring high and far enough to clear the cemetery wall. I can't say whether it actually did or not, or would have, because it caught fire at the top of its arc – simply burst into flames as it flew on out of sight. We never found any charred fragments, though Stewie Hauser hunted for two days, determined to prove that it hadn't outdistanced his legendary home run. Nobody else cared, but I understood. Those things mattered then.

Mrs. Poliakov looked briefly after my shot, said *"Hanh,"* to herself, pushed her fedora down hard on her head, and turned back toward her house. We never moved, but stood watching her, sensing perhaps that the game – or whatever it really was – might be ended, but that *something* was not yet complete. Just before entering her yard, she turned again to face us, waiting there in the street. Her face was dark and warning under the old hat, and not at all friendly.

"Next ugly in my yard," she said clearly, "next nasty" – and she pointed to indicate the last flight of the Spaldeen – "same thing you, all you." Now she waved both arms as high as she could reach, and went, *"Whoooaww! All heads, all heads, like you ball. Whoooawww!"*

We must all have been at least halfway home when I heard her call after us, "You come get balls! Balls, okay!" I *think* she was laughing, but I've never been sure. In any case, it took me a week to get Junius Dinkins' nerve up, but then we went together and rescued all the abandoned Spaldeens littering her front yard. Mrs. Poliakov didn't put in an appearance, though Junius swore that he caught a glimpse of that felt hat slipping around a corner – not her, just the hat, keeping an eye on us – which could have been true. Witches' hats are magic too, as any eleven-year-old can tell you. Or they could have then.

By Moonlight

"By Moonlight" was written for this collection, and has an odd history, even for one of my stories. It actually began as a one-act play, set at dawn on the morning after a night of revels in the Faery court of Titania and Oberon. The first characters to speak are a couple of cleaning fairies (of course there would have to be cleaning fairies: you don't think Titania does her own dusting, tidying, bedmaking, and cleaning up after an orgy, do you?) – named Halli and Halla.

> HALLI
> I hate Samhain.

> HALLA
> (anxiously)
> Don't let Herself hear you say that!
> You know how she gets –

> HALLI
> I've never made a secret of it. Oh, it's
> all very well for them as wants to go
> swanning around out there –
> (gestures)
> – luring farm boys and inspiring poets
> and such, and coming home so grand
> you can't even talk to them for days...
> but just look at what's left for us every
> time. Like the Wild Hunt had been
> through here –

> HALLA
> (a little wistful)
> Sometimes I think I'd like to go. I do,
> Halli. Just for the night, just to see...
> (laughs)
> I don't even know what I'd want to
> see. The houses, I expect...the houses
> in the moonlight. Just the way they
> live...

> HALLI
> Like pigs, trust me. They live like their
> own pigs. Next one finds his way here,
> ask him. If he's honest, he'll tell you.

In short order these two discover Paola, a country girl who had innocently wandered Under the Hill the previous night, had a grand time dancing with the faery folk, and then overslept. On being roused Paola is distinctly unhappy to learn that if she steps out into the morning of her own world it will be a hundred years later, with everything that made up her daily life gone forever. She then encounters Oberon and Titania, who urge her to stay (the latter with a certain edginess), and also someone identified only as The Man, who is obviously William Shakespeare. It's The Man who finally solves Paola's problem, by employing his own particular brand of magic – the magic of language – to send her home to her own time, and all's well that ends well.

But I couldn't quite make the concept work...and besides, I only found out after I'd completed my first draft that Neil Gaiman had already written the best Shakespeare/Titania story anyone's ever likely to do, back in 1990, in his "Midsummer Night's Dream" issue of *The Sandman*.

On my next attempt I radically altered the plot – no cleaning fairies, no Paola, no Shakespeare or Shakespearean magic – and turned the new version into a tale being told in a pub over pints of good English ale. But it came out generic, wearisome, distancing: an unmoving failure. Worth the try, because it forced me to look at my story in a completely different way, which is always a good thing; but otherwise useless.

Eventually it was suggested that I let the actual subject of the tale tell it himself – helped along by a touch of Alfred Noyes, and a hint of a hint of that bright boy from Warwickshire. I'm finally happy with the result.

DARLINGTON WAS desperately glad to see the little fire as he came over the moor from Bramham. *I can make it that far.* There was less snow on the ground here to betray him with footprints, but the cold was harder because of that, and while his coat could keep the wind off yet awhile, his boot soles had worn as thin as his hopes. He had sent the horse off in a different direction more than an hour ago, but he knew his pursuers too well to imagine that the trick would deceive them for long, if at all. At very best he was buying time; which, Darlington decided, could well be considered the entire story of his life. Wrapping his arms around his own shoulders, he stumbled up the low hill toward the fire. *I think I can make it that far.*

It was reassuring to see that there was only one figure observing his approach. He'd not have expected to encounter any but fleeing, freezing high-tobys like himself on the moor...but he had always found the supposed brotherhood of outlaws greatly overrated: none could be trusted after sunset, and few in broad daylight. But even from such a distance the man near the fire was clearly no bandit. He was tall and white-haired – white-bearded as well – and wrapped in a cloak of intriguing design that Darlington determined was coming away with him, should they survive the night. He saw, as well, that the man's face was curiously ageless in the feeble, wavering firelight, with a paradoxical mix of old sadness and equally profound tranquility. It made him nervous, as contradictions always did.

Showing no trepidation on his own part, the white-haired man beckoned Darlington to the fire, saying in a deep, quiet voice, "Warm yourself, good highwayman. I fear the pickings must have been slim on such a day."

Darlington's legs made the decision to sit before he did, and when he tried to speak, no sound at all came out of his mouth. The stranger nodded understandingly, and offered him a leathern flask plainly meant to contain brandy or *schnapps;* but what Darlington tasted was so astonishingly rich and alive inside him that he very nearly threw up, as though his body were trying to vomit out the whole terror of the day. When he was able, he gasped hoarsely, "Thank you. Whatever that was, thank you."

"Nectar of the gods," the stranger responded. "Or as close to it as either of us is ever likely to come. Rest now, and tell me what you will, or rest and be still. Those on your track will surely follow no further until morning, at the earliest. I will find more wood."

Too weary to wonder about anything, Darlington promptly fell asleep, and was only wakened by the increased heat of the revived fire on his face. The stranger offered him another swallow from the flask, and the heel-end of a battered loaf of brown bread. "The last of my provender, forgive me. I was making for Wetherby, more or less, but that's impossible now, in this cold. I may as well turn toward Ilkley – or even Harrogate, why not? Yes...perhaps Harrogate."

He was obviously debating an important issue with himself, and Darlington was near drowsing off again; but the unnerving oddity of a man who seemed neither mad nor a beggar knowing him on sight for an outlaw prodded him fully awake against his will. He spoke warily to his benefactor therefore, saying, "Sir, if your kindness is meant but to delay me until the High Sheriff's men have their hands on me, I feel bound to inform you that the pistol under my coat is pointed directly at your charitable heart. Let me be hanged at Leeds Assizes next month, I will at least swing for something grander than a mail coach that turned out to carry nothing but solicitors' accounts and begging letters from the colonies." And he patted his breast meaningfully and smiled what he dearly hoped was his most elegantly menacing smile.

"Roger Darlington, you would be," the stranger mused, smiling back at him. "A good Dalesman's name – I hear it everywhere on the moors lately, though I somehow feel I'll have forgotten it utterly by tomorrow's dawn. Wensleydale, most likely?"

Darlington let his hand fall, the pistol being empty anyway, since the last shot over his shoulder that had killed a trooper's horse. "Aye, born and bred in Skipton myself, but there've been Darlingtons in Wensleydale since the bloody Ark. But you have the advantage of me, sir."

"Ah, my name? Elias Patterson, at your service." The stranger offered his hand across the fire. "Reverend Elias Patterson that was, as you might say."

Accepting the handshake, Darlington frowned in some puzzlement. "You're a minister, then?"

Elias Patterson cocked his head slightly, as though the word were new to him. "Perhaps I am still. It's hard to know, you understand."

Darlington did know, having passed a fair number of entertaining evenings drinking, gambling, whoring and weeping with variously fallen clerics. "A woman, was it?" With this one, it would have to be a woman.

Again the thoughtful tilt of the head, the narrowing of the gray eyes, the least breath of a smile. "In a manner of speaking."

"Well, it's a good man's failing. Not like what I do."

He said it in his most swaggering manner, having once slipped into Lincoln's Inn Fields, with a price already on his head, to see *The Beggar's Opera*. Elias Patterson's eyes were neither impressed nor unsympathetic. "You hold a low opinion of your chosen trade, is it?"

"I never said that." Darlington found himself distinctly irritated with his own irritation. "But I hardly expect it to make me," – he gestured with his thumb toward the cold black sky – "welcome up there."

"But why not? You work hard, you have so far harmed no one – you see, I know a bit of you, Mr. Darlington – and the worst that can be said is that you have a certain passion for redistributing the doubtless ill-gotten wealth of that class which can afford to ride about in coaches, whether public or privately-owned. As a former man of the cloth, I can tell you honestly that the Savior might very well approve."

There was humor in the voice, but no mockery. Darlington had the alarming sense that the man meant exactly what he was saying. "I redistribute the wealth to *myself*, Reverend Patterson – Robin Hood's a long time gone. Now and then I do toss a coin or two into the poor box or the collection plate, but that's the end of it, believe me." Weary as he was, he leaned forward, elbows on his knees. "What sort of a minister *are* you, anyway?"

Elias Patterson did not reply, being occupied with placing more fallen branches on the fire. They blazed up quickly, sputtering a little because of the snow. He leaned toward the flames himself, his eyes and voice speculative, almost dreamy. "How strange, when you think about it," he mused in a near-whisper. "And we *should* think about it, you and I. A gentleman of the road and a – what? – a preacher who dares not even enter a church, for fear that the very blessed timbers might all come down on his head. Oh, we are indeed well met – one forever in flight, a poor fox, with no faithful vixen, no cubs waiting to warm and welcome him, celebrating him for losing the hounds one more time – "

"And just how would you know that, my wise *Reverend* Patterson?"

"– and the other in fact a hunter, a pursuer, wandering the same mazes over and over, endlessly searching for something he begins to feel he dreamed..." The voice dried to a meaningless insect drone.

Born a Dalesman, as Elias Patterson had guessed, Darlington had grown up with the silence of the moors. For him it was a sound in itself: a bleak, deeply elusive music, to be felt along the scalp, and in the soles of the feet, rather than heard with the ears. Tonight, listening intently for hoofbeats, for men's voices calling to each other and the yelping of hounds – suddenly he could not endure the stillness a moment longer. "No matter our need, it's clear that neither of us will be sleeping tonight," he said. "My story is entirely as you imagine it, barring perhaps a trifle more education than most robbers on horseback, and consequently a dream of my own. A dull dream, certainly, for it involves living to retirement and then starting up a good little inn in Whitby or Wensleydale, catering quietly to the profession...oh, an extremely dull dream, believe me. I would much prefer to hear any tale told by a minister of the Gospel who fears to walk into a church." Elias Patterson began to protest, but Darlington continued, "We haven't got wood enough to see us through the night. As an earnest of my intent, I promise to gather what we need before you begin. If you will begin."

They regarded each other for a long moment, during which Elias Patterson neither spoke, nor nodded, nor made any other sign to his criminal companion. Then Roger Darlington abruptly stepped away from the fire and set about collecting more branches. Elias Patterson sat motionless, staring into the darkness.

Darlington made three trips, and was sweating heavily despite the cold when he returned with the last armload. He rebuilt the fire entirely, so that it threw just as much heat but burned more slowly. "The one useful thing I learned from taking the King's shilling. I did leave two shillings for him when I deserted, so he can't be *that* annoyed with me."

"A king's bookkeeping is as mysterious as a woman's." Elias Patterson had not moved. "Thank you for the firewood."

Darlington peered sideways at him. "There was a price attached."

"Ah. My story. Are you certain you want to hear it? It is long, unlikely, and remarkably unedifying – shameful, even, to come from a minister's lips. Blasphemous, too, properly regarded."

"Better and better," Darlington responded. "On such a night, a little blasphemy might serve as well as a hot posset or a mug of mulled ale. I hold you to your word, sir."

Elias Patterson considered. "I suppose this would be as fitting a night as any for the tale, it being Imbolc, Bride's Festival – or perhaps you guise her as St. Bridget in Skipton?" Darlington stared back at him uncomprehendingly. "Come, I know they honor Bride in the Dales, no matter what we priests and preachers admonish them. I have seen the *Brideog* corn dollies made, and caught my own parishioners setting out the strips of cloth for Bride to bless when she walks the land on Imbolc Eve. You? Never?"

Darlington shook his head, forcing an embarrassed laugh. "Not in Skipton, believe me. Never in Skipton."

"A loss," said Elias Patterson. "Christianity was ever the better for a good brawl with the old gods. Now in the village where I lived – actually not too far from here, a bit west – every last sheep in my flock believed in every one of them. Come Beltane night, not a deacon, not an elder, not a First Soprano but was bound to be out till dawn, hunting till they dropped for faery gold. I was younger then, and I scolded them endlessly, shouting that it was an unholy pagan thing, and that those who trifled with such matters were placing their immortal souls in the gravest danger. Those were my very words, and every one of that lot sat mortified, when I called their names in church, and mumbled penitence, and went right on doing it, as I knew they would." He sighed. "It all shames me dreadfully to recall, Mr. Darlington. You won't understand, I expect."

"Well, I was never exactly a churchgoing man," Darlington answered him. "Be a better person if I had been, I've no doubt of it. But the world outside was so much more interesting. Always was."

"I knew nothing of the world in those days," Elias Patterson said. "I had my God, my work, my books and my cat, nor did it occur to me that these might not necessarily be sufficient for a man pledged to follow the Cross all his days. And for all my scorn of the old festivals as wicked folly, still I never left my house on Beltane, Samhain, Lughnasadh. My cat did, mind you, but not I."

"Never hurts to be on the safe side."

Elias Patterson looked directly into Darlington's face, and his gray eyes were very bright in the firelight. He said, "We give them different names, those nights lit only by fire and the moon, depending on the county and the calendar, but we know what they are. They call up the world that was before the Lord came down among us; the world where good and evil were not so certain, so *fixed* as they are today, where the known and the unheard-of could mingle as they chose…where truth had its doubts, do you see?" He laughed harshly. "Well, all that was a bit alarming for me to deal with then, so I stayed by my own neat little fire on those nights, and neither stepped out nor let anything in. Who knows what your door may open to – or upon – on Beltane eve?"

"I've usually taken Beltane off from work," Darlington reflected. "Girls are always so *cheery* at Beltane."

Elias Patterson was staring far into the fire. "But on one such eve, long ago, I opened my door three times. The first occasion was to let my cat out, for there's no Christianizing a cat, as I'm sure you know. They belong to gods older even than Bride and Angus, and our Lord grants them a special dispensation. Or so it was believed in my village, and I chose to believe it myself." This time the laugh was warm and genuine. "The second time I opened the door was to let Hannah Dawkins in. She was a widow, Mrs. Dawkins, but still youthful and pleasing enough to capture any man's eye, I must say. She brought me some of her own currant wine, I remember."

Darlington winked boldly at him. "Must have been a good deal of that coming to visit, hey? You being young and not bad-looking, and of course highly respectable. And unattached."

"She was as respectable herself as any in the village," Elias Patterson responded severely. "A handsome woman, as I say, well set-up, with money of her own, and a lively conversationalist in the bargain. And if she did come calling with a purpose, guessing that most of the other women were likely to be out jumping over the Beltane fires, or dancing in a circle widdershins...why, no blame to her, or to me either, for setting down my book and inviting her to my fireside."

"Man was not meant to be alone," Darlington quoted piously. "Isn't that what our Lord himself said? Something like that."

Elias Patterson looked mildly shocked. "No, certainly not, nothing of what I can see you thinking happened between us that night – nothing but a bit of excellent currant wine and a bit of conversation. And if – and I say *if* – she left in some slight disappointment...well, I may have led her on, though I never meant to. I may have done."

Darlington said, "I've always found these things a matter of the moment, myself. Another time – another hour, even – another place..." But the white-haired man shook his head.

"It would have taken another man," he replied softly. "Not owing to any flaw in the good Widow Dawkins, but because of a restlessness that I never could put words to, and never dared name, for fear that would give the thing more power over me than it already had. From my birth, it had always slept quietly in me for months, years at a time, that *thing*... and then it would rouse up to rack my sleep and trouble my reading in the Book, and turn my sermons on their heads. It was such a restlessness came on me after the Widow Dawkins left, and made me bank my hearthfire and open my door for the third time that night, and walk out into the wilderness of Beltane eve. As I had never before done – as I had always known better than to do. Because of that *thing*."

"Yes," Darlington murmured as though to himself. "Not the gold. It's never the gold."

Both men were silent for some time. Elias Patterson had his arms folded on his knees, and was bent almost double, staring into the flames. Darlington, his lethargy vanished, listened constantly for any sounds of pursuit, but he heard nothing except the hiss and crackle of the fire, and the occasional cold bark of a fox, signaling to his mate. The snow clouds were blowing away, and stars were appearing for the first time in several nights. *Be a nice clear day tomorrow*, he thought. *See for bloody miles, they will. Bloody wonderful.*

Elias Patterson finally stirred. "Mr. Darlington, do you believe there is a real place called Faery? We have spoken of Beltane and Imbolc, of

Bride and Angus, of corn dollies and old gods. Do you believe that there is an actual realm where such as these still dwell? Your answer is important to me."

Darlington did not laugh, but he slapped both his thighs and grinned with teeth that should not have been as healthy-white as they were, given the life he led. "You mean Under the Hill? The door in the mountain where you wander in and spend a night dancing and reveling with the fairy folk, and then you come out in the morning and it's a hundred years later? That place?"

"That place," Elias Patterson agreed quietly. "*Tír na nÓg,* the Irish call it. The kingdom of Oberon and Titania."

Something in his voice made Darlington's smile fade. After a moment, he said, "Well. I've nothing *against* believing in it, when I think of what I've seen in my time, and what I've had to believe. But I've never yet met anyone who could tell me he'd been there."

"Until now," Elias Patterson said.

Darlington said nothing, but simply held out his hand for the leather flask. He took a swig, handed it back, and remained silent for a long enough time that it became necessary to arrange more wood on the fire. He said at last, "You're a hundred years old."

"I don't know how old I am." Elias Patterson answered. "Do I count the years, or do I count the time?"

The silence was longer this time. Darlington got up again and relieved himself into the darkness. He did up his buttons, turned back to face Elias Patterson, and said, "So, then. Instead of doing the sensible with that nice, willing widow, you walked out alone after she left, and you walked straight Under the Hill. Straight into Faery."

"Nothing about Faery is straight, not as we understand the word." Elias Patterson's eyes seemed to be growing brighter as Darlington stared into them. "The doorway is not always in the side of a hill, or a mountain. Faery lights where it pleases, shows itself where it lists; and though that village of mine lay in country as flat as Norfolk or the Fens, yet even so, when I walked out that night there lay Faery just across the road...or was it across Roger Munro's upper pasture...or perhaps glimmering beyond old Hugh Hobden's rich, muddy bottomland. It danced on before me like a rainbow, Faery did, and I followed as best I might, always explaining to myself that I was looking for my cat. And when at last I was too weary to follow further, I simply laid myself down on a little low hillside, in a pile of fallen leaves, and fell asleep as trusting as a child. And while I slept, Faery came to me."

Darlington raised his eyebrows, but said nothing.

"It must have been an enchantment," Elias Patterson continued, "for I dreamed all that happened, but I could not waken. First there came the loveliest woman I had ever seen, tall and splendid and queenly, riding on a milk-white steed – as is told, you remember, in the rhyme of True Thomas. And after her came another, and then another – all on white horses, each woman so beautiful as to make the one who rode before look like a kitchen wench, a scullery maid – until there were a full dozen of them ranged in a circle around me, looking down on me as though from a far greater height than the back of a horse." His eyes were closed as he spoke, and his voice seemed far away, as though only a part of him still sat by the fire. Darlington knew the man believed every daft word; and in his own despite he felt himself starting to catch that belief, like a head cold.

Elias Patterson looked at him thoughtfully. "Had I actually awakened to that sight at that moment, I think I might well have gone mad. Humankind can only bear so much wonder and glory all at once, which is why I often worry about Heaven."

Darlington shrugged. "Not one of *my* problems. Go on."

"Ah," said Elias Patterson. "Last came Titania, stepping barefoot and alone. In my dream she knelt beside me, like no queen but a young girl, and she gazed long and closely into my blind face before she spoke. She said, "'This is he. I will have no other. Bear him to my bower.' And so it was done."

"'*And so it was done,*'" the highwayman mocked him. "And you mean to tell me that you went on sleeping in the arms of a dozen beautiful women bearing you away? And still knew what was going on, all along?" He shook his head. "Rot and moonshine, man."

"I am telling you what happened. I was lifted and borne directly into a farmer's hayrick, of all things – but through it I know I saw the lights of Faery rippling and flowing, on the far side of my closed eyelids. And I heard the music, for even a faery enchantment cannot altogether silence faery music. Titania told me later that I smiled in my sleep to hear it, and that my smile touched her heart. The women of Faery, glorious as they are, have no hearts, but Titania does. This is why she is often lonely."

Darlington thought he heard a horse somewhere nearby, but Elias Patterson's eyes held him fast, and he could not move. He asked, "How long did you sleep? When did you wake?"

"I was never sure," Elias Patterson replied. "What matters just now is that I woke in a twilight secrecy the like of which I had never seen. There were green and purple vines arching over, and strange birds singing their evening songs in great misty trees for which I had no names, and the thickest, gentlest grass beneath all. I smelled something like honeysuckle, and heard water somewhere, and Titania singing. It was hard to tell her voice from the voice of the stream, for it murmured and laughed by turns, and sighed too, soft as the grass on which I lay, warm as the breeze that ruffled my hair...or it might have been Titania's fingers, for my head was in her lap, and her own starlit hair was brushing my face. And I did not want to move, ever again."

"All most unChristian, to be sure," Darlington twitted him. "Why, I'd go so far as to name it pagan."

"You would be right, without question. And for that, in that moment, I could not have cared a fiddler's fart." Elias Patterson snapped his fingers at the end of that vulgar phrase, and the outlaw was hard put to it to determine whether it was the snap that startled him most, or the sudden startling bite of the words.

"When I sat up," Elias Patterson went on, "which seemed to take forever – and that was perfectly agreeable too – I found myself face to face with a face I could have drowned in, and welcome. I knew this could only be Titania, and this place Faery, and that I was bound under lifelong orders from my God and my bishop to cry out *Retro me, Sathanas!* and turn my mind from temptation and toward Heaven...if this were truly not it." He ran his hands through his white hair, and smiled helplessly. "But all I could say to that face, to those mischievous tender, fiercely wise eyes was, 'I pray you, madam, give me leave to go from here. For I in no way belong in your realm, as you well know.' Granted, I said this in a small and most tremorous voice, but I did say it."

"I said something similar to a lady in Wapping one time," Darlington offered. "Almost cost me a tooth."

Elias Patterson smiled briefly before continuing. "Then Titania laughed fully, and the sound of that laughter turned all my bones so weightless, and so...so full of sunlight that I could have flown up and out of that bower like a mayfly, if I could have moved at all. She caressed my face with her hands, that were like wings themselves, light and strong enough to bear us both to world's end and beyond, as just then I wished they would. But I was a Christian, even in Faery, Mr. Darlington, even with the Queen of Faery's hands on me, and to her laughter I repeated my request, saying honestly, 'Great lady, you know what I am. You know that I serve another God than yours, and you know further that my Lord's victory is foreordained in the firmament. With every respect, what word have we for one another?'

"'This,' said Titania, and she leaned forward and kissed me."

In a vague, faraway manner, Darlington realized that his eyes had become a child's eyes, stretched so wide that they almost hurt. He did his best to recover himself by saying, "Of course you showed some proper sense, for once, I trust, and abandoned Father, Son, and Holy Spirit on the spot?"

Elias Patterson did not laugh. He said, "On the contrary, my belief was strengthened by that kiss, for I well understood it to be a temptation set in my path to test me. So I straightened my back and put my hands behind it – for all that my mind was spinning in my skull, and my eyes could not focus on anything but Titania's eyes – and I spoke out as forcefully as I might, saying, 'I belong to my Lord and Saviour Jesus Christ. Your wiles have no power over me. Dissolve your enchantments, turn toward righteousness, and release me.'

"'But there are no charms chaining you here,' Titania answered me, and her speaking voice fondled my heart as her hands had done my skin. 'I would be shamed to hold a man so, lord or slave, mortal or faery. Rise and walk away then, if you will; indeed I'll send folk of mine to guide you home.' But she smiled, saying this...she smiled, Mr. Darlington, and suddenly...suddenly I was no reverend at all, nor ever had been, and all I could to was to stand very still where I was. Titania said, 'Or kiss me, for it's one or the other, my beautiful mortal. Choose.'"

"And you chose," Darlington said, surprisingly gently. "As I'd have done in a moment. Indeed, we're a bit alike, after all, as you say."

"And I chose," Elias Patterson said, and no more.

After a time Darlington asked, "You'd never been with a woman, of course? Meaning no offense."

"No, never with a woman. Nor with a man, either – nor was I ever drawn to boys, as happens. By nature I am a shy man, Mr. Darlington, shy even in my dreams and wishes. Imagine me now, if you will, lost in the wild miracle of the Queen of Faery in my arms, unable to take in the words she was saying and singing and sighing to me – let alone the things she was *doing...*"

"Please," Darlington said. "A rough outlaw I may be, but I'm still a little young for such details. How long did it go on, your – what's the word when it's with a queen? – your *liaison?*"

Elias Patterson said, "Time is a different thing in Faery, as you may have heard – sometimes longer than here, sometimes shorter. It rather depends."

"Depends on *what?*" When Elias Patterson did not reply immediately, Darlington said, "I have been hunted all this day, and it's entirely likely that I may be taken tomorrow and hanged in a month; in any case, we will certainly never see each other after this night. Depends on bloody *what?*"

Elias Patterson's white hair showed up his blush more noticeably. "When I was – ah – with her, Titania, in her bower, time simply ceased to exist in any way at all. I never knew how long we were together, or how often we...or what we...or when we slept, when we woke.... It was all one thing, one thing, do you understand me?"

"No," Darlington said. "No, and I don't think I want to. Did you never get out of that...bower of hers?"

He snickered at Elias Patterson's reply. "Those first days – or weeks, or months, whatever they were – we went nowhere else." But he bit his lips sourly when he was diffidently informed that in a little while Elias Patterson found himself grown strong enough – "grown *youthful* enough, perhaps; I had never been young before, you see" – to match the Queen's hunger, and even skilled enough to satisfy it in a few ways that rounded her twilight eyes. "So when she did bring me indoors at last, it was rather to show me off to Faery, not so much the other way around. They are more like us than we might imagine, those folk. In some ways."

To keep his mind off the day to come, Darlington asked, "And what's it like, then, that *indoors* Under the Hill?"

Elias Patterson was not looking at him, but plainly far beyond the flames. "All things, all at once – rather like Titania herself, if you will.

In Faery space is just as deceptive as time. For instance, there always seems to be as much forest as any hunter could desire, and those who dwell in Faery love the chase just as we do. Only their beasts of venery are a bit other than those we pursue: they'll be after the manticore for its claws and teeth, as we take wolf and bear; they'll shoot down griffins to make knives from their sharp-edged feathers; and there's a great serpent-thing that the hunter has to strangle, because no blade, no point will even scratch that hide. And the hunts themselves can last a month or a year, for they've got all the time in the world. Remember, *Tír na nÓg* means The Land of Youth."

After a considering moment, he added, "They won't take the fox or the unicorn, by the way – those two are sacred in Faery. I never knew why, but I was always glad of it. They can come and go as they desire between the worlds, though foxes clearly do it more often."

"You really were there," Darlington said softly. "By God, old man, you really walked in those woods, didn't you?" This time, it was his eyes holding Elias Patterson's eyes across the fire. "Bloody hell. You danced in the halls of Faery."

"They're full of light," Elias Patterson whispered, "bursting with it, *humming* with it. It's alive, that light. It moves as it pleases, stroking the faces of dancers and musicians, cooks and servants alike, just as Titania caressed me." Darlington could barely hear him. He said, "When you stay long enough in that light, you can feel yourself turning into it, becoming something neither faery nor mortal – nothing but the light. That's the only way those folk ever die, did you know? Dancing too long in the light. Titania told me that. She said sometimes they did it a-purpose."

The clearing sky had let the half-moon come out, and Darlington hunched down against its brightness. He said, "And the gold? The faery gold your church lot were always after?"

Elias Patterson raised his eyebrows. "My, I expected *that* question well before now. Well, yes, I saw a great deal of gold everywhere – there's another thing the faery folk love as much as we do. But they had too much of it to treat it as money, do you see; everybody had enough that more or less of it made no difference. I never worked out whether they had any actual notion of currency, but sometimes I thought it might be poetry." He smiled fondly at the night. "Say a poem to any one of Titania's people, and he'd be in your debt; the richest folk were those who knew the most poems by heart. Especially good long ones, the kind that can run on for an hour, more. They really like *long* poems."

"None of my sort in Faery, then. Pity." Darlington hesitated, and then asked, oddly but genuinely shy himself, "What about their music? You'd not think so, but my family had a music master come to the house for little Roger. I was to be a fiddler in some grand gentleman's private orchestra – that was the proudest career they could imagine for me, poor souls. Alas, all their hopes were dashed when I discovered how easy it was to pick the music master's pocket. I blame them – and him – for my becoming what I am. Tell me about the music you heard Under the Hill, good reverend."

He halted abruptly when Elias Patterson turned away, too late to hide the tears glittering in the firelight. Darlington waited, but on this subject there was plainly no answer to be had from the man. "Never mind the music, then. Tell me what sort of table they set in Faery."

"There was always food and wine," Elias Patterson said, when he could, "as there was always music. And whether or not I even recognized the dish, or the taste and fume of the drink, I learned to savor it and swallow it, and ask no questions. I remember one wine – they keep it for certain special occasions – that never tastes the same from glass to glass in the course of the feast. *He* makes that one himself. Titania told me so."

"He?" Darlington blinked in puzzlement.

"Oberon. Her husband." Elias Patterson's voice was completely without expression. "King of Faery since ever there's *been* Faery, just as she's been Queen. I went a long while without meeting him, or even catching a glimpse of him, for they spent far more time apart than they did together. They were forever fighting over this or that, like children – what one had, the other wanted, exactly like children. I was just as content to see no more of King Oberon than the shadow in Titania's eyes that always told me when she'd been with him. I became quite good at reading her whims and moods, as we all must learn to read our mates if we mean to keep them. Perhaps that was because she had a heart, as I've said, like a mortal woman. I don't think I could have fathomed any other woman of Faery in the same way."

"I've never *fathomed* a woman in my life," Darlington said shortly. "I never understood my mother and sisters, if you want to know – let alone the silly sluts who run after highwaymen." He stood up, moving to the edge of the firelight, as though he were about to relieve himself again. The night remained as deeply silent as he could have wished, but a life-time of flight had long since turned even silence chancy. Turning again, and looking down at Elias Patterson, he said, "And I have my doubts that you ever rightly knew the heart of the Queen of Faery. Meaning no disrespect."

"None at all," Elias Patterson assured him. "King Oberon certainly would have agreed with you." The fire flinched from a sudden cold breeze, and the reverend drew his cloak closer around his shoulders. He said, "Once I'd been introduced to company, as you might say, I saw something more of Oberon. Rarely alone, though, for his attendants were always on hand: musicians first of all, and then dancers, jugglers, faery clowns even, and others so strange that it made my eyes hurt to look at them for long, as though important bits of them were hidden around some other cor-ner and my eyes were trying to find the way there, and could not. On such occasion we met face-on – often during a dance, with Titania on my arm, and Oberon hand in hand with his latest elven beauty...why then, it squeezed my earthly heart to see how those two regarded one another, as though no one else existed, for good or ill. Minister no longer, to look at them was to understand where hell and heaven truly dwell, and harps and fire everlasting have no part in it."

"Aye, I'll drink to that one," Darlington swore. "There was this one bloody woman in Sussex – haven't seen her for years, and damned well don't want to, but when I think of her...aye, it squeezes. It does that. I *know* it was her turned me in for the reward money that time! How can you still wake up sad about someone who does that to you?"

Elias Patterson seemed not to have heard him. "It's a puzzling busi-ness, but while the lady Titania was, and surely remains, the most beauti-ful woman who ever walked this world or any other, I could have named you a dozen of my own parishioners handsomer than King Oberon. His cheekbones were too high and too prominent; his eyes too sharply angled, too wolfishly green; and his nose, chin and ears altogether too pointed for anything like beauty as we see it. Yet when Oberon looked at you, you felt naked as a white bone in the rain; and when he spoke, the voice of the Lord Himself would not have distracted you from his words. I was quite relieved that he spoke to me no more than necessary.

"But it happened one glorious Faery morning," Elias Patterson said, "while Titania yet drowsed in her bower, that Oberon came alone to me and drew me away with a single look to walk with him along the bank of that twittering little stream that I had heard on first waking with my head in Titania's lap. We said nothing to one another for a time, and then Oberon addressed me so: 'Do you imagine that my wife loves you?'

"'I would not presume,' I answered him, and that was true. But the shameless pride of having loved the Queen of Faery to sleep was on me, and for the life of me I could not keep from adding, 'But I do know that I make her happy.'"

"Aye, the Sussex woman always said that. No man but me had ever made her really happy, that's exactly what she said. Lying, conniving trull."

Elias Patterson said, "The contempt in Oberon's green eyes should have withered me where I stood, but I was younger then, and I could still hear Titania whispering her desire against my skin. Oberon said, 'You make her happy. And have you any notion of how many mortal men have made her happy? Of how many there will be after you?'

"'Jealous yourself,' I answered him – good God, how dared I speak so to such a king? – 'you'll not make me as bitter and spiteful as you are. I know well enough that my time in Faery is limited to seven years. All the old tales and ballads tell me that much, and I would howl at your gates for more, for a lifetime, if I thought it would do me any good. But my religion and my raising have both taught me the virtue of settling for less – less than my dreams, less than my visions – so that I will do when the time comes, and count myself the most fortunate of men, however empty the rest of my life may be. Can you understand that, Lord of Faery?'

"I like to think now that Oberon looked at me with a trifle less scorn after I spoke those words, but perhaps not. It was long ago. At all events, he replied most evenly, saying, 'It was I who laid a *geas* upon her, untold thousands of your years past, enjoining that she might take all the human lovers she chose – she had a fascination with your kind even then – but that none of her alliances might endure longer than seven years. For then she grieves each time, most movingly, and I comfort her, as I – *I* – know better how to do than any strutting, crowing mortal, and we are happy together for a while.' And after a moment, he added, more softly, 'Sometimes quite a long while.'"

Darlington put another log carefully on the fire. He said, "I should never have stopped here. Now I'm too warm to abandon your hearth,

Elias Patterson, and if the High Sheriff himself pops up right now, he's going to have to wait until I learn how the tale turns out. He couldn't have done better if he'd actually hired you to waylay me." He spat into the flame, smiled at the resulting hiss, and said, "Go on, then. What did you say back to His Majesty?"

"I asked a question in my turn," Elias Patterson replied. "I said, 'Is it a part of the *geas* that each of Titania's lovers returns to a world that is a hundred years older than he left it?' And Oberon answered, 'That is true. The dislocation, the shock of finding oneself an alien in one's own land, it keeps your lot fully occupied, far too busy merely remaining sane to be concerned with any notion of returning, any dream of a second chance at Faery. For if any man ever did succeed in returning to her, then the *geas* would be broken, and she free to fancy whom she chose, for as long as she chose. But that will never happen, Elias Patterson – never while I live. And I live forever.'

"'And you tell us all this?' I asked him. 'You take all your wife's men in turn for pleasant morning strolls, and inform them that there is a *geas* on her, and that it can be lifted if any of them should find his way back Under the Hill? Is that wise, my lord?'"

Darlington muttered, "I should have done something like that with that woman. I should have told everyone that she was diseased – something really horrible, really disgusting." He sighed. "I always think of things too late." A second fox barked, fairly close by, and Darlington said, "There's the vixen."

"Yes," Elias Patterson said. "I have spent a good deal of time studying the foxes in this district."

Darlington cocked his head, but the reverend did not explain further, choosing instead to continue his tale. "In response to my question, Oberon replied, 'I tell you about the *geas,* as I have told few others, because, of them all, you *will* try to come back to her. I know this. But you will fail, and fail again and again, and you will suffer endlessly and needlessly until you die. I am only trying to spare you such a fate.'

"'I am touched by your concern,' I said. 'Even honored.' And I was not mocking him, Mr. Darlington, truly. I said, 'But you and I both know that the three of us will do what God in his mystery has put it on us to do. I have failed Him, and I will be punished for it, but that changes nothing. That changes nothing at all.'

"'No,' Oberon answered. 'You are right – we will all do what we will do.' And then he smiled at me in a strange way, almost a sad way, and he said, 'And you may bear this triumph away, if you will, that I, undying Oberon, am indeed envious of a mortal man, which has only once before occurred in all my life Under the Hill. It will be long before my lady forgets you and forgives me what I do. Savor it, human. Savor it well.'"

Elias Patterson drew a deep breath, putting his hands out to the flames and looking straight at Roger Darlington. "Then he was gone, in the way he had of coming and going, and the little stream was still singing to itself. I walked slowly back to where Titania lay in her bower, awake now. And that was how the morning passed, and I envied nobody in the world, nor ever have again."

"I envy you," Darlington said quietly. "I'm telling you that right now."

"Envy nobody. It is the true secret of happiness, or at least the only one I know. So the years passed for me in Faery: not only in making love with Titania, but in hunting with her and her friends and her maidens – for she too loved the chase as well as any – and walking and sporting together in those sunlit woods that became my true home. And if I was happier than the priests and the ministers like myself think mortal man has any right to be...all the same, I never deceived myself into believing that my joy would have no end. One midnight I would fall asleep in Titania's embrace, as I had done every night for seven years, and awaken on the very same cold hillside where I had lain myself down, exactly seven years before. Then the payment would begin, and I was ready for that, too."

"You thought you were," the highwayman said somberly. "We always *think* we're ready."

"Not that I had any sort of calendar, or any way of marking my days: I only had to look in Titania's eyes to see the seventh Beltane come upon us. I had become well skilled at reading her moods, as I've told you – certainly better at it than Oberon, or any of her ladies. We gazed at each other for a long, wordless time, when that day came, and then she said, 'It is not my choice. It is my fate, and my doom.'

"And I answered her simply, saying, 'I know. There was never a moment when I did not know.'

"Faery folk do not – cannot – weep, Mr. Darlington. Only Titania. It is part of her loneliness. I held her that night for the last time, as she rocked and moaned and whimpered against me, and her tears scarred my face and my throat. This is why I grew my beard, you know, to cover the marks. She quieted a little after some while, and I said to her, 'Forget me, my love. It will be hard enough for me in my world without knowing you unhappy in this one. I beg you, forget even my name, as God has done. Will you do that for me, you for whom I forgot Heaven?' And I kissed her tears, though they burned my mouth.

"I could barely hear the words when she breathed her answer. 'If I say that, my beautiful, beautiful mortal, I will be lying, who never once lied to you.'

"'Lie to me now,' I told her then, and Titania did as I bade her."

"And even so." Darlington was not looking at him, but at the ground, his head low. "Even so, you're still never ready."

Elias Patterson smiled in some surprise. "You're quite right, Mr. Darlington. I certainly wasn't ready, on the last night of the last year, for her to shake me out of an exhausted sleep – when you know, as I did, that you will never do something unbearably wonderful ever again in your life, you see no reason to hold back anything for tomorrow – whispering, 'My love, my love, you must run! Please, *wake* – you are in terrible danger!'"

Darlington looked up, his mouth crooked. "I'm always hearing tales of brave women who risk their lives to warn their lovers of one approaching peril or another. Never met one in my life, you understand, but I'm sure there must be thousands."

"Titania never looked more beautiful than she did that midnight," Elias Patterson said, "bending over me, with the moon in her hair and the wild terror in her eyes. I reached out to pull her down once again – *once more, oh, once more* – but she resisted, tugging at my wrist, crying over and over, 'No, no, they are here, I feel them, you *must* fly!' When I dream of her, that is how she comes to me, always."

"What was the danger? I don't imagine they've got troopers or High Sheriffs in Paradise."

"She did not want to tell me at first. But I saw the figures moving in the darkness, and each time, pulling me along as she was, she would freeze in place, absolutely, like a fawn when the wolves are near, knowing that its only chance of life is not to move, not to make a sound, not to breathe." Elias Patterson shook his head in fresh wonder. "Titania, Queen of Faery, who hunted manticores."

Darlington waited, saying nothing. Elias Patterson said, "I never got a close look at them, thanks to her wariness and her skill. They were great shadows, for the most part, moving as silently as she under the ever-blooming trees and meadows of Faery. What I did see of them I will not tell you, for I still dream that, too. But I *felt* them, as she said: hungry shadows who knew my name, clawing at my mind and my soul to be let in – and if I let them in there would be nothing left of me but skin; nothing but a shadow inside, like themselves. And all the same, there was as well a terrible lassitude that came with that feeling – a sense that it would be so pleasant to surrender, even to invite them in, since what would life matter without Titania?" He laughed then, but there was no smile in the laughter. "And when I look back, that is probably just what I should have done."

"But you didn't." Darlington's voice was hoarse and expressionless.

"No. But if it had not been for Titania, holding me together and *them* outside with her faery hands and her human heart...well, I would be in another place than Yorkshire today. For what she said to me was that Faery exists on sufferance of the Hell – whatever it actually is – that you and I were both raised to believe in. 'It is a mere token tithe we pay, every seven years,' she told me, 'most often an animal, though I have known it to be as simple as a flower that grows only here, Under the Hill. But this time, this time –' and dark as it was, her face was white as a flower itself, white as alyssum, white as anemone, white as yarrow – 'this time, my darling, *you* are the tithe...'"

"Oberon," Darlington said through his teeth. "It was Oberon who shopped you."

"Aye, I never doubted that, nor did Titania. But it is a curious thing, how certain horrors are so vastly horrible to think about that they simply do not take hold on your imagination at the time, but go almost unnoticed – sooner or later to wake you screaming, surely, but not *now*. What was real was Titania, crouching beside me in a thicket while those – what were they? Demons, monsters, damned souls? I've no idea to this day – while those creatures who had been sent for me glided soundlessly by, close, so close, drawn perhaps by the ticking of my blood, perhaps by the chatter of my mind, the betraying rustle of the hair rising on my forearms." He paused for a moment, and then said in an oddly younger voice, "Or by the sweetness of Titania's breath on my cheek, which I *will* not think of, *will* not remember..." He caught himself, abruptly, but Darlington could hear the effort.

"If I had a shilling for every man, woman and child who's shopped *me*," Darlington murmured, "well, they'd not do me much good just now, all those shillings, would they? Except maybe to bribe a turnkey to let a wench into my cell. Go on."

Elias Patterson said, "Titania led me a long way, circling and doubling back at the least sign of danger, sometimes standing motionless for minutes at a time, even when I could sense nothing. It was a strange, slow flight, and a sad one, for we passed through fields where we had rambled together in sunlight, crossed a stream where the Queen of Faery had tucked up her skirts like a girl and shown me how to tickle fish with my toes; and rounded the golden corner of a wood where I had flattened myself, marveling, against a tree to see her take down a grimly boar with nothing but a slender oaken spear longer than she was. She had leaped into my arms afterward, and rubbed her bloody hands all over my face. But we could speak of none of this, or anything else, for fear of attracting my hunters' attention. We moved along in silence, her hand always in mine; and now and then, when we could, we looked long at each other. I remember."

He was silent for a few moments, and then continued, "We came very near to evading them altogether. Titania had just pointed to a grove of tall hemlocks a little way ahead, and whispered, *'There*, my love – pass under those trees and step safely home into your own world,' and I had turned for...what? A last look, or word, or hopeless embrace? Perhaps none of these, for I had sworn to myself long ago that there would be no such tormented farewell for us when the time came. But all at once my mind filled with fire and stench and despair bearing down on me from all sides. I could not see Titania – I could see nothing but howling shadows – and I cried out in fear, and felt her push me down, hard, so that I sprawled flat on the ground. Something was flung over me, covering me completely, and I knew by the dear scent of her that it was Titania's cloak. I cowered in her smell, feeling the shadows raging around me – around *her* – expecting my pitiful refuge to be torn away from me at any instant. All I could think, over and over, the one light trembling in my darkness, was *when I am in Hell, I will hold her with me, and eternity cannot be so dreadful then.*"

Darlington said quietly, "It's that cloak you're wearing, isn't it? That's Titania's cloak."

"I heard her laugh," Elias Patterson said, "and it was like the first time I had wakened to her singing – soft and clear and proud, as though she had just invented singing at that very moment. She was moving away slowly, back the way we had come – I could feel it, just as I felt the great shadows sullenly trailing behind, and felt their savage bewilderment. Under that cloak, I did not exist for them; and yet the Queen of Faery was laughing joyously at them, and they knew it. I could feel them knowing it, as their night lifted from my mind."

"It's a cloak of invisibility, like in the fairy tales." Darlington was talking aloud to himself. "But it can't be, for you're plain enough to see right now. How *does* the bloody thing work?" His voice had grown harsh and hungry when he raised his eyes to meet Elias Patterson's eyes.

"I wish I could tell you," Elias Patterson answered him sincerely. "It didn't make me invisible – un*thinkable*, really, is what I suspect. All I can say with any certainty is that it's quite a warm cloak. And easy to clean."

"Good to know." Darlington brought out his pistol, though not particularly pointing it at Elias Patterson. "For a man in my profession."

Elias Patterson smiled at him. "Your gun's empty, as we are both aware, but that doesn't matter. I'll give you the cloak, gladly – but if I might make a suggestion, you should wait a bit before you take possession. For your own good."

Darlington scowled, puzzled. "Why?"

"Trust me. I was, after all, a minister of the Gospel."

Darlington put his pistol away. "I do have bullets around somewhere," he said, but absently, still caught up in the tale, still eyeing Elias Patterson's cloak. "So she led them away, and you escaped back to this world."

"So it was. I waited until I could feel that I was safe, and then I scurried to that hemlock grove Titania had pointed out, like a frightened little mouse, with her cloak wrapped round me. Between one mouse-step and the next, I was walking English earth, under an English heaven, safe from the wrath of Hell and Oberon alike – and, if you'll believe it, already frantic to turn and go straight back, whatever the price, whatever the doom. But the grove was gone, the land was as flat and flavorless as I remembered it, and hemlocks don't grow in that soil, anyway. The country Under the Hill was shut to me. I was...home."

"And was it," – Darlington hesitated – "*is* it a hundred years later? Than when you walked out of your house, that Beltane eve?"

"It was a hundred and six, to be accurate, which such things rarely are. But yes, it turned out exactly as the ballads have it. All my friends and family were long gone, my house had apparently blown down in a storm – and been quite nicely rebuilt, by the by – and my church now belonged to a denomination that hadn't existed in my time. There was nothing of me left in that town, except for an All Hallows' Eve tale of the minister who was snatched away by the Devil – or by the Old Ones, if you talked to the most elderly of the villagers. *Tabula rasa*, you might say, and doubtless the better off for it."

Darlington was staring at him, his expression a mixture of superstitious awe and genuine pity. Elias Patterson laughed outright. "Believe me, good highwayman, there's something to be said for the completely blank slate, the scroll of perfect virgin vellum on which anything at all might yet be inscribed. I wandered away from my village for the second time, perfectly content, and I have never looked back. I have been...otherwise occupied."

"Doing what? If you're not a minister anymore –"

But the white-haired man was suddenly on his feet, half-crouched, his posture almost that of an animal sniffing the air. "Down," he said very quietly. *"Down."*

Darlington had not heard that particular voice before, and he did not question it for a moment. He knelt clumsily, briefly noticing Elias Patterson fumbling with the fastenings of his cloak; then he was flat on the cold ground, with the cloak over him, listening helplessly to slow, deliberate hoofbeats and the soft ring of light mail. He heard Elias Patterson's voice again, now with a strange, singsong boyishness to it, saying eagerly, "Welcome, welcome, captain! It *is* captain, isn't it?"

A growl, impatient but not discourteous, answered him. "Sergeant, sir, sorry to say. What are you doing up here alone?"

The reply, tossed back lightly and cheerily, chilled Darlington more than the ground beneath him. "Why, searching for Faery, sergeant. That's my appointed study in this world, and I flatter myself that I'm uncommon good at it."

Three horses, by the sound, so two other riders, and very bewildered riders they must be by now, Darlington thought.

The sergeant said, a little warily, "That's...interesting, sir. We've been all this day and night in pursuit of a dangerous highwayman named Roger Darlington. Would you have seen him the night, by any chance, or heard any word of him? There's five hundred pounds on his head."

Elias Patterson was saying, in his odd new voice, "No, sergeant, I'm afraid I hardly notice anything when I'm at my searching. It's terribly demanding work, you know."

"I don't doubt it," the sergeant rumbled agreement. "But isn't it cold work as well, on a night like this? That fire can't throw much heat, surely – and you without a proper cloak, at that. Hate to find you frozen stiff as a bull's pizzle on our way back."

Another rider's grunt: "Wager old Darlington'll be happy when we catch him, just to get in out of the weather."

I'm right at your feet, you natural-born imbecile! Practically under *your feet, and you can't see me!*

"Never fear, good sergeant," Elias Peterson chirped in response. "All the warmth I need is here in my hand." Darlington heard the leather flask gurgle. "Taste and see, I beg you."

Three clearly audible swallows – three distinctly louder gasps of *"Jesus!"* – then the third rider: "God's teeth, rouse a stinking corpse, this would. Where'd you come on it?"

Elias Peterson giggled brightly. "The Queen of Faery gave it me, as a remembrance. We are old friends, you see – oh, very old. Very old."

He'll never get away with it. But plainly he had done exactly that – Darlington could hear it in the sergeant's words: "Well, that's a fine thing indeed, sir, to be a friend of the Queen of...But you won't want to be passing it around so free, or there'll be none left to warm your old bones, hey?" The horses were stamping fretfully, already beginning to move away.

Another playfully demented giggle. "Ah, no fear there either," *Christ, don't overdo it!* "This is an enchanted flask, never yet empty in all the years it's companioned me on my quest. A wonderful gift now, don't you think?"

"Wonderful," the sergeant agreed. "Well, we'll be on our way, sir, and my thanks for your kindness. And if by chance you should hear any word of that Darlington fellow – "

"I'll pass it on to you directly, of course I will. On the instant." A knowing chuckle. "I know how to reach you on the instant, you see."

"I'm sure you do. Good night to you then, sir."

Darlington waited a good deal beyond the time when he could no longer hear the hoofs crunching the light snowcrust before he threw off the cloak and scrambled to his feet. "I wouldn't have believed it! I wouldn't have bloody *believed* it! I really *was* invisible, the same as you were!"

Elias Patterson shook his head. "No, I told you – they saw you, all right, just as those creatures come from Hell saw me. They saw that cloak covering some object, but it meant nothing to them, it suggested no connection, no picture in their minds, as most things we even glimpse do. The cloak breaks that connection in some way. I don't understand it, but I know that must be what it does, when sorely needed." He paused, watching Darlington staring after the departed horsemen. In a lower voice, he said, "And why Faery is only seen when it chooses to be seen."

"Well, however it works, it's bound to come in useful," Darlington said. "And so might that ever-full flask on a hard night, now I think of it." He held out his hand.

"I think not, Mr. Darlington," Elias Patterson said gently. Their eyes met, and though the reverend was a century and more older than the other, in a little while Darlington lowered his hand. Elias Patterson said, "It is growing light."

"Aye, I'd best be off, find myself a horse. First farm I come to – " Darlington grinned suddenly – "if the goodman's a bit easier to bluff than you."

He offered his hand again, in a different manner, and Elias Patterson took it, saying, "I'd head south and west if I were you. As far as Sheffield, and straight west from there. Dorset might suit you for a time, in my opinion."

"Poor as churchmice, Dorset. Nothing worth stealing but a bit of copper piping, a bit of lead off the roofs. Hardly my style." He shook Elias Patterson's hand firmly. "But south-west you tell me, so south-west it is. And good fortune to you on your own quest, Reverend."

"Faery is all around us, Mr. Darlington," Elias Patterson said. "The border never stays in one place – Oberon moves and maintains it constantly, to keep me from crossing back – but it is always permeable from the far side, not merely at Beltane and Samhain. That is how the fox and unicorn come and go as they please, as do the phoenix and the mermaid. Not even Oberon can bar their way." He folded his hands where he sat, and nodded again to Darlington. "And that is why I pay heed to foxes."

Staring at him, Darlington saw the madness fully for the first time. He said, "You really believe you can cross a border that the King of Faery is determined to hide from you forever? A border that will keep moving and moving away from you, even if you find it?"

"The Queen of Faery remembers me," Elias Patterson said. "I have faith in that, as I once had faith in something quite different; and what a fox knows a determined man may discover. Go now, Mr. Darlington — south and west — before those men come back. And do not trust my lady's cloak to hide you a second time. It never did for me. I think you must give it to someone else, in your turn, before it chooses to work again."

"No doubt I'll find reason to test that, Reverend."

"No doubt." Elias Patterson nodded once, placidly. "God be with you, my friend."

Darlington started off, fastening the cloak at his throat. The sky was pale green with dawn over the moors before he looked back. He could still see the hilltop, and even the last bright threads of the dying fire, but there was no sign of Elias Patterson. The highwayman stood for some while, waiting; then finally snugged Titania's cloak about him again, and walked on.

The Unicorn Tapestries

In 1938, a year before I was born, New York's Metropolitan Museum of Art opened an extraordinary extension in Manhattan's Fort Tryon Park which it called The Cloisters. The name comes from the fact that portions of five medieval French cloisters were incorporated into the construction of the building, and the general idea of the place was (and is) to present art, sculpture, and crafts from the Middle Ages in a setting which would reflect the time and spirit of their creation.

I loved going to The Cloisters as a child, even though something there would always trigger my allergies, causing me to lose my voice. It was worth not speaking for a few hours to see the stained glass and stonework, the covered walkways and open gardens, the view of the tree-lined Hudson River from the West Terrace...and especially to see the Unicorn Tapestries. Woven from silk, gold, and silver sometime around the end of the 15th century, brilliantly dyed with weld, madder, and woad, these seven hangings captured my imagination with their silent tale of a brutal unicorn hunt.

Some many years later an ambitious publisher in New York decided that he wanted to put out something new and different based on these tapestries, and concluded – thanks to The Last Unicorn – that I was exactly the person to tackle the subject in a poem cycle. His book, sadly, never appeared; and except for two rather obscure, small-edition reprints, neither did my poetry. I'm glad to end that invisibility here.

The poems are told from the point of view of a small boy who appears in the sixth tapestry, just behind the lord and lady who must have commissioned the hunt, and who might indeed be his parents. He is playing with his dog, and he is so careful not to look at the dead unicorn as it is carried by. The three young dandies in the first tapestry are his older brothers; and the dog's name is Pepée because I knew a nice dog by that name once.

The only other important note is that the ceremonial virgin who captures the unicorn is never actually seen. A long strip is missing from the center of the fifth tapestry, and the only thing left of the virtuous betrayer herself is a bit of her sleeve, and one hand toying gracefully with the unicorn's mane. The heavy-lidded minx who is often taken for the virgin is in fact her maidservant. I chose to imagine that the boy's mind had closed the woman out: literally refused to remember a person who could do what she had done. The truly terrible thing, however – as Jean Renoir reminds us in La Regle du Jeu – is that she probably had her reasons, like everyone else.

First Tapestry

The running-hounds woke us before the sun.
Under my window, we heard them call,
"The day is up, and the hunt's begun!"
And the greyhounds said never a word at all.

And we ran to the window, Pepée and I,
and saw my brothers go by below,
with the greyhounds eager as birds to fly,
and the air like honey and harps and snow.

The greyhounds' collars were silk brocade –
the running-hounds leaned on a twist of rope.
Their eyes were gold in the dappled glade,
and their coats were lilac and heliotrope.

And I leaned far out, until I could see
to the forest's edge, to the brim of day,
and fat Guillaume in a walnut tree
calling us to follow the wondrous prey.

Second Tapestry

My mother made me sit to board,
and then my tunic would not tie,
and then I could not find my sword,
so we were late, Pepée and I.

But in a clearing, all agleam
with morning dew, the hunt we found.
There was a fountain, and a stream,
and there were lions all around.

And stags; and genets, wicked-wise;
a panther, sweet-breathed as the morn;
hyenas, with their human eyes;
and rabbits, and a unicorn.

He was not white as ivory,
or snow, or milk, as men declare,
but white as moonlight on the sea –
oh, white as daisies! white as air!

The stream was thick and slow and spoiled:
he knelt and bowed, as though to pray –
and all the poison hissed and boiled,
and rose like mist, and fled away.

A pheasant was the first to drink –
he hopped upon the fountain's brim,
and gave a whistle and a wink,
as though it had been all for him!

Then all the other beasts drew near –
the lean hyena and the swan
the panther and the gentle deer
drank side by side, and he looked on.

The hounds all whimpered and lay flat;
the hunters fretted at delay.
My father in his feathered hat
lifted his hand and bade them stay.

He said, "We may not give him chase
till he is roused and starts to run.
Stand you a moment in his grace
and ask his pardon, every one."

Then I was glad to be his son.

Third Tapestry

And then he turned
and saw us, and he sprang
across the stream like thunder.
We blew our bugles till the morning rang,
He flew so fast, and left so little sign,
we might have lost him – but he had to shine,
and we went trampling where the great horn burned,

the silver seashell horn....
What must we look like to a unicorn?

Pepée and I,
we fell so far behind
I nearly started crying –
but then we heard my father's bugle wind
"He's gone to water!" and the dogs replying,
and we caught up in time to see him swim,
swift as a seal, bright as the seraphim.
Spears ringed him, but they fell to let him by
before his dazzling scorn....
What must we look like to a unicorn?

Fourth Tapestry

He came out of the water in one singing glory of wrath,
and flew at the spears like a storm gathered into a spear.
My father was calling them all to stand out of his path,
but the men had no knowledge of him, and the dogs had
    no fear.

The greyhounds went at him as they would have gone at
    a stag –
all harry and hold till the men can come up for the kill –
but his horn turned the brave Ogier to a poor tattered rag,
and his hoofs broke the huntsmen as millstones break grain
    in the mill.

I remember the barking, the chime of his hoofs on the ground,
and two peasants who came to cut wood when our play
    should be done,
and my brother Rene holding fast to my father's best hound
to keep him from running to death, as he wanted to run.

Then my father was calling the men and the dogs to his side –
oh, he was as angry as ever I saw him that day! –
saying, "Fools, you are led by a fool, will you pay for my pride?
There is only one way to capture a unicorn – only one way!"

Fifth Tapestry

I cannot remember her –
when I try,
I see only her handmaiden,
sleek and sly.

She may have been beautiful
past belief –
I thought her handmaiden
looked like a thief.

She may have been ugly,
a fool, a boor –
my father cared only
that she be pure.

She sat in a garden,
quiet and alone.
I would not have gone to her –
I would have known.

But the unicorn watched her
with his seadeep stare.
Perhaps he did know,
and did not care.

For he came to her call
and put his head down,
with a long white shiver,
in the folds of her gown.

She played with his mane,
she stroked his head;
and the dogs drew near,
sniffing where he bled.

He looked in her face –
she was still as a wall –
then he lay down beside her,
looking strange and small.

To see him so
made my inside ache,
but the handmaiden smiled
like a sleeping snake,

and she winked and she signed
that the beast was tame.
And a man blew a horn,
and the hunters came.

Sixth Tapestry

I still can see the killing,
as I saw it then:
the wholeness broken by the grunting men,
the beauty spilling,
his eyes brilliant with hurt,
neck starting to sag –
then the dim horn plowing the dirt,
and the dogs lapping his blood with their tails awag,
his white breath stilling.
His tongue hung out, all muddy, and his hide
turned stone-gray as he died.

They brought him to the castle, slung across
a horse's back, upon some sticks and moss.

Dogs yapped, trappings rang,
but no one sang.
My mother waited there,
and all her ladies with their crackly hair
whispered like fire,
and my father went to stand with her.
I saw how proud and sorrowful they were.

All my desire
was to wake up and see
him shining, fierce and free,
as he was meant to be.
And when they bore him past where I stood with Pepée,
we looked away.

Seventh Tapestry

But oh, in the morning —
Oh, in the morning!

Oh, in the morning, when we came
out to go walking, and saw him blaze
up from the field like a shout of praise,
shining and shining and shining,
too bright, too living, to have a name.
Pepée started barking and running in circles, and I —
Oh, then I did cry.

All in the morning, there he lay,
collared and kept with a silver chain,
red with the pomegranates' sugary rain,
shining and shining and shining,
with a fence like a ribbon to make him stay.
His horn was all sunset and spindrift, all rainbow and rose —
Pepée licked his nose.

All in the morning, feeling his breath
play in my hair as he stamped and blew,
just for a moment I knew what he knew,
shining and shining and shining –
that nothing could hold him, not even death;
that no collars, no chains, no fences, as strong as they seem,
can hold a dream.

Chandail

One of the great pleasures for me in *The Innkeeper's Song* – still my favorite of my own novels – is that it provided me with a world to sneak back to at the least opportunity, with characters new and old on hand to tell me their stories. This one came to me in the voice of my dear Lalkhamsin-khamsolal, also known as Sailor Lal, Swordcane Lal, Lal-Alone, Lal-after-dark...the black woman mercenary with, as she says sourly, an inconvenient conscience. She is an old woman now, long since returned to the life originally intended for her: that of a traditional storyteller, living alone in a desert hut, with an apprentice to provide for her and learn her ancient art. Here the story she shares concerns a mysterious sea creature and the one person Lal has hated all her life, for the best of reasons.

Lal says. Cape Dylee is not like other places.

Yes, it does resemble Leishai, Grannach Harbor and the Karpache headland in being almost perpetually cold and misty, clearing only when the shrill *laschi* winds of late summer dispel the haze for a little while. Myths and legends – gods, even – always seem to be born in such places, possibly because one's vision is generally so clouded. But Cape Dylee is different, all the same.

My full name is Lalkhamsin-khamsolal. In other times and lands I have been known by such names as Sailor Lal, Swordcane Lal, Lal-Alone and Lal-after-dark, but all that was very long ago. Now I am older than I ever expected to be, and I live here, in this desert hut, and I tell stories, which is what I was always meant to do, and people come far to hear them, as you have. Listen to me now, listen to an old woman, and perhaps I will make you very wise. Perhaps not.

Cape Dylee is indeed different from all other peninsulas isolated at the backside of nowhere, and not merely because of the fishermen's boots and trews and hooded capes for which it has become known. Cape Dylee is where you find the *chandail*.

No, they are altogether of the sea. I too have heard the tales that have them walking on land like men, but this is fable. As many legs as they have, and not all of them together capable of supporting their great soft bodies out of water. They *can* climb, slowly, but surprisingly well, employing all four of those finny arms to haul themselves up on any jutting bit of rock, or even a wharf now and then. Origin of the mermaid legend?

Naked half-women languidly combing their hair to lure poor sailors and fishermen? You have never seen a *chandail.*

They are not shapeshifters, *chandail,* though it is easy to see why folk believe them so. Ugly, yes, marvelously horrific; yet if you look at them long enough, sometimes something happens to your sight, and you can actually see them becoming beautiful right before you, so beautiful that your eyes and mind hurt together, trying to take in such splendor. And yet they remain exactly what they are: dankly reeking multi-legged monsters, like some grotesque cross between a jellyfish and a centipede. One knows that...one always *knows* that...and yet more than once I have forgotten to breathe, watching that impossible alteration, feeling my eyes filling with tears that I cannot lift a hand to brush away. Do *they* know – do they realize what is going on in the humans who stare at them so helplessly, repelled and yearning by turns, watching them ripple and shift like rainbows? Some days I think one thing, some days another.

You cannot ever tell from their faces. Oh, yes, they do have faces, in a sort of way; indeed, there are moments when they look heartbreakingly not quite human, nearly resembling plump-cheeked children, except for the huge slanted eyes (which are not really eyes) and the little parrot beak. Then – so subtly that you cannot tell where the transformation starts and ends – all features slide away, drift out of proportion into a shapelessness that the eye can never name or contain. What do they look like when that happens? Like clouds. Like massive, fleshy clouds, swollen with storm and stink. When the wind is right, you can smell them before you see them.

No, they cannot speak. They do not need to.

On Cape Dylee they say, "Ask advice of a wind in the grass – go to a rock-*targ* for comfort – but heed no word of the *chandail.*" Not that they chat with humans in words; you hear them inside. No, not in your head – I said *inside,* making pictures in your bones and belly and blood, pictures that you *feel* in the way that you feel who you are, without having to study or remember it. They can impart a wondrous truth in this manner – a truth that lives as far beyond language as I live beyond the place where I was born – or they can picture you such a lie that the word itself has no meaning, a lie you will forever exalt over the truth, knowing all the while, every minute, what it is. Believe this – oh, for your soul, believe it. *Lal says.*

Being a storyteller myself, I have been drawn all my life to this thing the *chandail* can do; yet I am no closer to understanding its nature, or theirs, than I am to knowing, finally, what I am *besides* a storyteller, and a wanderer, and...someone my mother would not have liked very much. What I do know certainly is that the *chandail* are neither sea monsters nor magicians, nor mindreaders, as those to whom the exact name matters so often assume. You might call them soulreaders, if you choose. It is no more accurate than the other words, but it will do.

The fishermen there have more ancient legends and superstitions about the *chandail* than they have about fish. Depending on where you drink and with whom, you can hear that the First *Chandail* fashioned a world before this one of ours: gloriously beautiful, by all accounts, but crafted all of water, which was no problem until the Second *Chandail* made the sun. More wondrous yet, that must have been for a while, what with the new, new light bending and shattering so dazzlingly through those endless droplets – a rainbow creation, surely. Except, of course, that it melted away, by and by, and sank back into empty dark until the world we know came to be. I have been told, over many a tankard of the equally legendary Cape Dylee Black, that the *chandail* grieve still for that lost wonder, and would gladly call it back to drown ours, if they could. A sailor I know tells me that he can hear them planning in the night, in the little waves that chime and murmur against the sides of his ship. He says that they will never give up.

Another tale has it that the *chandail* could speak once, when they were first born, at the beginning of things. They were given the waters of this world for their dwelling by the fishermen's god, Minjanka, who instructed them not to be greedy, to share the catch with their neighbors, and always to warn the humans when they sensed a storm coming. The legend says that for a time the *chandail* did as they were ordered; but presently they become restless and mischievous, and began sending the fishermen off with word of vast shoals of herring and *lankash* and roe-laden *jariliya* to be found along the south shore, while they gorged themselves giddy half a mile west. In the same manner, they would divert the fish from their usual sea-roads, teasing and cozening them to flee this unseen predator, or swarm in search of that promised prey. Fish are quite naïve, and lack humor.

The same could be said for gods, I have often thought. Minjanka grew angry at this and took speech from the *chandail,* which was a mistake, more of a mistake than perhaps even a god could have known. Silent and patient, forced to find some other way of communicating, the *chandail* learned to lie in pictures, in images – in waking dreams – and found themselves newly able to deceive human beings to a depth and a degree that words could never have achieved, while the great Minjanka remained as ignorant as a fish. Gods can send dreams themselves, but they cannot eavesdrop. Always remember this; it's the only true privacy we have. *Lal says.*

I am not sure, even now, whether the *chandail* actually understand the difference between our flawed reality and the perfection of falsehood. Why should they, when we ourselves hardly do? See now, I tell the old stories, and train a young disciple to tell them as they should be told, as she will tell them after me. But no one knows better than I that what I teach through those tales is not truth, not as you and I know what that word is supposed to mean. My truth is told through illusion, through fraudulence, through purest mendacity – why should it be any different with the *chandail?* In that way, if in no other, we may be kin.

They are sociable, in their way: it is not uncommon for a *chandail* – or several, for that matter – to follow a boat for days, keeping pace effortlessly while they babble to the crew in outlandish hallucinations, flooding them with antique gossip of the sea lanes, with uncanny fancies and foreshadowings, with memories most likely not their own. But they *feel* like our own – oh, that they surely do, even if one knows better. They feel like the memories we should have had, the dreams that belong to us, though we had no hand in their shaping. Even now, merely speaking of them, a dozen lives later, I can smell those memories. I can taste them.

I was very young when I met the *chandail* – at least it seems so to me now. It came about some time after I parted from the man I ever afterward called *my friend,* the wizard who took in, and sheltered, and trained, and loved (though he never once used the word) a child newly escaped from slavery and half-mad with terror. I had no desire ever to leave him. Indeed, I pleaded against it with all my heart. But he judged it time, and there never was any arguing with him. So I bundled what I owned, along with the gifts he gave me (not all of which needed to be packed up, or could be), and I set off along the road he recommended, which in time took me to Leishai, on the west coast. He always knew what I needed, that infuriating old man.

At Leishai I found work on a fishing boat called simply *The Polite Lady*. I was at home on that pitching, yawing deck the instant I set foot there, as though I had been bred and raised fishing day and night for *jariliya* and never coming ashore, like the families I used to see in the bustling harbor of Khaidun, where I was born. I did what I was told, scrubbing and shining, patching and sluicing down, and when I was ordered to lend a hand with the halyards or the anchor or the nets, I did that too, and felt as though I had come home. No...no, I do not mean that, not as it sounds. I already knew that I could never go home.

I was stolen and sold when I was very young. I never saw my family again. Perhaps they sought me and still do; perhaps they shrugged. The one thing I know is that they never found me. I was sure that they would, for a long time.

When that passed, between one moment and the next – I was cleaning fish at the rail, just abaft the galley, as I recall – then I became Lal, there on the spot, Lal-Alone. Nothing dramatic about it; hardly even any sorrow or pain. All done, that, all gone over the side with the fish guts, gone with the salt spray wind-whipped across my face. I barely noticed, to tell you the truth.

But the *chandail* did – at all events, they began calling to me that same night. Coincidence it very well may be. I am only telling you what happened.

It may have been only one *chandail* – you never do know – but at the time there was no way I could have believed that a single creature could overwhelm me so with visions of my parents and the lost life already so far behind me. I dropped all the fish and sagged against a bulkhead, weeping as I never had – *never* – when certain things were being done to me. Because these were no ghostly, wispy, transparent glimpses of scenes remembered wrongly: no, these were real, and more than real – beloved faces and voices and bodies, all pressing so close, so desperately joyous to have me back at last. My little brother's nose was running, as it always was, and my mother was already fussing with my hair, and my father called me Precious. He had other pet names for his other children, but I was Precious.

It was not an illusion. Whatever I know today about the powers of the *chandail,* I will die believing that it was no illusion. *Lal says – oh, Lal says.*

And yet...and yet, even then I did know that it could not be – that they were not real *here,* in this place where I was, alone on *The Polite Lady* with my blood-slick fish, my shipmates and the featureless, slow-heaving sea. I tried to tell them. With my arms around as many as I could hold – and I felt and bumped and smelled them all – I cried out to them, "Go away, I love you so, go away, *go away!*" But they stayed.

It was the Captain who finally came to my aid. She was a stocky, red-haired, middle-aged woman, an easterner who spoke with the strange, thick Grije accent that seems to swallow half the vowels. She marched through the crowd around me as though they were none of them there – which, of course, for her they weren't – and she lifted me roughly to my feet with one calloused brown hand, saying, "So, so, girl, and now you have know *chandail.* Welcome aboard."

I could not speak for the tears. The Captain took me down to her cabin – no more than a bunk that she had for herself, while the rest of us slept in hammocks – and she gave me a full schooner of barleywine and waited patiently until I grew quiet, only sniffling a little, before she said, "They will do it again. You must accustom."

"No," I said. "No, I cannot bear it. I will have to get off, get off the boat."

The Captain smiled. "Then no fishing ever here, no fishing anywhere near – you will go east, where folk talk like me, and no *chandail.* But you like here, yes?"

I nodded. I was sold east, the first time, and I swore before all the gods of my people that I would never in my life return there. I did, though, later on.

"So," the Captain said again. "So you learn not to listen. *Must* learn," and she caught me by the wrist, peering hard into my face with her hard blue eyes. "*Chandail* mean not much harm, not much good either. To them, our minds like – " she groped for a word – "like toyshop, like a playroom, our minds. Everything they find," and now she made a ges-ture and a face as though happily tossing invisible objects into the air with both hands, "play. You understand? All for *them,* no matter the rest, no matter *us.* You cry now – listen, we all cry over *chandail,* one time. One time, no more. You understand?" She waited until I nodded again. "Got to be, or we can't live. No cry no more – back on deck now, best thing."

She slapped my shoulder heartily, and we went up together.

But I cried a good deal more before I finally became immune to the sendings from the sea. The worst of it, in a way, was not the faces, racking as it was to feel myself surrounded again and again by all the loves of my amputated innocence, knowing beyond any self-deception that even though I could actually touch and hold them, I could not *touch* them, if you see what I mean. That was bad enough; but my particular horror was of the *places* – the sudden dazing visitations from gardens I had toddled through, woods where I had slipped away from my brothers, giggling happily to myself as I heard them shouting for me; the wharves and harbors where the sea-wonder had first taken hold of me. I was a long time learning not to see *them*, those hideaways of my heart. But the Captain knew. I did learn, like the others, because I had to.

And in so doing I came to hate the *chandail*, as I do not think I have ever hated even the ones whose hands and faces still wake me most nights, after so many years. Because at least those are long dead, all of them – someone else got Shavak before I found him, but I missed no others, for all the comfort I had of it – while these images daily and nightly brought back both the joy and the horror and despair of my childhood, and there was no revenging on that, nor ever would be. And the very worst thing was that I, like others, came to *desire* those visions, even as I loathed and dreaded their coming. As the Captain had said, the *chandail* were playing with me, *in* me, and I knew that I would forgive Shavak, and even Unavavia, before I forgave them.

In the years that followed, I traveled the sea, left the sea, came back to it, left it again...and so it has gone for me until more recently than you might think, to look at me. I'm done with the sea now – or it with me – but somehow in those days, journey as I might, I was never really away from it. Sooner or later, there I'd be, Sailor Lal once more – passenger, pirate or crew, it made no matter. And so, will-I, nil-I, I have had some dealings with the *chandail* in my time.

And I would hate them still, bitterly, heartlessly, mercilessly, without compassion, in that way of hating that does no one any good, except for a thing that happened when I was *not* a sailor, but a plain paid...until I was hired to hunt down an undeniably bad man in Cape Dylee. Yes, I found him, but that is not part of this story. What matters is that, having earned my fee, I was indulging myself somewhat, allowing myself a full night spent wandering the waterfront taverns before I set off for home the next day. Yet for some reason – perhaps because of a nagging doubt that the man was that much worse than I – no amount of ale, wine or that vile but curiously captivating fish sauce the folk there call a liqueur had the least effect on me, much as I wished it. Near sunrise, then, I was as dead sober as I'd been when I walked away down the long wharf, grateful for the kindly absence of the moon. Now, with the tide well on the ebb, I forced myself precisely back over my sandy footprints to see whether or no it had taken the body with it. Always so much simpler for everyone, for that to be the case.

Well, this time the sea had struck a bargain with me, as it has done once or twice since. The tide had indeed accepted my offering, but left for me, in return, an enormous pulpy mass of tangled – legs? or were they vines? strands of bladder-wrack? – four separate appendages that might almost be arms, each crested along its ropy length with a line of tiny, useless-looking fins; the whole dominated by a bulbous, more or less conical head with no recognizable features, except for the dainty little beak in the center. Not to mention the dizzying aroma, like an entire shoal of dead fish, all by itself. I had never seen a *chandail* close to before.

At first I was sure it was dead, because I saw, not only the blood dark on the sand under it, but the short spear half-buried in one of the still, flabby sides. It was a two-pointed stabbing lance, the kind the Cape fishermen use in shallow water – but I could not fathom why anyone with any sense would be hunting so plainly inedible a beast, nor what a *chandail* could have been doing so near shore. I came slowly closer in spite of the stench, in spite of the fear licking coldly along my nerves; not because of anything that helpless mass could possibly do to me, but out of a sailor's belief that a *chandail* can continue its making and sending – its *playing* – for some while after death. This is completely untrue, of course, and I knew it at the time. But it didn't matter, standing there with one foot in the sea and that great dead thing washing back and forth against it as the tide began to turn – nothing about it then to make you cry with wonder, I promise you. I wished that it would come to life for a moment, so that I could kill it again, and I bent and tugged the fish-lance out of its body, meaning to stab it once or twice, just for myself. I was a fine hater in those days.

And then it moved...and it *was* alive, though only the least bit so. It made a kind of floundering heave, slugging its helmet-shaped head like a horse fighting the reins. It pulled itself almost erect, turned blindly this way and that; then pitched over on its side once more, with the tiny, trusting sigh of a child falling asleep in a familiar place. I had expected a rush of blood to follow my removal of the lance, but there was almost none. The thing lived, that was plain enough, and either I ended it once and for all, or I took responsibility for keeping it alive. It's not important whether I yet abide by the ancient ethics of my people, I know what they are. *Lal says.*

Why did I make the choice I did? As long as it has been, I ask myself that question still. Perhaps my conscience was troubling me over the man I'd killed a few hours before – I have always had the most inconvenient conscience for the life I have lived – but much more likely it had to do with that first curious exchange at the water's edge. Somewhere in my long-gone child soul, there must have been a buried belief that it is bad *dree* – bad luck, you would say, bad business – to reject a gift from the sea. Abominate it or not, the wretched creature was mine.

And I hadn't any notion of what to do with it. The deep wound in its side had stopped bleeding altogether, but the *chandail* had shown no other sign of life after that one brief flurry. I stood over it (you don't ever get inured to the smell, but your nostrils go numb after a time) and wondered what to do. If there's a physicker in the world understands the innards of a maybe dying *chandail*, I've not met him, no more than I've again been that close to a living one: so close that I could see the fringes all along the undersides of the four arms quivering with the tide. They look very like hair, but it is thought that they serve the *chandail* as eyes in some way. I couldn't tell whether the motion meant that they were seeing, or not. I couldn't tell anything.

"Talk to me," I said aloud. "Here I am, talk to me."

I readied myself, bracing my mind – well I knew how to do it by now – against the shock that always comes with the first explosion of the *chandail* into their...playroom, as the Captain called it. But nothing happened. There came no apparitions, no impossibly responsive mirages such as I was bitterly accustomed to – only a silence in myself fathoms deeper than the mere absence of sound. Feeling almost as deep a relief, and something somehow absurdly close to guilt, I had begun to move away when there came a picture so tenuous, so frayed and shadowy, that I would never have recognized it as the sending of a *chandail*. As it was, in the darkness I could barely distinguish the figure of a woman, myself, bending over a huge inert form and lunging a swordcane blade into it, hard, over and over, all the way to the wooden hilt, on and on. The woman even twisted her wrist at the end of the thrust, as I always do.

Beyond the least doubt, the creature was begging me to kill it.

And I could not.

No. Before you even open your mouth, *no*. Mercy had nothing to do with it. Quite, quite the contrary. I could find no mercy in myself for a suffering *chandail*, but only cruelty of the purest sort, as I know better than many, and knew at the time. They had, at their whim, made my mind their theater, their sporting arena – very well, here was a chance, long overdue, to make one hurt as I had hurt when the creatures summoned my father from my heart to call me Precious again. And I need do nothing at all to cause this pain, nothing to alert that ever so self-conscious conscience of mine – nothing but to savor the beast's agony for as long or as little a time as I chose, and then walk away. How much more innocent could raw revenge possibly be?

But I couldn't do that, either. And I tried. *Lal says.*

I must tell you that it was one of the more interesting discoveries I have ever made. To have spent much of my youth, and all of my adult life, learning to kill more and more efficiently, with less and less pleasure, because pleasure gets in the way, and then to realize that even your taste for retribution has its limits...as I say, it was an interesting moment. I whispered, "I will help you," feeling the words rake the back of my throat as I dragged them out of myself. "What must I do?"

No response for another long while, with the *chandail*'s sides not stirring in the least, and then the same image over again, exactly: me with my swordcane vigorously putting the thing out of its pain. I said, louder now, "No. No, I'm not going to do that. Tell me how I can make you well." And all the gods in their idiot secrecy know that I never intended to say any such thing.

Silence. Night and silence, and the tiny giggles of the waves. The *chandail* was still alive – of this I was doggedly certain – but I knew enough to know that it could not long survive in the shallows, half out of the water. The first lunatic step, therefore, must be to tow it as far to sea as I could – which, considering that I had neither a boat nor a rope, seemed likely to prove troublesome. Not insurmountably so, however: in a tumbledown shed, located in an isolated corner of the harbor, I came across a derelict but serviceable fishing smack, just small enough to be managed by a lone sailor. I left a good portion of my assassin's wage atop a heap of ragged nets, skidded the boat down to the water, and warped her around to where I had left my malodorous charge. Having halyards and a tiller to manage was, as always, a dear comfort, and kept me from concerning myself with my own astonishing foolishness. Not altogether, but almost enough.

The *chandail* had not moved an inch, as far as I could see; but when I tried to bunch a few of its legs and bend a cable around them, then it suddenly began to struggle, hard enough to make it plain that I had no chance of rigging any sort of towline without the bloody thing's cooperation, moribund as it undoubtedly was. I splashed furiously away from it, aware that daybreak was near, and disinclined to be caught with someone else's boat, expensively borrowed or not. The *chandail* sank back into somnolence, but not before I felt a tremulous suggestion that it would drown if dragged through the water by its legs. Once I had reversed the rope and managed to find a way to snug it safely under the great bloated head, all went so swiftly and smoothly that it took me some while to realize that my old tormentor and I had communicated most matter-of-factly, to our mutual benefit. I found the thought disquieting, and put it out of my mind.

Away then, and out of the harbor with the sun and the little dawn breeze, sails nearly as limp as the *chandail*'s sides, and me tacking this way and that, desperate to make a little headway before someone recognized the boat, let alone what I was hauling. But no one did; and by the time the dripping red sun had climbed high enough to grow yellow and small, I was beyond sight of Cape Dylee. Even so, I cracked on as much sail as I could handle, convinced that the *chandail*'s one hope lay in its deep home, out where such small crafts as mine rarely venture, with good reason. I spied a weak patch in the caulking, and lashed the tiller down while I reinforced it as I could with what I had. *Teach you to steal boats you don't know,* I thought. How many more such weaknesses might there be below the waterline?

The *chandail* itself seemed none the worse for being employed as a sort of sea anchor to windward. If anything, it appeared even a bit revived by the rush of water through its...gills? Even today, I know exactly nothing about how the *chandail* breathe, mate and reproduce (I never could be certain whether mine was male or female), nourish themselves – well, fish, I know they eat various small fish – let alone how and when they die, in the normal way of things. I regret that now, but at the time I was much less interested in such affairs than in, first, seeing this one *chandail* healed and whole, and, second, trying to comprehend why its survival should matter so much to me, when I had loathed the entire species so fiercely for so long. In those days, it annoyed me mightily not to understand myself. I felt it a weakness, a luxury that I could not afford. I feel differently now.

When the wind dropped, near sunset, I took in sail, threw out an actual anchor, and fixed myself a barebones meal, the boat being well-stocked for its size with several days' worth of salt fish and ship's biscuits. I sat on a hatch cover to eat, staring down over the stern at the *chandail* floating passively just to starboard, looking oddly like a flower in the fiery sea, with all its legs spread out around it like grotesque petals. It raised two of its arms rather feebly, in what could have been a shaky salute, but which more likely meant that it was studying me very intently with those eye-hairs on the undersides. I waved and smiled at them. I said to them, "Yes, this is indeed me. Who are you?"

Nothing, for a long moment; nothing but the fading cries of a few seabirds and the deep whuff of a *panyara* briefly surfacing a few yards to port. Suddenly a very small girl, no more than perhaps eight or nine years old, was standing beside me: so present, so entirely human, so *there,* that I actually offered her a biscuit before realizing what she was. The *chandail* had ransacked my mind for some equivalent of its own identity, and presented with me with – no, not myself at her age; the thing knew better than *that* – but with a child who had bright blue eyes, a firm little mouth and chin, and a sprightly, self-confident carriage that I must have seen somewhere and somehow remembered. She was barefoot and wore the simple wraparound garment that most folk wear south of Grannach. The *chandail* pay great attention to detail.

I asked her name, and she told me. I could not have repeated it then, let alone now, but that was how I learned that the *chandail* do have individual names, which I had doubted. I said, as I had said before, "How can I help you? What must I do?"

Her voice was somewhere between a croak and a chime. She said, "Why do you help? You do not want to help. I know."

I was some while replying. I said finally, "It is something I have to do. I cannot tell you why. But from this moment, you will stay out of my memories – is that understood? One other creature appearing on this boat – one single vision of *anything*, anything at all – and I promise you that I will cast off the line and leave you to die here, and never look back. Is that understood?"

The girl uttered a low, rough chuckle: curiously chilling, coming from that small throat. "Very well," she said, "and what can you do about *this?*" She turned abruptly, loosening her single garment, and I saw the purple-lipped gash that took up so much more of her body than it had of the *chandail*'s great loose bulk. There was no blood, but I know the smell of rotting tissue. I'd have thought salt water would have done the infection some good, as it usually does with humans, but this was looking worse than when I had found the *chandail* helpless in the harbor. I asked the girl, "What happened to you? Who did this?"

The child shrugged, as lightly as a much older woman dismissing an importunate lover. "A fisherman. He was angry." I could picture the rest of it easily enough: some heartbroken deckhand, taunted one time too many by visions of vanished beloveds – as I had so often been – stabbing downward with the one weapon ready to hand, finding flesh and twisting the two-pronged lance as viciously as he could, until the *chandail*'s flailing struggles snatched it from him. The girl added casually, "There will have been poison on the tines."

"Yes," I said, for I knew of many such attempts, usually futile. I said, "I lived awhile in the South Islands. I have some skill."

She did not answer. Her image thinned and flickered – just for a moment, but it made me aware that the *chandail* was weakening steadily. I looked from her festering wound back to the creature lying so serenely in the darkening water. If it had had an expression I could read, I would have said that it appeared resigned, neither avoiding nor approving its fate. I turned to the child again and asked her, "If I heal you, am I healing...?" I could not quite finish the sentence, and there was no need. The girl nodded. I said, "Well, then."

I had only a very few salves and unguents with me, and none that would likely ease an injury such as hers. South Island cures are mostly a matter of the hands, anyway, of something that happens between one's hands and oneself – or one's soul, call it what you choose. I have never been able to explain it, nor to teach it to anyone else; and it does not always come when I call, if you understand me. But when it does work, I have seen it make bodies change their minds about being dead. *Lal says.*

"I must meditate now," I said. "We will begin at first light." The little girl nodded again, and was gone. I sat where I was for a long time, watching the thready infant moon rise, and the *chandail* stirring only with the stir of the tide. I thought about the South Islands, and the woman there who taught me the little I know of healing. Lean and bare and twisted as an old winter branch, yet she had a laugh to set butterflies dancing, and a way of being kind that one only noticed long afterward. To this day, I call her into my heart, or at least try to do so, on the rare occasions when I need to summon what I learned from her. She died many years ago, but I still sometimes pretend no one has yet told me.

The little girl was there precisely at sunrise – no, a bit before, it was, because I remember the sky being a cool, pale, translucent green behind her. She did not speak, but turned and let her dress fall, exposing the *chandail's* wound on her slender brown back. The smell was stronger than it had been only a few hours ago. I breathed it in deeply, as you have to do with South Islands healing. You have to take the pain all the way in.

"This will not hurt," I told her, "but it will feel very peculiar. And it will take a long time – perhaps all day, perhaps days."

The girl laughed again: that deep old laugh that could not belong to her. "*I* will feel no hurt," she said, "whatever you do." At my direction, she stretched out on the hard deck, face down, and I put my hands on the raw, oozing laceration and asked my long-dead teacher to be with me. I stretched my fingers as far as I could, from one edge of the wound to the other, not actually measuring its length and width, but only to let them spy out the battlefield before them. Then I simply waited for the feeling to come: the familiar sensation of near-boiling water flooding through my wrists and forearms and out of my body altogether, leaping all fleshly boundaries to pour itself over and into whatever suffering was calling it. I never felt that I was master of any healing that happened – nor did my teacher, as she often told me. I was merely grateful to be its conduit, its channel. Its riverbed.

But not that day. And not the next, nor the one after that. South Island healing comes when it comes, caring nothing for mere need. If I had needed more evidence that the *chandail* was dying, it was there in the little girl's behavior each day: not so much in her words, which were always terse and calm, but in the way she held herself, in the tension of the muscles I was so vainly kneading, and the increasing chill of her skin. I could do nothing for her but wait; there was no way that I could find by myself into either the *chandail*'s mystery or my own. Nothing to do but wait, with an unreal child fading under my futile hands, and the creature itself slipping lower and lower at the cable's end each day. I caught fish, yellow and blue, and patched the hull as best I might, and drank raw red wine, of which there was considerably more on board than there was water. It comes when it comes.

The *bruach* came first.

There were two of them, which is unusual. *Bruach* are solitary scavengers – and cannibals, to boot, as likely to turn on each other as on a dead whale or stranded *lankash*. They are more like eels than like anything else, I suppose, except that they run as much as twenty feet in length, and fear nothing, because nothing but a *bruach* would eat one. As a rule, they wait for their prey to die on its own, but not always.

The girl saw them first: the two long, swift swirls to left and right of the *chandail*, and then the sheep-snouted gray heads – sheep with teeth like sharpened little pegs – rearing high to get their bearings and submerging again. She gave one soft cry and vanished between my hands, leaving me clutching foolishly after her. The *chandail* shivered in the water.

The *bruach* imitated her in their eerie, twittering voices, as though mocking her fear. I searched frantically for a bow or even a throwing axe, my swordcane being of no practical use just then. The galley finally yielded up a couple of decently-balanced carving knives, and a butcher's cleaver as well. I have fought for my life with less, although at the time I couldn't remember when. I scrambled back on deck, and prepared to do battle.

By choice, they go for the belly, gnawing their way in, dining on the fatty organs, and often laying their eggs in the ruins. I leaned over the low railing, gripping my knives, praying for each sheep-head to rise above the waves just once more. When one did, I cocked my arm just so, as an old soldier who was drunkenly kind to a slave child taught me to do, and made sure to follow through from my legs. The head did not come all the way off, but close enough.

The second *bruach*, distracted by the sudden explosion of near-black blood, romped in the sticky ripples for a few moments, gnawed briefly on its late companion, and then turned its attention back to the *chandail*. I threw the second carving knife, but missed. The *bruach* dived deep, beyond my sight, but I knew that it would turn and straighten itself in the darkness, and begin to spin along its whole length, faster and faster, until it came hurtling up under the *chandail*, hard enough to knock it out of the water, using its leverage to grip and twist and bore through the toughest hide into the helpless body. I hefted the cleaver without much hope of hitting anything, if I should somehow be granted a second chance. It felt like a stove lid in my palm, and the handle was loose.

But as the *bruach* surged toward the surface, the *chandail* moved. Just a bit, no further than a slight eddy might have pushed it, but enough so that the *bruach* missed its mark, as I had mine. The *bruach* broke water instead of flesh, looked around unhurriedly, making no connection between its partner's death and me at the rail of the fishing boat – they are dull beasts – and turned to dive for a second strike. But the *chandail*, rolling halfway onto its side, struck out feebly with a pair of its arms, not stunning or even jarring the *bruach*, only holding it *still* for one brief moment, no more than I needed. This head did not come off, but it did make a very satisfying sound when it split. The cleaver was better balanced than I had thought, after all.

The girl did not reappear on board until near sunset. I sat on deck and watched the same yellow and blue fish I had been eating nibbling daintily at the bodies of the two *bruach*. My right shoulder ached from having hurled the heavy cleaver with all my strength, while my mind ached even more from puzzling over my reason for being where I was, doing what I was doing. After a time the *bruach* began to sink, and I prayed that others of their kind would not come and discover them, because I had nothing else to throw. I was so distracted that I almost failed to notice the child when she did return.

She was different – not drastically so, but unmistakably. There was at once a greater solidity about her, and a certain new clarity as well; even her eyes seemed to have changed from an indifferent, washed-out blue to something close to the color the sea would be again, when the blood was gone. She said, in that strange voice of hers, half ragged with age and pain, half clear as snow-water, "Thank you. You saved my life."

I said nothing. She continued, gently and innocently. "And now you are wondering why you should ever have done such a thing."

"Yes," I said. "Yes, I am."

"Because I am your memory," the little girl said...the *chandail* said. "I am the secret place where you hide it all – the beautiful room you cannot bear to enter – the cave where the monsters live – the dreams that make you dread sleep. You know this, Lalkhamsin-khamsolal."

No one had called me by my rightful name for a great many years. I was not even aware of having leaped to my feet, nor of shaking my head until my hair stung my eyes. I do not think I was screaming, but my throat hurt as though I had been. I said, *"No.* No, you are no part of me. You are parasites, like the *bruach* – no, worse than the *bruach* – and I despise you all, make no mistake. If I saved you, it was out of pity, as one or two others have had pity on me in my life. Nothing more. Nothing more."

The girl remained as serene as though I had soberly agreed with her. She said, "Despise us – hate us, if you will – but consider. What you are is also what you lost – what was taken from you – and if I and mine did not keep the key to that room, would you be fully yourself? Would you even truly exist?"

In her half-smiling child's mouth, my name sounded foreign and far-away, not connected to me at all. I said only, "You have a wound to treat. Come."

She laughed then, and lay down for me to try my poor back-country curing one more time. The infection was worse, the stench brought back places I wish I had never seen...but the feeling was there too, at last, rushing down from my shoulders, hurrying so hungrily toward the need that it seemed almost to stumble over itself on the way. The rotted skin sloughed away under my hands as I put them directly on the lesion, and I sensed the *chandail*'s suffering draining back into me, as it should if the healing is working right. There was pain, but it was happening a long way off, to someone who was at once me and not-me. I cannot say it any more clearly than that. I did nothing – only touched, and closed my eyes.

When I opened them again, the sky was black and starless, with no smallest rag of sunset left. The girl vanished, as she always did, and I went below to my bunk, where I lay awake the rest of the night, brooding over what she had said to me. It was at least a change from the dreams.

In the morning I could see no real difference in the wound, beyond a certain suggestion of knitting around the edges – most likely wishful thinking on my part, for the smell and suppuration were definitely unaffected. I told the girl that South Island healing is unpredictable and rarely instantaneous, that I would not give up until she was well, however long a time it might take. She answered simply, as she lay down, "It will not be long," and left me to take that how I would.

In the three days that followed, the power that coursed between the *chandail* and me never faltered; but the undoing of the damage that the fisherman's two-tined lance had wrought was a wearier business than I had ever dealt with. At times I convinced myself that the wound was smaller and cleaner-looking, and that the creature itself was plainly stronger; at others, it seemed dreadfully obvious that the *chandail* was not only failing, but that my treatment might very well be hastening its end. Even at my most hopeful, I never dared cut or loosen the cable, our only other connection, for fear that the creature might slip silently down out of sight, as the two dead *bruach* had done, too weak and damaged to stay afloat on its own. There came to be nothing else in the world but the same sun pouring down on us each day, and my little boat swinging in the same slow half-circle between sea and sky, between the *chandail* and me. I fished and swam, and drank my red wine in the evenings, and watched the stars flickering through the waves, quick as fish themselves. It was very peaceful, and there was no time.

Of real speech between us – between me and the *chandail* speaking through her – there was very little. As I have said, the creature seemed utterly unconcerned with its own life or death; and whatever pain it truly suffered, I never knew. But we did actually converse, now and again, through the little girl, and I slowly gained a sense of the cold and fearless arrogance under my hands – and something else, as well: something almost like a teasing desire to be known, to be understood, to be *seen* by a human being. I remember that once I asked her, "Why do you amuse yourselves with our grief? We have never fished for you, never harmed you in any way – we could not, even if we wanted to. Why do you toy with us as you do?"

She had the grace to look surprised by the question; or it could have been a trick of the light on the water. "But what else are you here for?

Of all beings on the earth, your folk alone were created especially for us, for our own particular delight. Have you kept me alive only to make you understand this?"

I did not trust myself to answer her. What she had told me was no more than I had feared, suspected – indeed, *known*, somewhere in myself where I rarely visited. The Captain had told me truly: the *chandail* did what they did in perfect simplicity, with neither malice nor pity, quite simply because we belonged to them. What particular delight could they have drawn, after all, from the memories of fish? The nightmares of *panyaras* or the *bruach*? The gods I was raised to worship never promised human beings their entire eternal attention, but neither did they advise us that we were to be forever the playthings of creatures with eyes on the underside of their four arms. I spoke no more for the rest of the day.

Then, on the cool, bright morning of the third day, it was she who posed a question. As though we were in the middle of an ordinary chat between friends, she asked suddenly, "And what harm have *my* people ever done *you*? Where is the great evil in bringing your memories to life for a little while? Where is our wickedness, that you hate us so?"

I cannot say how long it took me to find words – no, to remember language at all. I said, "You don't know? You really do not know?"

I will always think that she actually blushed – though, obviously, that couldn't have been possible. She said, "We have not given it much thought, I admit that. Nor are we likely to – I am speaking honestly to you. I am asking for myself, and no other." And that was how I learned that the *chandail* were indeed individuals, with their own desires and curiosities. Few believe me yet, after all this time. *Lal says.*

I told her why we hated them. I told her, I think, for hours – all the while trying as hard as I knew to transmit healing through her illusory body to the monster likely dying off my starboard bow. She listened in silence, never interrupting once – that would be a human sort of thing, after all – and when I was done at last, she did not speak for some time. Only when I was resting for a little, soaking my hands in seawater – South Island work is painless, but your hands get so hot – did she finally say one word, "Interesting."

I gawked as dumbly as any astonished yokel. She said, "I have never known a human being. This has been extremely interesting for me."

I forgot everything I ever knew about healing in that instant. I thought of the first time the *chandail* had had all their way with me, and I remembered the Captain, and though I directed my words at a little girl, I was speaking directly to the thing she was. "You know *nothing* of me. You know nothing of us – nothing – and you never will, because you have always been too busy raping our memories, sporting with our hearts, without thought, without even the notion of pity. No, forgive me, I must take that back. The truth is that you know everything about us but what we are – everything but what it is to have those memories, good or bad, cherished or denied...or dreaded. You need a heart to understand that, and a soul, and your kind have neither." I was shouting into her face, just as though she were real.

And for the smallest moment she responded as though she were, and I had my one true meeting with the *chandail*. Her tranquil, expressionless blue eyes darkened with anger – or it might have been disbelief, or perhaps even sadness. She said, "You are quite right – we have no hearts, not as you and *your* kind would understand them. But souls...souls we do possess. Whether *your* kind would call them so or not." A truly human voice could never, surely, have conveyed such contempt as I heard in her soft, lilting words.

I did not want to talk to her – to *it* – anymore. I gestured with my head for her to lie down on the deck again, and she obeyed. The great gash on her back looked far more hideous than it had the first time I had seen it, and no gainsaying that it stank like a slaughterhouse. I understood one thing at least then, very suddenly. I said, "I have been no use at all, have I? All this that I have done – tried to do for you – *nothing*, from the beginning. You have been dying every minute since that lance went into you, is that not true?"

The girl turned her head slightly to look back at me over her shoulder. "If you were no help, you did me no further hurt either. As I have said, it was interesting, and I was...curious. As I am about death." Her voice had become a placid mumble; she might have been drowsing in the sun.

I stood with my hands on her, still feeling the heat vainly racing down my arms into the wound, as though the healing were stubbornly refusing to admit its futility. My anger was gone, and every other feeling seemed to have flown with it. I had difficulty, not only in finding something to say, but in remembering what individual words meant. I managed finally to mumble clumsily, "I've never known South Island healing to fail."

"Not on humans, perhaps." She looked at me as she always had, from somewhere I had never been. She said, "I told you to kill me."

"It was not in me to do," I answered. "Killer as I am."

The child laughed her strange laugh, for the first time in some while. "I am grateful that you could not. I would not have cared to die where you found me, wallowing in the filthy shallows. This is better."

Neither of us spoke for a long time after that. I went on working mechanically on her injury as though my efforts still mattered, while she continued calmly sunning herself. At last I asked her, "Should I loose the cable? Is that what you wish?"

She shook her head. "Not yet. I can no longer swim, and that is a bad thing for us, a dishonor. Besides, I have," – she hesitated briefly – "something to do. A gift."

"Not for me," I said, as quickly as I have likely ever said anything. "Forgive the discourtesy, but I have had well more than enough of your *gifts* in my life. If you mean to say farewell, we can simply shake hands, and each say *sunlight on your road*. No gifts."

The girl's smile lifted the corners of her eyes, but not her mouth. She said, "Oh, you will like this one, I assure you. The word of a *chandail* undoubtedly means little to you, but it has some worth even so. Trust me, Lalkhamsin-khamsolal."

That was the second time she called me by my name, and the last. I neither nodded agreement nor shook my head. Only waited.

"Shake hands, is it?" she said. She reached out then, but did not take my hand, merely touched it – an instant's fiery tingle, and she was gone. And Bismaya was there.

Bismaya...

I had not seen her since a certain afternoon on a riverbank when we were children, but this Bismaya was full-grown, and pregnant, heavily, clumsily so, carrying herself with the weariness of a woman who has long since lost hope of ever *not* being pregnant. Her plain, broad face was lined and sagging, and her beautiful skin, richly dark and always smoother than mine, had aged to the color of wet slate. I would have known her in any guise, at any distance. I would have known her in my sleep, in the darkest and most dreadful of the dreams into which she sold me, my cousin, my dear deadly playmate. I will know her after death.

The *chandail* had outdone itself. Unreal as Bismaya had to be, she still paled with the motion of my anchored boat, and swayed slightly as it rocked in the swell. Bismaya had never had any sort of a stomach, even on the wobbly little rafts we used to make with boards and logs and *jan-shi* vines. I remember everything about Bismaya.

She was so occupied with being bewildered, frightened and queasy that she did not see me until I spoke her name. Then she turned, stared, and tumbled awkwardly to her knees, whispering two words. "Lal. Please."

I used to imagine her saying that, begging me for mercy before I tore her to pieces, one slow piece at a time. Gods, how many times had I put myself to sleep with that vision? How many times did I call it up to shut out what was being done to me? And here it was – here *she* was, helpless on her knees before me – and here *I* was, dumbstruck, horror-struck, knowing that it could not be happening, not like this. Even the *chandail* cannot do this.

You see, the sendings of the *chandail* look and feel absolutely accurate, perfect to the smallest detail strained out of your recollection, your imagining. They can touch you, and you can touch them; they can chatter endlessly of memories only you – and so they – could share; indeed, they often call up people and places and events that you had completely forgotten, for good or ill. What they cannot do is hear what you say to them and respond to it – they cannot *listen*, not to words, not to eyes or bodies. Bismaya could not possibly have seen what she so plainly saw in my face.

And yet the little girl had said of her gift, "Oh, you will like this one." As false as any *chandail* vision, this one, surely, but illusory in a completely different way. I managed to mutter, "Oh, get *up*, you stupid slut, get up," and Bismaya tried to rise, but her belly gave her so much trouble that I had to fight the impulse to help her to her feet. We faced each other in silence. She said finally, "You look well, Lal."

"Slavery agreed with me," I answered. "Rape has kept me young."

I spoke quietly, but Bismaya cringed away from me, catching hold of a railing to steady herself. "There was never a boat," she whispered. "All the dreams, every night, every night, but never on a boat. I will wake from this – I *will*." But her eyes knew better.

"The best is not to sleep," I said. "Take my word for it." She saw the *chandail* in the water then, and gave a little cry of boneless terror:

seeing one of them without warning does have that effect. I said, "You *are* dreaming, Bismaya. I cannot harm you, and I would not if I could. Now that I see you, the idea of it – the dream that cradled my heart every night for so long – seems silly and meaningless." She actually bridled at that: the same Bismaya who would rather have been flogged in the market square than ignored. I went on, "But I need to know something, and I think you need to tell me." She belched suddenly, as pregnant women will, and then looked horribly shamed and mortified. I savored the old bitter taste of the word for the last time before I let it leave me. *"Why?"*

She stammered and coughed, looking everywhere but at me. I said, "Later I heard that you received money enough to buy that singing bird you coveted so. Was that really the way of it, then?"

Bismaya shook her head, still not looking at me. Her hair – dusty graying shadow of the comb-defying black wilderness I remembered – hid her face when she finally replied to me. "It was your eyes. I could not bear your eyes."

I think my mouth actually dropped open. She said timidly, "Lal, you always had such beautiful golden eyes – always, from the first – and all I ever had was these muddy brown ones. They're too small, and the lashes are just *stubby,* and I wanted so much to have eyes like yours. I couldn't sleep for envying you, do you understand?" She made that maddening helpless *twittering* gesture with her hands that she used to make when explaining why some new disaster wasn't her fault. "I couldn't stand to see you, Lal, every single day. You remember how it was. How we were."

First up in the morning, first over at the other's house to play and laugh, and gobble breakfast, and swim in the river, and make up long, long stories about the adventures our toys had together...Bismaya went on, talking faster now, "I had to be rid of you – I had to make you go away, do you understand, Lal? So I wouldn't be thinking about you all the time." She stopped abruptly and stilled her hands, spreading them with something resembling dignity. "That was why. That was all."

I was suddenly very tired. There was nothing here for me: not retribution, not solace, not even poor old useless justice – nothing but a foolish woman whom all my hating had not made worthy of hatred. Had she been there in the flesh, I would still have...but how do you strangle a ghost? Beat a ghost to death? Claw out the stupid eyes the ghost so hungered to trade for yours? Instead I asked, "When is your baby due?"

"In two weeks' time. So they tell me." Changing the subject made her voice firmer, and strengthened her stance as she faced me. "My ninth, would you believe it? It would have been the eleventh, but we...lost two of them." I dislike people who cannot bring themselves to say *died,* but the pain in her eyes was as real as she – I had to keep reminding myself – was not.

I wanted to look away from her, so that she would vanish, as the *chandail*'s specters always did if I could ignore them long enough. It astonished me to hear myself saying formally, "I grieve your grief" to her, and I deliberately undercut any suggestion of sympathy by adding pointedly, "But you clearly lost no time in finding replacements." Bismaya winced visibly. I was glad.

"This one will be the last," she said. I must have made some sort of derisive sound, because her voice changed, becoming harshly flat in a way that I had never before heard from fluttery Bismaya. "This one will kill me."

I stared at her. She smiled a strange, almost exultant smile. She said, "I know this. I welcome it."

"No," I said. "No, you can't know such a thing certainly." But women can, and I had seen the look of her body and her face too many times on others not to recognize it, whether I would or no. There was nothing to say, so I said, "The child?"

"Oh, the child will live." The smile sidled wider. "It's healthy and strong – I can feel it – and my husband will have a new wife to raise it before the earth has settled on my grave." She mentioned his name. I recalled it, and his chubby face as well, from our shared childhood. She said, "So there you are, Lal. There you are. It is all to you, in the end."

"Nothing is mine," I said. "Victory, vengeance, the triumph of patient virtue – none of it worth a minute's waiting for. In a moment you will wake, when the *chandail* wearies of its play with us, and so will I rouse from my own old dream, and neither of us will ever awaken so again. It is over, Bismaya."

"Over?" she cried, stepping toward me for the first time. "Over for *you,* perhaps!" Marriage, or motherhood, perhaps, or simply the imminence of death – had given her distinctly more spirit than I recalled her ever possessing. "Lal, for every night you suffered for the wrong I did you, I promise you that *I* have spent *two* nights of weeping, of writhing in shame and horror inside my skin, hating myself as I hate myself now – of wishing I could die, welcoming it – "

My hands came up at my sides of their own accord, curled fingers beckoning death; if she had been solid flesh, they would have been on her throat, choking that insect whine to cinders. Very well, I was not – I *am* not – entirely free of Bismaya, after all. "You could have looked for me," I said. My own voice sounded like someone else's; it could have been an old man's voice. "You could have bought me back. As much money as your family had."

"I was a little girl!" She seized my hands, touching me for the first time with hands that felt like dead leaves. "I had done a terrible, evil thing, and I was afraid to tell my mother and father! I was afraid!"

I pulled free of her. I said, "I was a little girl too."

After that we only stared at each other, until it occurred to me that the *chandail* might easily have died by this time, without my knowledge. Surely she would have vanished instantly, if that were so – but what if she did not? Which would be the true Bismaya then? The illusion stranded here with me, or the body trapped in her own bed, swollen with life, empty of spirit? I turned from her and looked over the side at the massive hulk floating so inertly at my cable's end. There was no way to be certain whether it yet lived. I called to it loudly – no response – and then threw an empty ship's-biscuit tin to splash beside its head. Nothing.

"Excuse me for a little," I told Bismaya politely. She gaped as I swung myself over the side and went hand over hand down the cable to drop into the sea only a foot or two from the *chandail*. Close to, even half under water, the huge eyeless head still loomed over mine, and the jumble of limp legs was like one of those vast seaweed tangles that snare and drown ships much bigger than mine. Bobbing in the slow swells, I lifted the cold tip of one – more than that would have been beyond my strength – looking for the fringe of eye-hairs underneath. No way of telling whether they were open, of course; all I could do was hope to rouse whatever fading attention might linger there still. I said, or perhaps only thought – what difference now? – "Enough. It is enough."

The *chandail* did not stir. I gave up then, really, but I tried once more anyway. "I do appreciate your gift. Knowingly or not, you have lifted a great stone from my heart, and I thank you for it." I hesitated, and then added, "Sunlight on your road." Not that I truly cared – not exactly – but it is what we say.

Whether my words had anything to do with it or not, the *chandail* moved then. No more than a sluggish heave, granted – by comparison, its behavior in the oily shallows of Cape Dylee harbor was that of a spring lamb – but it lived, and for one last tremulous moment it began doing what they do, if you look too long: rising and flowing into radiantly misshapen beauty, the beauty of the *chandail;* shifting, not its shape, but its spirit, somehow, burning there on the water, casting its own light on the road it was taking. I said once again, "Enough," and I swam away and climbed back up the cable.

Bismaya was pacing the deck, rail to rail, left hand squeezing and twisting the fingers of the right, as she always used to do when fearful of being scolded. When she saw me, she wrinkled up her nose in her old annoyance at my messy habits. She said, "Phoo, you're all *wet,* don't come *near* me," exactly as she would have said it – did say it – when I was seven, and she was six and a half. Idiot compassion roused in me for an instant, but I smacked it on the head and it lay back down again.

"You are going home," I said. "I hope you are wrong, and that this baby will not be your death." And I did hope that, in a way that I do not think was any less genuine for being so cold.

She gave me that eerily triumphant smile once more. "Oh, it will. No fear."

I wanted to comfort, not her, but myself. I wanted to tell her, "Bismaya, live or die, we are quits. I cannot remember why you took up so much of me for so long." But it was not true, and never will be, and I did not want my last words to her to be a lie. So all I said in the end was, "Goodbye, Bismaya. I send my best greeting to your family." And she was gone.

I felt the *chandail* go very quickly after that, but I never looked up. I stayed on deck the rest of the day, patching the mainsail and the little jib, caulking and filling where I could, and salting down as many fish as I could catch. At sunset I cut the cable, and watched the creature slide away into the deep gray-green where I still think I will go one day, even though you find me here in this white-bone emptiness. Then, with the moon rising, I hoisted sail and set off for the place where I was living at the time. There is nothing at all to say about the journey, except that all the long way I was never once visited by any *chandail* come to play with the pieces of my life. I never have been again.

And that is all there is to the story you have come such a long way to hear. There is nothing to add – except, perhaps, that I did go home one day, many, many years later. There I learned that Bismaya had indeed died in childbirth, and that her husband had indeed remarried, and was himself long dead, as were my own parents. I found her grave, and stood by it for a time, waiting to feel something, anything – rage or triumph, or even watery compassion. But all that came to me was an ache in my left knee, almost as old as I – we both fell out of a tree, playing outlaws in its high branches – and a memory of the two of us spying on Bismaya's older brother and his sweetheart, hoping to see them...doing what, I wonder now? Kissing, I suppose; I really remember only the giggling together, which we would barely manage to smother before a glance at each other would set it off again. Her brother caught us, of course, and chased us all the way to the river – we had to dive in to escape him.

A week later, she sold me. No, it was nine days. I grow forgetful.

So, then? Have I told you anything you did not know before you came to me? Do my old eyes discern something besides attentive cleverness in those eyes of yours? No, do not answer – what my listeners take away with them on the journey home is their own concern and none of mine. Ah, but I did speak of wisdom, did I not? Very well, in that case I will tell you the one thing I know for certain...

Wisdom is uncertainty. Wisdom is confusion. Wisdom is a heartless trickster healing my heart, my worst enemy drawing pity up out of my lifetime of hating, like sweet water from a long-dry well. Wisdom is knowing nothing, and not even knowing how you feel about knowing nothing. Wisdom is finding joy in bewilderment, at the last. At the last. *Lal says.*

For news and information about Peter S. Beagle and his works, go to
www.peterbeagle.com.